Faithless

JOYCE CAROL OATES

Faithless

TALES OF TRANSGRESSION

 THE ECCO PRESS
An Imprint of HarperCollins*Publishers*

HarperCollins books may be purchased for educational, business, or sales promotional use. For information please write: Special Markets Department, HarperCollins Publishers Inc., 10 East 53rd Street, New York, NY 10022.

FIRST EDITION

Designed by Cassandra J. Pappas

Printed on acid-free paper

Library of Congress Cataloging-in-Publication Data
Oates, Joyce Carol, 1938–
    Faithless : tales of transgression / Joyce Carol Oates.—1st ed.
    p. cm.
    ISBN 0-06-018525-2
    1. United States—Social life and customs—20th century—Fiction.
I. Title.
 PS3565.A8 F35 2001
813'.54—dc21   00-060007

01   02   03   04   05 QW 10   9   8   7   6   5   4   3   2   1

These stories are for Alice Turner
and for Otto Penzler

CONTENTS

ACKNOWLEDGMENTS

MANY THANKS TO the editors of the following magazines and anthologies in which the stories in this volume originally appeared, often in slightly different forms.

"Au Sable" in *Harper's*

"Ugly" (previously titled "Ugly Girl") in *The Paris Review*

"Lover" in *Granta*

"Summer Sweat" in *Playboy*

"Questions" in *Playboy*

"Physical" in *Playboy*

"Faithless" in *The Kenyon Review* and in *The Best American Mystery Stories 1998* and *The Pushcart Prize: Best of the Small Presses 1998*

"The Scarf" in *Ploughshares*

"What Then, My Life?" in *Fiction*

"Secret, Silent" in *Boulevard* and in *The Best American Mystery Stories 1999*

"A Manhattan Romance" in *American Short Fiction*

"Murder-Two" appeared in *Murder for Revenge*, edited by Otto Penzler

"The Vigil" in *Harper's*

"We Were Worried About You" in *Boulevard*

"The Stalker" in *Press* and in *Unusual Suspects: An Anthology of Crime Stories,* edited by James Grady

The Vampire" appeared in *Murder and Obsession*, edited by Otto Penzler

"Tusk" appeared in *Irreconcilable Differences*, edited by Lia Matera

"The High School Sweetheart: A Mystery" in *Playboy*

"Death Watch" in *Story*

"In *COPLAND*" in *Boulevard*

When one does not love too much,
one does not love enough.

—Pascal

Part One

AU SABLE

*E*arly evening, August. In the stillness of the suburban house, the telephone rang. Mitchell hesitated only a moment before lifting the receiver. *And here was the first wrong note.* The caller was Mitchell's father-in-law, Otto Behn.

Not for years had Otto called before the phone rates went down at 11 P.M. Not even when Otto's wife Teresa had been hospitalized.

The second wrong note. The voice. "Mitch? Hello! It's me—Otto." Otto's voice was oddly lifted, eager, as if Otto were a farther distance away than usual and worried that Mitchell couldn't hear him. And he sounded affable, even buoyant—as Otto rarely was these days on the phone. Lizbeth, Otto's daughter, had come to dread his calls in the late evening: as soon as you picked up the phone, Otto would launch into one of his riffs, complaint-tirades, deadpan, funny, but with a cold fury beneath, in the long-ago style of Lenny Bruce, whom Otto had much admired in the late 1950s. Now, in his eighties, Otto had himself become an angry man: angry about his wife's cancer, angry about his own "chronic condition," angry about their Forest Hills neighbors (noisy kids, barking dogs, lawn mowers, leaf blowers), angry about being made to wait two hours "in a refrigerated room" for his most recent MRI, angry about politicians, including even those he'd helped canvass votes for in the first heady flush of his retirement from high school teaching fifteen years ago. It was old age that Otto was angry about, but who could tell the poor man that? Not his daughter, and certainly not his son-in-law.

Tonight, though, Otto wasn't angry.

In a warmly genial, if slightly forced voice he queried Mitchell about Mitchell's work, which was corporate architectural design; and about Lizbeth, who was the Behns' only daughter; and about their grown, beautiful, departed children, Otto's grandchildren he'd adored as kids—and this went on for a while until at last Mitchell said uneasily, "Uh, Otto— Lizbeth is out at the mall. She'll be back around seven. Should I have her call you?"

Otto laughed loudly. You could all but see the saliva glistening on his full, fleshy lips. "Don't want to talk to the old man, eh?"

Mitchell tried to laugh, too. "Otto, we've been talking."

Otto said, more seriously, "Mitch, my friend, I'm glad you picked up. Not Bethie. I can't talk long and I'd prefer, I guess, to talk to you."

"Yes?" Mitchell felt a touch of dread. Never in their thirty years of acquaintance had Otto Behn called him "friend." Teresa must be out of remission again. Dying? Otto himself had been diagnosed with Parkinson's disease three years before. Not a severe case, yet. Or was it?

Guiltily Mitchell realized that he and Lizbeth hadn't visited the older couple in almost a year, though they lived less than two hundred miles away. Lizbeth was dutiful about telephoning, usually Sunday evenings, hoping (usually futilely) to speak first with her mother, whose telephone manner was weakly cheerful and optimistic; but the last time they'd visited, they'd been shocked by Teresa's deterioration. The poor woman had had months of chemotherapy and was bone-thin, her skin like wax. Not long ago, in her sixties, she'd been exuberant, fleshy, sturdy as an earthenware pot. And there was Otto, hovering about, tremors in both hands that he seemed to be exacerbating out of comic spite, complaining brilliantly about medical workers, HMOs, and UFOs "in conspiracy"—what a strained, exhausting visit. On the drive home, Lizbeth recited lines from an Emily Dickinson poem—" 'Oh Life, begun in fluent Blood, and consumated dull!' "

"Jesus," Mitchell said, dry-mouthed, shivering. "That's it, isn't it?"

Now, ten months later, there was Otto on the phone speaking matter-of-factly, as you'd discuss selling some property, of a "certain decision" he and Teresa had come to. Teresa's "white-cell blood count," his own "shitty news"—which he wasn't going to discuss. The books were closed permanently on that subject, he said. Mitchell, trying to make sense of this, leaned against a wall, suddenly weak. *This is happening too fast. What the hell is this?* Otto was saying, in a lowered voice, "We decided not to tell you and Lizbeth, her mother was back in Mount Sinai in July. They sent her home. We've made our decision. This isn't to discuss, Mitch, y'understand? It's to inform. And to ask you to honor our wishes."

"Wishes—?"

"We've been looking through albums, old photos and things, and having a ball of a time. Things I haven't seen in forty years. Teresa keeps saying, 'Wow! *We* did all this? *We* lived all that?' It's a weird, humbling thing, sort of, to realize we'd been goddamned happy, even when we didn't know it. *I* didn't have a clue, I've got to confess. So many years, looking back, sixty-two years Teresa and I've been together, you'd think it would be depressing as hell but actually, in the right mood, it isn't. Teresa says, 'We've already had about three lives, haven't we?' "

"Excuse me," Mitchell said, through a roaring of blood in his ears, "—what is this 'decision' you've made?"

Otto said, "Right. I'm asking you to honor our wishes in this respect, Mitch. I think you understand."

"I—what?"

"I wasn't sure whether I should speak with Lizbeth. How she'd react. You know, when your kids first left home for college." Otto paused. Tactful. Ever the gentleman. Never would he speak critically about Lizbeth to Mitchell, though with Lizbeth he could be blunt and wounding, or had been in the past. He said now, hesitantly, "She can be, well—emotional."

On a hunch Mitchell asked where Otto was.

"Where?"

"Are you in Forest Hills?"

Otto paused. "No, we're not."

"Where are you, then?"

Otto said, an edge of defiance in his voice, "At the cabin."

"The cabin? Au Sable?"

"Right. Au Sable."

Otto let that point sink in.

They pronounced the name differently. Mitchell, *O Sable,* three syllables; Otto, *Oz'ble,* one elided syllable, as locals pronounced it.

Au Sable meant the Behns' property in the Adirondacks. Hundreds of miles away. A seven-hour drive, and the final arduous hour along narrow, twisting, mostly unpaved mountain roads north of Au Sable Forks. So far as Mitchell knew, the Behns hadn't spent time there in years. If he'd given thought to it—and he had not, for subjects pertaining to Lizbeth's parents were left to Lizbeth to ponder—Mitchell would have advised the Behns to sell the property, hardly a cabin but a six-bedroom lodge of hand-hewn logs, not winterized, on twelve acres of beautiful, desolate countryside south of Mount Moriah. Mitchell would not have wished Lizbeth to inherit this property. For they wouldn't feel comfortable selling it, something that had meant so much at one time to Teresa and Otto; yet Au Sable was too remote for them, impractical. They were people who quickly became restless away from what they called civilization: pavement, newspapers, wine shops, decent tennis courts, friends, and at least the possibility of good restaurants. In Au Sable, you drove an hour to get to— what? Au Sable Forks. Years ago, of course, when the kids were young, they'd gone each summer to visit Lizbeth's parents, and, yes, it was a fact: the Adirondacks were beautiful and waking early in the morning you saw Mount Moriah startlingly close like a mammoth dream and the air achingly fresh and pure piercing your lungs and even the cries of birds sharper and more defined than you were accustomed to and there was the conviction, unless it was the wish, that such physical revelations signaled a spiritual condition—but, still, Lizbeth and Mitchell were equally restless to leave, after a few days of this. They'd take to afternoon naps in their second-story screened-in room surrounded by pines like a vessel afloat on a green-tinctured sea. Tender lovemaking and dreamy, drifting conversations of a kind they never had anywhere else. Still, after a few days they were eager to leave.

Mitchell swallowed hard. He wasn't used to questioning his father-in-law and felt like one of Otto Behn's high school students, intimidated by the man he admired. "Otto, wait—why are you and Teresa in Au Sable?"

Otto said carefully, "We are planning to remedy our situation. We have made our decision, and this is to—" Otto paused, tactfully. "This is to inform you."

Mitchell felt, for all that Otto was speaking so reasonably, as if the man had kicked him in the stomach. What was this? What was he hearing? *This call isn't for me. This is a mistake.* Otto was saying that they'd been planning this for three years, minimum. Since his own diagnosis. They'd been "stockpiling" what was required. Good potent reliable barbiturates. Nothing in haste, and nothing left to chance, and nothing to regret. "You know," Otto said expansively, "—I'm a man who plans ahead."

This was true. You had to concede the point.

Mitchell wondered: how much had Otto accumulated? Investments in the 1980s, some rental properties on Long Island. Mitchell felt a sinking, sickening sensation. *They will leave most of it to us. Who else?* He could see Teresa smiling as she'd smiled planning her lavish Christmas dinners, her monumental Thanksgivings, the presentation of gifts to grandchildren, gorgeously wrapped. Otto was saying, "You promise me, Mitchell. I need to trust you," and Mitchell said, "Look, Otto," stalling, dazed, "—do we have your number there?" and Otto said, "Answer me, please," and Mitchell heard himself saying, not knowing what he was saying, "Of course you can trust me, Otto! But is your phone connected?" and Otto said, annoyed, "No. We've never needed a phone in the cabin," and Mitchell said, for this had been an old vexation between them, from years ago, "Certainly you need a phone in that cabin, that's exactly the place you do need a phone," and Otto muttered something inaudible, the verbal equivalent of a shrug, and Mitchell thought, *He's calling from a pay phone in Au Sable Forks, he's about to hang up.* Quickly Mitchell said, "Hey, look: we'll drive up and see you two. Is Teresa—all right?" Otto said, reflexively, "Teresa's fine. She's good. And we don't want company." Then, "She's resting, she's out on the sleeping porch, and she's all right. Au Sable was her idea, she always loved it." Mitchell said, groping, "But—you're so remote." Otto said, "That is the idea, Mitchell." *He's going to hang up. He can't hang up.* Mitchell was trying to stall, asking how long they'd been there, and Otto said, "Since Sunday. We took two days, we did fine. I can still drive." Otto laughed; it was his old anger stirring, his rage. A few years ago he'd nearly lost his driver's license and somehow through a doctor-friend's intervention he'd managed to hang onto it, and that had not been a good thing, that could have been a fatal error, but you can't tell Otto Behn that, you can't tell an elderly man he will have to surrender his car, his freedom, you just can't. Mitchell was saying they'd drive up to visit, they'd leave at dawn next morning, and Otto was curt in rejecting the idea, saying, "We've made our decision, it's not to discuss. I'm glad I talked with you. I can see how this would be going, with Lizbeth. *You* prepare her however you think's best, OK?" and Mitch said, "OK, but Otto—don't do anything," he was breathing fast, confused and not knowing what he said, in a sweat, a sensation like something cold and molten pouring over him, "—too quickly. Will you call back? Or leave a number? Lizbeth will be home in half an hour," and Otto said, "Teresa feels she would rather write to Lizbeth, and you. That's her way. She doesn't like the phone any more," and Mitch said, "But at least talk to Lizbeth, Otto, I mean you can say anything, y'know, any subject," and Otto said, "I've asked you to honor our wishes, Mitchell. You gave your word," and Mitchell thought, *I did? When? What word did I give? What is this?* Otto was saying, "We left everything in order, at the house. On my desk. Will, insurance policies, investment files, bankbooks, keys. Teresa had to nag me to update our wills. But I did, and I'm damned glad. Until you make out a final will, you just aren't facing facts. You're in a dreamworld. After eighty, you *are* in a dreamworld and you have to take control of the way the dream's going." Mitchell was listening, but he'd missed the beat. His thoughts crowded and flashed in his head like playing cards wildly dealt. "Otto, right! Yes—but maybe we should talk more about this? You can offer valuable advice! Why don't you wait awhile and—we'll drive up to see you, we'll leave at dawn tomorrow, or actually we could leave tonight—" and Otto interrupted, you'd have said rudely if you didn't know the man, "Hey, good night! This call is costing me a fortune. You kids, *we love you.*"

Otto hung up the phone.

WHEN LIZBETH CAME HOME, there was a wrong, slightly jarring note: Mitchell on the back terrace, in the dusk; alone, just sitting there, with a glass of something. "Honey? What's wrong?"

"Just waiting for you."

Never did Mitchell sit like this, wait like this, always his mind was engaged, this was something wrong but Lizbeth came to him and kissed his cheek, lightly. A smell of wine. Heated skin, damp hair. What you'd call a clammy sweat. His T-shirt soaked through. Teasing, Lizbeth said, indicating the glass in Mitchell's hand, "You've started without me. Isn't this early?" Strange, too, that Mitchell would have opened this particular bottle of wine: a gift from friends, in fact it might have been from Lizbeth's parents, years ago when Mitchell had been more serious about wine and hadn't had to cut back on his drinking. Lizbeth asked, hesitantly, "Any calls?"

"No."

"Nothing?"

"Not a thing."

Mitchell felt Lizbeth's relief, knowing how she anticipated calls from Forest Hills. Though of course her dad wouldn't usually call until 11 P.M. when the rates went down.

Mitchell said, "It's been quiet all day, in fact. Everyone seems to be away except us."

Their split-level stucco-and-glass house, which Mitchell had designed, was surrounded by leafy birch trees, evergreens, and oaks. It was a created and not a discovered house; they'd shaped it to their will. They'd lived here for twenty-seven years. In the course of their long marriage, Mitchell had once or twice been unfaithful to Lizbeth, and Lizbeth may have been unfaithful to him, in her intense emotions if not sexually, but time had passed, and time continued to pass, like random items in a drawer casually tumbled together their days, weeks, months, and years in the entrancement of adult life; and this was a peaceful confusion, like a succession of vivid and startling dreams which, after you've awakened, you will be unable to recall except as emotions. The dreams were good, but it's good to be awake.

Lizbeth sat on the white wrought iron bench beside Mitchell. They'd had this heavy thing, now weatherworn and chipped after its most recent repainting, forever. "Everyone is away, I think. It's like Au Sable here."

"Au Sable?" Mitchell looked at her, quickly.

"You know. Mom's and Dad's old place."

"Do they still own it?"

"I guess so. I don't know." Lizbeth laughed, and leaned against him. "I'd be fearful of asking."

She took Mitchell's glass from his fingers and sipped from it. "Alone here. Us alone. I'll drink to that." To Mitchell's surprise, she kissed him on the lips. The first she'd kissed him, like that, girlish and bold, full on the lips, in a long time.

UGLY

J knew there was something suspicious about the way I got the waitressing job at the Sandy Hook Inn. There was a sign in the front window WAITRESS WANTED INQUIRE WITHIN so I went in, just walked in off the street not bothering to comb my windblown rat's-nest hair or change my sweaty clothes, reasoning what difference does it make. I needed a job badly, I'd had two jobs in the five months since I'd moved out of my parents' house forever, but still I was stubborn, or resigned, fatalistic—another girl with a skin like mine would plaster makeup on her face and wear lipstick but my philosophy was what the hell. A profound and unerring philosophy that has guided me through life. And in the Sandy Hook Inn I had what you'd assume was a serious interview with the owner-manager Mr. Yardboro, this barrel-chested guy my father's age in a fancy knit sport shirt on top and swim trunks below, bulldog face and rude eyes inquiring where was I from, how old was I, what kind of restaurant experience did I have, all the while leaning on his elbows on the counter beside the cash register (we were up front in the diner that's open year-round, a place that surprised me it was so ordinary) sucking at a toothpick and eyeing me up and down my body like I was standing there naked in front of him, the bastard. Not even considerate enough to ask me to sit on a stool, have a cup of coffee.

(He was drinking coffee himself.) It was hard to figure out why the diner was so noisy, since at least half the stools and booths were empty. Mid-morning of a weekday just after Labor Day and already in Sandy Hook, a small oceanside town forty miles north of Atlantic City, it was the off-season. A wet wind like spit blew sand and litter along the narrow streets; there were many empty parking places on Main Street and at Sandy Hook Pier. There was that tacky left-behind look to which losers are instinctively drawn, even at a young age. In the diner were strong odors of hot grease, cigarette smoke, and something sweetly-oily I would discover later was the ointment Mr. Yardboro rubbed into his flushed face and forearms as a precaution against skin cancer. And a sharper acrid smell that was the man's underarms, and just possibly his crotch. "I just remembered, honey, the job's been filled, that sign shouldn't still be up," Mr. Yardboro said with a smirky smile, like the interview had just been a joke, and I must have looked shocked (I thought I'd learned by that time to keep my feelings to myself but I guess not always) so he added, "Why don't you leave your telephone number, just in case?" Like an act of charity. As if I were this craven dog that had crawled in and was groveling at his feet, to be pitied. A hot blush came over my face like scalding water and I thought, *Go to hell, mister,* but I told Mr. Yardboro thanks and quickly scribbled down my number on the back of a torn receipt he pushed at me. Conscious of the man staring at my breasts in the loose-fitting tank top as I leaned over the counter to write, no choice but to lean over, and my bare knees pressed tight together as if that would make them thinner.

Two days later the phone rang and it was a woman asking if I was the girl who'd applied for a waitress position at the Sandy Hook Inn, it turned out I'd neglected to include my name (!), so I told her yes I was and she asked if I could start work at seven o'clock the next morning and I told her, trying not to stammer I was so excited, "Yes! Thanks! I'll be there."

2

MY SUSPICIONS weren't unfounded: apparently there hadn't been anyone hired when I'd been interviewed.

Maxine, the woman who'd called me, who was a cousin of the owner-manager and his "associate" in the inn, laughed and shook her head fondly when I told her what Mr. Yardboro had said about the position being filled, saying, "Oh that'd just be one of Lee's games, you have to take him with a grain of salt. He teases a lot but he don't mean harm." I smiled to show I was a good sport. Still, I was puzzled. I said, "Maybe Mr. Yardboro had hoped to hire someone better-qualified than me? Better-looking?" Maxine laughed saying, "Hey, no. Lee isn't partial to pretty-pretty girls, believe me. We mostly hire them in the summers—college girls. But off-season is a different clientele and sometimes the diner can be a rough place and a pretty-pretty girl won't work out. Too sensitive, and not strong enough to carry heavy trays, and doesn't want to get her hands dirty. Can't take the pressure, frankly." Maxine spoke warmly, vehemently. We smiled at each other. We were both homely females. Maxine was on the far side of forty, I was twenty-one.

3

IN THE DINING ROOM I wore a powder blue nylon waitress's uniform with SANDY HOOK INN and an anchor stitched above my left breast, and in the diner I could wear my own clothes, Maxine told me. Even jeans were OK as long as they weren't obviously dirty.

Maxine said, without a trace of irony, "The main thing for a waitress is to be efficient, and of course to smile. You'll find that one without the other isn't enough."

I'd been a waitress once before, part-time while I was taking business courses at a community college in my hometown. I hadn't told Mr. Yardboro details of my brief experience in a restaurant adjoining a Greyhound bus station, where plates fell through my clumsy fingers to shatter on the floor and more than once I'd spilled scalding coffee on the counter, and on a customer. At the time, at the age of nineteen, I was taking diet pills, the kind you can buy in any drugstore without a prescription, and the effect of the pills was weirdly visual—I saw shimmering halos around lights and auras around people's heads that so captivated me, my reflexes would come almost to a halt. At the same time, the rest of the world swerved past at a heightened speed. The diet pills failed to suppress my appetite but made me ravenous in a frantic way. In secret I devoured leftovers from customers' plates. After twelve days I was fired. The last dishes I'd dropped had possibly not been by accident.

My job waitressing at the Sandy Hook Inn was not what I'd anticipated. I'd had a vision of working in an airy, spacious dining room overlooking the ocean but the dining room of the Sandy Hook Inn overlooked a marina of small, dispirited-looking boats with names like "Ship Ahoy!" and "Mad Max II." After Labor Day, the dining room was open only on weekends, and on Sundays open only for brunch. My hours were mainly Sundays, when being a waitress was reduced to minimal services—mainly hauling enormous trays of dirty plates and garbage back to the kitchen. I smiled doggedly at entire families, even babies in high chairs. It soon became clear that I was the least popular of the several dining room wait-resses, for my tips were the lowest. This made me try harder, smile harder. My smile was wide and fixed like something clamped onto my face and I scared myself seeing the wet gleam of my teeth in the aluminum surface of the swinging kitchen door.

Mr. Yardboro eyed me with what appeared to be grim amusement. In a sport coat that fitted him tightly around the shoulders, worn without a tie, he overlooked the Sunday buffet and was alert to customers' requests and complaints. All the waitresses were fearful of him; his remarks to us were made in fierce barking asides masked by a clenched smile. On my second Sunday, when I was frantically serving three large family tables, Mr. Yardboro followed me into the kitchen and pinched the flesh of my upper arm, saying, "Slow down, babe. You're panting like a horse." I laughed nervously, as if Mr. Yardboro had meant to be funny. His teeth were bared in a grin and the clusters of broken capillaries in his cheeks gave him the look of a cheery, friendly guy, but I knew better.

AT FIRST, the imprint of Mr. Yardboro's fingers in my fleshy upper arm was a dull pink, then it darkened into an ordinary yellow-purplish bruise.

It was a fact that Mr. Yardboro was the first man to touch me in a very long time but this was not a fact that required interpretation.

4

I WASN'T BORN UGLY. I've seen snapshots of myself as a baby, as a toddler, as a beautiful little girl with springy dark curls, shining dark eyes, a happy smile. (Possibly if the snapshots were in sharper focus you'd see imperfections.) There aren't many of these snapshots and there's a mysteri-ous absence of others in them, now and then adult arms positioning me or lifting me, an adult in trousers seen stooping from behind (my father?), a woman's lap (my mother?). When I lived at home I'd stare at these old wrinkled snapshots in the family album—they were like riddles in a foreign language. I had to resist the impulse to tear them into shreds.

In Sandy Hook, it came to me. One night in my rented room I woke in a sticky sweat and the thought came fully formed like the little ticker-tape fortune in a Chinese fortune cookie—*That little girl was your sister, and she died. When you were born, they gave you her name.*

As good a solution as any.

5

"HEY, WAITRESS, over here!"

"Where you been, taking a leak? More coffee."

After two weeks, I was waitressing only in the diner. There, the atmosphere was breezy and casual. There were a number of regular customers, men, friends of Lee Yardboro's who whistled to get the attention of waitresses, often called out their orders from where they sat. These were men who ate quickly and with appetite, lowering their heads to their plates, talking and laughing with their mouths full. Such customers were not hard to please if you did as they asked, and their needs were simple, predictable; they ate and drank the same things repeatedly. They would not notice if their waitress was smiling or if the smile was forced, pained, faked, or ironic; after the first few days, they scarcely glanced at my face. My body engaged their interest, though—my heavy swinging breasts, my sturdy muscular thighs and buttocks. I weighed one hundred forty-six pounds, at five feet six. During a hot spell in September I wore loose-fitting tank tops with no bra beneath. I wore Sandy Hook Pier Day-Glo blue T-shirts and a short denim skirt with metallic studs that glittered like rhinestones. My single pair of jeans, bleached white and thin from numerous launderings, showed the bulging curve of my ass, and the crevice of its crack, vivid as a cartoon drawing. (I knew, I'd studied the effect in a mirror.) My bare legs were fleshy, covered in fine brown hairs; I wore sandals and, as a joke, painted the nails of my stubby toes eye-catching shades of green, blue, frosty-silver. Often, at rush hours, I was out of breath, my mouth moist and slack, my long snarly hair damp and clotted as seaweed at the nape of my neck. Hauling trays bearing eggs, sausage, thick hamburgers oozing blood, french fries and fried fish filets and clattering bottles of beer, I was a conversation piece, an impersonal object over which men could exchange sly grins, roll their eyes, sniff provocatively in the area of my crotch and murmur innuendos as I set plates before them—"Mmmm, baby, this looks *good*." I learned to obey, like a good-natured dog, ear-splitting whistles, even to laugh at my own haste. If in the diner I sweated and panted like a horse, no one minded. My employer Lee Yardboro, who was happiest in the diner, mornings, drinking coffee and smoking with his buddies, seemed not to mind. Or, maybe, since it was the diner and not the dining room, he didn't notice. He laughed a lot, smiled without baring his teeth. Called me "babe," "sweetheart," "honey" without sneering. Rarely did he scold me, in the diner. Rarely did he pinch me, though sometimes, for playful emphasis, he'd poke his forefinger into the soft flesh of my waist. I despised him even as I yearned to please him. I took a curious pride in the fact that, in Sandy Hook, population 7,303, where once he'd been a star high school athlete, Lee Yardboro was well known and liked by both men and women. Though he was married and the father of several nearly grown children, there was something boyish and wounded in his bulldog face as if, an American kid, he'd woken to discover himself trapped in a middle-aged man's body, burdened with a middle-aged man's responsibilities. (Maxine confided in me that her cousin Lee and his wife had a family tragedy—an artistic child who'd caused them much sorrow. I stared at Maxine looking so blank that she repeated her words and still I stared and at last I realized she must have said "autistic" and not "artistic" but by that time the confusion struck me as funny, so I laughed. Maxine was shocked. "Better not let Lee hear you. There's nothing funny about mental defects." This time, the term "mental defects," in Maxine's grimly censorious mouth, set me off. Laughed and laughed until tears ran down my cheeks.)

From above, serving Lee Yardboro as he sat in a booth with friends, I observed, with a pang of absurd tenderness, his flushed, scaly scalp through his thinning hair that he wet-combed with care across his head. I observed his rough, mottled skin, the always slightly bloodshot pale blue eyes that bulged with mirth, mock credulity, or contempt. *Don't touch me you bastard. Please touch me.*

6

BECAUSE THE Sandy Hook Diner was a place where I couldn't fail.

Because, if I failed, and was fired, as I'd been fired from other jobs, what difference would it make?

I smiled, sucking this small unassailable fact like a loose tooth.

7

THE WEATHER TURNED. I wore rust-red corduroy trousers with a fly front, so tight across my buttocks (I seemed to be gaining weight, must've been nibbling the remains of sausage, Danish pastry, french fries off my customers' plates) the seams were beginning to part, showing a flirty minuscule trace of white nylon panties beneath. Still I wore the eye-hurting blue Sandy Hook Pier T-shirts and over them unbuttoned shirts, sweaters. Often I wore, with jeans, a pebbly-green sweatshirt I'd bought at the community college bookstore with POETRY POWER on the front in stark white letters. Seeing me, my hair in a ponytail, my waitress-smile distending my lower face, you'd think, *A girl who has overcome her shyness. Good for her!*

I'd come to notice a frequent if not regular customer in the Sandy Hook Diner. He'd signal for a waitress by raising his hand and actually lowering his head, his eyes swerving downward in a kind of embarrassment, or shame. He had physical mannerisms—tics. Moving his head repeatedly as if his neck was stiff. Moving his shoulders. Clenching and unclenching his fists. I'd catch him frowning, staring at me. Looking quickly away when I turned in his direction. As if he recognized me? In fact he reminded me of a math teacher at our junior high (my hometown was an hour's drive inland from Sandy Hook, in central New Jersey) who'd quit or been fired when I was in seventh grade; but this man, who hardly looked thirty, was too young to have been Mr. Cantry, I thought. That had been nine years ago.

This customer, who always wore a tweed suit and a buttoned-up white shirt and no tie, came into the diner a few times a week, mostly for breakfast. He walked with a slight limp. He was a big man, well above six feet tall, with a boyish-fattish pale face and an oblong head like an exotic squash, and heavy-lidded, hooded eyes that settled on me, or upon my body, with a look of frowning disapproval. *Ugly girl. How can you show your-self in public.*

He was ugly, himself. Weird-ugly. But ugliness in a man doesn't matter, much. Ugliness in a woman is her life.

This character seemed always to be seated in my section of the diner. He preferred the farthest corner booth. There, he'd read a book, or give that impression. A shadow seemed always to be passing over his face as I approached with my pert waitress smile and sauntering hips, order pad and pencil in hand. There would be no small talk here. No crude-sexy banter. No laughs. Even before he ate his meals (fastidiously, but there was no dis-guising the fact that, with that big gut, he was a glutton) he looked as if he was having exquisite gas pains. His big body was as soft as something decomposing and his suits looked as if they'd belonged to his dead father. I felt a physical repugnance for him but I had to admit he was always cordial, courteous. Called me "waitress"—"miss"—and spoke slowly giving his order, watching anxiously as I wrote it down as if I might be dim-witted, not to be trusted; then he'd have me read it back. His voice was hollow and fading like a voice on a distant radio station.

One of the weird things about the man in the tweed suit was his hair, which he wore clipped short, in a crew cut. It was a flat metallic color, a no-color, like his eyes. It exaggerated his boyish appearance but made you wonder if there was some clinical reason for such short hair, like a scalp-skin ailment, or head lice.

In the off-season in the Sandy Hook Diner customers rarely tipped beyond ten percent of their bill. Some sons of bitches, under cover of not having change, or being mentally incapable of calculating ten percent, left even less. A handful of nickels. Pennies. The man in the tweed suit some-times left as much as twenty percent of his bill, though frowning, not meeting my eye, hurrying out of the diner. I'd call brightly after him, "Thank you, sir!" as much to embarrass him as to express gratitude, for in truth I didn't feel gratitude; I was more contemptuous of customers who tipped me well than of those who didn't. Next time he came in, he wouldn't look at me directly—as if I'd never been his waitress, he'd never been here before.

Because he hadn't any name and was always alone and looked so weird, the man in the tweed suit drew the ridicule of Mr. Yardboro and his friends, and my coworkers in the diner, even Maxine if she was around. Their name for him was "Lover Boy"—"Fag Boy." The word "fag," on anyone's lips, aroused particular hilarity. You'd have thought that Lee Yardboro, owner of the Sandy Hook Diner, might feel protective of any customer, and grateful, but that wasn't the case. The impulse to mock, to ridicule, to share contempt for another was too strong. (There were other customers they joked about, too, but with more tolerance. I was fascinated, wondering what they said about me behind my back.) When Mr. Yardboro cracked one of his jokes in my hearing I laughed in a way I'd cultivated in high school, overhearing guys' dirty remarks, that was laughing-not-laughing; making hissing-giggling sounds as if I was trying not to laugh, I was "shocked," eyes screwed up and shut tight and shoulders and breasts shaking in a feminine, helpless way. Mr. Yardboro glanced around, grinning. Like any bully he needed an audience.

The man in the tweed suit stepped outside the diner and two minutes later everyone forgot him. Except I'd watch him walk away, as if his legs hurt him, carrying all that weight. He came on foot, didn't have a car. Must have lived close by. One evening I saw him in the local library, frowning over reference books, taking fussy notes. One day I saw him walking on the pier, wearing an old-fashioned trench coat with a flared skirt over his tweed suit and a visored cap pulled tight onto his odd-shaped head so the wind couldn't tear it off; he was staring at his feet, oblivious of the choppy, glittering ocean, the waves crashing and throwing up spray only a few yards from him. I wondered what he was thinking that was so much more important than where he was. I envied him, sunk so deep in himself. As if he mattered!

If he glanced around, saw me, recognized me—I sure wasn't going to recognize him.

I NEVER FOLLOWED the man in the tweed suit, I only observed. From a distance. Unseen. When I wasn't working I had a lot of time to kill. My rented room (in a converted Victorian "single-family" residence) depressed me, so I avoided it. Even as I had to admit (I'd boasted to my family) it was a bargain, at off-season rates, and only five minutes from the ocean. There was a telephone for my use even if I had no one I wanted to call, and no one to call me. There was a double bed with a mattress soft as marshmallow in which, every night, for as long as ten hours if I could manage to stay asleep that long, I was sunk in a deep fantastic near-dreamless sleep like a corpse at the bottom of the ocean.

8

WHAT DID I look like, aged twenty-one? I wasn't sure.

Just as fat people learn not to view themselves full-length in mirrors, so ugly people learn to avoid seeing what it's pointless to see. I wasn't what you'd call fat, and took a perverse satisfaction in contemplating my dumpy, mock-voluptuous female body in my ridiculous clothes, but I'd stopped looking at my face years before. When, for practical purposes, I couldn't avoid looking, I'd stand close to a mirror, sidelong, to examine parts, sections. An eye, a mouth. A minuscule portion of nose. I didn't wear makeup and didn't pluck my eyebrows (I'd plucked my eyebrows more or less out in high school, furious at the way they grew together over the bridge of my nose, wrongly confident that they'd grow back) and there was no problem about scrubbing my face with a washcloth, brushing my teeth stooping low over the sink as I did once a day, before going to bed. My hair was no problem, I didn't need to look into a mirror to brush it, if I bothered to brush it; I could snip off ends myself with scissors without consulting a mirror when it grew too long, snarly. Sometimes I wore a head rag for an Indian-funky look.

Now and then I thought, not altogether seriously, about bleaching my hair platinum blond, wearing it in some chic sexy style. One of my vivid childhood memories (there aren't many) was seeing two teenage boys observing a girl in high heels walking ahead of them on a sidewalk, a girl with a glossy blond pageboy, a good figure, and when they caught up with her to get a better look she turned to them and she was plain, homely—she wore glasses, she was horse-faced. One boy groaned rudely, the other laughed. They poked each other in the ribs the way boys do. The girl turned away, pretending not to know what all this meant. I hadn't been that girl but I'd seen, and I'd heard. Already, not ten years old, I knew my fate.

One advantage of *ugly:* you don't require anyone to see you the way a good-looking person does, to be real. The better-looking you are, the more dependent upon being seen and admired. The uglier, the more independent.

Another advantage of *ugly:* you don't waste time trying to look your best, you will never look your best.

What I remember of my face is a low forehead, a long nose with a bulblike tip, dark shiny eyes set too close together. Those dark thick eyebrows like an orangutan's. A mouth of no distinction but well practiced, before I entered my teens, in irony. For what is irony but the repository of hurt? And what is hurt but the repository of hope? My skin was darkish-olive like something smeared by an eraser. My pores were oily, even before puberty. In some eyes I looked "foreign." I'd looked "foreign" as far back as grade school, when the teasing began. I came to like the feeling—"foreign." Like "foreign substance"—"foreign object"—in food, in an eye, on a radar screen. Though no one on either side of my family has been "foreign" for generations. All proud to be "one hundred percent American" though none of us had a clue what "American" meant.

9

BUSINESS WAS SLOW at the Sandy Hook Inn, now the weather had turned. Tourists avoided the northern New Jersey seashore where always there was a wet, whining wind and the brightest sun could be eclipsed within minutes by glowering thunderheads. Each morning before dawn the wind woke me, rattling my single window like a cruel prank. My legs, feet, and spine ached profoundly from the previous day's waitressing, yet I was excited by the prospect of enduring another day at the Sandy Hook Diner. *I've come to the right place by instinct. Here is the edge.*

The Sandy Hook Diner, its exterior built to resemble a railroad car. Glinting like cheap tin.

The Sandy Hook Diner, in the early morning: a row of ten frayed black vinyl stools at the Formica counter. Eight frayed black vinyl booths along the outer wall.

The Sandy Hook Diner, fluorescent tubing overhead that glared like an eye impairment. In a smiling trance I'd rub, rub, rub the worn Formica and aluminum surfaces with a sponge as if charged with the holy duty of restoring to them their original lustre, beauty.

Who did all this? Shining like a mirror?—Mr. Yardboro would exclaim. Then they would tell him who did it.

The Sandy Hook Diner, careening through my sleep, dragging me beneath its wheels. God, was I excited! Hurrying to work breathless in the wind, arriving at 6:50 A.M. Eyes darting to see if, in the parking lot, Mr. Yardboro's slightly battered Lincoln Continental was parked in its usual place. (Some mornings, Mr. Yardboro came in late. Some mornings, he didn't come in at all.)

I wondered if his autistic child was a son or a daughter. If a daughter, whether she showed obvious signs of mental deficiency. Whether what was strange and wrong in her shone in her eyes.

Do not cry in contempt, *The dumb bitch is in love with*—*him? That ass-hole? Without knowing it?* Always I knew, from the time of the interview. One of my jokes, on myself. Providing plenty of laughs.

Because business was slow in the Sandy Hook Diner my shifts were erratic. Another, older waitress had disappeared; I made no inquiries. I worked hard, harder. I smiled. I smiled at the upturned faces of customers, and I smiled at the departing backs of customers. I smiled fiercely as I wiped down the greasy grill, cleaned the Formica-topped surfaces until, almost, they shone. I fantasized that, if dismissed by Mr. Yardboro from the Sandy Hook Diner, I would have no choice but to wade out into the Atlantic Ocean and drown myself. I would have to choose a remote place and I would have to act by night. But the vision of my clumsy, sodden body on the beach amid rotting kelp and dead fish, picked at by seagulls, was a deterrent.

10

"SWEETHEART, more coffee!"

One morning, Artie, who was a trucker-friend of Mr. Yardboro's, whistled to get my attention, and afterward the man in the tweed suit who'd been sitting in a corner booth said severely, "They are rude! You should not have to tolerate it! Why do you tolerate it?" I stared in disbelief that he'd actually spoken to me. He was on his feet, preparing abruptly to leave, glaring down at me. I couldn't think of a thing to say, not a word; all that came to me was an apology, but an apology for another person's rudeness made no sense. So I said nothing. The man in the tweed suit wheezed in disgust, on his way out of the Sandy Hook Diner. Afterward I would remember how his puffy-pale face had flushed unevenly, like an attack of hives.

Later that morning, when the diner was nearly empty, the man in the tweed suit returned. He was looking for a glove he'd left behind, he said. But we found no glove in the area of the booth in which he'd sat. Embarrassed, working his mouth in a complicated tic, he said, in a lowered voice, "I hope—I didn't upset you, miss. It isn't my business of course. You, and this environment." We stared grimly at each other, like losers pushed together on a dance floor. I saw that he wasn't so young after all—there were sharp indentations beneath his eyes, lines in his forehead. I was trying to think of an intelligent, conciliatory, or even witty reply, but though I was smiling automatically a sudden ringing in my ears drowned out my thoughts. As, in school, called upon by a teacher, or made to write a crucial exam, I'd be overcome by a kind of malicious static. The man in the tweed suit had obviously planned this speech, it was to be a gallant and noble speech, but he'd become self-conscious and was losing his confidence. Doggedly he continued, "It's—ugly to witness. I realize you need the employment. The tips. For why else. Of course. You seem not to expect better."

I heard myself stammer, "But I like it here. I—I'm grateful."

"What is your age?"

"My age? Twenty-one."

It seemed a shameful admission, suddenly. I wanted to scream at the bastard to leave me alone.

He saw the misery in my eyes, and turned away. Cleared his throat with a tearing, ripping sound, and must have had to swallow a clot of phlegm. "I think—you were a student of mine, once? Years ago."

Mr. Cantry? He *was*?

But he'd left the diner. I stared after him, stunned. Earlier, he'd left two crumpled dollar bills on the tabletop for me in his haste to escape, and a breakfast platter of eggs, sausage, and home fries only partly eaten. I'd pocketed the bills like a robot not knowing what they were. I'd eaten the sausage and most of the home fries not knowing what they were.

11

NEXT DAY, the man in the tweed suit stayed away from the Sandy Hook Diner, and the next. I was anxious and resentful watching for him each time someone his size pushed through the door. I was relieved when he didn't show up.

I tried to remember what had happened to Mr. Cantry nine years ago. I hadn't liked him as a teacher—but I hadn't liked most of my teachers, ever. There'd been rumors, wild tales. He'd quarreled with the school principal one day in the cafeteria. He'd slapped a boy. He'd been stopped for drunk driving and he'd resisted arrest and been beaten, handcuffed, taken to the police station, and booked. Or he'd had a breakdown in some public place—a doctor's waiting room. A local grocery store. He'd started shouting, he'd burst into tears. Or had he gotten sick, had major surgery. He'd been hospitalized for a long time and when at last he was released, his job teaching seventh- and eighth-grade math was no longer waiting for him.

A popular young woman had subbed for him and was eventually hired to take his place. Within a few weeks Mr. Cantry had been totally forgotten even by the few students who'd admired him.

IN THE DOORWAY of a dry cleaner's, up the block from the Sandy Hook Diner, he stood out of the rain waiting for me. Impossible to believe he wasn't waiting for me. Yet, clumsily, he expressed surprise at seeing me. He stepped quickly out onto the sidewalk, unfurling a large black umbrella. "Hello! A coincidence! But I'm afraid I've forgotten your name?"

He held the umbrella over me, gallantly. The rain came in feathery slices, thin as ocean spray. He was smiling eagerly, and already I despised myself for not running away. "Xavia."

" 'Zavv-ya'?"

"It's Romanian."

Xavia was not a name I'd ever heard of until that moment. Like static it had flown into my head.

So we walked together. Blindly it seemed. I would have turned at the next corner on my way home but, Mr. Cantry beside me, talking in his strange halting voice, I forgot where I was going. Again he apologized for speaking as he had in the diner—"But I don't believe that place is a healthy environment for a girl like you." I said, "What kind of girl would it be healthy for, then?" but Mr. Cantry didn't respond to the joke. He was speaking vehemently of "environment," "health," "decency," "justice." I couldn't follow the thread of his remarks. As we stood at a corner waiting for a light to change—there was no traffic in either direction—he introduced himself as "Virgil Cantry" and put out his hand to shake mine. I had no choice but to take it—his hand was firm, fleshy. "Would it be permissible for me to accompany you home, Xavia?"

I yearned to say, *No! No it would not be permissible!* but instead I said, in my bright waitressy voice, "Why not?"

Loneliness is like starvation: you don't realize how hungry you are until you begin to eat.

*   *   *

"I'M NO LONGER a teacher, I would describe myself as a private citizen now. A witness." Mr. Cantry held the umbrella over me at a gallant distance, choosing to walk in the rain himself. His large oddly shaped head bobbed and weaved as he spoke; he was constantly shifting, shrugging his shoulders inside his trench coat. He seemed both excited in my presence and acutely nervous. As we walked, an awkward couple, Mr. Cantry a head taller than me, I tried to avoid knocking against his arm; my heart was beating quickly, with a kind of fainting, incredulous dread; yet I had to resist the impulse to snort with laughter, too. For wasn't this a kind of date? A romantic encounter? I wondered what the two of us looked like, a couple walking along a near-deserted commercial street in Sandy Hook, New Jersey, in the rain. If it was the movies you wouldn't have a clue how to respond without music—is the scene solemn, sad, touching, comical? "I was sick for a while," Mr. Cantry said, "and in my sickness my ego was dissolved. I discovered that our historical existences are not our essence. I believe I'm free now of ego-contamination and distraction. It's enough that I *exist*. For to exist is to *witness*. My astigmatism is so severe, ordinary glasses would be inadequate, so I must wear contact lenses, yet—it's with clear eyes that I have learned to *see*."

I said, "I wear contact lenses, too. I hate them."

I smiled, it wasn't the right response. But Mr. Cantry seemed hardly to be listening. He said, "You were one of my students, Xavia? I thought I recognized you weeks ago, in the diner, but I don't recall the name— 'Xavia.' I think I would recall such an exotic name."

"I wasn't an exotic student. I didn't do well in math."

"I remember you as an intelligent, serious student. But shy. Perhaps anxious. You asked for 'extra credit' assignments in homework and they were always diligently done."

I heard myself laugh harshly, in embarrassment. "That wasn't me, Mr. Cantry."

"Please call me Virgil. Yes, surely it was you."

I resented it, that this man, a stranger, should claim to know more about me than I knew about myself.

Because I hadn't turned up the street to my apartment house, I was obliged now to improvise a route back in that direction. Mr. Cantry, earnestly speaking of his teaching years, his illness, and his convalescence and his "transmogrification" of ego, took no evident notice of where we were going. Like a blinded bull, he might be led by the lightest touch in any direction. He seemed not to mind or perhaps not to notice the rain, which was quite cold; he continued to hold the big black umbrella out over my head. I fantasized that I could have led this strange man any-where—out to the Sandy Hook Pier, where, at this hour, teenage boys would be playing video games in a hangar-sized garishly lit arcade, or along the windswept, littered beach in the direction of scrubby Sandy Hook, at the far end of which was a white-painted lighthouse, a local monument, unused as a lighthouse for decades. It seemed strange to me, it made me uneasy, that this man who didn't know me at all was so trusting.

"You have moved away from your home, Xavia? Are you living alone now?"

I yearned to say *I prefer not to discuss my private life with you, thank you!* but instead I said, in my bright waitressy voice, "Alone."

"*I* have never married," Mr. Cantry said fastidiously. "It was never an occasion."

"That's too bad."

"No, no, no! Some natures, it isn't for them to marry. To sire children, in any case."

"You can be married without having children, Mr. Cantry."

Mr. Cantry said vehemently, "What purpose is there of marriage, then? The marital bond is legalized, reinforced *nature*. It is a social embod-iment of *nature*. To reproduce the species, to nurture the offspring. If there are no offspring, there need be no marriage."

I couldn't quarrel with Mr. Cantry there. I wondered what we were talking about. At least, he wasn't proposing marriage.

Now we were on the narrower, darker street where I lived; it seemed that Mr. Cantry and I were blundering against each other more frequently. Several times he murmured, "Excuse me!" I was thinking sometime in eighth grade, around the time I'd begun to menstruate, my skin had started to go bad; it was possible that Mr. Cantry remembered me before the onslaught of the pimply infections. I could not seem to remember him at all now.

It crossed my mind that I might lead Mr. Cantry to another apartment house and say good night to him there. Yet he appeared so oblivious of his surroundings, I reasoned he wouldn't remember which house was mine. He walked with me up onto the porch of the house, out of the rain. He was panting from the few steps and his voice was strained. As if we'd been discussing the matter all along, he said, "So, you see, Xavia—I realize my opinion is unsolicited—I feel strongly that you should search for another job. A more civilized environment, yes?"

"*You* could eat somewhere else, Mr. Cantry."

"That isn't the point! *You* are the one who is being demeaned."

I yearned to say with a vulgar laugh, *Fuck you! Who's demeaned?*

I said, annoyed, "Look. I didn't graduate from college, Mr. Cantry. I barely graduated from high school. I'm lucky to have any job at all. And I told you—I like the Sandy Hook Diner."

This was the most I'd uttered to another human being in weeks, maybe months. I felt brash and invigorated, as if I'd been running.

Mr. Cantry said, sniffing, "Well, then. I stand corrected."

I'd disappointed him. He'd been mistaking me for an A-student and now he was learning otherwise.

I thanked Mr. Cantry for his concern and said good night. He was backing away uncertainly, as if suddenly aware of our situation beneath a porch light, our aloneness together. I saw that he contemplated shaking my hand again and discreetly I hid both my hands behind me. He said, hesitantly, "Maybe if, another time, you wished it—we might have dinner together? Not at the diner." It was an attempt at a joke but I failed to catch the joke, saying quickly, before I heard myself say *yes*, "Well. I don't know. Maybe."

From inside the musty-smelling vestibule of the old house I observed my former math teacher carefully descend the porch steps and walk away in the rain. It was clear that he limped slightly, favoring his right leg. His shoulders distinctly sagged. On the porch, not seeming to know what he did, he'd shut up the umbrella as if preparing to come inside the house and now, out in the rain again, he'd forgotten to open it.

THAT NIGHT, I had a rare dream. One of my lurid hurt-fantasies (as I called them: I'd had such fantasies since grade school). *At the Sandy Hook Diner having to serve the male customers who were Mr. Yardboro's friends though no one I exactly recognized. And Mr. Yardboro was calling me, whistling for me. I had to serve the men naked. A filmy strip of cloth like a curtain wrapped around me, coming loose. My breasts were exposed, I couldn't conceal myself. My coarse-hairy groin. The men called* waitress! here! *the way you'd call a dog. But it was meant to be playful, they were just teasing. No one actually touched me. I had to come close to them to serve them their food, but no one touched me. They were eat-*

ing pieces of meat, with their fingers. I saw bright blood smeared on their mouths and fingers. I saw that they were eating female parts. Breasts and genitals. Slices of pink-glistening meat, picked out of hairy skin-pouches the way you'd pick oysters out of their shells. The men laughed at the look on my face. They tossed coins at me, nickels and pennies, and I stooped to pick the coins up and my face heated with blood and I felt a strong sexual sensation like the pressure of a rubber balloon being blown larger and larger about to burst and I woke anxious and excited, my heart beating so rapidly it hurt, and cold, slick sweat covered my body inside my soiled flannel nightie and it was a long time before I got back to sleep. I didn't dream about Mr. Cantry at all.

12

BY THE END of November my hours at the Sandy Hook Diner had been cut back considerably. My shifts were unpredictable, depending upon the availability of other waitresses (I gathered). One day I might begin at 7 A.M., the next at 4:30 P.M.—the hour of the Early Bird Dinner (a senior citizens' special platter, $7.99). Other days, I didn't work at all. I slept.

When I worked the evening shift at the diner, somehow Mr. Cantry seemed to know. He'd linger over coffee as late as 10 P.M. when the diner closed, in the hope of "escorting" me home.

Politely I told him thanks but I had another engagement.

I whispered fiercely to him, not wanting anyone else to hear.

I was in perpetual terror of being fired from the Sandy Hook Diner and so moved in a trance of energy, high spirits, and smiles. My wide, fixed smile was so deeply imprinted in my face, it was slow to fade after my shift ended; sometimes, waking in the middle of the night, I discovered that it had returned. *Waitress! waitress!* I heard myself summoned impatiently and turned to see no one, no customer, there.

Though Mr. Cantry was there, often. In his corner booth, which was usually in my section. Brown tweed suit, stiff-starched white shirt. The metallic glimmer of his crew cut. Shifting his shoulders and odd-shaped head as if the alignment of his neck required continuous adjustment. Since the evening he'd walked me home, we hadn't spoken at any length; still, when I approached, he smiled eagerly, shyly. I gave him no encouragement. I dreaded anyone at the diner guessing that Lover Boy—Fag Boy— and I knew each other, however remotely we knew each other. When Mr. Cantry greeted me, "Hello, Xavia! How are you this morning?" I smiled like a robot and said, "What may I get you, sir?" If Mr. Cantry dared to leave me too large a tip (for instance, a $5 bill for a seafood platter costing $9.99!) I'd call after him, "Sir, you forgot your change." Blushing, contrite, he'd accept the money back from me with a murmured apology.

At such moments my heart pounded in vengeful triumph. My cheeks glowed with the heat of my blood. As in my high school gym classes when I'd outscored, outrun, intimidated, and frankly bullied other girls in our rowdy games of basketball and volleyball, at which, being so much stronger than the others, I'd excelled.

13

ONE EVENING at closing time there was no one in the Sandy Hook Diner except Mr. Yardboro and me.

How's about a ride, honey? Mr. Yardboro said and there we were in his slightly rusted but still glamorous, sexy Lincoln Continental cruising along the shore road. Beyond the Sandy Hook lighthouse, beyond Sandy Hook State Park. A moon like polished bone, moonlight rippling on the dark water. Lee Yardboro was a man to drive fast and unerringly with one arm resting on the steering wheel and the other on my shoulders. The interior of the car was warm, dreamy. My head on Mr. Yardboro's shoulder, forehead against his throat. It wasn't clear what we talked of, maybe we talked of nothing at all, there was no need. His distinctive smell, his smoker's breath, his body, his armpits, the ointment he rubbed into his roughened skin made me dizzy, delirious. *Where are we going? What will you do to me?* If I looked too closely, however, at the girl with her head on Lee Yardboro's shoulder, I saw that her hair was shimmering blond. Her face was a heart-shaped pretty-pretty face, no face I knew. Even the pearly moonlight rippling on the ocean dissolved, sheerly vapor.

Yet there was another evening, and no one in the Sandy Hook Diner at closing time except Mr. Yardboro and me. And I wiped down the booths for the final time that day, and the counter. And turned off the lights. And in the kitchen doorway Mr. Yardboro stood, hands on his hips and watching me, smiling in that teasing way that could be friendly or mean. Saying, "C'mon into the kitchen for a few minutes, honey, I've got some special instructions for you."

14

AT THANKSGIVING I took a bus home not wanting to go home but my mother pleaded with me angrily on the phone and I knew it was a mistake but there I was, in the old house, the house of one thousand and one associations and all of them depressing, the smell of the roasting turkey sickened me, the smell of the basting grease, the smell of my mother's hair spray so I realized I wouldn't get through it within minutes after walking through the door and that afternoon we were working together in the kitchen and I said excuse me, Mom, I'll be right back and when I came back with the old photo album the palms of my hands were cold with sweat and I said, "Mom, can I ask you something?" and guardedly my mother said, for years of living with me had made her wary, "What?" and I said, "Promise you'll tell the truth, Mom?" and she says, "What is the question?" and I said again, "Promise me you'll tell the truth, Mom," and she said, annoyed, "How can I promise, until I hear the question?" and I said, "All right. Did I have a sister born before me, given my name, and did she die? That's all I want to know," and my mother stared at me as if I'd shouted filthy words right there in her kitchen, and said, "Alice, *what?*" and I repeated my question which was to me a perfectly logical question, and my mother said, "Of course you didn't have a sister who died! Where do you get your ideas?" and I said, "Here. These snapshots," and I opened the album to show her the snapshots of me as a baby and as a little girl saying, in a low, furious voice, "Don't try to tell me this is me, it isn't," and my mother said, her voice rising, "Of course she's you! That's you! Are you crazy?" and I said, "Can I believe you, Mom?" and she said, "What is this? Is this another of your jokes? Of course that's you," and I said, wiping at my eyes, "It isn't! Goddamned liar! It isn't! This is someone else, this isn't me! This is a pretty little girl and I'm ugly and *this isn't me!*" and my mother lost it then as often she did in our quarrels, lost it and began shouting at me, and slapped my face, sobbing, "You terrible, terrible girl! Why do you say such things! You break my heart! You *are* ugly! Go away, get away! We don't want you here! You don't belong here with normal people!"

So I left. Took the next bus back to Sandy Hook so it seemed, when I went to bed that night, early, hoping to sleep through twelve hours at least, that I'd never been gone.

15

THE FOLLOWING Sunday evening Mr. Cantry dared to come to my apartment house. Ringing my buzzer as if I were expecting him! It was the first time the buzzer to 3F had been rung in the weeks I'd been living in this shabby place and the sound was as deafening as the amplified screams of maddened wasps. I wished I hadn't known who it it was, but I knew.

Taking my time I went downstairs, in my soiled POETRY POWER sweatshirt and jeans. And there was my former math teacher squinting up at me out of his puffy face the color of lard. He wore the trench coat with the flared skirt, he was turning his visored cap nervously in his fingers. "Xavia, good evening! I hope I'm not interrupting? Would you like to join me in a meal?—not at the Sandy Hook Diner." He paused for my response but I didn't smile, I said only that I'd already eaten, thank you. "Then to go for a walk? To have a drink? Is this a possible time? I saw you were not on duty at the usual place so I presumed to come here. Are you angry?"

I intended to say *Thank you, but I'm busy.* I heard myself say, "I could take a walk, I guess. Why should I be angry?"

I'd been cool to Mr. Cantry in the diner, the last couple of times he'd come in. I didn't like him brooding in his corner booth watching me. Frowning-smiling as if sometimes he didn't actually see *me*, God knows what he was seeing. And the day before, some guys had been teasing me the way some of the regular customers do, passing around a copy of *Hustler;* I was supposed to catch a glimpse of these photos of female crotches in stark closeup as in an anatomical text. My part was to pretend I didn't see, didn't know what it was I didn't see, my face blushing in patches. *Hey guys, I wish you wouldn't!* My embarrassed downcast eyes. My wide hips, my hubcap breasts inside a Sandy Hook Pier T-shirt and unbuttoned sweater. *But it's OK. I'm a good sport.* Not begging exactly, guys hate females who beg, like females who cry, makes them feel guilty, reminds them of their mothers. More as though I was asking for their protection. And it was OK, or would have been except there was Mr. Cantry looming up behind me, in his old teacher-voice and his mouth twisted in disdain, "Excuse me! Just one moment, please!" and the guys gaped up at him in astonishment not knowing what the hell was going on but I knew, I believed I knew, quickly I turned and tugged at Mr. Cantry's sleeve and led him back to his booth and whispered, "Leave me alone, God damn you," and he whispered back, "They are harassing you, those disgusting louts," and I whispered, "How do you know? How do you know what's going on?"—did he have X-ray eyes? Could he see through the backs of booths? So I got Mr. Cantry to settle down and returned to my other customers and they were laughing, making remarks, and I more or less pretended not to catch on to anything, just a dumb waitress, smiling hard and trying to please her customers—*Hey, guys, have a heart, will you?* So finally it worked out, they left me OK tips in small coins scattered across the sticky tabletop. But I was sore as hell at Mr. Cantry and would've asked him please never to come into the Sandy Hook Diner again except frankly we needed the revenue.

"I hope you are not upset, about yesterday? You didn't seem pleased."

"Those customers are the owner's friends. I have to be nice to them."

"They are crude, vulgar. They are—"

"They're the owner's friends. And I like them, anyway."

"You like them? Such men?"

I shrugged. I laughed. "Men, boys. 'Boys will be boys.' "

"But not in my classroom."

"You don't have a classroom now."

We were excited. It was like a lover's quarrel. I walked in quickened steps, ahead of Mr. Cantry. I believed I could feel the sharp stabbing pains in his legs, bearing the weight of his ungainly body.

We went to Woody's, a café I'd seen from the outside, admiring the winking lights, a preview of Christmas. Through an oval window in a wall of antique brick I'd often seen romantic couples by firelight, holding hands at the curving bar or at tables in the rear. Once Mr. Cantry and I were inside, seated at a table, our knees bumping awkwardly, the place seemed different. The firelight was garishly synthetic and a loud tape of teenage rock music played and replayed like migraine. Mr. Cantry winced at the noise but was determined to be a good sport. I ordered a vodka martini—a drink I'd never had before in my life. Vodka, I knew, had the most potent alcohol content of any available drink. Mr. Cantry ordered a club soda with a twist of lemon. Our waiter was young and bored-looking, staring at Mr. Cantry, and at me, with a pointedly neutral expression.

"A person yearns to make something of himself. Herself. A being of distinction," Mr. Cantry said, raising his voice to be heard over the din. "You must agree?"

I hadn't been following the conversation. I was trying to twist a rubber band around my ponytail, which was straggling down my back, but the rubber band was old and frayed and finally broke and I gave up. My vodka martini arrived and I took a large swallow even as Mr. Cantry lifted his glass to click against mine, saying, "Cheers!"

I said, feeling mean, "But why should a person make something of himself?—herself? Who gives a shit, frankly?"

"Xavia. You can't mean that." Mr. Cantry looked more perplexed than shocked, the way my mother used to look before she caught on to the deep vein of ugliness to which she'd given birth. "I don't think that's an honest response. I challenge that response."

I said, "Most people aren't distinctive. Most lives come to nothing. Why not accept it?"

"But it's human nature to wish to better oneself. That the inner being becomes outer. Not to sink into desolation. Not to—*give up*." He spoke with a fastidious curl of his lip.

"Haven't you given up, Mr. Cantry?"

This was a cruel taunt. I surprised myself, aiming for the man's heart. But to his credit Mr. Cantry took it well. He drew his shoulders up, took a deep breath, brooded. Then he said, "Outwardly, perhaps. Inwardly, *no*."

"What's 'inward'? The soul? The belly?"

"Xavia, you shock me. This is not truly you."

"If you look in a mirror, Mr. Cantry, do you seriously think that what you see isn't you? Who is it, then?"

"I am disinclined to mirrors," Mr. Cantry said, sniffing. He'd finished his club soda, ice and all, and was sucking at the lemon twist. "I have never taken mirrors as a measure of the soul."

I laughed. I was feeling good. The vodka martini was a subtler drink than I'd anticipated, and delicious. Blue jets of flame raced along my veins, antic as the synthetic gas jets in the fireplace. "*I'm* ugly. I don't need to kid myself."

Mr. Cantry stared at me, pursing his lips. "Xavia, you are not *ugly*. What a thing to say!"

"I'm not? I'm not ugly?" I laughed, slapping my fleshy cheeks. The flames were passing over me, my skin was feverish.

Mr. Cantry chose his words with care. "You are a young woman of an exotic cast. You are not conventionally attractive, perhaps—in the bland, banal way of American 'girls.' Your eyes, your facial structure—intriguing! But not ugly."

I was fed up with this bullshit. I signaled the bored-looking waiter. He was about my age, with a round-button boy's face, long eyelashes, and a rosebud mouth. A pretty boy, and he knew it. "Waiter," I said, and when the waiter nodded agreeably, if a bit guardedly, I said, "Am I ugly?"

"Excuse me?"

Mr. Cantry hissed, like a scandalized parent, "Xavia! Please."

"Well, waiter—am I? You can tell the truth, it won't affect your tip."

The embarrassed young man stared at me, his face reddening.

"I mean," I said, flirtatiously, "it *will* affect your tip. If you don't give an honest answer."

The waiter tried to smile, to make the exchange into a joke.

"Am I ugly? Just tell the truth."

But the waiter mumbled words of apology, he was wanted in the kitchen, he escaped.

Mr. Cantry scolded, "You should not embarrass people, Xavia. If you are unhappy with yourself—"

I protested, "But I'm not. I'm not unhappy with myself. I'm happy with myself. I just believe in telling the truth, that's all."

A few minutes later the waiter returned, probably with a witty rejoinder prepared, but by this time Mr. Cantry and I were discussing other matters. The vodka had gone to my head, I was in a good mood. "Another round," I said, snapping my fingers. "For both."

Mr. Cantry took out a large white handkerchief and carefully, loudly blew his nose. If I'd begun to feel something for the man, these blasts of sound dispelled it. I said, leaning forward solemnly, "Mr. Cantry, do you think much about death? Dying?"

It was like holding a lighted match to flammable material.

For a pained moment Mr. Cantry could not speak. His eyes quavered as if on the verge of dissolution. I saw that his skin, like what I recalled of my own, looked stitched-together, improvised; as if he'd been smashed into pieces and carelessly mended. "Death, yes. Dying. Yes. I think about dying all the time." He went on to speak of his parents, who were both deceased, and of a sister he'd loved who had died of leukemia at the age of eleven, and of a dog he'd brought here to Sandy Hook to live with him, a cocker spaniel who'd died in August at the age of only seven years. Since this dog's death, Mr. Cantry confessed, he'd had to face the prospect of, each morning, wondering where he would get the strength to force himself out of bed; he slept long, stuporous hours and believed he came very close to death sometimes—"My heart stopping, you know, like a clock—the way my father died. In his sleep. Aged fifty-two." As Mr. Cantry spoke, I saw tears gathering in his eyes; his eyes seemed to me beautiful, luminous; his moist loose lips, even the glistening of his nostrils; my heart beat quickly in resistance to the emotion he was feeling, the emotion which pumped through me yet which I refused to acknowledge. A mean voice taunted, *So that's why he's been dogging you. He's lost his only friend—a dog.*

I was fascinated by this ugly man who seemed not to know he was ugly. When rivulets of tears ran down both his cheeks, and in embarrassed haste he wiped them with a cocktail napkin, I leaned back in my seat and glanced about the crowded café, in a pose of boredom. Mr. Cantry's nose was seriously running and once again he blew it loudly, in a cocktail napkin this time, mine. By the time he was finished, I was well out of my sentimental mood.

I finished my vodka martini and stood. Mr. Cantry fumbled to stand beside me, like a man wakened from a dream. His bulbous forehead gleamed with perspiration. He followed close behind me as I pushed my way toward the door of the café, saying, "Xavia, I think you must know—I am attracted to you. I realize the difference in age. In sensibility. I hope I don't offend you?"

There was a crush of people at the coatrack. Almost, I managed to escape my companion.

Out on the sidewalk, in the freezing air, a second time Mr. Cantry said, pleading, "I hope, Xavia—I don't offend you?"

Pointedly, I didn't answer. I'd thrown on my windbreaker and crammed my knit cap down tight on my head. The windbreaker was unisex and bulky and the navy blue cap made my head look peanut-small. I caught a sidelong glance at myself in a beveled mirror banked by ferns in the café window and winced even as I laughed. God, I was ugly! It was no exaggeration. Almost, such ugliness is a kind of triumph, like a basket you sink after having been fouled.

RETURNING TO my apartment house I walked quickly, forcing Mr. Cantry to hurry beside me. His breath was audible, like sandpaper rubbed against a rough surface. Poor man, I wondered if varicose veins raddled his pulpy-white legs. I wondered if his feet, like mine, swelled like twin goiters and required nightly soaking in Epsom salts. Yet Mr. Cantry tried to catch his breath, and to regain some of his squandered dignity. "As to death, Xavia—I believe the subject is pointless to discuss. For when you are dead, you are in a state of blissful nonexistence; and in nonexistence is non-knowing. And where there is non-knowing—"

He spoke passionately, gesturing with his hands. I might have been moved, but the effect of his speech was weakened by the abrupt way in which, seeing a Sandy Hook police cruiser passing on the street, he became rattled; he shrank back as if fearful of being seen. I made a joke about the vigilance of the local police in this place where nothing ever happened but Mr. Cantry was too distracted to respond. He didn't relax again until the cruiser was out of sight.

I said, annoyed, "The fact is, Mr. Cantry, you *die*. It's an active verb. You *die*, I *die*. We *die*. It isn't a blissful state, it's an action. And there's terror, there's pain. Like drowning in the ocean—"

But Mr. Cantry was distracted, and maybe demoralized. I left him on the sidewalk in front of my house, thanked him for the drinks, and hurried up the porch steps before he could accompany me, wheezing and wincing. He called after me, "Xavia—good night?"

16

"THAT LEE!—he's so damned softhearted. Leaves the dirty work to *me*."

It was Maxine on the phone, her horsey face drawn downward in fond exasperation at her cousin. Though he owned the Sandy Hook Inn, or anyway held a sizable mortgage on the property, Maxine was the one who, at his command, routinely laid off or dismissed employees.

I hadn't been meant to hear this remark, of course. Maxine didn't know I'd drifted within earshot.

To my horror, a new waitress had been hired. I hadn't seen her but had heard rumors of her—a redhead, good-looking it was said. Since November, business in the diner had dropped a bit farther, then stabilized. A shrine-like McDonald's had opened a mile away and would surely draw more of our customers. We never acknowledged such rivals; even to allude to them would be to stir Mr. Yardboro's fury.

I believed that, in his way, Mr. Yardboro liked me. Yet he watched me closely, as he watched all his employees. His pale-blue bulging eyes following me, jaws working as he sucked at a toothpick. *Hey, sweetheart. Hey, honey—speed it up, eh? But don't go barging around like a goddamn horse.* I tried to obey Mr. Yardboro without his needing to give instructions. I tried to anticipate his smallest wish. I was very nice, never failed to smile, while waiting on his noisy pals. I never complained behind Mr. Yardboro's back, bitterly, like the others. Never cut corners, never hid away in the lavatory cursing and weeping. My only weakness, which I tried to keep secret, was eating leftovers from customers' plates. Like most food workers, I had quickly developed a repugnance for food; yet I continued to eat, despite the repugnance; once I began eating, no matter what the food, no matter how unappetizing, my mouth flooded with saliva and it was impossible for me to stop eating. The day I'd overheard Maxine on the phone, which had been a hectic, nervous day for me, a day of stingy tips and picky customers, a day of profound metaphysical repugnance, I pushed into the kitchen with a tray of dirtied platters and no one was watching so quickly I devoured the remains of a cheeseburger almost raw at its center, leaking blood, and several onion rings, and french fries soaked in ketchup. In an instant I was ravenous, dazed. I started in on another platter, devouring the remains of some batterfried perch, a foul-fishy taste even ketchup couldn't disguise, and at that terrible moment Mr. Yardboro slammed through the swinging door whistling, must have seen me, my guilty frightened eyes and greasy mouth and fingers, but in a gesture of unexpected tact—or out of simple embarrassment, for there were things that embarrassed even Lee Yardboro—he continued on his way back into the office, pretending he hadn't seen.

Though at closing time saying, with a disdainful twist of his mouth, and his blue gaze raking me up and down, "Eat as much leftover-crap as you want, honey. Saves wear and tear on the garbage disposal."

17

MR. CANTRY HAD STOPPED eating in the Sandy Hook Diner, it seemed. Only by accident did I learn, from a remark made by another waitress, that "that big weird-looking guy with the crew cut" had come in a couple of weeks ago, when I hadn't been on duty, and Mr. Yardboro had told him please not to patronize his diner any more because other customers—meaning Mr. Yardboro's pals, who'd been pissed at Lover Boy over the *Hustler* incident—had complained about him. "And what did the man say?" I asked. It was curious how my mouth twisted in a smile of childish complicity as if, talking with this mean-spirited woman whom I didn't know and didn't like any more than she liked me about an individual helpless to defend himself, we were establishing rapport. We were behaving like friends! "He said something like, 'Thank you, it is exactly my wish as well.' And walked out. Like this weird teacher I had in high school, always making speeches toward the ceiling." I laughed, trying to imagine the scene. Thank God he hadn't said anything about "Xavia." I was relieved no one could connect the two of us.

Did I think about Mr. Cantry, my old math teacher? No I did not. Erased him from my thoughts like wiping down a sticky Formica table.

Except, the blowy, dark afternoon of Christmas eve, when we were closing early (it was a lonely time—Mr. Yardboro and his family were spending a week in Orlando, Florida), there came Mr. Cantry to ask if he might see me that evening. He was wearing a bulky black wool overcoat and a black homburg pulled down tight on his forehead. His no-color eyes, fixed to my face, shone with yearning and reproach in about equal measure—as if I'd been the one to bar him from the Sandy Hook Diner. I wanted to say *What? Are you kidding? Christmas eve, with you?* but I heard myself say, sighing, "Well. All right. But only for a little while."

The diner was minimally but colorfully decorated for Christmas. Maxine and I had decorated it together, and I was sort of proud of it. There were strips of tinsel, plastic mistletoe, and holly above the booths; there was a three-foot plastic evergreen with winking bubble lights in a window; there was a comical fat-bellied Santa Claus beside the cash register whose nose could be lighted (the joke in the diner was, this Santa Claus resembled Mr. Yardboro with his flushed cheeks and bulging blue eyes). I asked Mr. Cantry what he thought of the decorations, making my question ironic, and Mr. Cantry looked around as if taking inventory, slowly. There was no one else in the diner at the moment and, seeing it through Mr. Cantry's eyes, I felt a wave of horror pass over me—the Sandy Hook Diner was only this, the sum of its surfaces. It was like one of those trendy hard-edged realist paintings of city scenes, neon, chrome, Formica, plastic, and glass you stare at trying to comprehend why anybody's asshole enough to have painted it.

Mr. Cantry said, meaning to be kind, "It does capture a kind of Christmas spirit."

★   ★   ★

DESPITE HIS PAINED WALKING, Mr. Cantry insisted upon coming to escort me to his place. I was surprised to discover it was on a street parallel with my street, a few blocks away; a stucco apartment building of five floors. His apartment, on the second floor, was high-ceilinged, with a fireplace (unused) in the living room, crowded with old furniture. Embedded in the grimy oriental carpet as if woven into the fabric were strands of coppery dog hairs, and there were more dog hairs on the Victorian horsehair sofa on which Mr. Cantry invited me to sit. The heavy velvet draperies had been pulled across the windows, though not completely. There was a pervasive odor of something medicinal. A voice teased, *The scene of the seduction!* While Mr. Cantry fussed about in the adjoining kitchen, heating up, as he called it, appetizers in the oven, I examined a table laden with numerous dust-coated framed photographs of Mr. Cantry's kin, oblong-headed, earnest persons, most of them middle-aged or elderly, in the clothes and hairstyles of bygone times. In the front row of photos were bright color snapshots of a butterscotch cocker spaniel with watery eyes. Mr. Cantry entered the room humming, in high spirits, carrying a silver tray containing a tall champagne bottle and two crystal goblets and a platter of still-sizzling sausages and cheese bits. He said loudly, "Ah, Xavia. Monuments to my dead. It should not dampen our spirits, though. On Christmas eve."

Smelling the appetizers, I was immediately hungry. Though I felt slightly sickened, too—the medicinal odor, and an underlying odor of dust, dirt, grime, loneliness were so strong. Ceremoniously Mr. Cantry set the tray down in front of me as if I were a tableful of people. His eyes were moist with effort and his fingers trembled. When I said nothing, beginning to eat, he added, in a wistful tone, "When you are the last of your blood-line, Xavia, as I am—you look backward, not forward. With children, you would of course be tugged forward. Your attentions, your hopes, I mean. Into the future."

"Well, I'm not in the mood for having a baby. Even if it's Christmas eve. Count me out, Mr. Cantry."

"Xavia, you say such things!"

Mr. Cantry blushed, but with pleasure, as if I'd leaned over suddenly and tickled him. I'd become the brash smart-aleck student some teachers inexplicably court. "I was not speaking of either of us—of course. I spoke only in theory." He sat on the sofa beside me; the piece of old furniture creaked. I was surprised he'd sit so close to me—Mr. Cantry seemed to have gained, in the seclusion of his apartment, a degree of masculine confidence. With some effort he uncorked the champagne—it was a French champagne, with a black label and pretentious gilt script—and poured brimming glasses for us both. He laughed as some of the bubbly liquid spilled onto my fingers and corduroy slacks. "To the holiday season, Xavia! And to the New Year, which I hope will bring us both much happiness." There was something giddy and ominous in the way he smiled, and clicked his glass against mine, and drank. I said, on a hunch, "Are you supposed to drink, Mr. Cantry?" He said, hurt, "Christmas eve is a special occasion, I believe."

If you're an alcoholic there's no occasion that can be special, I thought. Actually I'd had a drinking problem myself, a few years before. But I kept all this to myself.

Within a few minutes Mr. Cantry and I had each drunk two goblets of champagne. We'd eaten most of the greasy little sausages and cheese bits. Mr. Cantry was telling me of his sources of income—a disability pension from the state of New Jersey and a small family trust. "I have never yet married," he said, belching softly, "for the very good reason that I have never yet been in love." There was a buzzing sensation in my head like miniature popping bubbles, or brain cells. I smiled, seeing a man's fattish hand reach fumblingly for mine, one hairless creature groping for another. *Now the seduction! Now the rape!* I laughed, though I was beginning to feel panic. Mr. Cantry said, "You are so mysterious, Xavia! So exotic. Unlike the other young women waitresses I have come to know in Sandy Hook, you are special." I didn't like to be told that there'd been other waitresses in Mr. Cantry's life. "Why am I so special?" I asked ironically, staring at Mr. Cantry's fingers locked around mine, and both our hands resting on my knee. His knuckles were enlarged and hairless and his fingernails were neatly clipped, as clean as or cleaner than my own. "Because you were my student. Always there is something sacred in that relationship." I laughed, disappointed. I wasn't sure I'd actually been in Mr. Cantry's class, in fact. I pulled my hand from his and upset my champagne glass and it fell onto the horsehair sofa, spilling what remained of its contents. Mr. Cantry fussed with napkins, muttering under his breath. I said, "I think I should go now, Mr. Cantry. I don't feel well."

He said, breathing harshly, "You could lie down! Here, or in the other room. This is meant to be a happy occasion." I stood, and the room spun. Mr. Cantry lurched to his feet as if to steady me but he was unsteady himself, lost his balance, and we fell together to the floor in a clumsy heap. I was laughing. I was on the verge of hyperventilating. *He will strangle you now. Look at those eyes.* I was crawling to escape, on my hands and knees. A lamp must have been unplugged, the room was partly darkened. Mr. Cantry was on his knees panting beside me, awkwardly stroking my hair. "Please forgive me! I did not mean to upset you." Something blocked my way as I crawled—a heavy chair. I pushed at Mr. Cantry's hand, which was stroking my hair and neck in a way that might be interpreted as playful, the way Mr. Yardboro and certain of his friends bounced boyish punches off one another's upper arms. But Mr. Cantry was strong, and he was heavy. He was stroking my back now and kissing the nape of my neck, his mouth damp and yearning as a dog's. "I would love you. You are in need of strong, devoted guidance. In that place, you demean yourself. If you are punished long enough, you become guilty. This is a fact I know. Xavia—" I panicked and pushed him, he lost his balance and fell against a table, a cascade of framed photographs toppled to the floor and their glass shattered.

I crawled desperately, got free, and jumped up and grabbed for my windbreaker. Mr. Cantry shouted after me like a wounded beast, "What have you done! How could you! Please! Come back!" I ran out of the apartment and down the stairs and when I returned to my own place and bolted the door I saw with wild, teary eyes that it was only 8:10 P.M. of Christmas eve—it had seemed so much later.

I thought possibly Mr. Cantry might follow me, to apologize. But he didn't. The phone didn't ring. I wasn't expecting my mother to call to wish me happy Christmas, as I hadn't planned on calling her, either, and this turned out to be so.

18

CHRISTMAS DAY, the Sandy Hook Diner was closed. The next day, a Friday, when I went in to work in the late afternoon, I learned that Mr. Cantry had been arrested the previous day, for prowling in backyards and trying to look into a woman's downstairs windows. Gleeful Maxine showed me a copy of the local newspaper, a brief paragraph in the police blotter column and an accompanying photo showing Virgil Cantry gaping at the camera's flash, one hand feebly raised to shield his face in a classic pose of shame. "That's him, isn't it? That guy who used to come in here all the time?" I took the paper from her and read, astounded, that on Christmas eve, a local woman had reported a male prowler in her backyard, a man peering into her windows; she'd screamed, and he'd run away, through neighboring backyards; she called the police, who came and found no one. Next day, working with the woman's description, and other information, the police had arrested Mr. Virgil Cantry, 39, who'd denied the charges. "I don't believe this," I said numbly. "Mr. Cantry wouldn't do such a thing."

Maxine and the others laughed at me, at the look on my face.

I said, "No! Really. He wouldn't, ever."

I went to hang up my windbreaker, dazed as if I'd been hit over the head. Behind me, I could hear them talking, laughing. That hum and buzz of jubilance.

On my break I half-ran to the police station a few blocks away. I asked to see Virgil Cantry and was told that he wasn't there; he hadn't been arrested, as the paper had stated, only brought in for questioning. I was excited; I insisted upon speaking with one of the investigating officers; I said that Mr. Cantry and I had been together on Christmas eve, Mr. Cantry couldn't possibly have been prowling in backyards—"And he couldn't run, either. He has a problem with his legs."

The woman making the complaint had called the police at 8:50 P.M. of Christmas eve. It was ridiculous, I thought, to imagine that Virgil Cantry had gone out after I'd left him, to behave in such a desperate way. I insisted that we'd been together until sometime after nine. I gave an official statement to the Sandy Hook police, signed my name. I was trembling, incensed. "This man is innocent," I said repeatedly. "You have no right to harass him."

I would learn afterward (I made it a point to follow the case) that Mr. Cantry had been one of several men brought into the station for questioning. Though he hadn't fit the woman's description of a portly dark-haired man in a leather jacket, with a scruffy beard, the police had brought him in anyway, for questioning, since he was one of the few local residents with a police record (for public intoxication, disturbing the peace, and resisting arrest nine years before—charges to which he'd pleaded guilty in exchange for probation and fines instead of a prison term). Four days later, the prowler–peeping tom was arrested, and confessed.

When Mr. Yardboro returned from Florida, trimmer by ten pounds, tanned, and ebullient, he learned of the "arrest" of his former customer and how I'd gone to police headquarters, what I'd said. It had become a comical sort of tale at the Sandy Hook Diner, repeated frequently, laughed over. Mr. Yardboro thought it was very funny and laughed loudly; he was a man who liked to laugh. "What, honey-bun, you're Lover Boy's girl? How the hell long's this been going on?"

My face burned as if it was on fire. "No. I just wanted to help him."

"You were with him, like you said? Christmas eve?"

Mr. Yardboro laughed, laughed, his warm heavy hand falling on my shoulder.

19

IN MID-JANUARY, I discovered a letter for "Xavia," neatly typed, in a plain white unstamped envelope slipped into my mailbox.

Dear Xavia,

Thank you! I am deeply grateful to you. But so humiliated. I see I am "fair game" in this terrible place from now on.

Your friend,
Virgil Cantry

I never saw Mr. Cantry again; I suppose he moved away from Sandy Hook. But he'd loved me for an hour, at least. I hadn't loved him and that was too bad. But for that hour, I was loved.

20

ONE DAY in late January Mr. Yardboro called me into the kitchen to give me instructions in fish-gutting. One of the kitchen help had just departed the Sandy Hook Diner. Sucking at a toothpick, Mr. Yardboro pointed to the cleaver, already moist with watery blood, and told me to take it up. Eight whole fish had been placed belly up on the butcher-block table. "Start with the heads, sweetheart. Chop-chop. Careful. Then the tails. Don't swing crooked. Don't be shy. Good girl."

My fingers were like ice. I was excited, nervous. Mr. Yardboro smiled at my squeamishness.

Rainbow trout, perch, halibut. These fish were bought unfilleted from the supplier because they were much cheaper that way. They were to be gutted and cleaned and boned and rinsed in cold water and fried in greasy bread crumbs or baked and stuffed with a gummy substance described in the menu as mushroom-crab dressing which was in fact chopped mushroom stems and that repulsive synthetic food imported from Japan, "sealegs."

The fish were slithery-cold. Like snakes. Their scales winked in the harsh overhead fluorescent light. Weirdly round black button-eyes gazing up at me bland and unblaming. *One day you'll be in this position, too. You won't feel a thing.*

I swung the heavy cleaver in a wilder arc than Mr. Yardboro wished. The sharp blade neatly decapitated a trout and sank a half-inch into the wood. "Not so hard, sweetheart," Mr. Yardboro said, grinning. "You're a strong girl, eh?"

"Don't know my own strength," I said cheerfully.

The fish-stink was making me nauseated and there was a ringing in my ears but energetically I chopped, heads and tails, and pushed them into a bucket on the floor. Without the round black eyes looking up at me, I would feel calmer.

"Now the guts and innards. Go right in."

"Right *in?*"

Mr. Yardboro, who often boasted he'd gone ocean fishing since he'd been a kid, cleaning his own fish, showed me how it was done. His fingers were stubby but deft and quick. My fingers were less certain.

When our cook cleaned fish, he used rubber gloves. I was certain of this. But Mr. Yardboro didn't present this as an option.

I was clumsy. Guts stuck to my fingers. Blood, tissue. Bits of broken bone beneath my nails. I must have reached up to touch my hair, nervously. Later I'd discover a strand of translucent fish gut in my hair and I'd understand why Mr. Yardboro smiled at me in that way of his. A dimple in his cheek like a nick made with a razor.

Next came deboning. "Never mind trying to get one hundred percent of the bones," Mr. Yardboro said. "This isn't the Ritz." I was having difficulty extracting backbones from flesh. It drew my attention, how exquisitely fine the bones were. Curving translucent-white bones, some of them no larger than a hair, a filament. Inside the snaky exteriors, a maze; a maze so easily destroyed by a clumsy human hand. "What're you waiting for? Get rid of that crap."

Embarrassed, I pushed the bones into the bucket. What a stink arose from that bucket.

"OK, honey. Let's see you do the operation by yourself, beginning to end. Chop-chop."

Mr. Yardboro wasn't much taller than I was but he loomed over me. Nudging my shoulder with his own. As if we were equals almost, but I knew better.

Through my life I'd never be able to eat fish without smelling the odors of the Sandy Hook kitchen and feeling a wave of excitement shading into nausea. Raw fish guts, fried fish, greasy bread crumbs. I was sickened but still I ate.

LOVER

You won't know me, won't see my face. Unless you see my face. And then it will be too late.

Now the spring thaw had begun at last, now her blood, too, began to beat again. The earth melting into rivulets eager and sparkling as wounds.

Since the man who'd been her lover would have recognized her car, she acquired another.

Not one you know or would expect, but of a make she'd never before owned, never driven or even ridden in—an elegant yet not conspicuous Saab sedan. It was not a new model but appeared, to the eye, pristine, newly minted, inviolate. In bright sunshine it gleamed the beautiful liquidy green of the ocean's interior, and in clouded, impacted light it gleamed a subtler, perhaps more beautiful dark, steely gunmetal grey. Its chassis was strongly built to withstand even terrible collisions. It had a powerful transmission that, as she drove, vibrated upward through the soles of her sensitive feet, through her ankles, legs, belly, and breasts; through her spinal column, into her brain. *This is a car you will grow into,* the Saab salesman was saying. *A car to live with.* She felt the reverberations from the car's murmurous hidden machinery as of an intense, fearful excitement too private to share with any stranger.

It was the weekend of Palm Sunday.

So now in the thaw. Miles of puddled glistening pavement, staccato dripping. Swollen, bruised clouds overhead and a pervasive odor as of unwashed flesh, a fishy odor of highway exhaust, gases like myriad exhaled breaths of unspeakable intimacy. In this car that responded so readily to her touch as no other car she'd ever driven.

She was patient and she was methodical. Taking the route her former lover took on the average of five evenings a week from his office building in the suburb of Pelham Junction to his home in the suburb of River Ridge; three miles along a highway, Route 11, and five-and-a-half miles along an expressway, I-96. Memorizing the route, absorbing it into her very skin. *Unless you see my face. And then it will be too late.* She smiled; she was a woman made beautiful by smiling. Gleam of perfect white teeth.

And her ashy pale hair dyed now a flat matte black. Swinging loose about her face. And sunglasses, lenses tinted nearly black, disguising half her face. Would she be willing to die with him? That was the crucial, teasing question. She'd kick off her shoes in the car, liking the feel of her stockinged feet, the sensitive soles of her feet, against the Saab's floor and pedals.

Sometimes, pressing her foot against the gas pedal, feeling the Saab so instantly, it seemed simultaneously, respond to her lightest touch, she experienced a sharp, pleasurable stab in her groin, like an electrical current.

How many times she would drive the complete route, exiting for River Ridge and returning on southbound I-96, like a racing driver preparing for a dangerous race, rehearsing the race, in full ecstatic awareness that it might be the final, lethal race of his life, she would not know, would not recall. Sometimes by day, but more often by night, when she could drive unimpeded by slow-moving traffic, the Saab like a captive beast luxuriating in release, yearning for higher speeds. Like one transfixed, she watched as the speedometer needle inched beyond seventy-five toward eighty, and beyond eighty, risking a traffic ticket in a sixty-five-mile zone. *At high speeds, unhappiness is slightly ridiculous.*

It was in the second week of her preparation, near midnight on Saturday, that she passed her first serious accident site in the Saab. On southbound I-96, near the airport exit, four lanes funneled to one, traffic backed up for a mile. As she approached, she saw two ambulances pulling away from the glass- and metal-littered concrete median, sirens deafening; saw several squad cars surroundng the smoking wreckage, revolving red lights, blinding red flares set in the roadway. Yet, as soon as the ambulances were gone, an eerie silence prevailed. What had happened, who had been injured? Who had died? The Saab, sober now, was one of a slow and seemingly endless stream as of a funeral procession of mourners. Strangers gazing in silence at the wreckage of strangers. Only death, violent and unexpected and spectacular death, induces such silence, sobriety. She did not believe in God, or in any supernatural intervention in the plight of mankind, yet her lips moved in prayer, as if without volition. *God, have mercy!*

The Saab's driver's window was lowered. She hadn't recalled lowering it but was leaning out, staring at the wreckage, sniffing, her sensitive nostrils stung by a harsh yet exhilarating odor of gasoline, oil, smoke; she was appalled and fascinated, seeing what appeared to be three vehicles mangled together, luridly illuminated by flares and revolving red lights. Two cars, of which one appeared to have been a compact foreign car, possibly a Volvo, and the other a larger American car, both crushed, grilles and windshields and doors shoved in; the cars looked as if they'd been flung together from a great height with contempt, derision, supreme cruelty by a giant-child. The third vehicle, an airport limousine, was less damaged, its stately chrome grille crumpled and discolored and its windshield cracked like a cobweb; its doors flung open crudely, like exclamations. She was disappointed that the accident victims had all been taken away, no one remained except official, uniformed men sweeping up glass and shattered metal, calling importantly to one another, taking their time about clearing the accident site and opening the expressway again. The Saab was moving forward at five miles an hour, a full car length behind the car that preceded it, as if reluctant to leave the accident site, though a police officer was brusquely waving her on, and, behind her, an impatient driver was tapping his horn.

The sleek black stretch limo was one of a kind in which her former lover frequently rode on his way to and from the airport, on the average of three times a month; several times, in the early days of their relationship, she'd ridden with him, the two of them intimate and hidden in the plush back seat, shielded by dark-tinted windows, whispering and laughing together, breaths sweetened with alcohol, hands moving freely over one another. How eagerly, how greedily touching one another. *If it had happened then. If, the two of us. Then.* She could have wept, that opportunity lost.

NEXT DAY she slept late, waking dazed at noon. Bright and chill and fresh, and the sun glaring in the sky like a beacon. It was Easter Sunday.

The man who'd been her lover, and whom she had loved, was an executive with an investment firm whose headquarters were in a corporate park off Route 11. Beautifully landscaped, like a miniature city, this complex of new office buildings glittered like amber Christmas-tree ornaments. It had not existed five years before. In the bulldozed, gouged, and landscaped terrain of Route 11, northern New Jersey, new lunar-looking cities arose every few months, surrounded by inlets of shining, methodically parked automobiles.

She'd visited her former lover in his office suite on the top, eighth floor of his gleaming glass-and-aluminum building; she'd memorized her way through the maze of the corporate park, past cloverleafs, past a sunken pond and Niobe willows—she could not attract the unwanted scrutiny of any security guard. For in her beautiful sleek Saab, with her good clothes, styled hair, and sunglasses, with her imperturbable intelligent face, her poise, she looked the very model of a female inhabitant of Pelham Park, a young woman office manager, a computer analyst, or perhaps an executive. She would have her own parking space, of course. She would know her destination.

Her former lover's reserved parking space was close by his office building. She hadn't had to worry that, like her, he might have acquired a new car, for his car was identifiable by the reserved space; in any case, she'd memorized his license-plate number.

His telephone number, too, she'd memorized. Yet had never once dialed since he'd sent her away. Pride would never allow her to risk such hurt, guessing he'd changed the number.

You won't see my face. But you will know me.

Weekdays he left his office sometime after six-fifteen P.M. and before seven P.M., crossing briskly to his car, which was a silvery-grey Mercedes, and departing on his north-northwest drive to River Ridge. (Except for the days he was traveling. But she could tell at a glance when he was away, of course.) The Mercedes aroused in her a wave of physical revulsion; it was a car she knew well, had ridden in many times. The sight of it made her realize, as she hadn't quite realized before, that he, her former lover, had not felt the need to alter anything in his life since sending her away; his life continued as before, his professional life, his family life in River Ridge in a house she had never seen and would not see; nothing had been altered for him, above all nothing had been altered in his soul, except the presence of her from whom he'd detached himself like one shrugging off a coat. A coat no longer fashionable, no longer desirable.

Circling the parking lot, which was divided into sectors, each sector bounded by strips of green, bright and fine-meshed as artificial grass though in fact it was real, and vivid spring flowers. Waiting at a discreet distance. Knowing he would come, must come. And when he did, quite calmly following him in the Saab, giving herself up to the instincts of the fine-tuned motor, the dashboard of gauges that glowed with its own intelligence, volition. *You will know me. You will know.* The first time she followed him only on Route 11, as far as the exit for I-96; she was several cars behind him, unnoticed by him of course. The second time she followed him on to I-96, which was trickier, again keeping several vehicles between them, and on the expressway the Saab had quickly accelerated, impatient with holding back; moving into the outer, fast lane and passing the Mercedes (traveling at approximately the speed limit, in a middle lane) and continuing on, at a gradually reduced speed, past Exit 33, where he departed for River Ridge; again he hadn't noticed her of course, for what reason could he have had to notice her? Even had he seen her in the swift-moving Saab he could not have identified her in her new matte-black hair, her oversized dark glasses.

The third time she followed him was in a sudden, pelting April rain that turned by quick degrees to hail, hailstones gaily bouncing on the pavement like animated mothballs, bouncing on the silver hood and roof of the Mercedes, bouncing on the liquidy-dark hood and roof of the Saab. She'd wanted to laugh, excited, exhilarated as a girl, daring, on the expressway, to ease up behind him, directly behind him in a middle lane, following him unnoticed for five-and-a-half dreamlike miles at precisely, teasingly, his speed, which was sixty-nine miles an hour; when he exited for River Ridge, the Saab had been drawn in his wake, and she'd had to tug at the steering wheel to keep from following him onto the ramp. *You never knew! Yet—you must know.*

Sometimes cruising the expressway after he'd left. For she was so strangely, unexpectedly happy. Strapped into the Saab's cushioned dove-gray seat, a band across her thighs, slantwise between her breasts, tight, as tight as she could bear, holding her fast, safe. It was at the wheel of the Saab, passing a second and a third accident site, she'd understood that there are no accidents, only destiny. What mankind calls accident is but misinterpreted destiny.

Now the days were warmer, she felt naked inside her clothes. Now the thaw had come at last, the earth glistened with melting, everywhere shining surfaces, oil-iridescent puddles like mirrors. *So happy! You can't know.* She surmised that her former lover might be thinking that she'd disappeared or was dead. He'd expressed concern that she was "suicidal"—with what disdain he'd uttered the word, as if its mere syllables offended—and now he would be thinking, quite naturally he would be thinking she was dead. If he thought of her at all.

Naked inside her clothes, which were loose-fitting yet clinging, sensuous against her skin. Her buttocks pressed into the cushioned driver's seat, her thighs carelessly covered by the thin, silky synthetic material of her skirts. (For always she wore skirts or dresses, never trousers.) And her legs bare, pale from winter but smooth, slender, and graceful, like the sleek contours of the Saab's interior. She kicked off her high-heeled shoes, placed them on the passenger seat, liking to drive barefoot, liking the intimacy of her skin against the Saab's gas and brake pedals. Sometimes at night truckers pulled up alongside her, even if she was traveling in the outer, fast lane, these strangers in their high, commanding cabs, not readily visible to her, maintaining a steady speed beside her for long tension-filled minutes, peering down at her, at what they could see of her slender body, her bare ghostly-glimmering legs in the dashboard light of the Saab, they were talking to her of course, murmuring words of sweet, deranged obscenity, which she could not hear and had no need of hearing to comprehend. *Not now, not yet! And not you.*

Once, sobbing in the night. Her knuckles muffling the sound. And the pillow dampened with her saliva. And she'd felt his hands on her. In his sleep, his hands groping for her. Not knowing who she was, perhaps. Her exact identity, as in the depths of sleep, in even the most intimate sleep, lying naked beside another we sometimes forget the identity of the other. Yet he'd sensed her presence, and his hands had reached for her to quiet her, to subdue. To cease her sobbing.

WEEKS AFTER Palm Sunday and the Saab entering her life. A mild, misty evening of a month she could not have named.

By this time she'd memorized the route, every fraction of every mile of the route, absorbed it into her brain, her very skin. The precise sequence of exit ramps, the succession of overhead signs she might have recited like a rosary, stretches of median that were made of concrete and stretches of median that were weedy grass; how beyond Exit 23 of I-96 there was, on the highway's shoulder, a litter of broken glass like fine-ground gems, part of a rusted bumper, twisted strips of metal that looked like the remains of a child's tricycle. And in a railroad underpass near Exit 29 a curious disfigured hubcap like a skull neatly sheared in half. By day you could see secreted on certain stretches of pavement, on both Route 11 and I-96, hieroglyphic stains, a pattern of stains, oil or gasoline or blood or a combination of these, baked into the concrete, discernible as coded messages to only the sharpest eye. And there was Exit 30, where you turned in a tight hairpin, scary and exhilarating as a carnival ride if your car was moving above twenty miles an hour, circling a marshy area of starkly beautiful six-foot reeds and cattails, at its core pools of stagnant water, black and viscous as oil on the sunniest days. How drawn she was, how unexpected her yearning, to such rare remaining pockets of "nature"—relics of the original landscape where, in theory, perhaps in fact, a body might be secreted for years; a body quietly decomposing for years, never discovered though passed each day by hundreds, thousands of people. For in such a no-man's-land, at the very core of the complex highway system, no pedestrians ever ventured.

From six P.M. onward she waited until, at six-fifty P.M., her former lover appeared. Carrying his attaché case, walking quickly to his car. Unseeing. As she sat in the Saab, motor off, some fifty yards away, calmly smoking a cigarette, betraying no agitation, nor even alert interest; knowing herself perfectly disguised, her sleekly styled matte-black hair covering part of her face. Her makeup was flawless as a mask, her mouth composed, eyes hidden by dark glasses. Her nails were filed short but fastidiously manicured, polished a dark plum shade to match her lipstick. Calmly, in no haste, turning the key in the ignition, feeling the quick, stabbing response of the Saab's motor waking, leaping to life.

Yes, now. It's time.

An insomniac night preceding, a night of cruising I-96, and yet she felt fully rested, restored to herself. Tightly strapped into the passenger seat like a pilot at the controls of a small plane, yet controlled by the plane; secured in place, trusting to fine-tuned, exquisitely tooled machinery.

At a careful distance she followed her former lover through the winding lanes of Pelham Park. Waited a beat or two to allow him to ease into traffic on northbound Route 11. Then following, with utter casualness. Once on the highway, a mile or so after entering, the Saab demanded more mobility, more speed, so she shifted into the outer, fast lane; she'd lowered both the windows in the front, her hair whipped in the gassy, sulphurous air, and she'd begun to breathe quickly. Now there was no turning back; the Saab was aimed like a missile. The Mercedes was traveling at about sixty-five miles an hour in a middle lane; her former lover would be listening to a news broadcast, windows shut, air-conditioning on. It was a hazy evening; overhead were massed, impacted storm clouds like wounds; at the western horizon, brilliant shafts of fiery, corrupt sun the color of a rotted orange; the industrial-waste sky was streaked with beauty of a kind, as a girl living elsewhere, she'd never seen. By degrees the misty air turned to a light feathery rain, the Saab's windshield wipers were on at the slowest of three tempos—a caressing, stroking motion, hypnotic and urgent. Now she was rapidly overtaking the Mercedes and would exit close behind it for I-96; once on I-96 she would swing out again into the fast lane to pass slower vehicles including the Mercedes, one of a succession of vehicles, at which she need not glance. She had five-and-a-half miles in which to make her move.

How many times she'd rehearsed, yet, on the road, in the exhilaration of the Saab's speed and grace, she would trust to instinct, intuition. Keeping the silvery, staid-looking car always in sight in her rearview mirror even as she maintained her greater speed; hair blowing about her heated face, strands catching in her mouth. Her eyes burned like headlights; there was a roaring in her that might have been the coursing of her own fevered blood, the sound of the Saab's engine. *At high speeds, unhappiness is not a serious possibility.*

He hadn't loved her enough to die with her; now he would pay. And others would pay.

The glowing speedometer on the Saab's elegant dashboard showed seventy-two miles an hour; the Mercedes, two cars behind, was traveling at about the same speed. She would have wished a higher speed, eighty at least, but hadn't any choice; there was no turning back. Pinpoints of sweat were breaking out on her tense body, beneath her arms, in the pulsing heat between her legs, on her forehead and upper lip. She was short of breath, as if she were running or in the throes of copulation.

Switching lanes, shifting the Saab into the next lane to the right, so abruptly she hadn't time to use her turn signal, and the driver of a car in that lane protested, sounding his horn. But she knew what she meant to do and would not be dissuaded, allowing two cars to pass her in the Mercedes's lane; then moving back into that lane, so that now she was just ahead of the Mercedes, by approximately two car lengths. Rain fell more forcibly now. The Saab's windshield wipers were moving faster, in swift, deft, percussive arcs, though she didn't recall adjusting them. In sensuous snaky patterns rain streamed across the curved glass. In the rearview mirror the Mercedes was luminous with rain and its headlights were aureoles of dazzling light, and staring at its image she felt a piercing sensation in her groin. She believed she could see, through the rain-streaked windshield, the pale oval of a man's face; a frowning face; the face of the man who'd been her lover for one year, eleven months, and twelve days; yet perhaps she could not have identified the face; perhaps it was a stranger's face. Yet the Saab propelled her onward and forward; she could almost imagine that the Saab was propelling the Mercedes forward as well. She was bemused, wondering: how like high-school math: if the Saab suddenly braked, causing the Mercedes to ram into its rear, with what force would the Mercedes strike? Not the force of a head-on collision, of course, since both vehicles were speeding in the same direction. Would both swerve into another lane, or lanes? And which other vehicles would be involved? How many individuals, at this moment unknown to one another, would be hurt? How many injuries, how many fatalities? Out of an infinity of possibilities, only one set of phenomena could actually happen. The contemplation of it left her breathless, giddy; she felt as if she were on the edge of an abyss gazing blindly out—where?

It was then that she saw, in the rainwashed outside mirror, another vehicle rapidly approaching at the rear. A motorcycle! A Harley-Davidson, by the look of it. The cyclist was a hunched figure in black leather, his head encased in a helmet and shining goggles; he seemed oblivious of the rain, weaving through lanes of traffic, boldly, recklessly, now cutting in front of a delivery van, provoking an outraged response of horn-blowing, now weaving out again, into the lane to the Saab's right, just behind the Saab. She pressed down quickly on the gas pedal to accelerate, to allow the cyclist to ease in behind her if he wished; there was no doubt in her mind he would do so, and he did; bound for the outer, fast lane in a breathtaking display of driving skill and bravado. And in the rain! *Because he doesn't care if he dies. Because there is no other way.*

She felt a powerful sexual longing for him, this hunched, bearded stranger in his absurd leather costume, this stranger she would never know.

Acting swiftly then, intuitively. For Exit 31 was ahead, with its two exit-only lanes; many vehicles on I-96 would be preparing to exit, shifting their positions, causing the constellation of traffic to alter irrevocably. Within seconds the cyclist would have roared ahead, gone. In the dreamy space of time remaining she felt a rivulet of moisture run down the left side of her face, like a stream of blood she dared not wipe away, gripping the steering wheel so hard her knuckles ached. She saw admiringly that the Saab was free of human weakness; its exquisite machinery was not programmed to contain any attachment to existence, any terror of annihilation; for time looped back upon itself at such speeds and perhaps the Saab and its entranced driver had already been annihilated in a multivehicular crash involving the Harley-Davidson, the Mercedes, and other vehicles; perhaps it was a matter of indifference whether the cataclysm had happened yet or was destined to happen within minutes or, perversely, not to happen at all. But her bare foot was pressing on the brake; her toes that were icy with fear, pressing on the Saab's brake as a woman might playfully, tauntingly press a bare foot against a lover's foot; a quick pressure, but then a release; and another quick pressure, and a release; jockeying for position, preparing to move into the left lane, the cyclist might not have noticed, for a low-slung sports car was approaching in that lane out of a tremulous glimmer of headlights, quite fast, possibly at eighty miles an hour, lights blinding in the rain; the cyclist was rapidly calculating if he had time to change lanes, or had he better wait until the sports car passed; he was distracted, unaware of the Saab's erratic behavior only a few yards ahead of him; and a third time, more forcibly, she depressed the brake pedal. Unmistakably now, the Saab jerked in a violent rocking motion, and there was a shriek of brakes that might have been the Saab's, or another's; the Harley-Davidson braked, skidded, swerved, seemed to buckle and to right itself, or nearly; she had a glimpse of the bearded man's surprisingly young face, his incredulous eyes widened and wondering inside the goggles, in her rearview mirror, in the very fraction of an instant the Saab was easing away, like a gazelle leaping away from danger. Within another second the Saab was gone, and in its wake a giddy drunken skidding, swerving, a frantic sounding of horns; faint with excitement she held the gas pedal to the floor, racing the Saab to eighty, to eighty-five, the car's front wheels shuddering against the rain-slick pavement yet managing to hold the surface, while behind her it appeared that the motorcycle had swerved into the outer lane, and the sports car had swerved to avoid a direct collision yet both vehicles careened onto the median, and there they did collide and crash; at the same time the Mercedes, close behind the motor-cycle, had turned blindly into the lane to its right, and what appeared to be a delivery van had narrowly managed to avoid hitting it. The Mercedes and the van and a string of dazed, stricken vehicles were slowing, braking like wounded beasts, passing the flaming wreckage that would be designated the accident site. She saw this spectacle in miniature, rapidly shrinking in her rearview mirror and in her outside mirror; by this time the Saab itself was exiting the expressway, exhausted, safe; she was trying to catch her breath, laughing, sobbing, finally rolling to a stop in a place unknown to her, near a culvert or an underpass smelling of brackish water and bordered by wind-whipped thistles, and her spinal cord was arched like a bow in a delirium of spent pleasure and depletion; her fingers rough between her legs trying to contain, to slow, the frantic palpitations.

Next time, she consoled herself.

SUMMER SWEAT

*D*ying *versus Dead*. It's a fact. In the throes of the most destructive love affair of her life, with the composer Gregor Wodicki in the summer of 1975, Adriana Kaplan frequently wanted *to die*, washing down prescription Benzedrines with vodka in some desolate beautiful place (the Catskills, possibly), yet Adriana was never so distraught as to wish *to be dead* in any permanent way.

She was too restless, inquisitive, troublesome a young woman for *deadness*. She especially wouldn't have wanted her lover's wife to outlive her.

She wouldn't have wanted her lover to outlive her by even a few hours.

No choice! That's why I'm happy. In those days *happiness* was only subtly distinguishable from *misery,* yet Adriana would not have wished her life otherwise. Running breathless to meet Gregor in the pine woods down beyond the old, rotting stables of the Rooke Institute, where they were young, brilliant, and neurotic together, forty minutes north of Manhattan on the east bank of the Hudson River. In the dense pine woods where on achingly bright summer days the shade was too dark. Splotched sunlight and shadow: neurological anxiety. So in dreams of subsequent years and even decades Adriana would see the unnaturally straight, tall trees more like telephone poles than trees, or like the bars of a labyrinthine cage. Few branches on their lower trunks and thick, pungent-smelling needled boughs over head. *Why am I here, what am I doing risking so much, am I crazy?* was not a question she could retain seeing Gregor loping toward her with his expression of rapt, dazed desire. How like a young wolf he seemed to her, greeting her by digging his strong pianist's thumbs and fingers into her ribcage and lifting her above him as if Adriana, twenty-seven years old, and not a small-boned woman, was one of his children with whom he played rough (she'd witnessed this, from a distance) though with Adriana it was deadly serious, and no play in it. Gregor would pant greedily, "You came. You *came*"—as if, each time, he'd frankly doubted she would come to him. Eagerly Adriana embraced the man, a man she scarcely knew, her arms gripping his head, her heated face buried in his thick, often matted and oily hair, in a delirium of desire that allowed her, as with a powerful anesthetic, not to think if her lover doubted her love for him, and how she doubted his for her. Yet they couldn't keep away from each other. And when they were alone together, they couldn't keep their hands off each other. Adriana loved even the rank animal smell of the man's body, her sweat-slick breasts and belly flattened beneath him, and her arms and legs clutching him as a drowning woman might clutch another person to save her life. *Don't don't don't don't leave me. DON'T LEAVE ME.* As in animal copulation the frenzy is to be locked together not out of sentiment or choice but physical compulsion. As if bolts of electric current ran through both their bodies and would only release them from each other when it ceased.

After their secret meetings Adriana went away alone, back to her initially unsuspecting husband. She was bruised, dazed, triumphant. She was covered in sweat, and shivering. This was love, she told herself. Yet also it was sickness. *I love you, Gregor I would die with you that's why I'm so happy.*

Fatal. Rarely that long deranged summer did they find themselves in a car together. In the Wodickis' battered station wagon filled with family trash and smelling still, as Gregor complained, of diapers, though his youngest kid was three now and by this time the stink should have faded. This was risky, driving anywhere in the vicinity of the Institute. For there was no reason for Gregor Wodicki and Adriana Kaplan to be alone together except the obvious. *They're screwing each other? Those two?* The average IQ of any resident of the Rooke Institute for Independent Study in the Arts and Humanities was perhaps 160; it would have required an IQ of 80 to figure that one out. So there was the risk, and Gregor's rushed, reckless driving, and in a fine misty rain he hit a slick patch of pavement on a country road and the station wagon skidded and his arm leaped out reflexively to protect Adriana from lurching forward into the windshield—"Watch out, Mattie!"—in his alarm mistaking her for one of his daughters. He didn't seem to realize his mistake, nor did Adriana choose to notice, for they were laughing together relieved, thank God they hadn't crashed. "We can't be together in an accident," Adriana said, more tragically than she'd intended, and Gregor said, "Not unless it's fatal for both. Then, who cares?" He grinned, baring his imperfect, stained teeth. The left canine was particularly long and distinctive.

Afterward Adriana deconstructed this incident. It was a good sign, she believed. *He loves me as he loves his daughter. I'm not just one of the women he's fucked in his lifetime, mixed together like family junk in a drawer.*

A family man. Though he had love affairs, some secret and some not, it was said of Gregor Wodicki by both friends and detractors that he was *a family man* despite being a frequent drunk, a user of speed, an unreliable citizen, a primitive-cerebral composer descended from Schoenberg, and a general son of a bitch. *A family man* who adored his kids and may have feared his wife, whose name, Pegreen, filled Adriana with mirth and anxiety— "Pe*green?* No, really?" Gregor Wodicki was thirty-two years old in the summer of 1975. The father of five children of whom the three eldest were his wife's from a previous marriage. He was one of the defiant, unapologetic poor. He borrowed money with no intention of repaying. He bargained with the director of the Institute for an increase in his stipend though he was already the youngest of the senior fellows in the music school. He was hotheaded, difficult, scheming even among a community of temperamental artists and scholars. It was said admiringly, grudgingly, that his music was brilliant but inaccessible. It was said that he'd been getting by on his "genius" since adolescence. The Institute director, Edith Pryce, disapproved of his behavior but "had faith" in him. He went for days even in the humidity of midsummer in upstate New York without showering. How's that my problem? he laughed at the notion he might offend someone's sensitive nostrils. It was said that Gregor and Pegreen smelled identical if you got close enough. And the kids, too.

If you visited their house (as Adriana never did, though she and her husband were invited to big brawling parties there several times that summer)
you'd be shocked at the disorder, yes, and the smells; particularly scandalous was a downstairs "guest" bathroom where towels hung grimy and
perpetually damp and the toilet, sink, and tub badly needed scouring.
There were dogs in the Wodicki household, too. A rented ramshackle
shingleboard house at the edge of the Institute grounds. *A family man* who
nonetheless quarreled publicly with Pegreen his wife, and exchanged
blows with her to the astonishment of witnesses—slaps rather than full-
fledged blows, but still. Sometimes in the late evening as summer heightened in a crescendo of nocturnal insects, lovesick Adriana drifted by the
Wodicki house taking care to keep far enough away from the lighted windows so as not to be seen by anyone inside. A mere glimpse of Gregor
through an opened window even if his figure was blurred was reward
enough for her, and simultaneously a punishment. *Aren't you ashamed. How
can you bear yourself.* She was struck by the very shape of the Wodickis'
sprawling house, like an ocean vessel, every window blazing light and casting distorted rectangles out into the night.

   *You could walk up onto that porch, you could knock on that door if you want.
You could open that door and walk inside if you want.*

   But never. Adriana never did.

   A family man though he confided frankly in Adriana, in a lumpy bed in
the Bide-a-Wee Motel outside Yonkers, that his children were a burden
upon his soul. The three older kids he tried to love but couldn't, even his
own kids, the three-year-old especially he found himself staring at in
astonishment and disbelief—"Did I really cause that kid to come into the
world? *This* world? Why? Yet he's beautiful. He breaks my heart." A knife
turned in Adriana's heart, hearing this. Though she wanted intimacy from
her lover yet she was wounded easily as an adolescent girl. She said carefully, "Of course Kevin is beautiful, Gregor. He's your son."

   Frowning, Gregor corrected her, "Pegreen's, too."

Pegreen the Wife, the Earth Mother. Six years older than Gregor, whom
she'd seduced as a youth of nineteen; she'd been the wife of one of
his music instructors at the New England Conservatory. A slovenly-
glamorous woman with gray-veined black haystack hair; a fleshy, sensual
body; and a beautiful ruined face like a smeared Matisse. Pegreen exuded a
derisive sort of sexuality like an oily glistening of sweat; in fact she was

noticeably warm in public, flush-faced, with damp half-moons beneath her arms and tendrils of hair stuck to her low, broad forehead. Her eyes were malicious and merry and she wore bright red lipstick like a forties screen actress. She wore tight-fitting summer-knit sweaters with drooping necks and ankle-length skirts with alarming slits to midthigh. She, too, was a musician and played piano, organ, guitar, mouth harmonica, and drums with a gay, giddy imprecision, as if mocking the deadly serious art of her husband and his colleagues. She had a loud, contagious laugh very like her husband's and like her husband she had a weakness for vodka and gin, beer and wine, whiskey, whatever. She was said to be more experimental and therefore more careless in drug use than Gregor, with a sixties hashish habit. It was said that Pegreen was devoted to her difficult "genius" of a husband unless she was bitterly resentful of her difficult "genius" of a husband. Certainly they quarrelled a good deal, and exchanged blows harder than slaps in private. (So Adriana learned, marveling at a cascade of purple bruises on her lover's back.) Pegreen was the Earth Mother grown ironic about mothering and wifeing and womaning in general. She would appear to have been a manic-depressive, though mostly manic, in high spirits. Yet one day following a quarrel with Gregor she bundled the two youngest children with her into the station wagon and drove as fast as the vehicle would go on the New York Thruway, the children screaming and crying in the car when a state trooper stopped her; she'd lost her license for six months, and began to see a psychotherapist. At one point she spent some time in a psychiatric clinic in Manhattan. Gregor said, "Pegreen meant to crash the station wagon, I'm sure. Yet she could not. Her ties are as deep as mine. She isn't truly mad, she has only the showy outward energies of madness." The most disturbing thing Adriana knew of Pegreen was that she'd acquired from somewhere a .32-caliber revolver which, she boasted, she carried "in my purse and on my person" when she went into the city. She laughed at the alarm and disapproval of her husband's colleagues. She was a firm believer, she said teasingly, in the right to bear arms and in the survival of the fittest.

Adriana protested, "But does your wife have a permit for this gun? Is it *legal?*" and Gregor said, shrugging, "Ask her." Adriana said, "But aren't you frightened, a gun in the house? Does your wife know how to use it? And what about the children?" Lovemaking left Adriana exhausted and close to tears and her voice dismayingly nasal. You can't make love with another woman's husband for most of an afternoon without fantasizing a certain power over his thoughts, a claim to his loyalty. Though knowing it was risky to pump Gregor about his family beyond what he chose to volunteer, Adriana couldn't resist. Her heart thumped in the callow hope of hearing him speak harshly of her rival. Instead, he turned irritably away from Adriana and rubbed his eyes with both knuckles. They were lying amid the mangled, damp sheets of the Bide-a-Wee. A smell as of backed-up drains pervaded the room. No longer clutched together in each other's arms devouring each other's anguished mouth, they lay side by side like carved effigy figures. Gregor swung his hairy, brutal legs off the edge of the bed and sat up, grunting. "Pegreen does what Pegreen will do. I'll use the bathroom first, OK?"

Twenty-three years later at a memorial service at the Institute for the deceased Edith Pryce, and a decade after Pegreen's death (in an alleged auto accident on the Thruway at a time when Pegreen was undergoing chemotherapy for ovarian cancer, fifty-one years old, and still married to Gregor Wodicki), Adriana will hear again that cruel koan-like phrase. *Pegreen does what Pegreen will do.*

In the Bide-a-Wee there was not the eerie labyrinthine cage of too-straight pine trees but instead a low water-stained ceiling and a single window with a water-stained blind and that pervasive odor of drains, and sexual sweat. Where they'd lain the sheets looked torn, trampled. There was a sweetly sour odor of matted hair, underarms. The window unit rattling air conditioner was defeated by July heat rising toward 100° F. and humidity like a gigantic expelled breath. Hours in a delirium of angry yearning they'd strained together kissing, biting, sucking, tonguing each other's livid body. Like great convulsing snakes they were. A percussive music in their groans, in their frightened-sounding whimpers and shrill spasm-cries. If either had wished to believe this might be their final meeting, and afterward each would be free of the other, neither believed so now. There was a hook in their bodies impaling both. There would be no easy release. Their eyes rolled glassy-white in their skulls in a mimicry of death. Saliva sprang from the corners of their mouths. Their genitals were tender, smarting as if skinless. Everywhere Adriana's skin smarted from her selfish lover's unshaven jaws and the wiry hairs of his body. Gregor's back was scribbled red from Adriana's mad raking nails. He laughed—she would tear off his head with her teeth, like the female praying mantis of legend. Yet perhaps he was afraid, a bit. Where he gripped her shoulders, the reddened imprints of his fingers remained. Her breasts were bruised and the nipples sore like a nursing mother's. (Though Adriana Kaplan had never nursed any infant, and would not.) Afterward Adriana would stare at the marks her lover left on her body, sacred hieroglyphics she alone could interpret. She was cunning, clipping her pubic hair with her husband's nail clippers; her pubic hair which was a bristling bushy black, scintillant, like the hair of her head which she wore in a single braid like a bullwhip halfway down her back. She wanted nothing to come between her and Gregor, nothing to muffle her physical sense of him. For she seemed to know that this was the only knowledge she would have of him, and this fleeting as breath: their sexual contact, to be protracted as long as possible. Long shuddering waves of what was called pleasure yet for which, to Adriana, there was no adequate term.

If I'm hurting you, tell me and I'll stop.
No. Don't stop. Never never stop.

"*It just ends.*" So Adriana remarked of one of Gregor's compositions performed by a string quartet and Gregor stiffened saying, "No, it's broken off," and Adriana said, "But that's what I mean. It ends with no warning to the listener, you keep waiting to hear more," and Gregor said, "Exactly. That's what I want. The listener completes the music in silence, himself." Adriana realized that her lover, so casual about others' feelings, was in fact offended by this exchange; it offended him further to be obliged to spell things out, and to know that the woman with whom he was involved was musically ignorant. Adriana said, hurt, "I suppose Pegreen gets it? Yes?" Gregor shrugged. Adriana said, "If your music is so rarefied, then the hell with it." Gregor laughed, as if one of his children had said something funny. He kissed her aggressively on the mouth and said, "Right! The hell with it."

The cage. There was the terrible week in late August near the end of their affair when Adriana believed she was pregnant. Several times in haste they'd made love without using precautions so it shouldn't have been a surprise, yet it was a surprise, a shock that triggered both terror and elation. Her wish to die was as pervasive as a dial tone: you lift the receiver, it's always there.

But no. Why die? Have the baby.
Maybe you'll wind up your lover's one true love.

Even Adriana's mocking voices were shrill with hope.

Every new Institute fellow was summoned to have tea with Edith Pryce in her airy, high-ceilinged office in the old pink limestone manor house, and Adriana's turn had come. This would be a polite ritual visit during which the distinguished older woman would query the younger about her work. Edith Pryce was a dignified woman in her early sixties so severely plain as to exude a kind of beauty; she wore her ashy white hair in a tight French twist and had a way of elevating her chin as if gazing at you across an abyss not only of space but of time. She'd been a protégée of Gregory Bateson in the 1950s and had a degree from the New York Psychoanalytic Institute. In her elegant office there were antique furnishings, an Aubusson carpet, and a baroque brass birdcage suspended from the ceiling. It was known at the Institute that each tea with Edith Pryce began with admiring reference to the cage and to the red-gold canary inside, which Adriana supposed was the point, for Edith Pryce was a shy, coolly self-protective woman who did not like surprises. Adriana, blinking tears from her eyes, which were already raw and reddened, exclaimed, "How beautiful your canary is! Will he sing?" Edith Pryce smiled and said that Tristan sang usually in the early morning, inspired by wild birds outside the window. Originally, she told Adriana, she'd had two canaries, this "red-factor" German male and an American yellow female; while Tristan was courting Iseult, he sang continuously, and passionately; but once they'd mated and Iseult laid her five eggs, and five tiny fledglings were hatched, both canaries were frantic to feed their offspring and Tristan ceased singing. "I finally gave away Iseult and the babies to a dear friend who's a canary breeder," Edith Pryce said, with a stoical air of regret, "and for weeks Tristan was mute, and hardly ate, and I thought I would have to give him away, too—then, one morning, he was singing again. Not as beautifully as before but at least he was singing, which is what we expect of canaries, after all. Chickadees and titmice are his favorites."

Adriana was attentive and smiling. She wore tinted glasses to disguise her ravaged eyes and a not-quite-clean white shirt tucked into a denim skirt that, in other circumstances, showed her trim, sexy, tanned legs to advantage. Her hair seemed to have grown coarse overnight and strands were escaping the thick unwieldy braid damp as a man's hand on her upper back. She opened her mouth to speak but could not. *Help me. I think I'm going crazy. I've misplaced my soul. I married the wrong man and I love the wrong man and I want to die, I'm so exhausted but I don't want my lover to outlive me, I know he'll forget me. I'm so ashamed, I despise myself but I'm afraid, afraid to die—*

Suddenly Adriana was crying. Her face crumpled. She was stammering, "I'm so sorry—Miss Pryce, I d-don't know what's wrong—" Tears burned like acid spilling from her eyes. Through a vertiginous haze she saw Edith Pryce staring at her appalled. A telephone began to ring and Edith Pryce waited a moment before picking up the receiver and saying in an undertone, "Yes, yes—I'll call you back immediately." By this time Adriana understood that Edith Pryce had no interest in her emotions, that the emotional life was in itself infantile and vulgar, and that in any case she, Adriana Kaplan, was far too old for such behavior. She rose shakily to her feet and stammered another apology which Edith Pryce accepted with a frowning nod and evasive eyes.

As Adriana fled the office she heard Tristan, excited by her weeping, chittering and scolding in her wake.

The first time, the last time. The first time, in an unexpectedly hot May. Swift and sweetly brutal. A kind of music. Gregor Wodicki's kind of music. Afterward Adriana would recall it sheerly as sensation. *My God, I can't believe this is happening, is this me?* yielded to a dazed, gloating *I can't believe I did that, and am innocent.* It had seemed to her an accident, as if two oncoming vehicles had swerved into each other on the Thruway. She and her husband had attended an Institute recital featuring the premiere of a bizarre composition of Gregor Wodicki's, a trio for piano, viola, and snare drum; Gregor himself played the piano with minimalist savagery, grimacing at the keyboard as if it was an extension of his own body. During the tense eighteen minutes of this piece, Adriana fell in love. So she would tell herself and, in time, Gregor. (Except, was this true? Undressing for bed that night she and Randall joked that contemporary music "made no sense" to their ears, they much preferred Mozart, Beethoven, the Beatles.) But shortly afterward Adriana and Gregor Wodicki met again, and were immediately attracted to each other, and drifted off together in earnest conversation that ended in an abrupt encounter down beyond the old, rotting stables and in the romantic pine woods. This was an ordinary weekday afternoon in May.

Recalling long afterward that first, probing touch of Gregor Wodicki's. The man's fingers on her wrist. A question, yet also a claim. Like touching a lighted match to flammable material.

How am I to blame, I'm not to blame, it's something that is happening, like weather.

The last time, after Labor Day, in sultry-humid heat illuminated by veins of distant lightning, they'd met in the pine woods though each was fearful by this time of the other. Adriana knew by this time she wasn't pregnant, after her humiliating encounter with Edith Pryce she'd begun to bleed and bleed and bleed, and it was over now, the hysterical pregnancy, though in weak moments through her life she would fantasize that in fact she'd been pregnant, with Gregor Wodicki's child, the single pregnancy of her life and this precious fetus she'd miscarried because of the extremes of emotion to which she and Gregor subjected each other. In her dreams Adriana sees the stricken young woman making her way like a sleepwalker through the maze of bar-like trees. Determined not to notice the evidence of other careless lovers in these woods, teenagers who trespass, leaving behind the debris of burned-out campsites, beer cans, junk food wrappers, condoms. Condoms strewn like translucent slugs amid the pine needles. Adriana saw a used, wrinkled condom and a flurry of tiny black ants crawling excitedly into it, and she gagged and turned away.

But the last time was very different from the first. Gregor's breath was fumy with alcohol, his face was beaded with sweat, and his eyes were dilated; he'd stared at her as if not recognizing her and was reluctant to touch her, not gripping her ribcage and lifting her as always with his hard, hurting hands. Their kisses seemed misdirected, tentative without being tender. Despite the heat, Gregor carried a jacket with him; Adriana expected him to spread it on the ground but he did not; his manner was vague, distracted, and he made no effort to defend himself when Adriana accused him of not loving her, of only just using her, and she slapped him, struck him with her fists weeping not in sorrow but in rage. *Can't believe this is happening! And I have no choice.*

There was a moment when he might have struck her in return, and hurt her, Adriana saw the flash of pure hatred in his eyes, but he only shoved her from him muttering, "Look, I can't. I've got to get back. I'm sorry."

The slut. Adriana would one day think calmly, with the wisdom of Spinoza, *It must happen to everyone. The last time you make love, you can't know it will be the last.*

After Gregor, and after her marriage dissolved in sullen slurs and recriminations, Adriana embarked upon a number of love affairs. These were explicitly *love affairs,* so designated beforehand. Some were single-night encounters. Others, not even an entire night. By the age of thirty-three she'd acquired a reputation as a bright young aggressive critic of American culture who lived a good deal in Rome. She was a sexy, witty girl. She wore blue-tinted metallic designer glasses and consignment-shop clothing of the highest, most quirky quality. She favored black: silk, brocade, cashmere wool. She would wear her trademark braid like a bullwhip halfway down her back and would not dye it as her hair began to turn prematurely silver. Women were attracted to her as well as men. Gay men "saw something" in her: a deep erotic fury not unlike their own. *You made me into a slut,* Adriana wanted to inform Gregor Wodicki, but she wasn't certain he'd have appreciated her humor. Or that this was evidence of humor.

In memoriam. Twenty-three years after that steamy summer, Adriana Kaplan has returned for the first time to the Rooke Institute, to attend a memorial service for Edith Pryce, recently deceased at the age of eighty-four. One of the first people she sees is, not surprisingly, Gregor Wodicki: now "Greg Wodicki" as he prefers to be called, the current director of the Institute. Adriana knows, because malicious informants have told her, that Gregor, or Greg, has gained weight in recent years, but she isn't quite prepared for the bulk of him. No other word so fitting: *bulk.*

Adriana thinks, shocked and offended, *Am I expected to know that man? I am not.*

Not that Gregor Wodicki is obese, exactly. He carries his weight, an extra sixty or seventy pounds, with dignity. His face is flushed and gleaming; his hair has turned gunmetal gray, grizzled, lifting about his dome of a head like magnetic filings. He's wearing a dark gray pinstripe seersucker suit into which his bulk fits like a swollen sausage. Adriana feels a stab of hurt, that that body she'd known so intimately and loved with a fanatic's passion is so changed; yet she seems to be the only visitor who's surprised by his appearance, and Gregor, or Greg, seems wholly at ease in his skin. Seeing Adriana, he makes his way to her with an unexpectedly predatory quickness for a man of his size, and shakes her hand. There's a moment's hesitation and then he says, "Adriana. Thank you for coming."

As once, years ago, he'd murmured in triumph, *You came!*

Adriana manages to say politely that she's come for Edith.

"Of course, dear. We've all come for Edith."

Dear. A quaint, ambiguous word. *Dear* he'd never called her when they were lovers.

During the ceremony, Adriana studies the face of "Greg Wodicki." Though this is a solemn public occasion, clearly her former lover is relaxed in his role as organizer and overseer. Where once he was contemptuous of such formalities and distrustful of words ("You can't lie in music without exposing yourself, but any asshole can lie in words. Words are shit") now he speaks graciously and with winning frankness. He introduces speakers, musicians. He's become a fully responsible adult. His eyes are rather sunken in the creases of his fattish face yet they're unmistakably *his eyes*; inside the middle-aged mask of flesh there's a young, lean, handsome face peering out. The mouth Adriana had kissed so many times, sucked and moaned against, more familiar to her once than her own, is a curiously moist red, like an internal organ. Where Gregor was, now Greg is. Amazing.

Adriana never returned to the Rooke Institute after quitting her appointment but of course she's been aware, at a distance, of her former lover. He hasn't been a practicing composer or musician for years. Adriana had avoided musical occasions when his compositions were performed and skimmed reviews of his work in New York publications—these were infrequent, in fact—and never attended a concert or recital. There were recordings of his work but she made no effort to hear them. He'd wounded her too deeply; it was as if part of her had died and with that the entirety of her feeling for him. What she'd heard of him was unsought and accidental: he and his wife Pegreen never formally divorced though they lived apart a good deal, and there was trouble with one or more of the children, and Gregor remained at the Institute and Pegreen came to live with him during her ordeal with cancer, until the time of her death. Surely Gregor had had other affairs, for he, too, had powerful attractions for both women and men, and sexuality seemed to have been for him as natural an expression as touching, with as few consequences. The surprise of Gregor Wodicki's life would seem to have been his late-blooming talent for administrative work. He'd been appointed by Edith Pryce as her assistant, and had taken over after she retired.

A vague rumor had it that Gregor had been a lover of Edith Pryce's. Adriana rather doubted this, but—who knows? She came to suppose she'd never really known him, except intimately.

Three beautiful pieces of music are performed during the memorial service by resident musicians. One is by J. S. Bach, another by Gabriel Fauré, and the concluding piece a quartet for strings and piano by "Greg Wodicki." A spare, delicate, enigmatic piece that ends not abruptly but with a dreamy fading-away. Adriana, listening closely, blinks tears from her eyes and wonders bitterly if "Greg" might have revised the piece since Edith Pryce's death, to emphasize its elegiac tone. The date of the composition is 1976, the year following their breakup, and the music he'd written in the seventies had been harsh and uncompromising, indifferent to emotion.

Hypocrite, Adriana thinks, incensed. *Murderer.*

Adriana M. Kaplan. Adriana had declined an invitation to luncheon after the memorial service yet somehow she's prevailed upon to remain; fortunately she isn't placed at the head table with Gregor, or Greg, and distinguished elderly friends and colleagues of the late Edith Pryce. Midway through the lengthy meal she becomes restless and excuses herself from the dining room and drifts about the first floor of the old manor house, which had been deeded to the Institute in 1941 with ninety acres of land and numerous outbuildings. Since 1975, Rooke House, as it's called, has been attractively remodeled and refurbished. In a large, paneled library, Adriana skims shelves of books by current and former members of the Institute and is flattered to discover two of her five books; one is her first, a study of American modernism (art, theater, dance), a slender work published by the University of Chicago Press, well enough received in its season but long out of print. Here it is on the library shelf without its jacket, looking naked and exposed; probably it's been here for fifteen years, unopened. Stamped on the spine, faded and barely legible, is the author's name: *Adriana M. Kaplan.* ("M" for Margaret.) Beside Adriana's books are titles and authors she's never heard of. She feels a wave of vertigo but overcomes it, managing to laugh. *Have I exchanged my life for this?*

As if she'd had that choice.

In the pine woods. Though Adriana intended to return to the city immediately after the luncheon, somehow she finds herself in the company of her former lover, who insists upon showing her around the Institute grounds—"D'you like the changes you've seen, Adriana? We've been fixing things up a bit."

This is a modest understatement. Adriana knows that since "Greg Wodicki" became director of the Institute, he's singlehandedly embarked upon a ten-million-dollar fund-raising campaign, and the most immediate results are impressive. Several new buildings, a beautifully renovated barn now a concert hall, landscaping, parking lots. Adriana says yes, yes of course the changes are wonderful but she rather misses the old slapdash style of the place: leaking roofs, rotting barns, water-stained facades, uncultivated fields. "But that was another era," Gregor points out. "A nonprofit foundation like the Rooke could survive on low-investment returns and the occasional quirky millionaire donor. But no longer."

Adriana wants to ask, Why not?

After the initial shock of their meeting there was a suspended space of time (the memorial service, the luncheon) during which Adriana and her former lover seemed to have come to terms with seeing each other again. But now, suddenly alone together, in the stark June sunshine, they are entering another phase, of belated excitement and apprehension. Heavyset Gregor is breathing through his mouth, Adriana is feeling stabs of panic. *Why are you here, what the hell are you trying to prove? And to whom?* Our most fervent wish is for a former lover's defeat, deprived of our love; at the very least, we wish to appear transcendent, indifferent, wholly free of that lost love. During the luncheon Adriana noticed Gregor glancing in her direction but she'd ignored him, talking earnestly with guests at her table. But now they're walking along a graveled path side by side, like old friends. Gregor glances down at his bulk with mild exasperation and bemusement and sighs, "I've changed a bit, eh, Adriana? Not like you. You're beautiful as ever."

Adriana says coolly, "I've changed, too. Even in ways that can't be seen."

"Have you?" Gregor's tone is skeptical.

As if mildly brain-damaged, or drunk, the two are walking haphazardly along a path between two stone buildings; away from Rooke Hall and toward the pine woods. Now, in midafternoon, the air has turned humid, almost steamy. A sudden sharp odor of pine needles makes Adriana's nostrils pinch in dread.

Where are the old stables? Razed to make way for a parking lot.

Where is the old, overgrown path she'd taken into the woods? Widened now, neatly strewn with wood chips.

Though they descend a hilly slope into the shadowed woods, Gregor's breathing becomes steadily more audible and his now rather clammy-sallow skin is beaded with sweat. He's removed his seersucker jacket and tie and rolled up the sleeves of his white dress shirt, but much of the shirt is sweated through. If this man were a relative or friend, Adriana would be concerned for his health: the bulk of that body, at least two hundred forty pounds, dragging at his heart and lungs.

Inside the woods, there are the sweet, clear cries of small black-capped birds overhead. Chickadees?

Impulsively Adriana says, "That brass birdcage of Edith's."

Gregor says, "We still have it, of course. In Edith's former office, now my office. It's an expensive antique."

"And is there a canary in it?"

Gregor laughs explosively, as if Adriana has said something slyly witty. "Hell, no. Who has time to clean up bird crap?"

They walk on. Adriana takes care not to brush against Gregor, whose big body exudes, through his straining clothes, an oily sort of heat. She hears herself saying, in a neutral voice, "I never told you. Near the end of—us—I broke down in Edith Pryce's office. She'd invited me for 'tea.' I began crying suddenly and couldn't stop. It was like a physical assault, I was a wreck, I seem to have thought I was—pregnant."

"Pregnant? When?"

Gregor's reaction is immediate, instinctive. The male terror of being trapped and found out.

Adriana says, "Of course, I wasn't. I hadn't been eating much and I was taking Benzedrine some irresponsible doctor was prescribing for me and I was clearly a little crazy. But I wasn't pregnant."

"Jesus!" Gregor says, moved. He would pause to touch Adriana's arm but she eases out of reach. "You went through that alone?"

"Not alone exactly," Adriana says, with subtle malicious irony. "I had you."

"But—why didn't you tell me?"

Adriana considers this. Why? Their intense sexual intimacy had somehow excluded trust.

"I don't know," she says frankly. "I was terrified you'd want me to have an abortion, you'd never want to see me again and I—I wasn't prepared for that." She pauses, aware of Gregor staring at her. *His eyes:* wetly alert, blood-veined, living eyes peering through the eyeholes of a fleshy, flaccid mask. "I thought it might be easier somehow to—die. Less complicated."

This preposterous statement Gregor Wodicki accepts unquestioning. As if he knew, he'd been there.

"And what did Edith say to you?"

"Nothing."

"Nothing?"

"As soon as I started to cry, she cut me off. She didn't want to be a witness. Maybe she knew about us, in fact. But she didn't want to know more. She allowed me to see myself for what I was: a hysterical, selfish, blind, and neurotic woman."

"A woman needing help, for Christ's sake. Sympathy."

"It was a good thing, I think. Edith Pryce's response."

"Do you!" Gregor says, snorting.

"Yes! Yes, I do."

In angry silence Adriana walks ahead. What are they quarreling about? Adriana's heart is beating rapidly; she isn't prepared for such emotion after so many years, it's like ascending to a too-high altitude, too quickly. She's recalling their last time together in these woods. She'd anticipated love-making and there had been none. Gregor's strange edgy behavior. His breath that smelled of whiskey, his queer dilated eyes. She sees the tall, straight pine trees, so like the bars of a cage, a vast living cage in which, unknowingly, they'd been trapped. Erotic love. Deep sexual pleasure. Those sensations you can't speak of without sounding absurd and so you don't speak of them at all until at last you cease to experience them and in time you can't believe that others experience them, you can only react with derision. You're anesthetized.

Telling yourself, *It's behind me now, I've survived.*

"That last time we saw each other, somewhere around here, I think?" Gregor says casually, wiping his forehead with a much-wadded tissue. "Or, maybe—farther down by the river?"

As if the point of this is *where.*

Adriana glances at Gregor and sees that he's smiling. Trying to smile. His teeth are no longer uneven and discolored but have been expensively capped. Yet there are the sunken, damp eyes. The flaccid froggy skin. Is she falling in love with this man again? Adriana Kaplan's "genius"-prince, turned into a frog.

Never. She'll never fall in love with anyone, again.

Nor does she like the drift of this conversation. Tempting her to betray twenty-three years of stoic indifference.

They walk on. The air is slightly cooler here, a quarter-mile from the river. Gregor begins to speak impulsively, ramblingly. "Y'know, Adriana—I don't remember every minute of that summer, to be frank. I'd been 'mixing'—taking speed, drinking. Pegreen was giving me hell. *She* was seriously suicidal. But I couldn't leave the woman, and I couldn't give you up. I was obsessed with you, Adriana. And jealous of you and your marriage. And my 'youth' passing. And my 'genius.' My fucking music like ashes in my mouth. That last time we met here, you never knew—I brought with me, in the pocket of my khaki jacket—Pegreen's revolver."

Adriana is sure she hasn't heard correctly. "The—gun? You had a gun with you, here—?"

"I must've thought—it was crazy of course—I'd use it on you, and then on myself. *Jesus!*" Gregor blows out his cheeks and rolls his eyes in the adolescent-boy gesture Adriana recalls from twenty-three years ago when he'd narrowly missed crashing the station wagon.

In the pine woods, in the strangely peaceful airless air of summer, Adriana Kaplan and Gregor, or Greg, Wodicki stare at each other. Then, unexpectedly, they begin to laugh. Pegreen's .32-caliber revolver, in the pocket of Gregor's jacket. How absurd, how embarrassing. Gregor's laughter is deep-bellied, a contagious hyena laugh. Adriana's laughter is almost soundless, quivering and spasmodic, like choking.

QUESTIONS

She was thirty-one years old, her lover was twenty years old, should that have worried her? She knew it was a mistake to get involved with him but she couldn't prevent it from happening. She hadn't known he was suicidal at the time.

His name was Barry, which didn't suit him—he might better have been called Jerzy, or Marcel, or Werner. He had a look, Ali thought, both American and exotic. He was an undergraduate in the college, not one of her students, a tall thin boy with lank dark hair, mushroom-pale skin, accusing gray-green eyes, a habitually pinched expression. Two gold studs in his left ear, overlarge shirts and sweaters, Nike running shoes worn without socks. Could you guess he'd gone to Exeter?—his father was a State Department official? He had been a pre-law student originally but was now interested in "theater arts." His life would be devoted to acting and to writing poetry, he said; one day—soon—he hoped to be acting in his own plays. Ali regarded him with both affection and skepticism. Didn't he imagine himself, as so many undergraduates did these days, as a performer in a film or video of his own life? As Ali, though not of his generation, imagined herself, at times, an actress in a film of unknowable proportions?

Ali had fallen in love with Barry while watching him perform in a campus production of Peter Weiss's "The Persecution and Assassination of Jean-Paul Marat as Performed by the Inmates of the Asylum of Charenton Under the Direction of the Marquis de Sade." The production was billed as a revival, since the play had been originally performed on campus back in 1968. Barry played the role of the erotomaniac Duperret, and played it with near-hysterical intensity; he had no natural gift for the stage that Ali could see, but something about his tall gaunt slope-shouldered frame, his bony elbows, his sullen air, quite won her. She was a full-blooded woman of some experience who liked to be "won."

She was high too; she and her friend Louis (who taught East Asian studies, and was faculty adviser to the campus gay organization) were both high, having shared some of Louis's prescription Dexedrine before coming to the play. Ali turned to Louis with tears in her eyes and whispered, "Who is that beautiful boy?—is he one of *yours?*" and Louis whispered back with mock primness, "Ali, he's too young for you."

Ali thought, That's for me to decide.

SHE WAS BORN and baptized Alice; she'd long ago named herself Ali. For a while during their marriage—while they were living together, that is; they were in fact still legally married—her husband called her Alix: the word's second syllable, *-ix,* given a hissing malevolence he'd thought was amusing. "Al*ix,* dear, where are you? Al*ix,* darling, why don't you answer?" She had not seen her husband for nearly two years now though they spoke on the telephone sometimes, as a matter of practical necessity. He lived in their old loft on Greene Street, just south of Houston, where he painted during the day (and taught art at the New School, at night); Ali lived in Vermont where she taught film and film criticism at a small liberal arts college famous, or infamous, for its experimental curriculum and its "unstructured" atmosphere. She was a popular, audacious teacher, a campus celebrity of sorts—who else reviewed fairly regularly for New York publications? Who else would organize a film festival of "banned" films?—a fierce fleshy woman with long dense curtains of jet-black hair, dramatic slanted eyes, full lips. She dressed and behaved provocatively though she was an ardent feminist—"provocation" was simply her style, as meticulously observed as the styles of the great film directors whose work she admired. Certainly Ali Einhorn was highly intelligent but she was also—was primarily—a very physical woman: a ripe rich Concord grape, as a lover once said of her. Delectable!

Ali had made an early reputation as a bright young film critic—she'd published books and essays on Fellini, Buñuel, Truffaut, Fassbinder, Herzog, Schlöndorf, Bergman, and many others; she'd even published her abstruse Ph.D. dissertation on André Bazin's ontological concept of the photographic shot as the "deconcealment of Being." For the past several years she had been working, in alternately frenzied and desultory cycles, on "magic realism" in contemporary West German film. In the little college town up in the mountains all sorts of wild and extravagant rumors circulated about Ali which she rarely troubled to correct; she reasoned that they made her appear more interesting. Wasn't she married?—Wasn't her husband gay?—Didn't she have affairs with colleagues, even with students? Hadn't she once had an affair with the dean of the college (now relocated on the West Coast with his wife and children)? On the door to her office was a large full-color poster of Klaus Kinski in Herzog's *Aguirre, Wrath of God*—Kinski's extraordinary face so radiantly composed in madness one could hardly bear to look at it. Above the poster was Buñuel's militant NOTHING IS SYMBOLIC in bright red letters. Though Ali didn't give high grades as promiscuously as many of her colleagues her classes were always jammed with students; for which reason, as he said, Barry Hood had avoided her for two years. He thought too highly of himself to succumb to mass movements. He'd once quoted Nietzsche to Ali, in the early days, or hours, of their relationship—" 'Where the rabble worships, there is it likely to stink.' "

Ali was both wounded and delighted by the boy. What arrogance! What assurance! She leaned forward impulsively to kiss his mouth; she ran her fingers roughly through his hair. You'll pay for that, you smug little bastard, she was thinking. But really she adored him.

THEIR "FRIENDSHIP," as Ali called it, was sporadic and whimsical on her part, carried on while she was negotiating another more serious affair with a man, a film director, who lived in New York City and worked on the Coast. Each affair kept the other in perspective—Ali knew the risk of expecting too much from a single source. Barry Hood fascinated her as a presence, a phenomenon, twenty years old yet in a way aged, worn out, though in other ways he was much younger than twenty—he was shy and arrogant and clumsy, brattish, spoiled, yet, at times, almost unendurably sweet as a child is sweet, in utter unself-consciousness. "A child of his times," Ali said of him, but not to him. They were not to sleep together very many times and never (in Ali's secret opinion) altogether satisfactorily but she was quite taken with his style, as she called it—those distinct, pure, unmistakably American-aristocrat features beneath the sullen glowering boy.

Much of their time together was spent in talk—passionate talk. The kind Ali never remembered the next morning but quite enjoyed at the time. Barry and Ali and often Barry's black roommate Peter Dent—"black" only nominally, since he was fair-skinned as Ali herself—in one or another of the campus places or in Ali's apartment, smoking dope. Peter Dent's father was a lawyer too, like Barry's, but he was in show business law, he divided his time between New York City and the Coast, and was evidently very successful. Ali knew that when students spoke with bitter humor of their families it meant only one thing: success. Scholarship students whose families were relatively poor invariably spoke of them in warmer terms. Then, dear God, you were likely to get heart-wrenching tales of sacrifices, grandmothers, older brothers and sisters, complicated illnesses with difficult medical names. Ali much preferred her boys Barry and Peter who dismissed bourgeois convention as "shit" and never spoke of their families except in terms of lofty contempt.

Barry was not as beautiful close up as he'd appeared onstage but he had remarkable gray-green eyes that darkened, or lightened, or welled with tears, depending upon his mood. When they made love he fairly quivered with passion—his ribs rippled beneath his skin; his very skeleton seemed to tremble in ecstasy. Ali liked to stroke his body, running her soft fleshy hands over his bones, reminded of Buñuel's camera in its erotic glidings and circlings of Deneuve's perfect body in *Belle du Jour*. Buñuel had understood that sensuality is a matter not of the whole but of parts; the wholeness of the human being—the "human" being—hardly exists at such times.

Barry was moody, capricious, unpredictable. How seriously he took himself!—daring to pay Ali the compliment, one night, of telling her she was the first woman in his life who didn't try to make him eat. He wrote poetry of an "experimental" kind and kept a voluminous journal in longhand which he refused to let Ali read: it was the only place, he said, he could tell the truth. "I feel pure and innocent and redeemed only when I'm writing or acting," he said, in a slightly contentious tone, as if he believed Ali might protest. She did not. She said, "*I* feel pure and innocent and redeemed only when I'm making love." It was a provocative statement, certainly not true.

Like most of the undergraduates at the college Barry smoked dope at least once a day and took drugs whenever they were available. Yet he held himself aloof from his classmates; he never went to the parties that were held at different dormitories each weekend and had become notorious, throughout the Northeast. Barry belonged neither to the "druggies," nor to the "straights"—there were only a few people he believed he could trust. Ali was moved and flattered that she was one of them, but how had it happened so quickly? One night he told her in a sudden rush of words that his mother had committed suicide during his freshman year at Exeter and that he often felt her "lure"—even when he was happy. In bright daylight, he said, in a voice tremulous with pride, he felt the powerful attraction of night.

Ali had not known how to reply except to say, "How terrible, how tragic"—words that offended with their banality. She knew she was expected to say more, much more, to ask how? and why? and had they been close? and how had his father taken it? but she resented the boy telling her, at least at this time, when she'd been feeling so buoyant. They were lying together on a quilt on the floor of Ali's darkened apartment, they'd made love, they were sharing a joint, in a few minutes Barry would leave to return to his dormitory—why had he sprung this ugly revelation upon her? She knew that if she dared touch him, if she dared comfort him, Barry would shove her away with disdain.

NOT LONG AFTERWARD Ali broke off with Barry Hood, telling him that she and her husband were working on a reconciliation. He didn't protest or telephone her but over Thanksgiving break, when she supposed he had gone home to Washington, he tried to kill himself by taking all the pills in his and Peter Dent's medicine cabinet—including Peter's prescription Quaaludes—and slashing his arms. When the news came Ali was watching a video of Murnau's *Nosferatu* with friends, which struck her as the most ghastly of coincidences. When she hung up the phone she was white-faced, giddy, as if someone had kicked her in the stomach. "What is it, Ali? Is it an emergency?" she was asked. The drama of the scene thrummed and vibrated about her, beat against her, out of her control. "Yes," she said carefully. "It's an emergency. But not mine."

WHEN SHE WENT to the hospital she was told that Barry Hood was in the intensive care unit, in critical condition; he was expected to live but could not receive visitors. Only members of his immediate family would be allowed to see him. A young Arabic intern named Hassan whom Ali knew from the campus film society told her what had happened: Barry had taken the drugs—slashed at his arms—collapsed in his room—revived—stumbled out into the hall—again collapsed, in front of the resident adviser's door. The RA had telephoned an ambulance at once, and the ambulance had come within three minutes. "So he didn't really want to die," Ali said. The intern said, "Nobody really *wants* to die, but it happens all the time." His tone was sarcastic: Ali was chilled and chastened but a bit resentful—she'd meant her remark to be an innocent statement of fact.

She told Hassan that the boy's mother had committed suicide a few years ago. If it was anyone's fault it was that woman's fault.

JUST AS WELL, Ali thought afterward, that they hadn't let her see Barry. She could imagine his bruised reproachful eyes; she knew how wretched, how aged, postsuicidal people looked—she'd visited several in the hospital over the years.

And hadn't Ali been one herself?—a long time ago.

It was emotional blackmail, pure and simple. You had to feel sorry for the boy but you had to feel impatience too; outright anger. What a trick! What manipulation! She'd taken two Libriums to steady her nerves and now her nerves thrummed like a radio turned low. Why, why did you do it? she would have asked Barry, why, why, *why?*—no matter that that was precisely the question he wanted Ali, and others, to ask.

Or why, if you decided to do it, did you change your mind?

That was the question no one would ask.

Years ago Ali had wanted to die and she too had taken an overdose of drugs—prescription barbiturates. She'd woken in Bellevue emergency where terrible things were being done to her: a hose forced down her throat into her stomach, attendants holding her in place as she convulsed. Like the freeze-frame at the end of Truffaut's *400 Blows*—Ali sprawled helpless and broken on a table—forever and ever. In weak moments she saw that sight. Forever. It might be deferred but it could never be erased. And the man she had hoped would be devastated by her death, the man she'd actually hoped might want to join her in death—he had broken off with her immediately. Hadn't even come to see her in the hospital.

But that was a long time ago. Ali was a big girl, now.

*   *   *

TWO DAYS LATER Barry's father telephoned Ali and asked if he might see her. He sounded hysterical over the phone—speaking in short staccato phrases Ali could barely understand. She had known he was in town and she had thought perhaps he might call and she'd considered simply not answering her phone but knew that was a cowardly and ignoble thing to do. So she answered it. And there was Mr. Hood, distraught and choked, telling her that his son had slipped into a coma and he was desperate for someone to talk to—someone to explain what had happened. He promised to take up no more than an hour of her time.

"A coma?" Ali asked, frightened. "I hadn't known."

Mr. Hood was speaking so rapidly Ali could barely follow his words. She wondered who had given him her name, and how much he knew. And did he intend to accuse her of—anything?

He insisted he would not take up more than an hour of her time. Ali didn't see how she could refuse to see him, under the circumstances.

"—THE LAST TIME Barry was in the hospital here I wasn't able to get to see him," Mr. Hood was saying. "That was his freshman year—did you know him then, Miss Einhorn? Of course it was only mononucleosis—which he'd had before, in prep school—but that can be deadly; it can lead to hepatitis. I was in Europe at the time on crucial business and I simply couldn't get back and my wife—Barry's mother—wasn't able to get up here either, for personal reasons." Mr. Hood was speaking rapidly and not quite looking Ali in the eye. One of his eyelids was twitching; from time to time he rubbed his knuckles roughly against it. "I don't feel that the boy has ever forgiven me for that—and other things. Though I tried, God knows, to explain my circumstances to him. And I've certainly tried to make it up to him." He paused. He was smoking a cigarette which he stubbed out now, briskly, in the ashtray. He looked at Ali and tried to smile. "Has Barry ever said anything about this to you, Miss Einhorn? Has he ever said anything about—me, or his mother? Or—" His voice trailed off into the cocktail hubbub around them. (They were having drinks in the Yankee Doodle Room of the Sojourner Inn, where Mr. Hood was staying.) "Has he ever shared any of his feelings about his family with you—?"

It was an awkward question though not awkwardly asked—Mr. Hood was an articulate man. Ali chose her words carefully in reply. She must not upset Barry's father any more than he was already upset but she must not humor him, or lie. She'd seen at once that he was the kind of man—a Washingtonian, a State Department attorney—intelligent, acute, steely-eyed, hardly a fool, who, for all his anxiety, would see immediately through any ordinary attempt at subterfuge. She said, "I didn't really know Barry that well, Mr. Hood. Only the past few weeks—and then not really well. Your son isn't an easy person to get to know—he doesn't open up very readily. A very private—" Ali was ashamed of the weak dull flat tone of her voice but Barry's father, staring so intently at her, made her extremely self-conscious. She said, "There must be teachers of his who know him better than I do. His resident adviser? And his roommate—he might in fact have several roommates?"

"Oh, I've talked with the roommate," Mr. Hood said impatiently. "The colored boy with the—what was it? Quaaludes! For schizophrenia, or manic depression, my God!—right there in the medicine cabinet staring Barry in the face day after day! And he's always been such an excitable, impressionable boy—much less mature than he looks. Yes of course I've talked with the roommate," Mr. Hood said. He was breathing hoarsely. But he managed to smile at Ali, a reassuring smile showing perfectly capped white teeth. "I wound up trying to comfort *him*—the poor kid is so scared Barry might die. Nice sweet boy—Peter's his name. But he doesn't seem to know Barry any better than I do."

Mr. Hood laughed, his nostrils darkly distended, as if he'd said something particularly funny. Ali smiled uneasily. She asked, casually, "Was it the roommate who gave you my name?"

But Mr. Hood went on to speak wonderingly of Barry's friends, or lack of friends, in prep school, grammar school, nursery school. How Barry had never seemed to mind their moving from city to city—claimed he looked forward to it. "Did you ever hear of a child expressing such a sentiment, Miss Einhorn?—*Ali,* is it? From the beginning this penchant for—" He stared at the cigarette freshly lit and burning in his fingers. "—something you might call irony. If that's what it was."

Marcus Hood resembled his son only slightly, about the eyes—which was a relief. As soon as Ali shook hands with him in the hotel lobby she knew that her worries were groundless—he didn't appear to be angry with her. He was eminently civilized, civil, a gentleman; an American patrician, in his middle or late fifties, impeccably well groomed and conspicuously well dressed—camel's-hair topcoat, powder-gray pinstripe suit, dark blue silk tie, gleaming black shoes. He was a handsome man, or had been at one time; now his eyes were raw-looking and his skin was sallow. He reminded Ali just slightly of that brilliant actor in Bergman's repertory—Max von Sydow, of years ago—the facial structure all verticals; eyes sunken deep in grief and mouth wounded. Sorrow stitched into the very flesh.

After his second martini he began to speak with some bitterness. He accused himself of having let things slide in his family; of having neglected his only son. He'd been blind to certain danger signals: Barry's habit of dropping courses or taking incompletes, Barry's disinclination to come home for holidays, Barry's disappointing grades. And though he'd always asked Barry if there was anything he wanted to talk about Barry never took him up on the offer. And he'd supposed that meant things were all right.

Ali said carefully, "I suppose that, at a time like this, the instinct is to blame yourself. But—"

"Who else should I blame?" Mr. Hood said.

He talked, talked. Sometimes not even looking up at Ali, as if he'd forgotten she was there. What had gone wrong? How could he have done things differently? It was the pressure of his job, his jobs, all that moving around the country—New York, Los Angeles, Connecticut, Washington—when Barry was a small child. And his domestic situation which, he said, was "difficult." His wife Lynda—

"Barry told me about her, actually," Ali said.

"He did?"

Ali wondered if she had made a tactical error. She said hesitantly, "—That she'd committed suicide when he was in prep school. And—"

"Committed suicide? What?"

"Didn't she? Barry's mother—"

Mr. Hood stared at her in utter astonishment.

"Lynda has done some extreme things, she's an extreme personality," he said carefully, "—but to my knowledge she has never attempted suicide. We're separated—not officially, but *de facto*—I don't in fact know her precise whereabouts at this moment, but I'm certain that she is alive."

"She's—?"

"Barry must have been lying," Mr. Hood said. "I mean of course he was lying. Suicide! Lynda! His mother! Of course it's a symptom of his general disturbed state but I wouldn't have thought him capable of such a—low thing. Such a—libel."

Now Mr. Hood was terribly upset. Ali could not think of a graceful way out. She said, "Well—you should probably know that Barry tells his friends that when he feels depressed he finds himself thinking of his mother—of what she did. And he feels a certain attraction. A 'lure,' I think he calls it."

"That's just self-dramatization," Mr. Hood said dismissively. "It's typical of him—of that kind of highly articulate, highly verbal temperament of his. Barry always had a morbid imagination and of course he was always encouraged to express it—every school we sent him to! Without fail! Still, to think he'd deliberately lie like that, saying such a thing about his mother—misrepresenting his own family to strangers. I can see that he might want pity, but—" Mr. Hood paused. His mouth twisted as if, for a moment, he couldn't bring himself to speak. After a pause he said, "You don't—do you?—think he might be—?"

"Gay?"

Mr. Hood winced at the word. "Homosexual," he said. "Do you think—?"

"No," Ali said.

For a while they sat in silence. A red-headed youngish man was playing desultory tunes at the cocktail piano; the lounge was gradually filling up. Ali's nerves were beginning to tighten again and she wondered when she could slip away to the powder room to take another Librium. She always carried a small supply of six capsules in her purse, and replenished them at frequent intervals.

"Actually, Mr. Hood," Ali said, "Barry didn't seem to want pity. He had—has—too much self-respect. I think you underestimate him."

"Thank you," Mr. Hood said. "I very much appreciate your saying that."

Over a third martini—Ali was having her second margarita, and it was reassuringly strong—he asked Ali again her personal impressions of Barry. Ali felt distinctly uncomfortable as if, now, her own interrogation had begun. She explained carefully that she had not known Barry that well. He wasn't, for instance, enrolled in any of her courses.

"But you're involved in the theater, aren't you?"

"I teach film. But Barry hasn't taken a course of mine."

"I see," he said slowly, though it was evident he didn't. He said, "But Barry is very—attached to you, Miss Einhorn. I gather you know that?"

Ali said, brazening it out, "There are a number of students who are 'attached' to me, Mr. Hood," she said. "Because of the subjects I teach, primarily. And what they see to be my iconoclastic approach. But Barry is only one of them. And, as I said, he hasn't ever taken a course of mine. He doesn't seem to think that film is a serious subject."

"Well—. I guess I'd been led to think something else," Mr. Hood said. He appeared subtly disappointed, perhaps a bit puzzled.

He asked Ali if he might take her to dinner here at the Inn?—since it was getting late, and he'd kept her for so long anyway. But first, if she didn't mind, he wanted to call the hospital to see if—anything had developed.

AT DINNER in the Inn's walnut-paneled candlelit dining room Ali began to feel more relaxed. She volunteered information about Barry she wouldn't have had to give Mr. Hood. One of his son's "distinctive" traits, she said, was his honesty—which could be abrasive. And he frequently asked questions of a rhetorical nature. " 'Why is there Being, and not rather Nothing?'—Heidegger's question," Ali said. Mr. Hood asked her to repeat this but made no comment. "Another question I remember was— 'Do we get what we deserve, or deserve what we get?' " Ali said. She paused, feeling, for a moment, rather excited. Marcus Hood was staring at her so intently. "It's a profound question, really, when you consider it."

Mr. Hood lit a fresh cigarette though there was still food on his plate. In the soft sepia-tinted light his hair looked crisp as fine handworked silver; his eyes were shadowed. He said, exhaling smoke through his nostrils as if sighing, "It *is* a profound question—I'm damned if *I* know the answer."

Near the end of the meal he told Ali a story—something that had happened when Barry was ten years old. It was meant, he said, to illustrate his own failure of integrity. "Just so you know that, when I say I've been a poor father, you'll know I'm telling the truth—" His words were just perceptibly slurred.

It happened that his wife Lynda's older sister Elise came to stay with them in Rye, Connecticut, where they were living at the time; she was a beautiful, extremely intelligent woman but, unfortunately, irremediably neurotic—"high-strung" the family used to say. "Almost immediately

Elise began to affect our household in various disruptive ways," Mr. Hood said. "She rang up exorbitant telephone bills. She used Lynda's credit card—forged her signature. She cruised the bars and hotels and picked up men—went out with blacks from the third world embassies— stayed away for days at a time. Lynda, who had her own problems, was terrified that Elise would be found dead in a hotel room somewhere. The woman was a pathological liar yet you couldn't help but believe her—she had a certain charismatic power. But no—I didn't fall in love with her, or have an affair with her, if that's what you're thinking," he said, with an unexpected smile. "In fact I was away most of the time, as usual; I tried to stay clear of the problem. I hadn't been the one to invite Elise to stay with us, and I didn't feel I could ask her to leave. Still— I should have known it was an unhealthy situation for Barry to be in." He paused, sighed, rubbed at both eyes with his knuckles. "Well—what happened was: it came out one day that Elise was caressing my son in certain ways. The woman—thirty-five, -six years old!—was undressing a ten-year-old boy and caressing him in an intimate way. Can you imagine anything so perverse—so sick! And it had been going on, evidently, for months."

"How did you discover it?" Ali asked.

"Lynda discovered it. Just by accident. She found them in the pool house together—but of course Elise denied everything. She's always been a superb liar. Cool and bland while Lynda slips into hysteria at the slightest provocation—what a pair! Elise said she was simply helping Barry with his swimming trunks and Barry pipes in and says that's all she was doing too. Lynda had had a bit to drink and there was a terrible fight and by the time I got back home Elise was gone; moved out. But the damage had been done—Lynda with her hysteria had only made things worse."

"But Barry denied it?"

"He didn't know what to 'deny,' he was so young. I didn't have the heart to interrogate him."

Ali said carefully, "Of course it's a disturbing story—if it really happened as your wife says—but I don't quite see why you have to blame yourself, Mr. Hood." She'd taken a second tranquilizer before dinner; she'd had a fair amount to drink. She was buoyantly high but lucid. "And, for all you know, your sister-in-law might have been innocent, as she said. How would you really know?"

"Lynda swore it happened the way she said. And she was so upset she must have seen something."

Ali knew better than to fall in with Mr. Hood in what must have been an old dispute. He said, "In any case—hysterical women aside—the blame lies with me for letting things slide the way I did. For not knowing, or not wanting to know, how disrupted my household was." For a sharp painful moment Ali felt the man's self-loathing as if it were her own.

"But how could you have known?" Ali persisted. "You had to be away on business."

Ali was suffused with emotion, ripe with it—her skin felt dewy, moist, warm. She was conscious of her rings glittering in the candlelight. She said impulsively, "We're all guilty of behaving in ways we don't like from time to time. We're human after all." She paused, smiling. She tried to imagine how she might look to Marcus Hood. "It's the human condition—fallibility."

"You're very kind, Ali, very generous, but—I don't think I behaved judiciously. And of course there had been other times too—more than I care to remember. He holds them all against me, you can be sure of that."

"Barry doesn't strike me as a punitive person," Ali said, not entirely truthfully.

"As you said—you don't know him very well."

Ali did feel generous. Magnanimous. She decided to tell Mr. Hood a story about something that had happened to her a few years ago: "Just to illustrate my own failure of integrity."

She was married then, living with her husband, an artist, in a loft on Greene Street. In their wide circle of acquaintances were a sculptor and his wife, both flamboyant personalities, notorious, really—the wife no less than the husband. The wife had tried to befriend Ali from time to time, but Ali kept her distance, fearful of getting involved. She knew the couple had serious problems; and she and her husband had serious problems of their own. (Mr. Hood was listening sympathetically. "You must have married very young," he said.) The sculptor was a violent man, a drinker, it was generally thought he might even be emotionally disturbed; and one night while they were quarrelling his wife fell, or was pushed, out a window in their apartment, and died in the fall—it was eight stories to the pavement. Ali thought afterward that she'd been a coward to withdraw when the woman had approached her. She felt sick with guilt and self-disgust but the worst of it was, the sculptor claimed his wife had killed her-self, had jumped out of the window during the quarrel, and most of their friends seemed to believe him, and rallied around him. That is—the men rallied around him, helped him make bail. "There was a memorial service for the woman, and I wanted to attend," Ali said, her voice swelling with emotion, "—but my husband refused to let me. He said I couldn't appear to be supporting *her* and not *him*. 'She's dead, he's alive,' my husband said. 'And you know he's a vindictive man.' We quarreled bitterly but in the end I stayed away from the service—the way so many of our friends did. I did what my husband wanted me to do because I was too cowardly to resist." Ali's heart was beating erratically; in telling the story, she had made herself frightened. She said vehemently. "But I vowed that would be the last time I ever let men push me around. Any men."

Mr. Hood had listened sympathetically. He laid his hand lightly on her arm, to soothe her. He said, "I can see that you're upset—it's an ugly story—but I don't see, really, that you were a coward. Aren't you being awfully hard on yourself? You did defy your husband to a degree. And, after all, that maniac might have killed you too. Don't tell me he's still free—?"

"The jury voted to acquit," Ali said, her voice shaking. " 'Insufficient evidence,' they said. Imagine!"

They sat staring at each other, silent for a long impassioned moment. Mr. Hood's hand still lay, lightly, upon Ali's arm. His lips moved; his words were nearly inaudible.

". . . 'Insufficient evidence,' " he whispered.

AT ALI'S APARTMENT Barry's father telephoned the hospital another time. Ali, making drinks in the kitchen, could hear his questioning aggres-sive voice but could not make out his words. When she came out she saw him standing motionless, staring at the floor with a quizzical smile.

"Is there any news—?" Ali asked.

He shrugged his shoulders irritably and took the glass from her. "None at all," he said.

In Ali's fussily decorated living room he paced restlessly about, not wanting to sit down. He examined the framed movie posters on the walls, the many photographs, the aluminum bookshelves jammed with books and video cassettes. Atop Ali's television set was the tape of Murnau's *Nos-feratu*—Mr. Hood picked it up absently and stared at the garish illustration on the box cover. " 'Classic vampire tale'—?" he said.

Ali said quickly, "I'm writing an essay on Herzog's *Nosferatu*—comparing the two," as if that explained everything.

Mr. Hood laid the tape down without comment.

Ali's apartment was on the twelfth floor of a new high-rise building a few miles from the college campus. She'd taken it primarily because it overlooked a small lake and an expanse of pine-covered hills but by night the living room seemed rather narrow and cramped. She wondered how it looked to Marcus Hood in his elegant gray pinstripe suit, Marcus Hood of Washington and the State Department—Barry's "successful" father—as he strolled about peering into corners. "Attractive place," he said. "I gather you live here alone?"

Ali told him yes. She lived here alone, and always had.

His lips were tightly pursed and his nostrils distended as he breathed heavily, audibly. His skin was unevenly flushed though, like Ali, he could certainly hold his liquor well.

In a casual voice he said, turning back to Ali, smiling, "You know, Miss Einhorn, Ali, I read my son's diary the other day—or whatever he calls it—I thought I had better. And there's a good deal in there about you. About—you and Barry." He paused, still smiling. "I assume it's mainly fantasy? Or entirely fantasy? A kid's erotic fantasy? That sort of thing?"

Ali said evenly, "Since I haven't read the diary I don't know what you mean but I think, yes—I'm sure—it would probably be something like that. Fantasy." She swallowed a large mouthful of her drink and held the thick squat glass steady in both hands. "Barry had—has—a strange imagination. A lively imagination."

"A damned *morbid* imagination," he said with some heat. "But we've already been over that ground."

From that point onward things became confused. Ali would not remember afterward precisely what happened. They must have talked about Barry a while longer; then Mr. Hood was denouncing his wife, who was an alcoholic of the very worst kind, the kind that doesn't really want to be cured: "I don't even know where she is! Barry tries to kill himself, and I don't even know where she is! She might even be with Elise—two of a kind!" Then, suddenly, with no warning, Mr. Hood was crying, Mr. Hood was broken and sobbing, gripping Ali in his arms.

He was holding her so tight she was terrified her ribs might crack. She could hardly breathe. She tried to push him away, saying, "Mr. Hood, please—You're hurting me—*Please*—"

They stumbled together like a drunken couple. Ali's glass fell clattering to the floor. "You're so good, so kind, you're the one good decent person," Mr. Hood was saying extravagantly, burying his face in her neck, "—the one good decent person in my life. You're so beautiful—" Ali, utterly astonished, tasted both panic and elation. She tried to pry his fingers loose, tried without violence to disengage herself from him, but he held firm. His body seemed enormous, pulsing with misery and heat. He sobbed helplessly, in a virtual frenzy of desire, besotted, whispering, "—so good, so kind. So beautiful. Beautiful, beautiful woman—" Gripping her tight as a drowning man.

So Ali thought, as she'd so often thought, Why not?

IN HER BATHROOM, 3:20 A.M. She has locked the door behind her out of superstition though Mr. Hood is asleep in her bed and will be asleep for a long, long time: Ali knows the symptoms. Slipped sly and sweaty out of his embrace, staggered swaying across the tilted floor to get to the safety of the bathroom where, hidden behind a bottle of Advil, is what remains of a small supply of cocaine her New York lover brought her the previous week. She also has a small cache of crystal meth but even in her disoriented state reasons that it might be contraindicated here. Psychopharmaceutical error. "Death, my dear," Ali says wisely in a voice not her own. In Mr. Hood's crushing arms beneath Mr. Hood's thrusting desperate body she had felt perhaps a pinprick of pleasure that faded almost at once to be replaced by a churning sensation at the back of her head, churning and screeching like the hundreds of death's-head monkeys overrunning Aguirre's raft at the end. She can still hear them in the bathroom, the door locked.

Only a few grains remaining of the coke and she thought there'd been more. Spreading the snowy glittering grains across the mirror trying not to worry that her hands are shaking so.

What is the difference between something and nothing, Ali thinks. Shutting her eyes and sharply inhaling.

After a few minutes her hands are no longer shaking. Or if they are, it isn't visible.

Naked beneath her untied robe, hair in her face, panting, she kneels on the floor presses her forehead against the rim of the bathtub. Whispers, "Barry—we are going to save you. Barry—we are going to save you. Barry—"

When she'd held him she could see his skeleton shuddering inside the envelope of skin the way they said the Hiroshima survivors could see their own bones through their flesh when the great bomb exploded. When she'd held him tight, tight, her eyes shut tight in triumph.

Her breasts are aching and she doesn't want to remember why. Her thighs are aching too. Fatty ridges of flesh on the curve of her hips she can't bear to look at or to touch but still they say she's beautiful—luscious ripe Concord grape. Her head is clearing rapidly because of the lovely blizzardy white and she is able to see things with remarkable lucidity. Methedrine comes in handy if she isn't feeling precisely herself on teaching days; you need that demonic edge, white-hot energy for fifty minutes, not fooling around the way the kids did but for therapeutic reasons, for professional reasons, to get back to the Ali Einhorn most truly *herself*—not some slow sad dragging cunt-cow. Then a Librium or two to bring her back down if she can't sleep. But there is nothing like coke and she's half-sobbing with relief and gratitude, pressing her forehead against something hard and white and cold and ungiving.

"Barry—we are going to save you. Barry—we are going to save you."

4:10 A.M. and Ali makes her way groping back to the bedroom where a man lies in the center of her bed breathing in long deep chopping strokes. Is he asthmatic, has he a mild heart condition, will he die one day in her arms? He has told her he loves her; he has told her he is so lonely he can't bear it; can she believe him? A wise voice asserts itself through her own: "He is sleeping the merciful sleep of oblivion, *do not wake him.*" Ali does not intend to wake him.

She stands barefoot in the doorway, her bare toes flexing against the floor. It is early morning but still hours from dawn. The white walls of the bedroom gleam faintly, mysteriously, as if from a distance. She feels good, in fact very good, back in control and contemplating the options before her. Return to bed? slip in quietly beside Mr. Hood and try to sleep? Or should she sleep on the living room couch, or try to?—as she has done in the past, never in comfort. Or should she give up entirely on the idea of sleep? She sees herself in that long brilliant tracking shot at the end of Buñuel's *Viridiana.* All the cards have been dealt out but what do they say?

PHYSICAL

Good news!"

Temple's doctor was smiling, glancing through a sheaf of X rays as he entered the waiting room where Temple sat, shivering. Temple thought, *Not lymphatic cancer, then.*

What he was suffering from was—severe muscle spasm in his upper neck? overstretching of ligaments? possible disk injury? Temple listened with a dutiful show of interest. It was mildly surreal that Freddie Dunbar whom he knew from the Saddle Hills Tennis Club should be delivering the news—Dunbar whose tennis game was dogged, mediocre. Temple's heartbeat had quickened when Dunbar entered the room bearing what Temple had assumed was his death warrant ("Hmmm! The lymphoid glands appear to be swollen, that's not good," Dunbar had murmured, startled, during the physical examination preceding the X rays) but now it was *good news,* not *bad,* Temple's heart was returning to normal, or what passed for normal. Temple would live, after all—it was only a physical problem.

Temple's former wife (how like *former life* that sounded) had accused him of not caring if he lived or died. But really she'd meant not caring if their marriage lived or died. (Was that true? Temple had vehemently denied it.) It was just that, after forty, Temple had became one of those men who in middle age plunge into physical activities—in Temple's case jogging, cycling, tennis, downhill skiing—with the avidity of youth, when a man believes not only that he's immortal but that his body is protected by a sacred aura. *Not me! not me! I can't be stopped, not me!* Now Temple was forty-five—no, forty-six: his birthday, unheralded, had been the previous Saturday—he hadn't any less energy or enthusiasm, nor any less skill—he would swear to this!—but things seemed to be happening to him. Like being struck by lightning, *he* was blameless. A skiing accident in Vail, ankle in a cast for weeks last winter; a fall on the tennis court, bruises and lacerations on his right forearm. And his (minor but annoying) heart problem. (Which he hadn't indicated on the medical form he'd filled out at the front desk. Dunbar was a neck man, not a cardiologist.) And this latest problem he guessed must be from tennis, too, recurrent pain in the upper right side of his neck.

Why was *pain in the neck,* like *pain in the ass,* some sort of dumb joke? Temple had had his for eleven weeks now, and it was no joke.

Dunbar had been holding the X rays to the light for Temple to examine if he wished, discussing Temple's physical problem in a thoughtful, measured voice. It was a voice Temple knew, for he employed it frequently himself: one professional to another. One man to another. Above all it was the kindly yet magisterial voice doctors employ in such settings—these breathtaking new quarters of the Saddle Hills Neck and Back Institute—to forestall patients' panicky fear that they would have a hand in paying for such luxury. Temple, a moderately successful Saddle Hills developer of the eighties, knew the price of such high-quality custom-designed construction: enormous landscaped lot, octagonal two-floor building with an atrium foyer, lots of stylish solarium features, Spanish-looking tiles. The waiting room, to accommodate the patients of the Institute's eight physician-partners, was spacious and plush as the lounge of a luxury hotel. In fact, Temple had initially gotten lost as he'd entered the building, wandering off the atrium foyer into the physical therapy wing. So many chic gleaming machines! So many attractive young people in attendance, at the check-in desk and scattered through the unit! Through a glass partition a pool of impossibly aqua water shone like crystal. There were potted rubber trees, elegantly abstract wall hangings in the mode of Frank Stella. Soft-rock music issued from invisible speakers as somber-looking men and women pulled at weights, pedaled dutifully on stationary bicycles, lay outstretched on the floor on mats and tried, under the close scrutiny of therapists, to lift parts of their bodies that seemed, to Temple's eye, ominously heavy. Temple noted with interest that the therapists appeared to be exclusively female. And young. White-clad in stylish slacks, cotton-knit tunic tops with names stitched in pink above their left breasts. One curly-haired young woman walking briskly past with an armload of towels glanced in Temple's direction with a quick smile—did she know him? Another, tenderly overlooking a damaged-looking man of Temple's age who was trying, face contorted with pain, to do a single push-up, had china-doll features and hair the color of apricot sherbet. But it was a petite, dark-haired girl who caught Temple's eye, as, her own posture ramrod straight, she massaged the neck of a woman lying limp on her stomach on a table—a pretty girl, not beautiful, with dark Mediterranean hair and an olive-pale slightly blemished skin. Temple's heart went out to her. You just didn't see girls with pimply complexions any longer in America, where had they all gone?

"It isn't uncommon," Freddie Dunbar was saying. "You say you've been flying a lot recently? Here's what I'm guessing: you picked up a viral infection from stale air circulating and recirculating in the plane, it settled in a neck muscle already strained from exertion and poor posture. Once the muscle goes into spasm, as yours has, it can take quite a while to heal."

" 'Poor posture'?" Temple said, hurt. He'd immediately straightened his shoulders, elevated his head. "How can you assume that, Freddie?"

"*Assume* it?—I can see it."

Dunbar was a short, peppy-wiry man who may have been a few years younger than Temple. He had ghost-gray eyes, a congenial but guarded smile; Temple would have to reassess him, in the light of this multimillion-dollar medical investment. He sat on the edge of the examining table to demonstrate. "This is proper posture, see?—at the back of the neck, the cervical lordosis it's called—" touching the nape of his neck, head uplifted and chin slightly retracted, "—a small inward curve. And, here, at the lower back, a similar hollow. When you slouch as you've been doing, everything sags, your head protrudes, and a considerable strain is placed on your neck muscles. And if these muscles have been infected or injured in any way, the injury can be exacerbated, and quite painful. Your muscle has gone into 'spasm.' The X ray shows a kind of knot."

Temple's awkwardly corrected posture made his neck ache more. He kneaded the sore muscle at the back of his head. "A knot," he said, puzzled. "How do you untie it?"

Dunbar said, not ungraciously, "That's what we're here for."

The consultation was over. It had not seemed hurried, yet only eight minutes had passed. Temple had spent most of the hour shivering in the X-ray unit. Dunbar quickly wrote out a prescription for a muscle relaxant—"Be sure not to drink while taking these, Larry, and be careful driving, all right?" as if Temple had to be cautioned about such an elementary measure—and a prescription for Temple to take to the physical therapy clinic downstairs. Somehow, Temple was in for three therapy sessions weekly until his pain subsided.

The men shook hands, as if after a tennis match Dunbar, the weaker player, had unaccountably won. It was only then that Dunbar asked, his expression subtly shifting, an actual light coming up in his eyes, "And, Larry—how is Isabel?"

"Who?"

"Isn't that your wife's—former wife's—name? Isabel?"

"Oh, you mean Isabelle." Temple gave the name the French intonation Isabelle preferred. Coolly he said, "I'm afraid I don't know, Freddie. Isabelle moved to Santa Monica after the divorce and remarried. It's been three years since she's spoken to me on the phone and more than five years since I've seen her—except in the company of lawyers. As for my son Robbie—we seem to be out of communication." Temple was breathless, angry. He was still smarting over that crack about poor posture and he couldn't have said whether he resented Dunbar's asking about Isabelle, or only that he'd asked belatedly, about to walk away. And Temple knew, even before he presented his Visa card at the front desk, he'd be criminally overcharged: $338 for the visit!

The glamorous young woman who processed his bill smiled at him anxiously. "Mr. Temple, are you all right?"

"Thanks, I'm fine, I'm in agony," Temple said, smiling in his affable, charming way, "—I'm in *spasm,* actually. It sounds sexual but it isn't. I always walk with my head under my arm."

Thinking on his way downstairs he'd simply walk out, get into his car and drive away—what the hell. Quit while he was out only $338. Physical problems embarrassed him. He'd always been a healthy, unreflective person—intelligent enough, with a reputation in some quarters for being shrewd, and more than shrewd; but not neurotic. Never been comfortable discussing physical matters. Or "spiritual," either. As when Isabelle tried to insist he make a will. "It's something that has to be done," she'd said provocatively, "—like dying itself." The woman had known how to needle him, upset him. It was part of her style. But Temple had been so damned busy making money those years he'd postponed the meeting with their lawyer until at last it was too late and he and Isabelle required two lawyers, dueling lawyers, to negotiate the breakup and artful dismantling of their thirteen-year marriage and its considerable assets. Now that he was a bachelor again, and not even, in any practical sense, a father, Temple still didn't have a will; but he intended to get around to it soon. He doubted he'd die before he was fifty.

He was sweating, wincing with pain in his neck and head. It wasn't that smug hustler Dunbar he was furious with, it was his former wife Isabelle. *Damn you: what a way to treat a man who loved you. Crazy for you and what did I ever get out of it? Kick in the teeth, in the neck. In the balls.*

DESPITE THE CODEINE in the muscle relaxant, washed down with beer, Temple had a wretched night. Alone with his *physical self.*

Defeatedly then next morning he checked into the Physical Therapy Clinic of the Saddle Hills Neck and Back Institute and, after a restless wait of forty minutes, was assigned a therapist. "Hello, Mr. Temple? I'm Gina. Will you come this way?" Dazed with pain Temple squinted at whoever it was with the somber equanimity of a condemned man greeting his executioner. He saw the petite young woman with the fine dark hair that fell to her shoulders, olive-dark skin and very dark, thickly lashed eyes. GINA in pink script above her left breast. His heartbeat quickened. Oh, ridiculous!

Temple was a man besieged by women. A solitary well-to-do male in Saddle Hills, New Jersey. Not about to fall in love with a "physical therapist" with no last name.

The young woman led Temple, more briskly than he could comfortably follow, a steel rod of pain driven through his neck. Through the large airy L-shaped space, past ingenious torture machines of pulleys, rings, bars, pedals, into which shaky men and women were being helped, victims of what physical mishaps, what unspeakable muscular or neurological deterioration one could only imagine. Temple did not want to stare. He feared seeing someone he knew, and being seen and known in turn. A muscular young man stood poised atop a curious disk, gripping a bar and trying desperately to balance himself; terror shone in his eyes as his legs failed, he began to fall, and two attendants deftly caught him beneath the arms. Another man, Temple's age, with thick bushy receding hair very like Temple's, lay stretched out groaning on a mat, having collapsed in the midst of an exercise. Back trouble, Temple guessed. Bad back trouble. Quickly, he looked away.

"In here, Mr. Temple. Would you like me to help you lie down, or can you manage, yourself?" Gina shut the door: thank God, they were in a private room. Temple climbed up upon, and stretched out upon, unassisted, an eight-foot padded table; a warm rolled towel beneath his neck, exactly fitted to the aching hollow of his neck. He shut his eyes, terribly embarrassed. Flat like this, on his back, he felt—unmanned. An overturned beetle. *What was this girl seeing, what was she thinking?* Luckily the crises of the past several months had burned off most of Temple's excess weight at the waist and gut: one hundred eighty pounds packed into a five-foot-ten frame, upper-body muscles still fairly solid, Temple didn't look—did he?—like a loser. He was wearing a freshly laundered T-shirt and chino trousers, jogging shoes. He'd showered and hastily shaved within the hour and his jaws stung pleasantly. He knew that, upright, he was a reasonably attractive man; looked years younger than his age on good days. But this was not a good day. He hadn't slept more than two or three hours the previous night. His eyes were ringed with fatigue and finely threaded with blood. It touched him to the quick that a young woman, a stranger, should see him in so weakened and debased a state.

"Mr. Temple, please try to *relax*."

Gina's voice was intense, throaty. Kindly. Temple did not open his eyes as she began to "stretch" his neck, as she explained—standing behind him, gripping the base of his skull and pulling gently at first, then with more strength. A woman's touch like ivory against his burning skin. Christ! He thought of masseuses, prostitutes. But no: this was therapy prescribed by Freddie Dunbar the neck specialist. This was legitimate, the real thing. Temple tensed expecting excruciating pain and could not quite believe it, that none came. He forced himself to breathe deeply and by degrees he began to relax. "Now retract your head, please. No, like this. Farther. Hold for a count of three. Release, relax, and repeat, ten times." Unquestioning, Temple followed instructions. Gina then began to knead the "knotted" muscles at the base of his skull, slowly on both sides of his neck, down to his shoulders and back up again, again. At the injured muscle, the fingers probed pure white-hot pain and Temple cried out like a stricken animal. "Sorry, Mr. Temple!" Gina murmured. Fingers easing away quickly as if repentant.

Crazy about you and what did I ever get out of it?

An exhausting drill of exercises. Invariable sets of ten. Again, again. Retracting the head, side-bending the neck. On Temple's stomach, sitting up, on his back again. When he gasped aloud Gina said gently, as if reprovingly, "Initial pain increase is common. Just go slowly." Temple realized he was floating on an island of pain like sparkling white sand. One of the numerous tropical-resort white-sand beaches of his late marriage. And Isabelle close beside him. So long as he did not look at her, she would remain. Warm oiled supple woman's body, the sunlit smell. When he opened his eyes, blinking, Isabelle was gone. But the dazzling sand remained. Blinding sand. An island of pain from which he kicked off, swam away in cool caressing turquoise waters, and returned; returned to the sparkling dazzling pain, and kicked off again, swam away again and again returned. Always, he returned. A woman's deft fingers were fitting a snug thick collar around his neck through which (Temple gradually gathered) hot water coursed. Fifteen minutes. Temple sweated, panted; observed his pain draining away, the tension dissolving like melting ice. His eyes filled with moisture. He was not crying, but his vision swam. Panting with happiness, hope. The young woman therapist in white stood beside the table making notations on a clipboard. Only now did Temple cast a sidelong glance at her—she was probably in her mid-twenties, slender, small-boned, with dark, thick-lashed eyes and a narrow, thin-tipped nose. Her complexion wasn't perfect yet you wouldn't call it blemished— tiny pimples at her hairline, like a rash. She had sensitive skin, so what? Not the smooth poreless cosmetic mask of glamorous Isabelle and her glamorous female friends.

"Are you feeling any better, Mr. Temple?"

"I am."

"You were terribly tense when you first came in. But you did relax, finally."

"I did."

Temple spoke heartily. He wanted to cry, to burst into laughter. Wanted to seize Gina about the hips, her slender hips, and bury his heated face against her, life seemed suddenly so simple, so good.

HE WENT AWAY, with a set of instructions for exercises to do at home, and an appointment with Gina for the morning after next. Secretly, he planned not to return—the sessions were $95, for fifty-five minutes! And he certainly wasn't going to see Dunbar again in a week, as "Freddie" wanted. You don't get to be a millionaire several times over by wasting good money.

FAR FROM BEING a loser, Temple was a winner. One of the winners of the world as he'd become, to his surprise, one of the adults of the world. In another lifetime it's true he'd been *poor.* No other way of describing it—*poor. Poor* rural county in northwestern Pennsylvania, *poor* family background. His prospects as a child must have been *poor.* Yet as a kid Temple hadn't seemed to know this. He'd been so eager, so hopeful and—what was Isabelle's word?—*grasping.* "A man who knows how to grasp," she'd said. "Grasp and not let go." Though he'd let go of Isabelle, finally.

The story Temple told himself and others was of a dreamy young kid ascending from a farm in Erie, Pennsylvania, as if hitchhiking through the void to his destiny: Saddle Hills, New Jersey. How he'd come to learn his business, which was essentially the borrowing of money in order to make money, wasn't clear; or wasn't in any case part of the story. What he told of himself might have been illustrated by Norman Rockwell for the old *Saturday Evening Post.* A freckled face, a gap-toothed smile. Intense brown eyes, a frank handshake and manner. Once so good-looking, women would glance at him and smile quizzically, as if they knew him. Since approximately his fortieth birthday, when his hair began to recede and knife-creases began to appear between his eyes, that rarely happened. Unless the women knew his name, and, knowing his name, knew who he was. And hoped he'd smile at them in return.

At about the time of the divorce, Temple began to experience odd heart "symptoms." An erratic, jumpy heart. A speedy heart. A sensation as of hiccups in the heart. So he'd begun taking heart medicine, digitalis. His condition wasn't serious, he'd been led to believe. But it could be embarrassing. In lovemaking, for instance, as he pushed to climax, if too much adrenaline was released in his blood, his heart might be triggered into fibrillation. Temple wouldn't die—anyway, he hadn't died, yet! But an attack could last as long as an hour and was not a comforting experience for either Temple or his lover, whoever the lover might be.

★　　★　　★

"WHY?—to help people, I guess. To play a role in a person's recovery."
This second therapy session, Gina spoke more readily. As gently but
forcibly she stretched Temple's neck, massaged the "soft tissue" at the base
of his skull, secured him into the remarkable hot-pack collar through
which steaming water coursed nourishing as blood. ("Is it tight enough? Is
it too tight?"—there was something disturbingly intimate, even erotic,
about being trussed up in the thing. Just a little more pressure on his neck
arteries and Temple's entire head would be tumescent.) Partly Temple was
quizzing Gina to distract himself from his misery and partly it was
Temple's habit to quiz strangers who intrigued him—*How do you live?
What is your life? Is there some secret to your life that might help me?*—but
mainly he was fascinated by the girl. Waking the previous night from restless dreams, a dream riddled with pain like pelting raindrops and someone
was standing silently beside his bed and she reached out to touch him,
calm him with her ivory-cool fingers. They were such strong fingers.

Gina was saying earnestly, "I knew I wanted to be a physical therapist
since—oh, sixth grade, maybe. Our teacher went around the room asking
us what we wanted to do when we grew up and I said, 'Help sick people
get better.' There was a cousin of mine, a boy who had cystic fibrosis. I
always wished I could have helped him walk! For a while I wanted to be a
nurse, then a doctor—but they don't really play a role in a person's recovery, over a period of time, like a physical therapist." How proudly she
spoke, in her shy way.

Play a role. A curious expression. It evoked a world in which people
played roles in one another's lives and had no lives of their own except for
these roles. Maybe it made sense, Temple thought. What is an actor, apart
from a play? A role? You can't just *be*—brute raw existence twenty-four
hours a day.

"I never knew that I wanted to be anything, I guess," Temple said.
Except a winner. "It's like, well—falling in love. A life can just happen." *Cut
the crap! Who was angling, negotiating, push-push-pushing to make it happen?*
"Uh—how many patients do you work with every day, Gina?" Temple
tried, in the exigency of the hot-pack collar, to keep his voice level and
casual.

"Ten, sometimes twelve. It varies."

"Ten! *Twelve!*" Temple's face burned. He didn't want to think this
was sexual jealousy. When he'd arrived that morning he peered in to

see Gina's 9 A.M. patient: a bearish young man of about thirty with sullen handsome features, wearing a neck brace, walking unsteadily with a cane. A cane! Football player's physique but the look in the poor bastard's eyes wasn't one you associated with the sport of football. Temple had looked quickly away, shuddering. "And do you work at the clinic every day?"

Gina hesitated as if these questions were becoming too personal.

"Well—most weeks, yes. I don't like holidays. I mean, to take them. People need their therapy." She spoke almost primly.

"And what are your hours?"

Again she hesitated. Flat on his back, Temple could see the girl only obliquely; wavy dark hair that fell to her shoulders, the set of her jaw. Was she frowning? In distaste? Quickly she answered, "Monday-Wednesday-Friday, eight to one; Tuesday-Thursday-Saturday, one to six."

Temple said, with forced exuberance, "That's symmetry!"

"What?"

Gina had removed the hot-pack collar—too bad—and now Temple was sitting up, steeling himself against pain. Next came the dreaded neck side-bends, retract chin, lower head slowly to the right shoulder, hold for a count of three, raise head, now the left shoulder, repeat, repeat. Gina's deft fingers were there to help, exerting pressure so that Temple could maintain the tremulous position. She hadn't really heard Temple's remark and he didn't repeat it.

Just like Isabelle. Like any woman. If you get abstract with them too quickly they turn vague, uneasy. Even the most harmless playful abstraction.

Temple had tried to stay away. He'd tried. Endured two wretched nights before giving in and returning here. The unpredictability of the pain as well as its severity had frightened him. And he'd discovered from examining the Institute's bill that where he'd been thinking *neck*, he ought to have been thinking *spine*. His official classification was *cervical spine strain*. That was sobering.

Next, on his stomach. Sweating forehead pressed against a rolled towel. Temple felt chastened anew. One thing about the therapy unit, you were all body here. Attempting "push-ups" from the head: God, how clumsy! A rod of molten-white pain in his neck. He was dizzily aware of Gina's slender hips and thighs in the white slacks close by his elbow. She murmured words of encouragement such as one might murmur to a child being potty-trained.

Next on his back, panting. Winded like a horse. But not wanting to lose control entirely, Temple remarked he thought he'd seen Gina a few nights before?—"Out at the Mall, at my theater?"

" 'Theater'?" This attracted her attention. Like a lovely silvery fish rising to the bait.

"The Cinemapolis, at the Mall. I own it."

Gina was making detailed notations on her clipboard. Temple waited for her to respond, glance at him impressed, *Hey: you're somebody of importance after all.* Most people did, even those who should know better. Developers and investors like Larry Temple. Certainly, most women. As if, being a vendor of movies, as another man might be a vendor of hardware, fencing, frozen pizza by the crate, Temple was associated with Hollywood glamour? Tabloid publicity, moneymaking on a grand scale? It's true, Temple had once been excited by the prospect of "exhibiting important films locally"—and so had Isabelle, for maybe a season. But that was a decade ago. Twelve years. Now, Temple rarely dropped by the six-screen cinema complex and more rarely still troubled to see a film. If he drove out tonight he'd see teenagers waiting in long rowdy lines to see *Crimson Tide, Die Hard with a Vengeance, Congo, Batman Forever.* Fewer customers for *Party Girl* but attendance was OK. As for the Russian film, Academy-award-winning *Burnt by the Sun*—Temple had dropped by to see it last Friday for the 7:10 P.M. showing and there'd been thirteen people scattered about the plush low-slung one-hundred-fifty seats.

Gina said, with a flicker of interest, unless it was merely a young person's politeness to an elder, "*You* own the Cinemapolis, Mr. Temple?"

"You could call me 'Larry,' actually."

Gina led Temple into the next exercise. Stretching a length of oddly fire-engine-red rubber diagonally across his body, shoulder to hip. It should have been easy except each time Temple moved, a jolt of pain illuminated his neck and upper spine like an X ray. He said, panting, "I—I've been doing a lot of flying lately. To L.A., and back. Sometimes business, sometimes personal. My former wife remarried and moved to Santa Monica." He heard these words with a kind of horror, as if they were issuing from an artificial voice box. "Dr. Dunbar thought—I might've picked up an airborne virus, in a plane. A neck muscle was infected."

"That can occur." Gina spoke solemnly. *Occur* seemed purposefully chosen, a clinician's word, out of a textbook. She said, "Once the muscle spasms, if the tissue has been overstretched—it can take a while to heal."

Casually Temple asked, "How much of a while?"

"Oh, I wouldn't want to say."

"Weeks?"—silence. "Months?"

"Dr. Dunbar might have an estimate."

Temple had a quick sense of the position of a young woman therapist, an hourly wage-earner, in the hierarchy of the Saddle Hills Neck and Back Institute. Not for Gina to overstep her authority.

"It wouldn't be—years? Would it?"

Gina said, in a lowered voice, though she and Temple were alone together, "Sometimes you see a person who can't hold or move his head normally? The pain is so severe?"

"Yes?"

"It might be someone who let the pain go for so long, not wanting to see a doctor—it can be too late."

"Too late?"

"To do much about the pain. You have to catch it in time."

Catch pain in time. There was a thought!

"This poor man who's my patient now," Gina said, "—he let his back pain go for twenty years! Imagine. He thought it would go away by itself, he said. Now it never will." Gina sighed. "*I* feel bad, there's so little I can do for him."

Absentmindedly she dabbed at Temple's flushed face where sweat ran in oily rivulets like tears.

There was Temple floating on his island of pain. Dazzling-white sand. And him flat upon it, fearful of moving. In the arm-flung leg-flung posture of a child making a snow-angel. The turquoise water lapped close by but Temple couldn't get to it. There was a shape beside him, warm and nudging. One of those teases: they can touch you, but you don't dare touch in turn. Don't dare look.

Then suddenly he was walking somewhere. Approaching a door marked PAIN MANAGEMENT CENTER. *Asleep yet sufficiently awake to register skepticism— there wasn't any such center at the Institute! What did they take him for, a credulous asshole?*

★   ★   ★

IT WASN'T TRUE that Gina had no last name. Right there on the bill her name was provided in full: *Gina LaPorta.*

There were several listings for *LaPorta* in the telephone directory. G. *LaPorta* in Saddle Hills Junction. Sleepless, damned neck aching, Temple drove by night in his ghostly-glimmering white BMW past the address—a stucco-facade apartment building on Eldwood Avenue. He didn't park but slow-cruised around the block. Deserted night streets of a part of town he'd known only as a onetime potential investor in some condominium properties. (He hadn't invested, fortunately.) It wasn't like Temple to behave like this, like a lovesick kid, weird behavior like his son Robbie back in prep school he'd never understood, or cared to understand—Robbie was Isabelle's pet, let the mother deal with him. But he was curious about Gina. Just curious! Wondered if she was living with someone. The telephone directory wasn't much help. He'd noticed a ring on her left hand, not a wedding band, nor a conventional engagement ring, turquoise-and-silver, but these days you couldn't tell—she might be married. Might even have a kid. *Physical life*—what a mystery! More mysterious than money, even, Temple had lately discovered.

First birds singing already?—only 4:40 A.M. There were cars parked at the curb on both sides of Eldwood Avenue and Temple saw, or believed he saw, Gina's little canary-yellow Ford Escort among them—he'd found out from her, in a casual exchange, what kind of car she drove and he'd checked it out in the Institute parking lot, at the rear. Economy car, compact and cute. And Temple's regal white BMW easing past, the motor near-soundless. Temple finished the lukewarm can of Molson's he'd been gripping between his knees as he drove. Something melancholy about night ending before you were ready. Always a melancholy tinge to the eastern sky when you've been awake with your solitary thoughts all night. Cruising the block, circling just one more time.

"HAVE YOU BEEN DOING your exercises, Mr. Temple?"

"More or less, yes."

"Has the pain lessened?"

"Definitely."

It wasn't exactly a lie. If Temple didn't move abruptly, or crane his neck forward as, in conversation with shorter people, especially attractive women, he had a natural tendency to do, he scarcely knew the pain was there. Though, like a dial tone radiating up into his head too, it was perpetually *there*. Too exuberantly he said, "I'm a thousand percent improved, Gina, thanks to you."

Gina blinked at him, startled. Her face colored in faint, uneven patches, like sunburn.

"Well—maybe just eight hundred percent," Temple said wryly, rubbing his neck.

Before coming to the Clinic, Temple had wandered about the Institute building. On the mezzanine floor he'd discovered a door marked SPORTS MEDICINE CENTER and, at the end of a corridor, another door marked PAIN MANAGEMENT CENTER. So it was real! He'd invented what was merely real.

Each time Temple stepped into the Physical Therapy Clinic its dimensions became just perceptibly smaller, friendlier. The first visit, he'd been confused by the mirrors that lined most of the walls and suggested an infinity of gleaming nightmare-machines and hapless anonymous people. But there were in fact just twenty-five machines, sleek stainless steel and black; there were six large mats on the polished tile floor, kept spotlessly clean. There were nine tables in the open clinic—more precisely, as Gina called them, *plinths*. There were racks of dumbbells, plastic yellow and blue balls of varying sizes. There was the shimmering aqua pool beyond the glass partition Temple looked at with longing. But Dunbar hadn't prescribed any sort of swimming therapy for him, yet.

Of course, Temple was beginning to recognize certain of his fellow patients, and guessed they were beginning to recognize him. No names here at the Clinic, just faces. And symptoms. It seemed to Temple he'd been in therapy for weeks, months! In fact, it was only Monday morning of his second week.

At the reception desk he'd glanced anxiously about, not seeing Gina at first. Then he saw her, doing paperwork at a desk; she looked up and smiled and his heart lifted. A ceramic barrette in her thick hair this morning and the turquoise ring prominent on her finger.

Temple's therapy began with the usual stretching and massage. Temple lay flat on the padded table—*plinth*—which he found almost comfortable now. He said, "The secret of happiness I think is to simplify your life, you know? My life has become simplified in recent years. When you're married and things are off-kilter life can be—well, complex." A pause. It was as if Temple's voice issued from his throat of its own capricious volition. "You're engaged, Gina?"

"Engaged? No."

"That ring."

"It isn't an engagement ring. Just a ring." Gina laughed sharply as if Temple had pushed too far. She retreated to the other side of the plinth. "Now sit up, Mr. Temple, please. We'll do neck rotation, three sets of ten." Neck rotation! When Temple flinched at the pain, Gina said, reprovingly, "This time rotate in the direction of the pain. Into the pain. It should centralize, or decrease. *Try*." He tried. He didn't want to disappoint her. His face was flushed like a tomato about to burst. He said, suddenly, "You've helped me so much, Gina. You've given me hope."

Gina murmured, embarrassed, "Well."

Again, on his back. On his stomach, forehead pressed against a rolled towel. Through a haze of pain he heard himself say, unexpectedly, "My ex-wife is *ex*. I mean literally. She has died." How strange that sounded, like an awkward translation: *She has died.* Temple amended, "I mean—she's dead. Isabelle is dead now."

There was a blank, systolic moment. "I'm sorry," Gina murmured.

Temple said, "Thank you." He was going to say *I miss her* but instead he said, as if it were a subtle, comic refutation of Gina's solicitude, "The alimony payments ended years ago"—an awkward joke, if it was a joke. It fell upon Gina's somber silence.

The therapy continued: again, Temple was sitting up. It was crucial for him to maintain perfect posture yet, oddly, the pain seemed to be pushing him out of alignment. He repeated, tasting the words, "My wife is dead. I could have gone to the funeral but—I wouldn't have felt welcome. Ex-wife, I mean. In fact, it's a double-ex. Gone first, and then dead. Pancreatic cancer. It's hard to believe—a woman like that—you'd have had to know her—*I* couldn't believe when I first heard—next, she was in the hospital. I mean, by the time I heard, she was already in. I flew out to see her, but—" What the hell was he saying? Why? His manner was affable, sane, matter-of-fact as if he were discussing a business deal; crucial for the other party to know that things were under control. It was the first time he'd uttered the remarkable words *My wife is dead.*

He was saying, with an air not of complaint but wonder, "My twenty-year-old son is a dropout from Stanford and he's in a drug rehabilitation center in La Jolla—I *think*. He hasn't spoken to me for five years except to ask for money." Temple laughed, to show he wasn't at all hurt, nor even much surprised.

Again Gina murmured, "I'm sorry." Not knowing what else to say, frowning and looking away from Temple, picking at a reddened bump on the underside of her chin.

"*I'm* sorry," Temple said. "But I don't let it affect my outlook on life."

Next was the hot-pack collar. Tight around his neck as he could bear. The eerie sensation of floating: feeling pain drain from his neck and skull like needles being extracted from flesh. Temple began to speak expansively, like a levitating man. A crisis had been met, and overcome. "Gina, suppose a man was to come into the Clinic here, as your patient? And he came three times a week as his doctor prescribed, and he's desperate to get well, and you got to like him—not just feel sorry for him, I mean, but like him—and he liked you; and he asked was it possible you might see him sometime, outside the Clinic? Where he wasn't a patient, and you weren't his therapist? What then?"

Gina didn't reply at first. She'd moved out of Temple's line of vision and he had only a vague blurry sense of her. "Is this a made-up story, or what?" She laughed sharply.

Temple said, "I'll continue. This man, your hypothetical patient, actually he'd seen you, without knowing your name of course, before he became your patient. Once at the Mall, possibly, or downtown—and at a property in the Junction, on Eldwood Avenue—he'd been looking into, as an investment. Isolated, accidental times. He wasn't looking *for* you, just happened to *see* you. And a few weeks or months later he develops a mysterious neck pain, and his doctor prescribes physical therapy, and he walks into the Clinic and sees you—just by chance. And he's excited, and anxious. He wonders is a patient allowed to request a therapist, not knowing her name?—or is that against regulations, would it be perceived as unprofessional? So he doesn't say anything; but he's assigned to you, anyway! And he thinks—oh, God, he thinks—if—if only—" Temple paused, breathing quickly. He was concerned that too much adrenaline might be flooding his veins.

Gina, out of sight, remained silent. Temple believed he could hear her quick shallow breathing.

"Hey, it's only a story," he said. "You're right, Gina—it's made up."

Quietly Gina said, "Excuse me, Mr. Temple."

She left the room, shut the door. In a paroxysm of embarrassment, unless it was mortal shame, Temple lay motionless as a man fallen from a great height, in terror of testing whether he can in fact move. Gina had gone to get the Clinic manager! She'd gone to inform Dunbar!

Steaming water coursed through the choking-tight collar. The *hydro-collator,* as it was called, $35 per session, was timed to run for fifteen minutes. Temple shut his eyes. He was doing the dead man's float. Close about him was the dazzling-blinding white-sand island and the shimmering turquoise water and he seemed, in his misery, to be enveloped by each simultaneously. *What a way to treat a man who loves you. Crazy for you and what did I ever get out of it?*

He must have slept. Didn't hear the door open behind him, or close. There came Gina's deft cool fingers against his neck, undoing the collar. She'd returned, as if nothing had happened? Therapy would continue, as if nothing had happened? "Forgive me?—I got a little carried away," Temple said. Gina was helping him sit upright. He was dazed, dizzy. The heat of the collar had spread through his body. Now came neck side-bends, and more pain: retract the chin, lower head toward right shoulder slowly, hold one-two-three; relax, return, repeat to left shoulder. Three times, sets of ten. There came Gina's steady hand on the side of his head, pressing gently downward, when Temple faltered. Zigzag bolts of pain shot upward into his skull, downward into his chest. Almost you'd expect jeering blipping sounds to accompany them, as in a kid's video game. Gina cautioned, "Retract your chin farther, Mr. Temple. You can hurt yourself in this exercise if you don't."

Temple was thinking: she'd gone away, and she'd considered his story. She was an intelligent young woman who could make the distinction between fiction and life, fable and fact. She could see that Temple was a worthy man. Obviously well-intentioned, decent. Possibly a troubled man but it was nothing he couldn't handle. If she was a normally curious young woman she might have noted her patient's address on the paper-work; might even have noted the BMW; made certain calculations. You wouldn't blame a woman—investments have to be worth the risk. Gina could foresee, surely, Temple's kindness? His affection and desperation in about equal measure? She could foresee—but Temple's vision began to blur, as in a dream rising abruptly to daylight, about to go out.

Temple lay another time on his back, winded. Gina resumed her position behind him, massaging his neck and upper shoulder muscles that were knotty and gnarled as aged tree roots. He shivered with pain he hoped she wouldn't notice, he didn't want to disappoint her. Hesitantly he opened his eyes and there was Gina's flushed face upside-down, above him. Just-perceptible strain lines at her eyes, her pursed mouth. Skin heated with emotion and she'd picked the tiny bump on the underside of her chin to bleeding. Maybe she wasn't so young as he'd thought? Thirty? Or more? He smiled happily, and it seemed to him that Gina smiled—anyway, almost. "Be serious, Mr. Temple," she said severely, fingers digging into his flesh. "You're in pain."

GUNLOVE

*T*he first? That's easy. My mom's Bauer semiautomatic snubbie, a .25-caliber "defense weapon" good for six rounds. It was made of stainless steel with a pretty ivory grip and a barrel so short—two inches!—it looked like a toy. When we moved to Connecticut after Dad left us, she carried it in her purse sometimes when she went out after dark, but we weren't supposed to know about this. She did have a homeowner's handgun permit. She kept the snubbie in the drawer of her bedside table in case of intruders. "Mom is really worried Dad's gonna break in and strangle her or something," my brother used to say. Whether this was truthful or to make me feel bad, I can't say. When we asked Mom who gave her the gun (we weren't supposed to touch it but we could sometimes look at it resting in the palm of Mom's hand) she laughed and said, "Who'd you think? Your dad." In fact, my brother said, it was a private detective who sold it to her, or gave it to her. Those years, Mom was a woman men liked to give presents to, especially men who were new on the scene.

THIS RIFLE BELONGING to my Uncle Adcock, before he got to be a multimillionaire developing a thousand acres on Mackinac Island and feuded with the relatives. It was a Springfield standard-issue .22- or .30-

caliber with a satin-nickel finish and a maple stock and it was so heavy, that long barrel, I staggered holding it. My cousins Jake and Midge got their dad's glass breakfront open (the key was beneath a loose brick in the fireplace) and smuggled the rifle outside. After they played with it awhile, aiming at birds and sailboats on the lake, they told me to "try aiming." I was afraid, but Jake insisted. He fitted the rifle onto my shoulder and my index finger against the trigger and helped hold the barrel steady. That rifle!—it had a cool oily smell, I'd remember afterward. And the smooth-polished stock against my cheek. I squinted along the barrel through the front sight (that looked bent) at white sails billowing in the wind. It was my imagination, the sails were magnified by looking through the sight. Uncle Adcock's big sailboat had candy-striped sails you could recognize anywhere. Jake said, "If it was loaded you could fire," then he said, "There's a recoil, so watch out." (I wouldn't think until afterward what he said, whether it made sense.) I wasn't sure what was expected of me. Jake and Midge were giggling. I suppose I looked comical, a potbellied little girl with glasses in shorts and a T-shirt holding a grown-up's rifle to her shoulder, and her skinny arms trembling with the weight. We weren't on the beach but in ankle-deep clover buzzing with bees. I was afraid of getting stung. Where the adults were, I don't know. Maybe on the lake. Jake was eleven, Midge was nine, and I was even younger. These were Michigan-summer cousins. When I wasn't with Jake and Midge it was like when I wasn't with my mom or dad or brother or anybody, I guess—I'd just forget about them, as if they didn't exist. But when I was with them, I'd have done anything they wanted.

THE STORY WAS, after the basketball game, around 4 A.M. the next morning, two or three carloads of black kids from Bridgeport drove past some Malden Heights basketball players' houses, plus the basketball coach's house, plus the principal's house, and sprayed the fronts with buckshot, breaking some windows. Or maybe it was only just BBs. You heard different stories. We'd moved from Darien that winter to live full-time with Mr. K. ("Kaho"), who was a Japanese-American ("Jap-Am") architect and a self-described cynic. He made my brother and me laugh, and embarrassed Mom because it was usually her stories he doubted, saying with a roll of his eyes, "Oh, yes? Interesting—if true." Which he said of the drive-by shootings. (How'd black kids from Bridgeport know where anybody lived? And why'd they give a damn, since Bridgeport won the championship?) By then, I was twelve. I was wearing contacts.

AT THE HUNGRY HORSE RANCH north of Hungry Horse, Montana, near Glacier Park, where Dad took us to learn horseback riding one August, I had a serious crush on Blackhawk (his actual name was Ernest, but he was from the Blood Reservation), who tended horses. I was always following Blackhawk. It got to be a joke, but not (I think) a mean joke. Once I trailed Blackhawk carrying a shotgun to where he shot at woodchucks running for cover. The gun was a .12-gauge double-barrel Remington belonging to the ranch owner. The shots were so loud! I pressed my hands over my ears; it was almost as if I couldn't *see*. Blackhawk, standing over a burrow and cursing and firing inside, ignored me. He'd missed every woodchuck except one he'd wounded (it looked like) that had dragged itself into the burrow, and now he was practically straddling the burrow and firing inside. The buckshot blasted into the earth! Blackhawk stood with knees apart horsey fashion and his dark face flushed and tight and clenched as a fist. Except for the noise, and the wounded woodchuck, and how Blackhawk could blast me in two if he whirled and shot like somebody on TV, it was such a funny sight I couldn't help laughing.

ASHLEY, my first roommate at Exeter, took me home at Thanksgiving and I was surprised at how old her father was, expecting a man like my dad. Mr. D. was a congressman from Maryland. They were living in Annapolis in this old stone house they said had been completely renovated. It was a beautiful house but I remember that the white walls were too much. Not a big house upstairs and Ashley's bedroom was close by her parents' and I heard Mr. D. snoring through walls and doors and I couldn't sleep. I tried, but I could not sleep. Ashley was asleep (or pretending: how she always dealt with things). I went downstairs in the dark and into a study off the living room and tried to read, pulling down books from shelves. One of them was a *Reader's Digest* edition, very old and dog-eared, but I got to reading *Lost Horizon* by James Hilton and liked it. About an hour later there came Mr. D. in a navy blue terrycloth bathrobe and barefoot staring at me. As if for a scary moment he didn't know who I was. His big belly tied in by the sash. How he knew I was there, I have no idea. Mr. D. scratched his chest inside the robe and tried to smile. In his right hand was what looked like a toy gun he might've hidden in his pocket but didn't. As though he had nothing to hide he was ashamed of. Making then like a joke of it showing me the "snubbie"—it was bigger than my mom's, with a three-inch stainless steel barrel—an Arcadia automatic "bedroom special" Mr. D. called it—a tough-looking little gun that fitted Mr. D's hand just right. I liked the blue finish and checkered walnut handle. He had a homeowner's permit for the weapon, Mr. D. wanted me to know. He kept the first chamber loaded with "just a .38 shot shell" (he showed me) to scare off an intruder, but the other chambers had the real thing, hollow-point bullets. I was too shy to ask Mr. D. if he'd ever actually fired his gun at a human being. I guessed I could see in his face he'd be capable of it, though. "Want to hold it?" Mr. D. asked. "The safety lock's on."

IN MOTHER'S SUMMER PLACE at East Hampton, I had my things spread out on the drawing board on the porch, radio turned up high, and I had a sort of idea something like this might happen; Kaho and I had had all we could take of Mother's shit. So the floorboards behind me give a little beneath my bare feet and I'm leaning over the drawing board and there's this poke, this jab against my rear (I'm in denim cutoffs cut pretty high in the crotch). My first thought is it's a gun barrel, I was going to be shot at the base of my spine!—but it turns out to be Mikal with just a hard-on.

"WHAT'S IT LIKE? For a guy it's like a gunshot going off. Before you're ready. And this stuff that shoots out of you . . . weird like something in a sci-fi movie. Christ."

I said, I'm glad I'm not a guy. It wasn't true, though.

When we made out, I pretended he was Blackhawk.

WERE WE IMPRESSED! In English class Mr. Dix read to us from a biography of Ernest Hemingway how, when Hemingway was eighteen, at his family's summer place in northern Michigan, sometimes he'd pick up *a loaded double-barreled shotgun* and draw a bead on his dad's head (where the old man, oblivious, was working in a tomato patch). Wild! Before this we'd just been thinking of Hemingway as one of those weird wrinkled old coots with white beards they wanted you to read.

Did you ever think of doing it? To yourself? Charl passed me the note. Charl S., coming on like Junior Dyke (the guys resented her terrific style). *Too lazy. Don't do anything myself.* I flicked back the note, and naturally we got caught.

THERE WAS Adrian L. we never saw again after Easter break our junior year. Adrian L., sixteen, from Rye, Connecticut, went home and died of a "gun accident" in the rec room of his family's house. In a Rye newspaper (some kids who'd been at the funeral brought it back to school) the coroner was quoted saying that Adrian had died "instantaneously" of a .45-caliber bullet in the brain discharged while he was cleaning his father's Army handgun. (A Government Model automatic.) Mr. L. had been a decorated U.S. Army lieutenant in Vietnam. Mr. L. insisted to investigators that the gun "was never loaded" but Mr. L. insisted too that his son had not shot himself deliberately. There'd been a single round of ammunition in the gun. At school we talked a lot about Adrian. We cut out his picture from last year's yearbook. "Adrian treated a girl with respect. Not like some of these assholes." We'd go around saying that, though actually none of us had known Adrian well. You couldn't get to know him, he was so quiet. High grades but the Math Club type. He'd dropped out of school activities and missed a lot of classes that semester, staying just (his roommate said) in his room. Somebody's dad (maybe my own?) made the remark that if you know guns, the Government Model .45 is a "classic." There'd be worse ways to go than a .45 in the brain, point-blank.

THERE WAS a more romantic way, though. "Teen Wedding" was a song we listened to, a lot. We never knew anybody who actually got married but we'd heard of kids who got in so deep they wanted to die together. A red-haired boy called Skix (he'd dropped out of Exeter a few years before; almost nobody remembered him but tales were told of him) who'd shot his girlfriend (nobody we knew, from the Rhinebeck public high school) in his car they were parked in overlooking the Hudson River, then turned the gun on himself. Both bullets in the heart. Guys who knew guns spoke knowledgeably about how Skix had used a Crown City Condor semiautomatic .45 (registered in an uncle's name). Skix had lived in Rhinebeck in what somebody described as "an actual castle, almost." It was a sign a guy took you seriously, if at least he'd twist your wrists till you cried. The sexiest was both wrists twisted at the same time.

*   *   *

THERE WAS a certain avant-garde drug called "ice" not everybody could handle. A guy I knew after college, Kenny B., who worked for Merrill, Lynch in Manhattan, made us laugh recounting tales of his high school days in Westchester County. He'd been so strung out and crazed from "sucking ice" he'd actually driven to school one morning with a carbine rifle!—a Safari Arms .30-caliber with a satin blue finish and a smooth walnut stock with a thumbhole design looking like, Kenny said, something Wild Bill Hickock might've used shooting up the Indians. This fantastic gun had belonged to Kenny's grandfather, who hadn't touched it in thirty years. Kenny sat in the parking lot with the gun on his lap, hidden under his jacket. Watching kids trailing into school. He'd had the intention of shooting somebody, preferably his math teacher. "I just wanted to waste some dude. Not any girl, though. I wouldn't have shot a girl, I'm sure."

SOME OF US still missed Adrian. We believed we would miss him all our lives. We were stubborn and loyal. I'd say suddenly, in rainy weather, "I loved him." Actual tears stung my eyes. We were young but prescient. These beautiful times! How they keep bringing you back to somebody gone.

WE WERE LISTENING to "Black Sabbath." We were frankly stoned, but cool. My dad (we weren't expecting him back so soon) came in, in this foul mood. The market was down, we knew. Everybody's dad was scared, and pissed. A few months ago my dad had been mugged by (he said) a "black Hispanic" with a gun outside the 30th Street Train Depot in Philadelphia. He'd given up his wallet, wristwatch, and briefcase with no resistance, desperate not to die. Reduced to "quivering cowardice" in five seconds, Dad said. White pride! Didn't save him from a pistol-whipping, though. So that spring he'd gotten a little crazed over the Tawana Brawley case, her photo and Reverend Al Sharpton's on the front page of the *Times.* Staring at Brawley's photo saying, this look in his face, "Who'd want to rape *her?*"

IN *The Tibetan Book of the Dead* some of us were reading spring of senior year (not on our honors reading list!) somebody had underlined in red ink,

In the Occident, where the Art of Dying is little known and rarely practiced, there is the common unwillingness to die.

DRIVING BACK from a weekend at Dartmouth. Four of us crammed into the backseat and three in the front of my roommate's boyfriend's step-mom's black Lincoln town car. We were totally wasted! The boyfriend was Nico W. from Peru; his dad was a diplomat and his stepmom an American. Nico was "100 percent Americanized." Insisted he knew a "scenic short-cut" to Bellows Falls but, sure, we got lost. Mountain roads turn and twist so, you can't get anywhere. Then the road turned into practically a ditch from so much rain. Nico was trying to turn the car around in like a six-foot space and we got stuck in mud. It was still raining! Just off the road was this crude house trailer resting on tires with a plastic Santa Claus on the roof and a giant satellite dish. Piles of trash around the place and a pun-gent odor of smoldering garbage. We were so pissed at the situation we were laughing like hyenas. Nico turns these tragic eyes on us, the pupils tiny as poppy seeds. He'd been snorting other people's coke all weekend and was burned out. But he was in the best shape of any of us to be driv-ing. We heard yelling and looked and in the doorway of the trailer there's this heavy woman in overalls, what looks like a shotgun over her arm. Double-barreled shotgun! Aimed at us! She was drunk or crazy, or both—"Get the fuck out of here, I'll blow your fuckin' heads off!" It was a TV scene. On TV it's funny, but in actual life it wasn't. We were scared we'd all be killed. Nico was desperate, gunning the engine and the car wheels spinning and the car sinking deeper into mud and all of us scream-ing and laughing so hard I almost wet my pants, or maybe did a little. How Nico got us out of there, I don't know. They would say the crazy woman fired the shotgun over our heads but I wasn't sure I heard it. I woke up later, my head bumping against the back of the seat, Nico flooring the gas pedal. We got lost another time, too, before we got to Bellows Falls.

SEAN STAYED with some friends in a high-rise off Bleecker Street. We didn't get much sleep. It was the Fourth of July weekend; through the night we'd hear firecrackers and gunshots like a war zone.

IN POUGHKEEPSIE, I ran a red light. Returning to school in a freezing rain. In one of those moods, thinking, *If it happens, it happens.* Like I wouldn't use the brakes if the car skidded. On the other side of some railroad tracks there was a New York state trooper patrol car, I saw too late. Turns on his lights and pulls out after me. I wasn't pregnant because I'd started bleeding in the car, into my clothes and onto the car seat. Here I'm stopping the car on the shoulder of the road shaking, crying, I'd been crying all the way up from the city. The cop is a youngish white guy, Italian-looking. He's got his gun drawn! I just about freak seeing that gun. He sees I'm a Vassar student, sees I'm alone, holsters the gun but talks kind of suggestively to me, asking for my driver's license, auto registration, etcetera and taking a long time examining them with a flashlight. All this, in the rain! He asks me then would I please step out of my car and accompany him to his car but by this time I'm crying so hard, I'm in no state to comprehend. My face all smeared and the crotch of my jeans soaked with blood. I can see he likes me crying but doesn't want too much of it. The last thing a guy wants is hysteria. I'm pounding the steering wheel, "Shoot me! I hate you! I want to die anyway!" The trooper looks at me disgusted and relents. Lets me off with just a traffic ticket, $60 fine and a mark for *moving violation* on my license, and a warning. "Lucky this time, Vassar girl," he says. I know I am.

LUCK RUNS in our family, Dad used to say. Maybe he was being ironic but it's a fact, it does. Like when Mother was knocked down, robbed, and raped in the ass, she wasn't murdered, too. See?

WHAT HAPPENED WAS: Mother was living in a two-bedroom apartment on East 77th Street, near Madison, in a building you'd think, she said, would be safe, except nowhere's safe in Manhattan any longer, returning from a performance of *Miss Saigon* (in which she was an investor) and absolutely *not drunk* (though she'd had a few drinks just possibly at Joe Allen's with friends), alone in the elevator to the ninth floor and alone (she swore!) in the hall, opening her door with her key and suddenly she's hit on the back of the head, hard as a sledgehammer, a man's fists, she's knocked inside, flat on her face, too panicked to scream, or hasn't the breath, he's pounding her on the back with his fists, grunting and cursing her, bangs her head against the floor, she's half-unconscious and he dumps the contents of her purse onto her back, back of her mink coat, paws through them to take what's valuable, unfortunately there's Mother's "snubbie" with the ivory handle, so her assailant presses the barrel of the little gun against the base of her skull, he's straddling her, panting and sweating, a dark oily smell she will swear, calls her *bitch* and *cunt,* a black accent, from the Islands she will swear, and he hikes up her skirt and what's called "sodomizes" her and he beats her unconscious with the gun fracturing her skull and tearing the scalp so she'll be found barely breathing in a pool of blood, but at least alive. She would beg my brother and me not to tell our father. Dad said, "What's she expect? Living alone."

WHEN I WAS with G. G. in his Varick Street loft, men wouldn't leave me alone. Not just strangers, guys on the street, but G. G.'s so-called friends. One of them led me into a storage room at a gallery opening, pushed his tongue into my mouth and brought my hand to his penis, where it protruded from the fly of his stonewashed jeans like an extra, eager hand. "See what I'm packing, baby." In a sleaze-porn film you'd be howling with laughter; in actual life you just stand there, waiting.

THEY WERE medical students high on some new amphetamine. They claimed they manufactured their own with Bunsen burners. We were telling nude stories. I was the blond, and blonds are listened to in a way that makes you uncomfortable until you get used to it, but it might be a mistake to get used to it. I told how in first grade at my friend Betsy's house, her older brother made us take off our clothes so he could "examine" us with a flashlight. Oh, did that tickle! In the telling, which I tried to dramatize, making them laugh, because I'd taken acting at Vassar and was said to have talent, I remembered suddenly it wasn't Betsy's house and it wasn't Betsy's brother but my own brother. It wasn't a flashlight he'd had but something else. Mom's little snubbie? He warned, "This is gonna tickle."

SHE HAD permanent nerve damage in her face and throat and internal injuries where he'd torn her anus. She had blurred vision in both eyes. Headaches. Spinal pain. Couldn't sleep without barbiturates and then mostly during the day. We begged her to move out of Manhattan. At least, to get married again. She was still good-looking, she had a flair about her like, who?—Lauren Bacall in those old movies. She wasn't yet sixty. She wasn't a pauper. And she'd tested negative for AIDS. "Don't tell me," I said laughing over the phone, "you're replacing that gun? Oh, Mother." Mother laughed too, in her nervous-angry way, saying she had a new friend who was a retired law enforcement officer (Nassau County) and he was advising her to purchase, for self-protection, a .38-caliber Colt Detective Special, a six-shot revolver more reliable than the Bauer semiautomatic, though the Colt, too, had a snubbie (two-inch) barrel. Mother said, "Next time, I'll be better prepared."

G. G. SIGNED FOR a Fox comedy series. The pilot was being filmed in L. A. and we'd be living in somebody's house in Pacific Palisades, a fantastic estate owned by a megawealthy record producer. If I came with him, which wasn't 100 percent certain. G. G. had this weird old west–looking six-shooter, a stainless steel .357 Magnum with an eight-inch barrel. One of his doper friends traded him for something. (Maybe me? I'd had my suspicions.) G. G. put a bullet in, spun the chamber (it wasn't too well oiled), saying, "How's about Russian roulette? Me first."

TARGET PRACTICE AT the town dump outside Greenwich. Rats and "garbage birds." He exploded a grackle in midair and wounded a furry panicked scuttling thing he called a "rabid raccoon." He was a pretty good shot. He closed my fingers on the rifle (a Winchester .22, nothing special), fixed my index finger on the trigger as if I couldn't have found it myself. He adjusted my arm. My shoulder. Breathing into my hair. He steadied the barrel. It was our first time. He was married, he took all that seriously. I was set to pretend to be afraid, upset by the noise of the gunshot and the recoil but in fact I didn't need to pretend. Afterward we made love so hard it hurt in the back of his Land Rover smelling of gunpowder, oil, grease, and aged running shoes and sweatsocks belonging to his sons.

RUSSIAN ROULETTE! I'd never do it, it's a guy thing. They say you need to get a coke high first, then there's no high like it.

AT SCOTT E.'S HOUSE, when we were living in Malden Heights and just kids. Scott went to Choate. His dad (whose own dad had been a World War II Air Force hero) was showing us his gun collection. I'd had so many beers I wasn't focusing too well. This guy I was with kept brushing against me, my breast. Scott was embarrassed of his father but sort of proud of him, too. We couldn't touch any of the guns but he'd answer questions if we had any. I remember a "German souvenir" and a "man-stopper" with a nasty long barrel made of what looked like iron. I asked Mr. E. if he kept any of his guns loaded, which was a silly question, but Mr. E. said with a sly smile, "Maybe. Guess which." It was like Scott, so quick, that guy was dazzling sometimes, in front of us all he picked up one of the fancy old revolvers, steely-blue with an eight-inch barrel at least, and silver engravings, and before his dad could stop him he turned the chamber and pulled the cock with his thumb, aimed at his own head and pulled the trigger. Click!

IN NEW YORK, I ran into my cousin Midge, now called Margery. I spoke of the time she and her brother Jake had been playing with their father's .22 rifle at the summer place on Mackinac Island. Midge, or Margery, said with this frozen face, "We never played with Daddy's guns. That's ridiculous. He'd have given us hell." (Uncle Adcock had died of cancer the year before, in Saint Petersburg. I'd meant to send a card or call.) I started to speak but Midge, or Margery, turned her back on me and walked away. I stared after her, shocked, as if I'd been slapped. I could remember the deafening crack of the rifle. The recoil against my shoulder that practically broke it. The burned smell of gunpowder in my nostrils. That exciting smell. And the way the white sails on the lake, billowing and slapping in the wind, looked almost, for a fraction of a second, like they'd been shot.

THAT EASTER BREAK, junior year at Vassar, I told my parents I was going skiing in Boulder with my roommate and her family but in fact I was with Cal at his stepfather's lodge in the mountains. We spent most of the time stoned, in bed, listening to heavy metal rock and getting up mainly when we had to use the john. (We'd see who could go the longer. We were drinking fruit juice and stuff like that. I was embarrassed at first having to pee so often but would've been more embarrassed to wet the bed. I had sort of a yeast infection I guess.) I walked around naked, a Yale sweatshirt around my shoulders and the sleeves tied beneath my breasts. The sunshine was too bright for our eyes, we had to keep the blinds mostly drawn. I was looking through cupboards and saw a rifle and an opened box of ammo. A Winchester .22, hadn't been cleaned in a long time and the blue-steel barrel coated with dust. On another shelf was a Sturm, Ruger six-chambered revolver, also dusty, stainless steel with a walnut grip and a barrel of about four inches. I liked this gun. I liked the feel and the weight of it. A heavy barrel and a sizable grip like you're shaking hands. Cal came in and saw me and about freaked. Like he hadn't known the guns were "on the premises." (Cal wasn't one to acknowledge his mother had married a paranoid schizophrenic who kept guns in all the places he lived and, being a criminal lawyer, had a permit to carry a concealed weapon.) Cal said, "Jesus, baby, put that down, OK?" I was stoned and really grooving with this fantastic piece. You hear talk like that, a man knowing when he connects with the right gun, but not women; but it was as though it was all between the Sturm, Ruger and me, and Cal was this third party, like a voyeur, looking on. I said, "Ever play Russian roulette?" Cal said, scared but trying to make a joke of it, "What the point of Russian roulette is, I never could figure." I'd clicked off the safety. I was checking to see if there were bullets in the chambers. I laughed, saying, "You take a chance, that's the point. If you win, you don't get a bullet in the brain." Cal said, as if it was philosophy class and arguing was part of your grade, "You don't have a bullet in the brain anyway. That means you're a winner?" "Hey, no," I said laughing. "You're a loser." Cal just didn't get it. A guy can be sexy and sweet and all that but just not get it.

AFTER MY MOM she was the first woman I knew who carried a gun in her purse. Kept it in her bedside table when not in her purse. It was a Sterling Arms Model 400 semiautomatic with a nickel finish and a three-inch barrel and a classy ivory grip. I was cool, holding it. Loaded, and the safety *on.* "Could you ever shoot this at a human being?" I asked. She just smiled, and took it back from me.

THERE WAS a rumor, Nahid A., this sexy rich kid from Kashmir we'd known at Vassar, had become a "mercenary arms dealer" in his native country. Other people said, "Bullshit. Nahid is a *poet.*"

SHOCKING NEWS! Charl S. (whom I'd been out of contact with for eight years at least) called to tell me. But I'd been reading about it in the *New York Times* and seeing it on TV. Lurid headlines on the front page of every tabloid. A pregnant social worker (white) and her unborn baby had been "riddled with bullets" and her husband wounded in their car in Worcester, Massachusetts, by a black male assailant believed to be (according to the husband's testimony) one of her welfare clients. The dead woman had been a wan, pretty blond from a well-to-do Boston family. Her husband, Charl pointed out, was our old mutual boy friend Nico. Nico, wounded by gunshot! Charl sounded thrilled. "Who'd ever suppose Nico would marry a social worker? He wasn't ever that type."

★   ★   ★

MUST'VE BEEN a month later when Charl called back, this time even more thrilled. Now there was truly shocking news! Nico's wife hadn't been gunned down by a black welfare client after all *but by Nico himself.* He'd just been arrested. He'd caused every black man in the Worcester area to be a suspect. It was national news. "Nico insured that poor woman for $1 million only a few months before he shot her. Isn't that terrible?" I was trying to feel that this was terrible news. Or even unexpected. I told Charl it hadn't been very bright of Nico to insure his wife for $1 million and then kill her himself. Thinking of Nico's velvety eyes and his weird lukewarm tongue thrusting and parrying in your mouth like some kind of sea urchin.

THE PHONE RANG during the night. It was my brother in Palm Beach. More bad news about Mother. But hadn't she just gotten married? Wasn't she on her honeymoon? The man sleeping beside me didn't stir. He was used to me prowling the place at night. Already my head was pounding with pain. "No, wait," I said, trying not to panic, "I already heard this. Didn't I?" My brother said rudely, "No, you haven't. This time she's dead."

HER COLT DETECTIVE SPECIAL WAS left to me, in Mother's hand-written words, *My only daughter. For her commonsense protection.* That and a box of tangled costume jewelry (what had happened to the good jewelry?) and family mementos and a couple of million dollars in bonds.

I CRIED all that spring. Couldn't stop. As though my heart was a block of ice now melting. Kaho held me for old time's sake. He wasn't so young and virile as he used to be, he warned. Kaho had been married, too, to an older woman who'd died in "mysterious" circumstances. (Not Kaho's fault!) After a while in my bed Kaho's ropey-muscled arm began to get stiff where I was lying on it, the weight of my body like a drowned girl's. Between us where we touched our skins were slick with cold sweat like gun oil. I was crying, "I love you, Kaho. I always have." But Kaho was embarrassed. It was all so long ago, he said. His big mariner's watch glowed pale green in the dark like a floating green fish, or an eye.

★   ★   ★

YOU CAN special-order gun grips in rosewood, zebra wood, birds-eye maple, ivory. I'd always wanted ivory. In Jackson Hole, this "Native American" (Crow Indian, but he didn't look anything like Blackhawk) carved gun grips out of blocks of wood with a knife that flashed so in his fingers, you'd swear it was throwing off sparks. Lyle Barnfeather carved custom orders for Smith & Wesson, had quite a back order, and wanted me to know he didn't "come cheap."

G. G. RETURNED TO my life. His TV career had bottomed out. Sometimes he seemed to blame me, for not coming with him. Other times, he borrowed money. When I kicked him out, he stalked me like a guy on TV. One of those serial killer specials. Except G. G. didn't have a van, or even a car. How'd he dump the body? He called me leaving messages, *Baby I love you don't do this to me.* It was all a bad TV movie except I didn't know how the script would end. I had my mom's Colt Detective Special, though, for *commonsense protection.*

AT THE READY-AIM-FIRE SHOOTING RANGE on Staten Island, we wore neutral (gray)-tinted glasses with adjustable nose pads. We were equipped with earmuffs approved by the EPA. Still, the noise was deafening. If you didn't hear it at full blast, you felt it vibrating through your body. Some of the men were firing machine guns. Like air hammers, and their faces shining. One of them, I saw drooling down his chin. My (male) instructor Buzz was patient with me. We started out with just lightweight practice pistols, then after a few months graduated to the Remington .44 Magnum ("most powerful hand-gun cartridge in existence"). Target shooting was like lovemaking with me, sometimes I hit the bull's-eye, but most of the time I miss. There was no logic to it. There was no design. My own wishes had nothing to do with it. My heart kicked when Buzz brushed against me, breathed into my hair. My bad habit was flinching. And shutting my eyes when I pulled the trigger. Buzz scolded gently, "That's how in actual life people get killed." The human silhouette is the hardest. You shut your eyes, breathe, and fire.

HOW MOTHER DIED was never satisfactorily explained. Her new husband who'd been seven years younger than Mother claimed he returned home after a two-day trip and simply "found" her. She'd been dead, lying part-dressed on top of her bed, for approximately ten hours, during which time, he claimed, and phone records would substantiate, he'd called six times, and no answer except the answering tape. The coroner declared her death a "natural" death. Yet it would remain a "mysterious" death. For why would Mother have taken her nighttime dosage of barbiturate at mid-day, why would Mother who was fastidious about such things have lain down on rumpled bedclothes, why would Mother who was obsessive about her nails have had several broken, cracked fingernails, the polish chipped . . . ? My brother was more stunned by Mother's death than I was. He spoke of hiring a private detective to look into it. I'd become more accepting, more fatalistic, like Kaho. The Asian stoicism.

Also as Dad said, "It was a tragedy bound to happen. Your mother's taste in men."

MIKAL HAD RETURNED to my life. I was trying not to be happy, hopeful. I did not believe I deserved happiness or even hope, if you knew my soul.

The primary responsibility of gun ownership is not gun safety but gun maintenance. Because you don't have gun safety without gun maintenance. I learned this at the Ready-Aim-Fire Range. I purchased in their front office:

    pistol cleaning rod
    proper size patches
    brass bore brushes
    special cleaning rags
    new toothbrush
    gunsmith screwdrivers
    Lewis Lead Remover
    Bore light/mirror
    Hoppe's No. 9 powder solvent
    bore oil
    lubricant
    bottle, bluing solution

Mother's Detective Special, my inheritance, had not been cleaned in years. Maybe it had never been cleaned. I held it in my hand, my hand trembled. I kept the chambers loaded. But would this gun fire?

You never know, until you know. But remember: You DO NOT OWE YOUR ASSAILANT THE FIRST SHOT.

MIKAL KISSED ME, and held my head pressed between his two hands in a way I'd remembered from years ago, and nobody else had done, ever. His kisses were like a child's, anxious, hopeful, not sexual (not yet: for this, I was grateful). "So life has wounded you, too." But mostly we didn't talk. Years away from me, married to other women, he'd become lean and nervy as an eel. I could feel the life-current moving through him. "My love. My love." Mikal's face was creased vertically as if with tears. His hair was graying at the temples but otherwise had the sheen of satin-blue finish. He was married, but separated from his (mentally unstable, suicidal) wife, whom I had met once, years ago, and could recall only as a flaming, blinding blond light. He was separated from his (vindictive, threatening) wife but deeply bound to her, and to their single child, a (somehow troubled? disabled?) daughter, that was clear. "Oh, hey, don't ask. Not yet." Long hours we lay together gripping each other's lean torsos, pressing cheeks together. Not speaking. Like survivors of a desperate swim across whitewater rapids. In the drawer of my bedside table was the Colt Detective Special, still uncleaned, unoiled. I liked the idea, it was a sort of sexy idea, that, when I left Mikal to use the bathroom, he'd roll over and quietly open this drawer and see this mean-looking "man stopper." My new custom-order ivory grip, glimmering out of the darkness.

BUZZ FROM the shooting range came by, a few times. Buzz, too, was "in a bad place, temporarily" with his wife and family. But Buzz was an ex-U.S. Army sergeant, and you see the world differently from that perspective. And if your name's Buzz, from age two. Still, seeing the condition of the Detective Special, the corroded finish, Buzz looked as if he was going to cry. Like stepping on something, and it turns out to be a crushed fledgling bird. "Jesus Christ. How could you. Even *you*." (He meant, even a woman. I knew that.) When I touched his wrist, he threw off my hand. He was, in his own words, seriously pissed. But we made up. Seeing where I lived, Buzz was always impressed. Expertly he dismantled the gun on a sheet of newspaper on the kitchen table, like an autopsy. His big fingers were deft and, in their way, loving. Using the items I'd bought at the shooting range he cleaned my mother's gun and reloaded it and clicked the safety *on*. "Always keep your safety *on*, see? When you're not preparing to fire." I thought there was something like a Zen koan in this, but I didn't pursue it. Buzz was the most silent lover I'd ever known. Maybe the word is stoic. When he came it was like somebody stepping on a nail barefoot, determined not to cry out or even grimace. How I knew Buzz came, he'd stop what he'd been doing and roll off me. He said I had "real class" but I knew he didn't respect me any longer, seeing the state of my gun. A gun in a bedside drawer like that, like a baby in its crib by Momma's bed, neglected. He'd seen into my soul. A man knows.

G. G. SEEMED TO HAVE disappeared. Maybe seeing me with Buzz scared him off. Or he'd gone underground, in disguise.

THERE WAS A campaign by the mayor of New York and the superintendent of police of New York for citizens to "turn in your handguns at your local precinct, no questions asked." Now the Detective Special was so beautifully cleaned and oiled I actually thought I might turn it in. I don't know why: to free myself of Mother, maybe. But I was superstitious, reasoning, *The day I turn it in, that night I'll need it.*

MIKAL OWNED an import business, leather goods, jewelry from Morocco. Or maybe (Mikal's business life was mysterious to me, like his personal life) he was partners with someone. His shop was on Madison at Seventy-fifth. One of those elegant little shops with window displays like something at the Metropolitan Museum. But he was never on the premises when I dropped in. One day he called me, agitated. He had to leave for Morocco that evening. It was an unexpected business emergency. Could I meet him in the park? I'd have preferred my apartment, but Mikal had a romantic attachment to Central Park. We'd actually made love there, to a degree, behind some boulders, once. He was twenty minutes late but arrived half-running and smiling, eager as a boy. His skin was waxy and gave off a clammy heat. He hadn't shaved for possibly two days. We held each other tight. So tight! I liked it, Mikal could feel my ribs, how slender I'd become and I knew he liked thin women. It was difficult to think such a precious moment wasn't being filmed. That melancholy twilight time when lights are coming on all over the city. Headlights of vehicles moving through the park, street lamps, lights in high-rise apartment buildings on Fifth Avenue.

In the west, flamey red streaks of the sun. And the rest of the sky dark roiling rainclouds. In Central Park there was a damp chill earth-smell. Rotted leaves, mulch. Dark glistening of tree trunks. Mikal and I were holding each other like swimmers who've staggered up on to shore neither knowing nor caring where we are. *He wanted us to meet here so we can't make love. Our parting will be spiritual.* I respected Mikal for this though I wanted badly to lie naked with him a final time before he went away, and to feel him inside my body. Mikal kissed me, fierce and hard, pressing into my arms a valise of the softest, most beautiful Moroccan kidskin. "Keep this for me, darling. Don't ask why. I love you." I weighed the valise in my arms. It was moderately heavy. "What is it?" I asked, though possibly I knew. Mikal said, kissing me again, "Darling, I'll know when I can ask for this back. When I can see you again, and love you. And we can be together permanently." Mikal was backing away. His eyes were ringed with fever-fatigue. I felt that my heart was being torn from my body. There were no adequate words to call after my lover. Back in my apartment I opened the valise slowly. *Until I actually see it, I won't know.* But I saw. Wrapped in a chamois cloth was a handgun with an unnaturally long barrel, about eight inches. Without touching it I saw it was a 9-millimeter semiautomatic Glock Hardballer, stainless steel frame and finish. I'd never seen a Glock before. It was a heavy gun, a man's gun. I wondered why the barrel was so long. I guessed the gun had been carefully wiped down. I didn't stoop to smell the barrel but rewrapped the gun in the chamois cloth. I shut up the valise and hid it away on a closet shelf with my other leather things. I had quite a collection, Mikal had given me things. He'd given me jewelry, too. I was feeling faint. A high ringing sound in my skull, unless it was a siren in the near distance. I wondered if I would see Mikal again. Maybe he would summon me to Morocco. I wondered if I would be questioned about Mikal, if anything had happened in his life to warrant my being questioned. I wondered if I would dispose of the gun but already knew probably I wouldn't, how could I, that beautiful Glock Hardballer. I just can't.

Part Two

FAITHLESS

*T*he last time my mother Cornelia Nissenbaum and her sister Constance saw their mother was the day before she vanished from their lives forever, April 11, 1923.

It was a rainy, misty morning. They'd been searching for their mother because something was wrong in the household; she hadn't come downstairs to prepare breakfast so there wasn't anything for them except what their father gave them, glutinous oatmeal from the previous morning hastily reheated on the stove, sticking to the bottom of the pan and tasting of scorch. Their father had seemed strange to them, smiling but not-seeing in that way of his like Reverend Dieckman too fierce in his pulpit Sunday mornings, intoning the Word of God. His eyes were threaded with blood and his face was still pale from the winter but flushed, mottled. In those days he was a handsome man but stern-looking and severe. Grizzled side-whiskers and a spade-shaped beard coarse and streaked too with gray, but thick springy-sleek black hair brushed back from his forehead in a crest. The sisters were fearful of their father without their mother to mediate among them; it was as if none of them knew who they were without her.

Connie chewed her lip and worked up her nerve to ask where was Momma? and their father said, hitching up his suspenders, on his way outside, "Your mother's where you'll find her."

The sisters watched their father cross the mud-puddled yard to where a crew of hired men was waiting in the doorway of the big barn. It was rye-planting season and always in spring in the Chautauqua Valley there was worry about rain: too much rain and the seed would be washed away or rot in the soil before it could sprout. My mother, Cornelia, would grow to adulthood thinking how blessings and curses fell from the sky with equal authority, like hard-pelting rain. There was God, who set the world in motion, and who intervened sometimes in the affairs of men, for reasons no one could know. If you lived on a farm there was weather, always weather, every morning was weather and every evening at sundown calculating the next day's, the sky's, moods meant too much. Always casting your glance upward, outward, your heart set to quicken.

That morning. The sisters would never forget that morning. They knew something was wrong, they thought Momma was sick. The night before having heard—what, exactly? Voices. Voice mixed with dreams, and the wind. On that farm, at the brink of a ten-mile descent to the Chautauqua River, it was always windy—on the worst days the wind could literally suck your breath away!—like a ghost, a goblin. An invisible being pushing up close beside you, sometimes even inside the house, even in your bed, pushing his mouth (or muzzle) to yours and sucking out the breath.

Connie thought Nelia was silly, a silly-baby, to believe such. She was eight years old and skeptical-minded. Yet maybe she believed it, too? Liked to scare herself, the way you could almost tickle yourself, with such wild thoughts.

Connie, who was always famished, and after that morning would be famished for years, sat at the oilcloth-covered table and ate the oatmeal her father had spooned out for her, devoured it, scorch-lots and all, her head of fair-frizzy braids lowered and her jaws working quickly. Oatmeal sweetened with top-milk on the very edge of turning sour, and coarse brown sugar. Nelia who was fretting wasn't able to swallow down more than a spoon or two of hers so Connie devoured that, too. She would remember that part of the oatmeal was hot enough to burn her tongue and other parts were icebox-cold. She would remember that it was all delicious.

The girls washed their dishes in the cold-water sink and let the oatmeal pan soak in scummy soapsuds. It was time for Connie to leave for school but both knew she could not go, not today. She could not leave to walk two miles to school with that feeling *something is wrong,* nor could she leave her little sister behind. Though when Nelia snuffled and wiped her nose on both her hands Connie cuffed her on the shoulder and scolded, "Piggy-*piggy.*"

This, a habit of their mother's when they did something that was only mildly disgusting.

Connie led the way upstairs to the big bedroom at the front of the house that was Momma's and Papa's room and that they were forbidden to enter unless specifically invited, for instance if the door was open and Momma was cleaning inside, changing the bedclothes so she'd call out *Come in, girls!* smiling in her happy mood so it was all right and they would not be scolded. *Come in, give me a hand,* which turned into a game of shaking out sheets, fluffing out pillowcases to stuff heavy goosefeather pillows inside, Momma and Connie and Nelia laughing together. But this morning the door was shut. There was no sound of Momma inside. Connie dared to turn the doorknob, push the door open slowly, and they saw, yes, to their surprise there was their mother lying on top of the unmade bed, partly dressed, wrapped in an afghan. My God it was scary to see Momma like that, lying down at such an hour of the morning! Momma who was so brisk and capable and who routed them out of bed if they lingered, Momma with little patience for Connie's lazy-tricks as she called them or for Nelia's sniffles, tummyaches, and baby-fears.

"Momma?"—Connie's voice was cracked.

"Mom-ma?"—Nelia whimpered.

Their mother groaned and flung an arm across one of the pillows lying crooked beside her. She was breathing hard, like a winded horse, her chest rising and falling so you could see it and her head was flung back on the pillow and she'd placed a wetted cloth across her eyes mask-like so half her face was hidden. Her dark-blond hair was disheveled, unplaited, coarse and lusterless as a horse's mane, unwashed for days. That rich rank smell of Momma's hair when it needed washing. You remember such smells, the sisters would say, some of them not-so-nice smells, all your life. And the smell in their parents' forbidden room of—was it talcum powder, sweaty armpits, a sourish-sweet fragrance of bedclothes that no matter how frequently laundered with detergent and bleach were never truly fresh. A smell of bodies. Adult bodies. Yeasty, stale. Papa's tobacco (he rolled his own crude paper cigarettes, he chewed tobacco in a thick tarry-black wad) and Papa's hair oil and that special smell of Papa's shoes, the black Sunday shoes always kept polished. (His work-boots, etcetera he kept downstairs in the closed-in porch by the rear door called the "entry.")

In the step-in closet close by the a bed, behind an unhemmed length of chintz, was a blue-speckled porcelain chamber pot with a detachable lid and a rim that curled neatly under, like a lip.

The sisters had their own chamber pot—their potty, as it was called. There was no indoor plumbing in John Nissenbaum's farmhouse, or in any farmhouse in the Chautauqua Valley well into the 1930s, or in poorer homes well into the 1940s, and even beyond. One hundred yards behind the house, beyond the silo, was the outhouse, the latrine, the "privy." But you would not want to make that trip in cold weather or in rain or in the pitch-black of night, not if you could help it.

Of course the smell of urine and a fainter smell of excrement must have been everywhere, the sisters conceded, years later. As adults, reminiscing. But it was masked by the barnyard smell, probably. Nothing worse than pig manure, after all!

At least, we weren't *pigs.*

Anyway, there was Momma, on the bed. The bed that was so high from the floor you had to raise a knee to slide up on it, and grab onto whatever you could. And the horsehair mattress, so hard and ungiving. The cloth over Momma's eyes she hadn't removed and beside Momma in the rumpled bedclothes her Bible. Facedown. Pages bent. That Bible her mother-in-law Grandma Nissenbaum had given her for a wedding present, seeing she hadn't one of her own. It was smaller than the heavy black family Bible and it was made of limp ivory-leather covers and had onion-skin pages the girls were allowed to examine but not to turn without Momma's supervision; the Bible that would disappear with Gretel Nissenbaum, forever.

The girls begged, whimpered. "Momma? Momma, are you sick?"

At first there was no answer. Just Momma's breath coming quick and hard and uneven. And her olive-pale skin oily with heat like fever. Her legs were tangled in the afghan, her hair was strewn across the pillow. They saw the glint of Momma's gold cross on a thin gold chain around her neck, almost lost in her hair. (Not only a cross but a locket, too: when Momma opened it there was, inside, a tiny strand of silver hair once belonging to a woman the sisters had never known, Momma's own grandmother she'd loved so when she was a little girl.) And there were

Momma's breasts, almost exposed!—heavy, lush, beautiful almost spilling out of a white eyelet slip, rounded like sacs holding warm liquid, and the nipples dark and big as eyes. You weren't supposed to stare at any part of a person's body but how could you help it?—especially Connie who was fascinated by such things, guessing how one day she'd inhabit a body like Momma's. Years before she'd peeked at her mother's big milk-swollen breasts when Nelia was still nursing, jealous, awed. Nelia was now five years old and could not herself recall nursing at all; she would come one day to believe, stubborn and disdainful, that she had never nursed, had only been bottle-fed.

At last Momma snatched the cloth off her face. "You! Damn you! What do you want?" She stared at the girls as if, clutching hands and gaping at her, they were strangers. Her right eye was bruised and swollen and there were raw red marks on her forehead and first Nelia then Connie began to cry and Momma said, "Constance, why aren't you in school? Why can't you let me alone? God help me—always 'Momma'— 'Momma'—'Momma.'" Connie whimpered, "Momma, did you hurt yourself?" and Nelia moaned, sucking a corner of the afghan like a deranged baby and Momma ignored the question, as Momma often ignored questions she thought nosy, none of your business; her hand lifted as if she meant to slap them but then fell wearily, as if this had happened many times before, this exchange, this emotion, and it was her fate that it would happen many times again. A close sweet-stale blood-odor lifted from Momma's lower body, out of the folds of the soiled afghan, that odor neither of the little girls could have identified except in retrospect, in adolescence at last detecting it in themselves: shamed, discomforted, the secret of their bodies at what was called, invariably in embarrassed undertones, *that certain time of the month.*

So: Gretel Nissenbaum, at the time she disappeared from her husband's house, was having her period.

Did that mean something, or nothing?

Nothing, Cornelia would say sharply.

Yes, Constance would insist, it meant our mother was *not* pregnant. She wasn't running away with any lover because of *that.*

That morning, what confusion in the Nissenbaum household! However the sisters would later speak of the encounter in the big bedroom, what their mother had said to them, how she'd looked and behaved, it had not been precisely that way, of course. Because how can you speak of confusion,

where are the words for it? How to express in adult language the wild fibrillation of children's minds, two child-minds beating against each other like
moths, how to know what had truly happened and what was only imagined? Connie would swear that their mother's eye looked like a nasty dark-
rotted egg, so swollen, but she could not say which eye it was, right or left;
Nelia, shrinking from looking at her mother's bruised face, wanting only to
burrow against her, to hide and be comforted, would come in time
to doubt that she'd seen a *hurt eye* at all; or wonder whether she'd been led to
believe she saw it because Connie, who was so bossy, claimed she had.

Connie would remember their mother's words, Momma's rising desperate voice, "Don't touch me—I'm afraid! I might be going somewhere
but I'm not ready—oh, God, I'm so afraid!"—and on, and on saying she
was going away, she was afraid, and Connie trying to ask where? where
was she going? and Momma beating at the bedclothes with her fists. Nelia
would remember being hurt at the way Momma yanked the spittle-soaked
corner of the afghan out of her mouth, so roughly! Not Momma but *bad-
Momma, witch-Momma* who scared her.

But then Momma relented, exasperated. "Oh come on, you damn little babies! Of course 'Momma' loves you."

Eager then as starving kittens the sisters scrambled up onto the high,
hard bed, whimpering snuggling into Momma's arms, her damp snarled
hair, those breasts. Connie and Nelia burrowing, crying themselves to
sleep like nursing babies, Momma drew the afghan over the three of them
as if to shield them. That morning of April 11, 1923.

AND NEXT MORNING, early, before dawn. The sisters would be awakened by their father's shouts, "Gretel? Gretel!"

2

*. . . never spoke of her after the first few weeks. After the first shock. We
learned to pray for her and to forgive her and to forget her. We didn't miss her.* So
Mother said, in her calm judicious voice. A voice that held no blame.

But Aunt Connie would take me aside. The older, wiser sister. *It's true
we never spoke of Momma when any grown-ups were near, that was forbidden.
But, God! we missed her every hour of every day all the time we lived on that
farm.*

I was Cornelia's daughter but it was Aunt Connie I trusted.

★   ★   ★

No one in the Chautauqua Valley knew where John Nissenbaum's young wife Gretel had fled but all knew, or had an opinion of, why she'd gone.

Faithless, she was. *A faithless woman.* Had she not *run away with a man: abandoned her children.* She was twenty-seven years old and too young for John Nissenbaum and she wasn't a Ransomville girl, her people lived sixty miles away in Chautauqua Falls. Here was a wife who'd committed *adultery,* was an *adulteress.* (Some might say a *tramp,* a *whore,* a *slut.*) Reverend Dieckman the Lutheran minister would preach amazing sermons in her wake. For miles through the Valley and for years well into the 1940s there would be scandalized talk of Gretel Nissenbaum: a woman who left her faithful Christian husband and her two little girls with no warning! no provocation! disappearing in the middle of a night taking with her only a single suitcase and, as every woman who ever spoke of the episode liked to say, licking her lips, *the clothes on her back.*

(Aunt Connie said she'd grown up imagining she had actually seen her mother, as in a dream, walking stealthily up the long drive to the road, a bundle of clothes, like laundry, slung across her back. Children are so damned impressionable, Aunt Connie would say, laughing wryly.)

For a long time after their mother disappeared, and no word came from her, or of her, so far as the sisters knew, Connie couldn't seem to help herself, teasing Nelia, saying "Mommy's coming home!"—for a birthday of Nelia's, or Christmas or Easter. How many times Connie thrilled with wickedness deceiving her baby sister, and silly-baby that she was, Nelia believed.

And how Connie would laugh, laugh at her.

Well, it *was* funny. Wasn't it?

Another trick of Connie's: poking Nelia awake in the night when the wind was rattling the windows, moaning in the chimney like a trapped animal. Saying excitedly, *Momma is outside the window, listen! Momma is a ghost trying to get YOU!*

Sometimes Nelia screamed so, Connie had to straddle her chest and press a pillow over her face to muffle her. If we'd wakened Papa with such nonsense there'd sure have been hell to pay.

Once, I might have been twelve, I asked if my grandfather had spanked or beaten them.

Aunt Connie, sitting in our living room on the high-backed mauve-brocade chair that was always hers when she came to visit, ignored me. Nor did Mother seem to hear. Aunt Connie lit one of her Chesterfields with a fussy flourish of her pink-frosted nails and took a deep satisfied puff and said, as if it were a thought only now slipping into her head, and like all such thoughts deserving of utterance, "I was noticing the other day, on TV, how brattish and idiotic children are, and we're supposed to think they're cute. Papa wasn't the kind to tolerate children carrying on for a single minute." She paused, again inhaling deeply. "None of the men were, back there."

Mother nodded slowly, frowning. These conversations with my aunt seemed always to give her pain, an actual ache behind the eyes, yet she could no more resist them than Aunt Connie. She said, wiping at her eyes, "Papa was a man of pride. After she left us as much as before."

"Hmmm!" Aunt Connie made her high humming nasal sound that meant she had something crucial to add, but did not want to appear pushy. "Well—maybe more, Nelia. More pride. After." She spoke insinuatingly, with a smile and a glance toward me.

Like an actress who has strayed from her lines, Mother quickly amended, "Yes of course. Because a weaker man would have succumbed to—shame and despair—"

Aunt Connie nodded briskly. "—might have cursed God—"

"—turned to drink—"

"—so many of 'em *did,* back there—"

"—but not Papa. He had the gift of faith."

Aunt Connie nodded sagely. Yet still with that strange almost-teasing smile.

"Oh, indeed Papa did. That was his gift to us, Nelia, wasn't it?—his faith."

Mother was smiling her tight-lipped smile, her gaze lowered. I knew that, when Aunt Connie left, she would go upstairs to lie down, she would take two aspirins and draw the blinds and put a damp cold cloth over her eyes and lie down and try to sleep. In her softening middle-aged face, the hue of putty, a young girl's face shone rapt with fear. "Oh yes! His faith."

Aunt Connie laughed heartily. Laugh, laugh. Dimples nicking her cheeks and a wink in my direction.

★   ★   ★

YEARS LATER, numbly sorting through Mother's belongings after her death, I would discover, in a lavender-scented envelope in a bureau drawer, a single strand of dry, ash-colored hair. On the envelope, in faded purple ink *Beloved Father John Allard Nissenbaum 1872–1957.*

BY HIS OWN ACCOUNT, John Nissenbaum, the wronged husband, had not had the slightest suspicion that his strong-willed young wife had been discontent, restless. Certainly not that she'd had a secret lover! So many local women would have dearly wished to change places with her, he'd been given to know when he was courting her, his male vanity, and his Nissenbaum vanity, and what you might call common sense suggested otherwise.

For the Nissenbaums were a well-regarded family in the Chautauqua Valley. Among the lot of them they must have owned thousands of acres of prime farmland.

In the weeks, months, and eventually years that followed the scandalous departure, John Nissenbaum, who was by nature, like most of the male Nissenbaums, reticent to the point of arrogance, and fiercely private, came to make his story—*his side of it*—known. As the sisters themselves gathered (for their father never spoke of their mother to them after the first several days following the shock), this was not a single coherent history but one that had to be pieced together like a giant quilt made of a myriad of fabric-scraps.

He did allow that Gretel had been missing her family, an older sister with whom she'd been especially close, and cousins and girlfriends she'd gone to high school with in Chautauqua Falls; he understood that the two-hundred-acre farm was a lonely place for her, their next-door neighbors miles away, and the village of Ransomville seven miles. (Trips beyond Ransomville were rare.) He knew, or supposed he knew, that his wife had harbored what his mother and sisters called *wild imaginings,* even after nine years of marriage, farm life, and children: she had asked several times to be allowed to play the organ at church, but had been refused; she reminisced often wistfully and perhaps reproachfully of long-ago visits to Port Oriskany, Buffalo, and Chicago, before she'd gotten married at the age of eighteen to a man fourteen years her senior. . . . In Chicago she'd seen stage plays and musicals, the sensational dancers Irene and Vernon Castle in Irving Berlin's *Watch Your Step.* It wasn't just Gretel wanting to take over the organ at Sunday services (and replacing the elderly male organist whose playing, she said, sounded like a cat in heat), it was her general attitude toward Reverend Dieckman and his wife. She resented having to invite them to an elaborate Sunday dinner every few weeks, as the Nissenbaums insisted; she allowed her eyes to roam the congregation during Dieckman's sermons, and stifled yawns behind her gloved hand; she woke in the middle of the night, she said, wanting to argue about damnation, hell, the very concept of grace. To the minister's astonished face she declared herself "not able to *fully accept* the teachings of the Lutheran Church."

If there was another more intimate issue between Gretel and John Nissenbaum, or another factor in Gretel's emotional life, of course no one spoke of it at the time.

Though it was hinted—possibly more than hinted?—that John Nissenbaum was disappointed with only daughters. Naturally he wanted sons, to help him with the ceaseless work of the farm; sons to whom he could leave the considerable property, just as his married brothers had sons.

What was generally known was: John woke in the pitch-dark an hour before dawn of that April day, to discover that Gretel was gone from their bed. Gone from the house? He searched for her, called her name, with growing alarm, disbelief. "Gretel? Gret-el!" He looked in all the upstairs rooms of the house including the bedroom where his sleep-dazed, frightened daughters were huddled together in their bed; he looked in all the downstairs rooms, even the damp, dirt-floor cellar into which he descended with a lantern. "Gretel? Where are you?" Dawn came dull, porous, and damp, and with a coat yanked on in haste over his nightclothes, and his bare feet jammed into rubber boots, he began a frantic yet methodical search of the farm's outbuildings—the privy, the cow barn and the adjoining stable, the hay barn and the corncrib where rats rustled at his approach. In none of these save perhaps the privy was it likely that Gretel might be found; still John continued his search with growing panic, not knowing what else to do. From the house his now terrified daughters observed him moving from building to building, a tall rigid jerkily moving figure with hands cupped to his mouth shouting, "Gretel! Gret-el! Do you hear me! Where are you! Gret-el!" The man's deep raw voice pulsing like a metronome, ringing clear, profound, and, to his daughters' ears, as terrible as if the very sky had cracked open and God Himself was shouting.

(What did such little girls, eight and five, know of God?—in fact, as Aunt Connie would afterward recount, quite a bit. There was Reverend Dieckman's baritone impersonation of the God of the Old Testament, the expulsion from the Garden, the devastating retort to Job, the spectacular burning bush where fire itself cried HERE I AM!—such had already been imprinted irrevocably upon their imaginations.)

Only later that morning—but this was a confused, anguished account—did John discover that Gretel's suitcase was missing from the closet. And there were garments conspicuously missing from the clothes rack. And Gretel's bureau drawers had been hastily ransacked—underwear, stockings were gone. And her favorite pieces of jewelry, of which she was childishly vain, were gone from her cedarwood box; gone too, her heirloom, faded-cameo hairbrush, comb, and mirror set. And her Bible.

What a joke, how people would chuckle over it—Gretel Nissenbaum taking her Bible with her!

Wherever in hell the woman went.

And was there no farewell note, after nine years of marriage?—John Nissenbaum claimed he'd looked everywhere, and found nothing. Not a word of explanation, not a word of regret even to her little girls. *For that alone we expelled her from our hearts.*

During this confused time while their father was searching and calling their mother's name, the sisters hugged each other in a state of numbness beyond shock, terror. Their father seemed at times to be rushing toward them with the eye-bulging blindness of a runaway horse—they hurried out of his path. He did not see them except to order them out of his way, not to trouble him now. From the rear entry door they watched as he hitched his team of horses to his buggy and set out shuddering for Ransomville along the winter-rutted Post Road, leaving the girls behind, erasing them from his mind. As he would tell afterward, in rueful self-disgust, with the air of an enlightened sinner, he'd actually believed he would overtake Gretel on the road—convinced she'd be there, hiking on the grassy shoulder, carrying her suitcase. Gretel was a wiry-nervous woman, stronger than she appeared, with no fear of physical exertion. A woman capable of anything!

John Nissenbaum had the idea that Gretel had set out for Ransomville, seven miles away, there to catch the midmorning train to Chautauqua Falls, another sixty miles south. It was his confused belief that they must have had a disagreement, else Gretel would not have left; he did not recall any disagreement in fact, but Gretel was after all an *emotional woman,* a *high-strung woman*; she'd insisted upon visiting the Hausers, her family, despite his wishes, was that it?—she was lonely for them, or lonely for something. She was angry they hadn't visited Chautauqua Falls for Easter, hadn't seen her family since Christmas. Was that it? *We were never enough for her. Why were we never enough for her?*

But in Ransomville, in the cinder-block Chautauqua & Buffalo depot, there was no sign of Gretel, nor had the lone clerk seen her.

"This woman would be about my height," John Nissenbaum said, in his formal, slightly haughty way. "She'd be carrying a suitcase, her feet would maybe be muddy. Her boots."

The clerk shook his head slowly. "No sir, nobody looking like that."

"A woman by herself. A—" a hesitation, a look of pain, "—good-looking woman, young. A kind of a, a way about her—a way of—" another pause, "—making herself known."

"Sorry," the clerk said. "The 8:20 just came through, and no woman bought a ticket."

It happened then that John Nissenbaum was observed, stark-eyed, stiff-springy black hair in tufts like quills, for the better part of that morning, April 12, 1923, wandering up one side of Ransomville's single main street, and down the other. Hatless, in farm overalls and boots but wearing a suit coat—somber, gunmetal-gray, of "good" wool—buttoned crooked across his narrow muscular torso. Disheveled and ravaged with the grief of a betrayed husband too raw at this time for manly pride to intervene, pathetic some said as a kicked dog, yet eager too, eager as a puppy he made inquiries at Meldron's Dry Goods, at Elkin & Sons Grocers, at the First Niagara Trust, at the law office of Rowe & Nissenbaum (this Nissenbaum, a young cousin of John's), even in the five and dime where the salesgirls would giggle in his wake. He wandered at last into the Ransomville Hotel, into the gloomy public room where the proprietor's wife was sweeping sawdust-strewn floorboards. "Sorry, sir, we don't open till noon," the woman said, thinking he was a drunk, dazed and swaying-like on his feet, then she looked more closely at him: not knowing his first name (for John Nissenbaum was not one to patronize local taverns) but recognizing his features. For it was said the male Nissenbaums were either born looking alike, or came in time to look alike. "Mr. Nissenbaum? Is something wrong?" In a beat of stymied silence Nissenbaum blinked at her, trying to smile, groping for a hat to remove but finding none, murmuring, "No ma'am, I'm sure not. It's a misunderstanding, I believe. I'm supposed to meet Mrs. Nissenbaum somewhere here. My wife."

SHORTLY AFTER Gretel Nissenbaum's disappearance there emerged, from numerous sources, from all points of the compass, certain tales of the woman. How rude she'd been, more than once, to the Dieckmans!—to many in the Lutheran congregation! A *bad wife. Unnatural mother.* It was said she'd left her husband and children in the past, running back to her family in Chautauqua Falls, or was it Port Oriskany; and poor John Nissenbaum having to fetch her home again. (This was untrue, though in time, even to Constance and Cornelia, it would come to seem true. As an elderly woman Cornelia would swear she remembered "both times" her mother ran off.) A shameless hussy, a tramp who *had an eye* for men. *Had the hots* for men. *Anything in pants.* Or was she *stuck-up, snobby.* Marrying into the Nissenbaum family, a man almost old enough to be her father, no mystery there! Worse yet she could be sharp-tongued, profane. Heard to utter such words as *damn, goddamn, hell.* Yes and *horseballs, bullshit.* Standing with her hands on her hips fixing her eyes on you; that loud laugh. And showing her teeth that were too big for her mouth. She was *too smart for her own good,* that's for sure. She was *scheming, faithless.* Everybody knew she flirted with her husband's hired hands, she did a hell of a lot more than flirt with them, ask around. Sure she had a *boyfriend,* a *lover.* Sure she was an *adulteress.* Hadn't she run off with a man? She'd run off and where was she to go, where was a woman to go, except *run off with a man*? Whoever he was.

In fact, he'd been sighted: a tower operator for the Chautauqua & Buffalo railroad, big red-headed guy living in Shaheen, twelve miles away. Or was he a carpet sweeper salesman, squirrely little guy with a mustache and a smooth way of talking, who passed through the Valley every few months but, after April 12, 1923, was never seen there again?

Another, more attractive rumor was that Gretel Nissenbaum's lover was a thirty-year-old navy officer stationed at Port Oriskany. He'd been transferred to a base in North Carolina, or was it Pensacola, Florida, and Gretel had no choice but to run away with him, she loved him so. *And three months pregnant with his child.*

There could have been no romance in the terrible possibility that Gretel Nissenbaum had fled on foot, alone, not to her family but simply to escape from her life; in what exigency of need, what despondency of spirit, no name might be given it by any who have not experienced it.

But, in any case, where had she *gone?*

Where? Disappeared. Over the edge of the world. To Chicago, maybe. Or that army base in North Carolina, or Florida.

We forgave, we forgot. We didn't miss her.

THE THINGS Gretel Nissenbaum left behind in the haste of her departure.

Several dresses, hats. A shabby cloth coat. Rubberized "galoshes" and boots. Undergarments, mended stockings. Knitted gloves. In the parlor of John Nissenbaum's house, in cut-glass vases, bright yellow daffodils she'd made from crepe paper; hand-painted fans, teacups; books she'd brought with her from home—*A Golden Treasury of Verse,* Mark Twain's *Joan of Arc,* Fitzgerald's *This Side of Paradise* missing its jacket. Tattered programs for musical shows, stacks of popular piano music from the days Gretel had played in her childhood home. (There was no piano in Nissenbaum's house, Nissenbaum had no interest in music.)

These meager items, and some others, Nissenbaum unceremoniously dumped into cardboard boxes fifteen days after Gretel disappeared, taking them to the Lutheran church, for the "needy fund," without inquiring if the Hausers might have wanted anything, or whether his daughters might have wished to be given some mementos of their mother.

Spite? Not John Nissenbaum. He was a proud man even in his public humiliation. It was the Lord's work he was thinking of. Not mere *human vanity,* at all.

THAT SPRING and summer Reverend Dieckman gave a series of grim, threatening, passionate sermons from the pulpit of the First Lutheran Church of Ransomville. It was obvious why, what the subject of the sermons was. The congregation was thrilled.

Reverend Dieckman, whom Connie and Nelia feared, as much for his fierce smiles as his stern, glowering expression, was a short bulky man with a dull-gleaming dome of a head, eyes like ice water. Years later when they saw a photograph of him, inches shorter than his wife, they laughed in nervous astonishment—was that the man who'd intimidated them so? Before whom even John Nissenbaum stood grave and downgazing?

Yet: that ringing vibrating voice of the God of Moses, the God of the Old Testament, you could not shut out of consciousness even hours, days later. Years later. Pressing your hands against your ears and shutting your eyes tight, tight.

" 'Unto the woman He said, I will GREATLY MULTIPLY thy sorrow and thy conception; IN SORROW shalt thou bring forth children: and thy desire shall be to THY HUSBAND, and he shall RULE OVER THEE. And unto Adam He said, Because thou hast harkened unto the voice of THY WIFE, and hast eaten of THE TREE, of which I commanded thee, saying, THOU SHALT NOT EAT OF IT: cursed is the ground for thy sake; in sorrow shall thou eat of it all the days of thy life: THORNS ALSO AND THISTLES shall it bring forth to thee; and thou shalt eat the herb of the field; in the SWEAT OF THY FACE shalt thou eat bread, till thou return to the ground; for out of it thou wast taken: for DUST THOU ART, and UNTO DUST SHALT THOU RETURN.' " Reverend Dieckman paused to catch breath like a man running uphill. Greasy patches gleamed on his solid face like coins. Slowly his ice-eyes searched the rows of worshipers until as if by chance they came to rest on the upturned yet cowering faces of John Nissenbaum's daughters, who sat in the family pew, directly in front of the pulpit in the fifth row, between their rigid-backed father in his clothes somber as mourning and their Grandmother Nissenbaum also in clothes somber as mourning though badly round-shouldered, with a perceptible hump, this cheerless dutiful grandmother who had come to live with them now that their mother was gone.

(Their other grandparents, the Hausers, who lived in Chautauqua Falls and whom they'd loved, the sisters would never see again. It was forbidden even to speak of these people, *Gretel's people*. The Hausers were to blame somehow for Gretel's desertion. Though they claimed, would always claim, they knew nothing of what she'd done and in fact feared something had happened to her. But the Hausers were a forbidden subject. Only after Constance and Cornelia were grown, no longer living in their father's house, did they see their Hauser cousins; but still, as Cornelia confessed, she felt guilty about it. Father would have been so hurt and furious if he'd known. *Consorting with the enemy* he would deem it. *Betrayal*.)

In Sunday school, Mrs. Dieckman took special pains with little Constance and little Cornelia. They were regarded with misty-eyed pity, like child-lepers. Fattish little Constance prone to fits of giggling, and hollow-eyed little Cornelia prone to sniffles, melancholy. Both girls had chafed, reddened faces and hands because their grandmother Nissenbaum scrubbed them so, with strong gray soap, never less than twice a day. Cornelia's dun-colored hair was strangely thin. When the other children trooped out of the Sunday school room Mrs. Dieckman kept the sisters behind, to pray with them. She was very concerned about them, she said. She and Reverend Dieckman prayed for them constantly. Had their mother contacted them, since leaving? Had there been any . . . hint of what their mother was planning to do? Any strangers visiting the farm? Any . . . unusual incidents? The sisters stared blankly at Mrs. Dieckman. She frowned at their ignorance, or its semblance. Dabbed at her watery eyes and sighed as if the world's weight had settled on her shoulders. She said half-chiding, "You should know, children, it's for a reason, that your mother left you. It's God's will. God's plan. He is testing you, children. You are special in His eyes. Many of us have been special in His eyes and have emerged stronger for it, and not weaker." There was a breathy pause. The sisters were invited to contemplate how Mrs. Dieckman, with her soft-wattled face, her stout corseted body, her fattish legs encased in opaque support hose, was a stronger and not a weaker person, by God's special plan. "You will learn to be stronger than girls with mothers, Constance and Cornelia—" (these words *girls with mothers* enunciated oddly, contemptuously) "—you are already learning: feel God's strength coursing through you!" Mrs. Dieckman seized the girls' hands squeezing so quick and hard that Connie burst into frightened giggles and Nelia shrieked as if she'd been burnt, and almost wet her panties.

NELIA ACQUIRED PRIDE, then. Instead of being ashamed, publicly humiliated (at the one-room country schoolhouse, for instance: where certain of the other children were ruthless), she could be proud, like her father. *God had a special feeling for me. God cared about me. Jesus Christ, His only son, was cruelly tested, too. And exalted. You can bear any hurt and degradation. Thistles and thorns. The flaming sword, the cherubim guarding the garden.*

Mere *girls with mothers,* how could they know?

3

OF COURSE, Connie and Nelia had heard their parents quarreling. In the weeks, months before their mother disappeared. In fact, all their lives. Had they been queried, had they had the language, they might have said, *This is what is done, a man, a woman—isn't it?*

Connie who was three years older than Nelia knew much that Nelia would not ever know. Not words exactly, these quarrels, and of a tone different from their father shouting out instructions to his farmhands. Not words but an eruption of voices. Ringing through the floorboards if the quarrel came from downstairs. Reverberating in the windowpanes where wind thinly whistled. In bed, Connie would hug Nelia tight, pretending Nelia was Momma. Or Connie was herself Momma. If you shut your eyes tight enough. If you shut your ears. Always after the voices there came silence. If you wait. Once, crouched at the foot of the stairs, it was Connie?—or Nelia?—gazing upward astonished as Momma descended the stairs swaying like a drunk woman, her left hand groping against the railing, face dead-white, and a bright crimson rosebud in the corner of her mouth glistening as she wiped, wiped furiously at it. And quick-walking in that way of his that made the house vibrate, heavy-heeled behind her, descending from the top of the stairs a man whose face she could not see. Fiery, and blinding. God in the burning bush. God in thunder. *Bitch! Get back up here! If I have to come get you, if you won't be a woman, a wife!*

It was a fact the sisters learned, young: if you wait long enough, run away and hide your eyes, shut your ears, there comes a silence vast and rolling and empty as the sky.

THERE WAS the mystery of the letters, my mother and Aunt Connie would speak of, though never exactly discuss in my presence, into the last year of my mother's life.

Which of them first noticed, they couldn't agree. Or when it began, exactly—no earlier than the fall, 1923. It would happen that Papa went to fetch the mail, which he rarely did, and then only on Saturdays; and, returning, along the quarter-mile lane, he would be observed (by accident? the girls weren't spying) with an opened letter in his hand, reading— or was it a postcard—walking with uncharacteristic slowness, this man whose step was invariably brisk and impatient. Connie recalled he'd sometimes slip into the stable to continue reading, Papa had a liking for the stable which was for him a private place where he'd chew tobacco, spit into the hay, run his calloused hands along a horse's flanks, think his own thoughts. Other times, carrying whatever it was, letter, postcard, the rarity of an item of personal mail, he'd return to the kitchen and his place at the table. There the girls would find him (by accident, they *were not* spying) drinking coffee laced with top milk and sugar, rolling one of his clumsy cigarettes. And Connie would be the one to inquire, "Was there any mail, Papa?" keeping her voice low, unexcited. And Papa would shrug and say, "Nothing." On the table where he'd dropped them indifferently might be a few bills, advertising flyers, the *Chautauqua Valley Weekly Gazette*. Nelia never inquired about the mail at such times because she would not have trusted her voice. But, young as ten, Connie could be pushy, reckless. "Isn't there a letter, Papa? What *is* that, Papa, in your pocket?"

And Papa would say calmly, staring her full in the face, "When your father says *nothing,* girl, he means *nothing.*"

Sometimes his hands shook, fussing with the pouch of Old Bugler and the stained cigarette-roller.

Since the shame of losing his wife, and everybody knowing the circumstances, John Nissenbaum had aged shockingly. His face was creased, his skin reddened and cracked, finely stippled with what would be diagnosed (when finally he went to a doctor) as skin cancer. His eyes, pouched in wrinkled lids like a turtle's, were often vague, restless. Even in church, in a row close to Reverend Dieckman's pulpit, he had a look of wandering off. In what might be called his earlier life he'd been a rough, physical man, intelligent but quick-tempered; now he tired easily, could not keep up with his hired men whom he more and more mistrusted. His beard, once so trim and shapely, grew ragged and uneven and was entirely grizzled, like cobwebs. And his breath—it smelled of tobacco juice, wet, rank, sickish, rotted.

Once, seeing the edge of the letter in Papa's pocket, Connie bit her lip and said, "It's from *her,* isn't it!"

Papa said, still calmly, "I said it's *nothing,* girl. From *nobody.*"

Never in their father's presence did either of the sisters allude to their missing mother except as *her, she.*

Later when they searched for the letter, even for its envelope, of course they found nothing. Papa had burned it in the stove probably. Or torn it into shreds, tossed into the garbage. Still, the sisters risked their father's wrath by daring to look in his bedroom (the stale-smelling room he'd moved to, downstairs at the rear of the house) when he was out; even, desperate, knowing it was hopeless, poking through fresh-dumped garbage. (Like all farm families of their day, the Nissenbaums dumped raw garbage down a hillside, in the area of the outhouse.) Once Connie scrambled across fly-buzzing mounds of garbage holding her nose, stooping to snatch up—what? A card advertising a fertilizer sale, that had looked like a picture postcard.

"Are you crazy?" Nelia cried. "I hate you!"

Connie turned to scream at her, eyes brimming tears. "Go to hell, horse's ass, I hate *you!*"

Both wanted to believe, or did in fact believe, that their mother was writing not to their father but to them. But they would never know. For years, as the letters came at long intervals, arriving only when their father fetched the mail, they would not know.

This might have been a further element of mystery: why the letters, arriving so infrequently, arrived only when their father got the mail. Why, when Connie, or Nelia, or Loraine (John's younger sister, who'd come to live with them) got the mail, there would never be one of the mysterious letters. *Only when Papa got the mail.*

After my mother's death in 1981, when I spoke more openly to my Aunt Connie, I asked why they hadn't been suspicious, just a little. Aunt Connie lifted her penciled eyebrows, blinked at me as if I'd uttered something obscene—"Suspicious? Why?" Not once did the girls (who were in fact intelligent girls, Nelia a straight-A student in the high school in town) calculate the odds: how the presumed letter from their mother could possibly arrive only on those days (Saturdays) when their father got the mail; one day out of six mail-days, yet never any day except that particular day (Saturday). But as Aunt Connie said, shrugging, it just seemed that that was how it was—they would never have conceived of even the possibility of any situation in which the odds wouldn't have been against them, and in favor of Papa.

4

THE FARMHOUSE WAS already old when I was first brought to visit it, summers, in the 1950s. Part red brick so weathered as to seem without color and part rotted wood, with a steep shingled roof, high ceilings, and spooky corners; a perpetual odor of woodsmoke, kerosene, mildew, time. A perpetual draft passed through the house from the rear, which faced north, opening out onto a long incline of acres, miles, dropping to the Chautauqua River ten miles away like an aerial scene in a movie. I remember the old washroom, the machine with a hand-wringer; a door to the cellar in the floor of that room, with a thick metal ring as a handle. Outside the house, too, was another door, horizontal and not vertical. The thought of what lay beyond those doors, the dark, stone-smelling cellar where rats scurried, filled me with a childish terror.

I remember Grandfather Nissenbaum as always old. A lean, sinewy, virtually mute old man. His finely cracked, venous-glazed skin, red-stained as if with earth; narrow rheumy eyes whose pupils seemed, like the pupils of goats, horizontal black slats. How they scared me! Deafness had made Grandfather remote and strangely imperial, like an old almost-forgotten king. The crown of his head was shinily bald and a fringe of coarse hair bleached to the color of ash grew at the sides and back. Where once, my mother lamented, he'd been careful in his dress, especially on Sundays, for churchgoing, he now wore filth-stained overalls and in all months save summer long gray-flannel underwear straggling at his cuffs like a loose second skin. His breath stank of tobacco juice and rotted teeth, the knuckles of both his hands were grotesquely swollen. My heart beat quickly and erratically in his presence. "Don't be silly," Mother whispered nervously, pushing me toward the old man, "—your grandfather *loves you*." But I knew he did not. Never did he call me by my name, Bethany, but only "girl" as if he hadn't troubled to learn my name.

When Mother showed me photographs of the man she called Papa, some of these scissored in half, to excise my missing grandmother, I stared, and could not believe he'd once been so handsome! Like a film actor of some bygone time. "You see," Mother said, incensed, as if the two of us had been quarreling, "—this is who John Nissenbaum really *is*."

I grew up never really knowing Grandfather, and I certainly didn't love him. He was never "Grandpa" to me. Visits to Ransomville were sporadic, sometimes canceled at the last minute. Mother would be excited, hopeful, apprehensive—then, who knows why, the visit would be canceled, she'd be tearful, upset, yet relieved. Now, I can guess that Mother and her family weren't fully welcomed by my grandfather; he was a lonely and embittered old man, but still proud—he'd never forgiven her for leaving home, after high school, just like her sister Connie; going to the teachers' college at Elmira instead of marrying a local man worthy of working and eventually inheriting the Nissenbaum farm. By the time I was born, in 1951, the acreage was being sold off; by the time Grandfather Nissenbaum died, in 1972, in a nursing home in Yewville, the two hundred acres had been reduced to a humiliating seven acres, now the property of strangers.

In the hilly cemetery behind the First Lutheran Church of Ransomville, New York, there is a still-shiny black granite marker at the edge of rows of Nissenbaum markers, JOHN ALLARD NISSENBAUM 1872–1957. Chiseled into the stone is, *How long shall I be with you? How long shall I suffer you?* Such angry words of Jesus Christ's! I wondered who had chosen them—not Constance or Cornelia, surely. It must have been John Nissenbaum himself.

ALREADY AS A GIRL of eleven, twelve I was pushy and curious, asking my mother about my missing grandmother. *Look, Mother, for God's sake where did she go? Didn't anybody try to find her?* Mother's replies were vague, evasive. As if rehearsed. That sweet-resolute stoic smile. Cheerful resignation, Christian forgiveness. For thirty-five years she taught high school English in the Rochester public schools, and especially after my father left us, and she became a single, divorced woman, the manner came easily to her of brisk classroom authority, that pretense of the skilled teacher of weighing others' opinions thoughtfully before reiterating one's own.

My father, an education administrator, left us when I was fourteen, to remarry. I was furious, heartbroken. Dazed. *Why? How could he betray us?* But Mother maintained her Christian fortitude, her air of subtly wounded pride. *This is what people will do, Bethany. Turn against you, turn faithless. You might as well learn, young.*

Yet I pushed. Up to the very end of her life, when Mother was so ill. You'd judge me harsh, heartless—people did. But for God's sake I wanted to know: what happened to my Grandmother Nissenbaum, why did nobody seem to care she'd gone away? Were the letters my mother and Connie swore their father received authentic, or had he been playing a trick of some kind? And if it had been a trick, what was its purpose? *Just tell me the truth for once, Mother. The truth about anything.*

I'm forty-four years old. I still want to know.

But Mother, the intrepid schoolteacher, the good Christian, was impenetrable. Inscrutable as her Papa. Capable of summing up her entire childhood *back there* (this was how she and Aunt Connie spoke of Ransomville, their past: *back there*) by claiming that such *hurts* are God's will, God's plan for each of us. A test of our faith. A test of our inner strength. I said, disgusted, what if you don't believe in God, what are you left with then?—and Mother said matter-of-factly, "You're left with yourself of course, your inner strength. Isn't that enough?"

THAT FINAL TIME we spoke of this, I lost patience, I must have pushed Mother too far. In a sharp stinging voice, a voice I'd never heard from her before, she said, "Bethany, what do you want me to tell you? About my mother?—my father? Do you imagine I ever knew them? Either of them? My mother left Connie and me when we were little girls, left us with *him*, wasn't that her choice? Her selfishness? Why should anyone have gone looking for her? She was trash, she was *faithless*. We learned to forgive, and to forget. Your aunt tells you a different story, I know, but it's a lie—*I* was the one who was hurt, *I* was the youngest. Your heart can be broken only once—you'll learn! Our lives were busy, busy like the lives of grown women today, women who have to work, women who don't have time to moan and groan over their hurt feelings, you can't know how Connie and I worked on that farm, in that house, like grown women when we were girls. Father tried to stop both of us going to school beyond eighth grade—imagine! We had to walk two miles to get a ride with a neighbor, to get to the high school in Ransomville; there weren't school buses in those days. Everything you've had you've taken for granted and wanted more, but we weren't like that. We hadn't money for the right school clothes, all our textbooks were used, but we went to high school. I was the only 'farm girl'—that's exactly what I was known as, even by my teachers—in my class to take math, biology, physics, Latin. I was memorizing Latin declensions milking cows at five in the morning, winter mornings. I was laughed at, Nelia Nissenbaum was *laughable*. But I accepted it. All that mattered was that I win a scholarship to a teachers' college so I could escape the country and I did win a scholarship and I never returned to Ransomville to live. Yes, I loved Papa—I still love him. I loved the farm, too. You can't not love any place that's taken so much from you. But I had my own life, I had my teaching jobs, I had my faith, my belief in God, I had my destiny. I even got married—that was extra, unexpected. I've worked for everything I ever got and I never had time to look back, to feel sorry for myself. Why then should I think about *her?*—why do you torment me about *her*? A woman who abandoned me when I was five years old! In 1923! I made my peace with the past, just like Connie in her different way. We're happy women, we've been spared a lifetime of bitterness. *That* was God's gift to us." Mother paused, breathing quickly. There was in her face the elation of one who has said too much, that can never be retracted; I was stunned into silence. She plunged on, now contemptuously, "What are you always wanting me to admit, Bethany? That you know something I don't know? What is your generation always pushing for, from ours? Isn't it enough we gave birth to you, indulged you, must we be sacrificed to you, too? What do you want us to tell you—that life is cruel and purposeless? That there is no loving God, and never was, only accident? Is that what you want to hear, from your mother? That I married your father because he was a weak man, a man I couldn't feel much for, who wouldn't, when it came time, hurt me?"

And then there was silence. We stared at each other, Mother in her glistening of fury, daughter Bethany so shocked she could not speak. Never again would I think of my mother in the old way.

WHAT MOTHER NEVER KNEW: in April 1983, two years after her death, a creek that runs through the old Nissenbaum property flooded its banks, and several hundred feet of red clayey soil collapsed overnight into the creek bed, as in an earthquake. And in the raw, exposed earth there was discovered a human skeleton, decades old but virtually intact. It had apparently been buried, less than a mile behind the Nissenbaum farmhouse.

There had never been anything so newsworthy—so sensational—in the history of Chautauqua County.

State forensic investigators determined that the skeleton had belonged to a woman, apparently killed by numerous blows to the head (a hammer, or the blunt edge of an ax) that shattered her skull like a melon. Dumped into the grave with her was what appeared to have been a suitcase, now rotted, its contents—clothes, shoes, underwear, gloves—scarcely recognizable from the earth surrounding it. There were a few pieces of jewelry and, still entwined around the skeleton's neck, a tarnished gold cross on a chain. Most of the woman's clothing had long ago rotted away and almost unrecognizable too was a book—a leatherbound Bible?—close beside her. About the partly detached, fragile wrist and ankle bones were loops of rusted baling wire that had fallen loose, coiled in the moist red clay like miniature sleeping snakes.

THE SCARF

A turquoise silk scarf, elegantly long, and narrow; so delicately threaded with pale gold and silver butterflies, you might lose yourself in a dream contemplating it imagining you're gazing into another dimension or another time in which the heraldic butterflies are living creatures with slow, pulsing wings.

ELEVEN YEARS OLD, I was searching for a birthday present for my mother. *Mom* she was to me though often in weak moments I'd hear my voice cry *Mommy*.

It was a windy grit-borne Saturday in late March, a week before Easter, and cold. Searching through the stores of downtown Strykersville. Not Woolworth's, not Rexall's Drugs, not Norban's Discounts where a gang of girls might prowl after school, but the "better" women's stores where few of us went except with our mothers, and rarely even then.

Saved jealously, in secret, for many months in a bunched-up white sock in my bureau drawer was eight dollars and sixty-five cents. Now in my jacket pocket, the bills carefully folded. This sum was sufficient, I believed, for a really nice really special present for my mother. I was excited, nervous; already I could see the surprised pleasure in my mother's eyes as she unwrapped the box, and this was to be my reward. For there was a delicious way Mom had of squinching up her face which was an unlined, pretty face, a young-woman face still (my parents' ages were mysteries to me I would not have dared to penetrate but clearly they were "young" compared with most of my friends' parents—in their early thirties) and saying, in her warm whispery voice, as if this were a secret between us, "Oh, honey, what have you *done*—!"

I wanted to strike that match bringing out a warm startled glow in my mother's face, that glistening in her eyes.

I wanted to present my mother with, not a mere store-bought item, but a love-offering. A talisman against harm. The perfect gift that is a spell against hurt, fear, aloneness; sorrow, illness, age and death and oblivion. The gift that says *I love you, you are life to me.*

Had I eighteen dollars, or eighty, I would have wished to spend every penny on the gift for my mother's birthday. To hand over every penny I'd earned, to make the transaction sacred. For I believed that this secretly hoarded money had to be surrendered in its entirety to the proper authority, to render the transaction valid; and that this mysterious authority resided in one of the "better" Strykersville stores and nowhere else. So there was a fevered glare in my eyes, a sense of mission; there was an eagerness to my slight body that propelled me forward even as I wanted to recoil in a kind of instinctive physical chagrin.

Naturally, I aroused suspicion in the primly dressed women who clerked in such stores. They were conspicuously "ladies" and had standards to uphold. The more gracious the salesclerk, the more acute her suspicion of me. I experienced several stores in a haze of blindness and breathlessness; no sooner had I entered one of these stores than I was made to know I'd better leave by a woman's sharp query: "Yes? May I assist you?"

At last I found myself amid glittery glass display cases and racks of beautiful leather goods hanging like the slain carcasses of animals. A well-worn parquet floor creaked incriminatingly beneath my feet. How had I dared enter Kenilworth's Ladies Fashions where mother never shopped? What gusty wind had propelled me inside, like a taunting hand on the flat of my back? The lady salesclerk, tight-corseted with a scratchy steel-wool bun at the nape of her neck and smacking-red downturned mouth, eyed my every movement up and down the dazzling aisles. "May I assist you, miss?" this lady asked in a cold, doubtful voice. I murmured I was just looking. "Did you come to look, miss, or to buy?" My face pounded with blood as if I'd been turned upside-down. This woman didn't trust me! Though I was, at school, such a good girl; such a diligent student; always an A student; always a favorite of teachers; one of those students who are on a teacher's side in the fray, thus not to be despised. But here in Kenilworth's, it seemed I was not trusted. I might have been a little colored girl for my dark hair was suspiciously curly-kinky like moist wires, and inclined to frizz like something demented. You would know, seeing me, that such a specimen could not drag a decent comb through that head of snarly hair. And my skin was olive-dark, not the wholesome buttermilk-pale, like the salesclerk's powdered skin, that was preferred. Here was a poor girl, an ungainly girl, a shy girl, therefore a dishonest girl, a sneaky little shoplifter, just give her the chance, just turn your back for an instant. You've heard of gypsies. There were no gypsies in the small country town of Strykersville, New York, yet had there been gypsies, even a single sprawling family, it was clear I was one of their offspring with my soiled skin, shifty eyes, and run-down rubber boots.

It was my ill luck that no other customers were in this department of Kenilworth's at the moment and so the clerk might fiercely concentrate her attention on me. How prized I was, not requiring the usual courtesy and fawning-over with which you must serve a true customer. For I was not a "customer" but an intruder, a trespasser. *She expects me to steal*—the thought rushed at me with the force of a radio news bulletin. What hurt and resentment I felt, what shame. Yet, how badly I would have liked, at that moment, to steal; to slip something, oh anything! into my pocket—a leather wallet, a small beaded handbag, a lacy white Irish linen handkerchief. But I dared not for I was a "good" girl who never, in the company of my gang of friends, purloined even cheap plastic lipsticks, fake-gold hair barrettes, or key rings adorned with the ecstatic smiling faces of Jane Russell, Linda Darnell, Debra Paget, and Lana Turner from Woolworth's. So I stood paralyzed in the gaze of the woman salesclerk; caught between the perception of my deepest wish (until that moment unknown to me) and my perception of the futility of that wish. *She wants me to steal but I can't, I won't.*

In a weak voice I said, "It's for my mother—a birthday present. How much is—this?" I'd been staring at a display of scarves. The price tags on certain of the items of merchandise—the wallets, the handbags, even gloves and handkerchiefs—were so absurdly high, my eye took them in even as my brain repelled them, as bits of information not to be assimilated. Scarves, I seemed to believe, would be more reasonably priced. And what beautiful scarves were on display—I stared almost without comprehension at these lovely colors, these exquisite fabrics and designs. For these were not coarse, practical, cottony-flannel scarves like the kind I wore most of the winter, that tied tightly beneath the chin; scarves that kept one's hair from whipping into snarls, kept ears and neck warm; scarves that looked, at their frequent worst, not unlike bandages wrapped around the head. These scarves were works of art. They were made of fine silk, or very light wool; they were extravagantly long, or triangular; some were squares; some were enormous, with fringes—perhaps these were shawls. There were paisley prints, there were floral prints. There were gossamer scarves, gauzy scarves, scarves boldly printed with yellow jonquils and luscious red tulips, scarves wispy as those dreams of surpassing sweetness that, as we wake and yearn to draw them after us, break and disintegrate like strands of cobweb. Blindly I pointed at—I didn't dare touch—the most beautiful of the scarves, turquoise, a fine delicate silk patterned with small gold and silver figures I couldn't quite decipher. Through her pinched-looking bifocals the salesclerk peered at me, saying, in a voice of reproach, "*That* scarf is pure silk, from China. *That* scarf is—" Pausing then to consider me as if for the first time. Maybe she felt in the air the tremor and heat of my blood. Maybe it was simple pity. This utterly mysterious transaction, one of those unfathomable and incalculable events that mark at rare intervals the inner curve of our lives, gratuitous moments of grace. In a lowered, more kindly voice, though with an edge of adult annoyance, the sales clerk said, "It's ten dollars. Plus tax."

Ten dollars. Like a child in an enchantment I began numbly to remove my savings from my pocket, six wrinkled dollars and nickels, dimes, a single quarter and numerous pennies, counting them with frowning earnestness as if I hadn't any idea what they might add up to. The sharp-eyed salesclerk said irritably, "—I mean eight dollars. It's been marked down to eight dollars for our Easter sale." Eight dollars! I said, stammering, "I—I'll take it. Thank you." Relief so flooded me I might have fainted. I was smiling, triumphant. I couldn't believe my good luck even as, with childish egotism, I never paused to doubt it.

Eagerly I handed over my money to the salesclerk, who rang up the purchase with that curious prickly air of impatience, as if I'd embarrassed her; as if I were not an intruder in Kenilworth's after all, but a child-relative of hers she did not wish to acknowledge. As she briskly wrapped the boxed scarf in glossy pink paper stamped with HAPPY BIRTHDAY! I dared raise my eyes and saw with a mild shock that the woman wasn't so old as I'd thought—not much older than my mother. Her hair was a thin, graying brown caught in an angry-looking bun, her face was heavily made up yet not pretty, her bright lipstick-mouth downturned. When she handed me the gift-wrapped box in a Kenilworth's silver-striped bag she said, frowning at me through her eyeglasses, "It's ready to give to your mother. The price tag is off."

MOTHER INSISTS *But I have no more use for this, dear. Please take it.* Rummaging through closets, bureau drawers of the old house soon to be sold to strangers. In her calm melodic voice that belies the shakiness of her hands saying, *If—later—something happens to me—I don't want it to be lost.*

Each visit back home, Mother has more to give me. Things once precious out of the ever-more remote, receding past. What is the secret meaning of such gift-giving by a woman of eighty-three, don't inquire.

Mother speaks often, vaguely, of *lost.* She fears papers being lost—insurance policies, medical records. *Lost* is a bottomless ravine into which you might fall, and fall. Into which her several sisters and brothers have disappeared one by one, and a number of her friends. And Father—has it already been a year? So that, for the remainder of her life, Mother's life grown mysterious to her as a dream that continues ceaselessly without defining itself, without the rude interruption of lucidity, she will wake in the morning wondering where had Dad gone? She reaches out and there's no one beside her so she tells herself, He's in the bathroom. And, almost, she can hear him in there. Later she thinks, He must be outside. And, almost, she can hear the lawn mower. Or she thinks, He's taken the car. And gone—where?

"Here! Here it is."

At the bottom of a drawer in a bedroom bureau Mother has found what she's been searching for with such concentration. This afternoon she has pressed upon me a square-cut amethyst in an antique setting, a ring once belonging to her mother-in-law, and a handwoven potholder only just perceptibly marred by scorching. And now she opens a long flat box, and there it is, amid tissue paper: the silk turquoise scarf with its pale heraldic butterflies.

For a moment, I can't speak. I've gone entirely numb.

Fifty years. Can it have been—fifty years.

Says Mother, proudly, "Your father gave it to me. When we were just married. It was my favorite scarf but you can see—it was too pretty to wear, and too thin. So I put it away."

"But you did wear it, Mother. I remember."

"Did I?"

"With that beige silk suit you had, for Audrey's wedding? And—well—a few other times." I can see in Mother's face that expression of veiled alarm. Any suggestion of her memory failing frightens her; she's seen, at close range, the ravages of age in others.

Mother says quickly, "Please take it, dear. It would make me happy if you did."

"But, Mother—"

"I don't have any use for it, and I don't want it to get *lost*."

Her voice rises just perceptibly. Somewhere between a plea and a command.

Staring, I lift the turquoise scarf from the box. Admiring. In fact its label is French, not Chinese. In fact the turquoise isn't so vivid as I remember. Fifty years ago! The salesclerk at Kenilworth's who'd seemed to want me to steal; who had (I'd come to this stunning conclusion years later) practically given away an expensive scarf, making up the difference out of her own pocket? And I, a reputedly clever girl of eleven, hadn't comprehended the nature of the gift? Hadn't had a clue?

Fifty years. My mother's thirty-third birthday. She'd opened my present to her nervously: the luxurious wrappings with ribbons and bows, the embossed silver KENILWORTH's on the box must have alarmed her. Taking the scarf out of the box, Mother had been speechless for a long moment before saying, "Oh, honey, it's—*beautiful*. How did you—" But her voice trailed off. As if words failed her. Or with her subtle sense of tact she believed it would be rude to make such an inquiry even of an eleven-year-old daughter.

The talisman that says, *I love you. You are life to me.*

This luminous silky scarf imprinted with butterflies like ancient heraldic coins. The kind of imported, expensive scarf women are wearing today, flung casually over their shoulders. I ask Mother if she's absolutely certain she wants to give away the scarf though I know the answer; for

Mother has come to an age when she knows exactly what she wants and what she doesn't want, what she needs and doesn't need. These encumbrances of life, that bind one to life.

In reply, Mother loops the scarf around my neck, at first lightly tying the ends, then untying them, beside me at the mirror.

"Darling, see? It's beautiful on *you*."

WHAT THEN, MY LIFE?

hy did Grandma Wolpert hate me? I was asking my mother in a confused dream of churning water, angry wind, and rows of towering cornstalks fluttering like living, convulsing things. I was in the shadowy interior of the kitchen in the old Wolpert farmhouse, and I was running in a cornfield, bladelike leaves and silky tassels brushing against my sweaty face. *Your Grandma didn't hate you! What a thing to say,* my mother protests. She's upset, guilty-eyed. I'm trying to hide against her; I must be a small child to be pressing myself so desperately against her legs, clutching at her. *What a terrible, terrible thing to say,* my mother says, her hushed voice confused with the churning water and wind, *What a terrible girl, to say such a thing.*

THIS IS an old dream, I'm sure. I don't believe I've had it for years, since my grandmother Wolpert died. I don't believe that I dream much at all any longer. Nor do I sleep through the night.

Terrible girl. It's something to be proud of, isn't it? That I could have sufficient strength, that I could be rebellious, mutinous. I'd like to think it was true. That it wasn't just a dream.

1. "Sleep Fugue"

THIS HAPPENED less than twelve hours ago, in New York City.

As my name was announced I arose from my seat onstage amid a blaze of TV lights and began to cross to the podium to speak, as we'd rehearsed—and in an instant, as a skilled butcher might cleave a side of raw, muscled meat in two, I was in another place, my grandmother's old kitchen, and I was running in a cornfield, running as if my heart might burst, and the need for sleep came over me like a dark cloud, as powerfully as if someone had clamped one of those old-fashioned rubber ether-masks over my mouth and nose. NO. NOT HERE. NOT NOW. There was a roaring in my ears as of an angry wind. There was that taste of panic, blackish acid in my mouth. My legs were leaden—what effort was required to move them!—yet I managed somehow to get to the podium, swaying, stumbling like a sleepwalker, forcing myself to smile to acknowledge a wave of courteous applause, trying to keep my eyelids open. I'd crossed a distance of perhaps twelve feet from where I'd been sitting in full view of fifteen hundred people and it was as if I'd been climbing, crawling, on my hands and knees up the side of a jagged rock face. *But I didn't give in.*

That I was in Lincoln Center, that I was the fourth in a succession of "presenters" at an annual awards evening broadcast over network TV, the circumstances of my life at this moment in my career—it's too complicated to explain. My role in the program wasn't very important, though of course it was important to me and to the program's organizers. For such occasions you arrive two hours before the broadcast to rehearse your two-minute spot, which is mainly reading from a prepared script from a TelePrompTer about eighteen inches away at eye level. The TelePrompTer is a remarkable invention, so small that even people seated in the front row of an audience perceive it as little more than a narrow horizontal bar floating in air; others perceive nothing at all. It's magic, scrolled words, words prepared beforehand, floating in midair for you to speak as if they were your own. If you happened to be watching the program, what you saw of me was a pale, startled-looking woman of young middle age managing a smile, hesitating just a moment before she began to speak, as a stammerer might do, then announcing the winner of the next award, reciting names, titles, facts, dates as if spontaneously, her oddly widened eyes fixed upon you (that is, upon the TelePrompTer positioned an inch or so left of center in front of a TV camera) in your living room. *Is there something wrong with that woman?* you may have thought uneasily, but the moment passed so swiftly, a brass plaque was being handed to a beaming goateed man in a tux, there was a vigorous handshake, a fanfare of trumpets, and a cut to a film clip of about sixty seconds. When the camera returned to Lincoln Center, to the live broadcast, the pale, startled-looking woman was gone and forgotten.

I didn't! Didn't give in.

Note: Once you've worked from a TelePrompTer you wouldn't wish to work again from a printed script held in the hand or flat on a podium.

Note: Once you move from one phase of perception to the next, you wouldn't ever wish to revert to the earlier phase.

As I'd sat in my seat among the other presenters, each of us formally dressed, women in black, men in tuxes, I had not been at all apprehensive, for I feel safest in public places. If fifteen hundred people are watching you, not to mention many times more over TV, you are defined by their perception as you can never be by your own. The more people who are viewing you at a given moment, the more "real" you are. "If I could die in front of an audience, a large, sympathetic audience, I wouldn't feel the slightest tinge of fear. It would all be part of the performance"—I'd once made this remark to a man with whom I'd been living, or almost living. (We'd each kept our own apartment, of course.) He'd laughed, startled, as if I'd meant to be funny, for I often joke, but I was serious, too, and would like to have been able to speak frankly with him on the subject. *How much easier is death in public, than in private.* It's self-evident, isn't it? Hasn't everyone come to this realization?

These "sleep fugues" come upon me abruptly, without warning, like fainting spells or epileptic attacks. Yet no neurologist has found any sign of pathology. Since the age of ten I've been vulnerable to these mysterious fits, which seem to have nothing to do with where I am, what I'm doing, with whom I might be speaking. Yet rarely do they happen in a public place, perhaps because I feel relatively safe in public, as I've said. I once had a sleep fugue overtake me while driving on the upper tier of the George Washington Bridge and I had to pull over immediately into the emergency lane; my eyelids were already shutting and I slid by rapid degrees into a dark, bottomless pit. The windy, thrashing Hudson River below was confused with the more familiar pit into which I sank and a voice consoled me, *Yes, this is good. It will be over soon.* That fugue lasted no more than two or three minutes, but others have lasted as long as ten minutes, leaving me dazed and disoriented as if I'd been sleeping for days, for weeks. You realize how "time" is purely a matter of consciousness: when you aren't conscious, "time" doesn't exist, for days and even weeks in a coma state can pass swiftly as a finger snapping. And where there's no memory, is there a "soul"?

Onstage at Lincoln Center I was somehow able to deflect the fugue by a desperate effort of will. I forced my eyes wide, I breathed so deeply my lungs ached, I was clenching my fists to make my nails dig into the soft flesh of my palms. The vision of the old farmhouse in the Chautauqua Valley, upstate in New York hundreds of miles away and thirty years ago, rows of hulking six-foot cornstalks and dried, crumbling dirt beneath my running feet—these were superimposed upon the bright, blinding scene around me like a film transparency. There came a loud trumpet fanfare, audience applause. I was blinking rapidly to stay awake, shook my head to clear it, heard my voice as if it were a stranger's performing my rehearsed role—reading "spontaneously" from the TelePrompTer, turning to present the shiny plaque to the Canadian documentary filmmaker, shaking the man's hand, trying not to notice how his face was pale as a corpse's. It was a big, formerly ruddy face, now the color had bled out of it as everywhere, everywhere I looked, the color had bled out of faces, things, surfaces. The roaring in my ears increased and I knew I must sleep. We were off-camera now, the master of ceremonies loomed beside me, quick and deft and kindly, gripping my elbow to walk me from the stage, murmuring in my ear, "You okay?" It was a rhetorical question; he knew I wasn't okay. The touch of this man whom I knew only slightly, his kind, concerned words jolted me awake temporarily as with a shot of adrenaline. Instead of returning to my seat as we'd rehearsed, I was escorted offstage; it seemed natural, easy, and no one would take much notice of my absence, though my chair would remain vacant for the remainder of the program.

What happened next isn't clear, and isn't important: as soon as I was safely backstage, evidently I lay down on some folded canvas on the floor, back behind the heavy fireproof stage curtains. I lay down, curled up like a child, and slept. I remember only that my consciousness went extinct like a candle flame blown out. *Yes, like this. This is good.* Dimly I was aware of concerned voices, being touched, a cold, damp cloth pressed against my forehead. At the same time I was sleeping, the sweetest, most consoling and refreshing sleep, a sleep of hours packed into minutes. And when I woke, revived, it was as if nothing, or almost nothing, had happened—I had no trouble standing, smiling in embarrassment, apologizing. I brushed at my clothes, my chic short-skirted black velvet suit, I smoothed my hair, I didn't want or require medical attention, I was eager just to go home, I explained that I'd been exhausted lately, under stress, but it was nothing— "A sleep fugue. They come out of nowhere, and they vanish. And I'm fine."

And so it was.

HOURS LATER, at home, I listened with dread to a half-dozen messages on my answering machine. Friends who'd guessed that something had been wrong with me, calling to inquire. I was touched by their solicitude. I was moved almost to tears, yet I felt guilty, too, arousing their alarm. One of these was the man with whom I'd almost lived, whom I no longer saw now, or no longer "saw" in the old way, and I replayed his message several times, thinking, *But of course you didn't know me, that's why you're calling now.* There were three hang-ups on the machine, so I supposed that my parents had called; they weren't comfortable with answering machines and never left messages. In fact they rarely called me at all, not wanting to intrude upon my life away from Ransomville. *She has her own life now,* my mother once remarked almost out of my hearing, at a family occasion, *her own life now, own life now* echoing strangely, as if in subtle hurt and reproach, though at the time Mother's voice had been brisk and matter-of-fact.

Is it wrong, I wonder, for a daughter to have her *own life* at any age? A daughter who loves her parents, I mean.

Is it even possible? For what is one's *own life* exactly?

The telephone rang. It was late, past midnight. This could not be my mother, I thought, for my mother goes to bed early while my father often sits up past midnight at the kitchen table, reading, smoking, sipping ale out of a can, but when I picked up the receiver it was my mother's voice I heard, and I began to cry, like a hurt, angry child, "Why did Grandma Wolpert hate me? I have to know."

FOR HOURS that night I lay awake unsleeping staring at the ceiling of my bedroom, which appeared gauzy in the dark, of no substance. At last I gave up, went to this desk and began to write, began to write feverishly in my journal, in my schoolgirl hand so conscientiously legible, each T neatly crossed and each I neatly dotted and not a comma, colon, or semicolon misused. A long, urgent entry that brought me safely through the worst hour of the night, the hour that yields to dawn, an entry beginning *This happened less than twelve hours ago, in New York City.*

2. The Edge of Nowhere

RANSOMVILLE, NEW YORK, where I was born and grew up, and where my parents and numerous relatives still live, was named for Joseph Edgar Ransom, who'd established a mill and fur-trading post on the Chautauqua River in the early 1700s when everything here was wilderness. Little is known of Ransom, this original settler, except that he'd died in 1738 and there's a mossy, melted-looking old stone marker in the Lutheran churchyard to commemorate this fact. Ransom had thirteen children with three wives of whom only a single son (who knew how many daughters; daughters couldn't bear the Ransom name and so didn't count) was said to have survived his death; this son became an itinerant minister in one of those Scots-Protestant sects whose most impassioned leaders ended in asylums. All this was so long ago it might have been a dream. For certain landscapes, especially in the mountains, must generate their own dreams. At school there were quaint old maps of the "original settlement of Ransomville," there were lists of Indian names we were made to memorize, to spell correctly. Out along the river there were broken stone foundations in the overgrown brush.

Does it matter where we're born? For we aren't after all made of the soil beneath our feet—are we?

I don't want to think this, I realize it's a high-flown, poetic way of thinking. Grandma Wolpert, who couldn't abide such talk from anyone, would've flared her big, black nostrils like a snorting horse.

In the early 1950s Ransomville was a small, thriving country town on the Chautauqua River, its population at a zenith of 3,700, but by the time I went to Ransomville Consolidated High School in the late 1960s, all but two of the half-dozen mills were shut down and you'd see FOR LEASE and FOR SALE signs on deserted gas stations out on the highway.

My Wolpert grandparents, my dad's parents, lived on a small farm eleven miles north and east of Ransomville in the foothills of the Chautauqua Mountains. You couldn't get there directly; you got there in a zigzag fashion first on the Falls Road, then turning off onto Church Hill, which was blacktop with a tendency to melt in heat waves, then a series of unpaved gravel and dirt roads. Shutting my eyes I can find my way to my grandparents' farm, unable to anticipate any of the roads until I actually see them. The names of these roads have long faded in my memory, or perhaps they had no names even then. That sprawling farm, most of its twenty acres too rocky and hilly to cultivate; the house that was the color of damp wood, the weather-worn hay barn, silo, outbuildings; a hill like a clenched fist looming behind the house cutting off half the sky so in winter there were days of virtually no sun. *The edge of the world* my mother called it, wrinkling her nose. *Out back of nowhere.* It wasn't a complaint exactly, more what you'd call teasing, a pretend-astonishment that this remote place was my dad's boyhood home and these people were his people.

Weekends, we'd drive out. Especially in summer. Always there was the excitement of driving into the country, not the tame countryside bordering Ransomville where we lived but the faraway countryside headed into the mountains. *Grandpa's farm* it was called, or just *the farm.* I was too young and heedless, too hopeful to realize that these visits were tense for both my parents, particularly my mother. For always there was the not-knowing beforehand if a visit would be one of the good visits or one of the awkward, uncomfortable ones at which Grandma Wolpert wouldn't talk, wouldn't look my mother in the face, or smile, only set platters of food on the table, working her jaws in silence. She was a husky, mannish woman with a face that could look swollen as a goiter. *Sure Ma likes you, hon, and the kids. It's just, you know—she's never been one to show her feelings. No one is, in her family.* Mom would turn from Dad when he said such things so he couldn't see her face. While she was young, it was a pretty, unlined face with a wrinkly-sniffy snub nose like a rabbit's. She'd wink at me and I could almost hear her thoughts. *What! Grandma Wolpert shows her feelings clear enough. You would not want those thoughts much clearer.* My older brothers sometimes bicycled out to the farm, mostly to fish for rock bass in a creek that ran through Grandpa's property, but by the time they were teenagers they'd lost interest, rarely rode out with us in the car. The summer she turned thirteen my sister refused to come along though she'd been a favorite of Grandpa's. "Oh, that, that place, it's so boring. It never *changes.*"

Of course it changed. The way she changed, and my brothers who moved away from Ransomville and my cousins Joey, Luke, Jake joining the navy one by one as each turned seventeen, gone for years and then returning as adult men so that seeing them on the street in Ransomville you'd hardly know who they were. By the time I was in high school, Grandpa Wolpert had had his first stroke, and by the time I graduated, he was dead. By the time I was a junior in college, Grandma Wolpert was dead of a kind of cancer (it must have been cervical or uterine) no one in the family wished to identify, and her youngest son Tyrone, who'd been working the farm, immediately sold it and moved away to Lackawanna to work in a factory and so there was no longer any reason for any of us to make the drive to the old farm ever again.

All this seems so long ago, too, it might've been a dream. But whose dream, I would not know.

BRISKLY SNIPPING STEMS, arranging zinnias in a vase, Mom might remark in that airy, poking way of hers to Dad, "I miss it, I do. I really do. It was always an adventure, visiting your folks. And that drive." She'd shake her head, smiling. "Out back of nowhere! But it was beautiful, in its way. And the kids used to love it, it was a place to take them. Your father— what a good, kind man in his heart even if he could be a little difficult at times. And your mother—" Mom's idle voice trailed off like a moth hovering in the air. I waited for my father to reach over and swat it with the flat of his hand, but he never did.

"YOUR GRANDPA loves you, honey. He doesn't mean any harm by just teasing."

I loved Grandpa Wolpert, too. His name for me was Big Kitten, but I was afraid of him; you never knew when his teasing and tickling would turn rough, his fingers that smelled of manure poking my ribs and catching in my hair and his laughing breath exploding in my face like rotted apples. "How's my Big Kitten? What's Big Kitten up to, eh? What you got to say to your Grampa, Big Kitten?" I shrank from him, shrieking and giggling, hiding beneath the table (so I was told, in later years) but quickly crawled out again if Grandpa didn't squat down to reach for me. He was a stout, whiskery man in overalls, soiled flannel undershirts that smelled of the barnyard, with a loud wheezing laugh, a creased dark-tanned face like a grinning moon. Where Grandma Wolpert was silent, Grandpa Wolpert was noisy as a blue jay—talking, laughing, whistling, humming to himself. He talked to animals as he'd talk to people. He was a practical joker: for instance you might be helping to clear the table after a meal and pick up an innocent-seeming plate or saucer and water would spill out—of where?—

onto your legs. You'd open the closet door and a mop would tumble out, upside-down, causing a fright. Grandpa had three or four flashy card tricks that left his grandchildren blinking in amazement, and tricks with his big, gnarled hands, thumbs curled inside fists, an acorn in the palm of his hand—"Now you see it, now you don't, eh, Big Kitten?" Nothing delighted him more than a child's small smile of puzzlement. Grandma Wolpert disapproved of these silly tricks, as she called them, sniffing and snorting under her breath, but Grandpa paid her no heed, or he'd make a show of staring around the kitchen as if Grandma weren't there or as if she were invisible, leaning his head toward me, saying, "Feels like the floor's shaking, there's some kind of big fat cow in here, eh? But I don't see 'er, do you?" And I'd giggle as if he'd tickled me. It was funny pretending Grandma wasn't there.

Grandpa played a harmonica; Grandpa liked to sing. Especially when he'd been drinking. He liked to gamble—dice, poker, euchre. "God whispers in my ear. Tells me what not to do, mainly. Like He'll say, seeing the hand I'm dealt, 'Uh-uh, Wolpert. You're a horse's ass if you do.' So I don't." Grandpa winked, telling such tall tales, yet it seemed clear he believed what he said. He was proud of himself, in fact; he had a reputation for being the shrewdest card player in the Ransomville area. Strange for me to learn when I was a little older that Grandpa Wolpert had numerous friends and was considered a good-looking man, tall, broad-shouldered, with curly silvery hair and whiskers that bristled not only over his jaws but beneath his chin, sprouting out of his throat. His big chunky teeth were stained with nicotine, and his breath often stank from hard cider (which he distilled himself in one of the barns) and Old Bugler tobacco (which he chewed lustily in juicy wads the size of a baby's fist), but this made no difference apparently; Hiram Wolpert was a man others regarded with respect, even a bit of a ladies' man for the racy way he spoke with women, teased them and made them laugh with pleasure. What drew people to admire a man, I came to see, was a man's way of admiring himself. Grandpa Wolpert had a manly swagger, opinions he wasn't shy about expressing, a habit of interrupting others while never allowing himself to be interrupted. (My father had inherited some of this but on a smaller scale; he was in fact a smaller man, more tentative and more self-conscious than his father. And not a drinker.) Grandpa was a loyal friend and (it was said) an even more loyal enemy. If he liked you, he loved you; if not, better stay out of his way. He was a part-time blacksmith at a time

when 'smithing' was nearly extinct and farmers would come from everywhere in the Chautauqua Valley to have their horses shod in exchange,
sometimes, for nothing more than one or another bartered item—a crock
of whiskey, a handful of cigars, an unwanted piglet. Once, it was said,
Grandpa shod a half-dozen horses for a well-to-do farmer and would
accept from him no cash, only a used tire for his John Deere tractor.
Grandma Wolpert cursed him for being the worst kind of fool—"Thinks
he's everybody's friend. Giving away what he hasn't got."

Grandpa's blacksmith equipment was kept in a dank-smelling,
earthen-floored barn behind the house. I never knew the names of
things—a kind of circular free-standing fireplace made of nailed-together
strips of tin, a bellows operated by a crank that required strength to turn,
heavy cumbersome implements. There were an iron anvil, a pair of
enormous tongs, a twenty-pound sledgehammer with a coarse, splintery
handle that was too heavy for me to swing, tugging painfully at my arm
muscles even when I was twelve years old. When my brothers still came
out to the farm, my grandfather let them help him, stoking the smoldering cinder fire, hammering heated semisoft iron horseshoes into
shape, clucking and talking to the horses that, easily spooked, had to be
tightly tethered, their staring eyes shielded by blinders. I begged to be
allowed to help, too. I was fearful of the gigantic horses but determined
to be as brave as my brothers. I was stroking a mare's shivery, surprisingly furry side while my grandfather sat, back to the horse, on a
wooden box with the horse's left rear leg, ankle, and hoof secured tightly
between his knees as he hammered nails into the horse's hoof; what a
thrill of pride I felt until without warning the horse snorted in alarm,
shook her head and lurched toward me, and her left front hoof came
down on the edge of my foot, causing me to scream as if I were being
killed. "Grandpa! Grandpa! *Grandpa!*"

Grandpa Wolpert, grunting and cursing, wrestled the horse away. With
a slam of his fist against her head he seemed to stun her, and I was freed.

A miracle, everyone said, my toes hadn't been crushed, every bone in
my foot broken.

Rare for Grandma Wolpert to speak directly to my mother, fixing her
eyes upon my mother's strained face, but she spoke so that day, in angry
contempt, "That silly little thing, she's a *girl*. She's not to do *men's things* on
this farm."

★　　★　　★

A MAN WAS making love to me and I fell asleep. A toxic cloud drifted across my brain. I was trying to explain, but I could not speak. *I want to love you,* I pleaded. *Help me love you.* I felt the slap slap slap of the cornstalks against my damp face. I felt the dried, crumbling earth beneath my running feet. I heard the slap slap slap of the raw bread dough Grandma Wolpert slammed onto the plank counter. Her flour-smeared fingers, wrists the size of a man's, hefty thighs and that single shelf of bosom like a camel's hump it must have been so heavy, awkward, to bear. Her graying skinned-back hair and the unexploded fury in her face. The bread dough like unshaped life thrown down, kneaded, and twisted—slap! slap! slap!—and after it was baked in blackened tins there was something crabbed and gnarled about these coarse, whole-grain breads with thick crusts that seemed to speak of Grandma's soul. *Here I am—food. But I won't nourish you.*

A man was making love to me and I fell asleep. But I woke almost immediately, laughing. "Well, it *is* funny," I said, wiping at my eyes. "Isn't it?" But I was the only one laughing in that silence.

A VIVACIOUS PUBLIC MANNER suggests happiness in private. Or its opposite.

Why does Grandma Wolpert hate us, Mommy? I'd asked her innocently when I was three or four. At that age when you don't yet know what you're allowed to acknowledge you know and what you aren't. And seeing their exchange of glances, Mommy's quick frown. *Nobody hates us, what a thing to say! Isn't that a silly thing to say.* But I remember a kerosene lamp exploding in Grandma's kitchen. Though they would laugh at such a memory. *Exploding? don't be silly, one of you kids knocked it off the table.*

At Grandma Wolpert's funeral many years later I embarrassed my family by falling asleep. My head slumped, my mouth opened, I died. That delicious black-pit sleep. Maybe I'd had a few glasses of red wine beforehand, though the funeral was at 10:00 A.M., a February morning dark as twilight. I was twenty years old, or ten. I was three or four years old. Trying not to cry, I'd been pinched. Or was I trying not to laugh because I'd been tickled? Trying not to wet my panties, which is the hardest, most urgent thing not to do when you are three or four years old and sometimes older, as old as ten and no longer a baby.

She had a shiny creased face of perpetual fury. They said she was near-sighted but refused to be examined and fitted for glasses. She saw enough of what was there, by God. More than enough. It wasn't just the kerosene lamp she'd caused to explode but a slippery, soapy china platter that was wrenched from my fingers to shatter on the floor. *Clumsy! look what you've done.* (Helping with the dishes after one of the long, heavy Sunday after-noon meals when the air was still thick with food smells, waning clouds of tobacco from the men's pipes.) Mommy's bleeding finger, the knife-gouge in the ball of the thumb, oh, how did this happen? Oh, what happened? There was a way, brisk, efficient, you cut noodle dough in three-inch strips, flat on the table, a long, sharp-bladed knife moving in flashes. And eviscerating chickens after they'd been steamed and their feathers plucked, their scrawny necks lacking heads. There was a trick to it but what the trick was, Mommy never quite caught on. *Here, let me do it. Give me that knife.* In warm weather she sweated like a man, wiping globules of grease from her forehead and her upper lip, where coarse dark hairs, so few you could count them, sprouted. Her eyes, nearsighted or not, were fierce as slivers of glass reflecting fiery light. Body like a fortress trussed in a girdle with numerous straps, hooks, and eyes, and a "brassiere" (I would not learn this strange, exotic word until years later) like a horse harness. Her fleshy raddled legs, pulp-pale with broken blue veins like cobwebs, that had to be encased in flesh-colored "support" stockings. Muscular arms, stubby strong fingers. A blood-smeared apron. For she butchered chick-ens—this was her task and she took a zestful pride in it, almost, her only playfulness, ordering whichever boys were around (my brothers, or my cousins Joey, Luke, Jake) to round up several selected chickens, good spec-imens they had to be, not scrawny, lice-ridden, feathers missing where they'd been pecked and made to bleed by other hens but healthy-looking, with red combs, clear eyes, an alert hop to their step. The boys caught the squawking, wing-flailing red hens and brought them to Grandma at the chopping block with her ax. This was Grandma's ax and not Grandpa's and there'd be hell to pay if you messed with it. She was frowning now, grim and vexed, angry, scolding the very chicken laid upon the chopping block, for of course the creature was in a panic, of course the creature knew very well what was coming, and I saw the boys grimacing and grinning and bit-ing their lips, and I saw Grandma's face as she lifted, swung the ax, bring-ing the already stained blade down onto the chicken's neck, and I thought, *It helps to kill if you're angry.* I understood this to be a principle of adult life.

Except in the shadowy front parlor where we were rarely invited, even on Sundays, she didn't want us fussing in there, you kids causing a ruckus, and the men trailing in mud and manure (of course they wiped their feet before entering the house and it was Sunday, they hadn't been mucking about the barnyard, but no matter), on the wallpapered wall above the rock-hard horsehair sofa there was Grandma's and Grandpa's wedding photograph, which I contemplated in wonder and maybe in fear, for how could that girl, that square-jawed but almost pretty young girl, be Grandma Wolpert? With her solemn dark eyes, thick dark hair gathered in an elegant thick braid like a crown, with a shy half-smile, in a white wedding gown with a high neck, lace, satin ribbons, a bouquet of roses clutched in her white-gloved hand; and her handsome bridegroom beside her, taller by several inches, Hiram Wolpert in his early twenties with startling black thick-tufted hair, sideburns, a neatly trimmed mustache, in a suit and a tie, a white carnation in his lapel. "Is that really you, Grandma?" I asked, pointing, and my mother tugged at my arm saying quickly, mortified, "Miss! Mind your manners," but Grandma Wolpert just laughed, loud gut-laughter without evident malice, "That's me as I used to be. Gramma before she was Gramma. Before she was Ma. Nearer in age to you right now than your Ma is to you," and this scared me, for Grandma talked like a riddle sometimes, her silence bursting out into such puzzlements; you knew she meant something but what? Saying with a look of satisfaction, "Before she turned sow for breeding and suckling litters of you-know-what." And she laughed again, at the look on my mother's face.

You-know-what. What?

I was intrigued to learn that the girl in the wedding photograph had had a name of her own: Katrina. And a 'maiden' name: Sieboldt. One day I would learn that Katrina Sieboldt had been married to my grandfather Hiram Wolpert at the age of sixteen, she'd become a mother for the first time at seventeen (though the baby, a boy named Hiram, Jr., would live only a few months, his name to be passed on to the next-born boy, my father); of six known pregnancies she'd had two miscarriages and four children who survived. In her early thirties she had began to suffer from "female trouble" (of which no one in those days spoke openly, even within the family), by thirty-eight she'd become a grandmother, and old. The summer I was ten, Grandma Wolpert must have been only fifty-two. Fifty-two!

3. *The Cornfield*

I DIDN'T SEE the bloody corncob. If that was blood. I believe I didn't see it.

This was the summer I was ten.

My father came out to the farm Saturdays to help his father and Tyrone, for Grandpa Wolpert had had a hernia operation and was semi-crippled, cursing his bad luck. Repairing rotted fences, shoring up the old barns, slaughtering pigs. Harvesting bushel upon bushel of tomatoes, sweet peppers, squash to be trucked into Ransomville to a farm stand. There were fields of potatoes, wheat, corn to be harvested. Goddamned exhausting work, my father called it, yet he seemed to find it exhilarating, too. He was restless with his work in town (clerking weekdays in the hardware store he part-owned, with its dour, dusty front window whose display had been unchanged for as long as I could remember) and craved working outdoors. Sometimes, not often, out of duty or guilt or because my father insisted, Mom came along to help Grandma Wolpert with her endless task of canning, but my brothers and sister never came any longer. Grandpa Wolpert would ask, "Where's them kids?" staring as if surprised each time, but Grandma Wolpert, pursing her mouth as if she'd been proved correct in some old quarrel, never said a word.

This Saturday I'm thinking of, the men were out working and my boy cousins Luke and Jake trudged into Grandma's kitchen for some ice water. They lived only about a mile away on a country highway and bicycled to the farm to check out their trapline set along the creek. Luke was fifteen, Jake was twelve, husky boys with sand-colored hair, blunt, bullhead faces. They went shirtless all summer and were tanned, as Grandma said, in that way you couldn't judge was admiring or disgusted, dark as niggers. I yearned to be noticed by my older cousins, but they rarely paid attention to me. Now Grandma was saying, "G'on, take her along. She's got nothing better to do. *I* don't need her here." The boys balked, staring glumly at me. Grandma said, with that low, snorting laugh, "Nobody's going to hurt your precious *traps*, you two." These words would have been a riddle to me if I'd heard them, but I didn't. Later I would hear them; or so I believe. But not then. Nor did the boys seem to hear. Luke muttered what sounded like "Shit," and Jake whined, "We're in a hurry, Gram." They went out of the kitchen, letting the screen door slam, and Grandma yelled after them, "Big men, eh? You get the hell out of my house, you got no better manners." To me she said, shoving my shoulder with the flat of her hand—so rarely did Grandma touch me that this shove had the force of a caress—"Go on, go. Curiosity killed the cat."

I thought, *Good! Mommy isn't here.*

My mother would never have allowed me to go tagging after the boys. She didn't like them, and she didn't like their mother, my father's older sister Dell. Dell and Dad weren't "on speaking terms" for some reason so tangled and bitter, dragging more and more relatives into it, it would never be sorted out through the years. All this was in Luke's and Jake's faces though probably they knew as little of the quarrel as I did. Years later at Aunt Dell's funeral I would ask my mother what on earth that had been about, a quarter-century feud? And my mother would insist she knew nothing about it. "Those Wolperts! You know what they're like. *Crazy.*"

Yes. I knew.

Though exactly what I knew, I've never been certain.

Back behind my grandfather's barns, along a rutted lane, there were my boy cousins Luke and Jake, walking fast. They reminded me of young horses trotting along. Not looking back. They weren't going to wait for me; possibly they'd forgotten me. Whatever Grandma Wolpert had told them to do, they weren't going to do it. I ran after them but I didn't call to them. I was just a little girl in their eyes: in shorts, T-shirt, sneakers. At the farm, my fair, thin skin was vulnerable to sunburn, my arms and legs were stippled with insect bites, scratches from thorns and prickly bushes. The boys crossed through a cornfield, rows and rows of tall cornstalks, browning leaves and tassels blown in the wind, and on the ground crows pecking at fallen corncobs, so many crows. I was a little afraid of crows, mistaking them sometimes for sparrow hawks; these crows cawed angrily at us, annoyed by our intrusion, but didn't fly off. Where crows were sometimes pecking, on a road for instance, in a ditch, you wouldn't want to look for fear of seeing something dead, nasty. I'd looked, and I was always sorry. Now my eyes swung away from the crows and I thought *They're not big enough to hurt me. Their beaks aren't sharp enough.* But I doubt this was truly so.

All I could see of Luke and Jake was their heads above the tall grasses, their sand-colored hair. They were descending an overgrown path leading steeply down to the creek. I was breathless, panting. It was a bright, heat-shimmering day. It was late August. I thought, *They don't want you, why are you following them?* I did not really want to see the boys' traps. I'd seen

Grandpa's rusty traps hanging in the barn, I knew what traps were. Luke and Jake trapped rabbits, muskrats, and raccoons and sold their pelts for a few dollars. I did not really want to see the creatures they'd trapped, whose bodies they would toss into a burlap bag. But I pursued them. I was excited, as if this were a game, maybe it was a game, my cousins were testing me by walking fast, testing me to see if I could keep up with them, if I wasn't afraid. I'd come to the creek many times, often with my brothers, I loved the creek we called Grandpa's creek for it wouldn't occur to us that the creek wasn't Grandpa's, that everything on his property wasn't his. At this time of summer the creek was low, yet its current ran swiftly, noisily, down a slope of enormous rocks; there were churning foam-specked pools of deeper water and splashing streams of white-water rapids as if the wide creek were several creeks flowing together. In a marshy area beside the creek, tall cattails and marsh grasses grew lushly. It was a jungle. Everywhere a buzz of wasps, dragonflies. The glitter of dragonflies in the sun. Small, quick-darting goldfinches in the scrub willow beside the creek. I shielded my eyes from the glare of long strips of water in the marsh like slivers of broken mirror. I heard my cousins' voices murmuring in excitement; I found them crouched over something on the bank. "What is it? What did you catch?" I asked. Their backs were to me. Luke's bare tanned back damp with sweat, and his hair damp at the back of his neck. Jake leered at me. He was a smallish boy, homely, with what Mom called the Wolpert nose, broad and snubbed. I'd seen older boys, including Luke, shove him around, and I'd seen his own father curse him out and cuff him like a dog. He said, jeering, "C'mon and see, nosy." It looked like a soft, mangled cat with dark-streaked fur. But there was a long, curving, scaly tail—a rat? Muskrat? As Luke extricated the creature from the trap's jaws, Jake pretended to be petting it, mock-crooning, "Pus-sssy," enjoying my look of repugnance. Luke carelessly tossed the limp body into the burlap sack. "How much is that worth? Where do you sell them?" I asked. I was shivering with sudden cold but I hoped to show my cousins that I wasn't afraid or disgusted. I'd asked a question anyone might reasonably ask, but the boys ignored it, baiting the trap with a piece of green pear and setting its ugly saw-toothed jaws apart again, replacing it at the very edge of the creek bank. I was struck by my cousins' seriousness, this adult-male solemnity, so like the way my father worked using his hands, head lowered, intent upon his task so he wouldn't hear my questions. "Was that a muskrat?" I asked. "Is that what it is? The poor thing." Luke and Jake moved on, Luke with the sack over his shoulder, and I followed after. I was used to my brothers ignoring me, too. I said daringly, "Don't you feel sorry for that animal? What if it happened to *you?* Caught in a trap." The boys were stomping in the creek bed; the path on the bank was so overgrown with briars, after hesitating a moment I stepped into the creek too, in about four inches of lukewarm water. At once my toes felt strange, squishy. I didn't like that feeling. It was as if there was something in the toes of my sneakers, something disgusting like mashed potatoes, oatmeal that made me feel sick to my stomach. My sneakers were water-stained and filthy anyway from playing in the creek. Nobody walked in Grandpa's creek barefoot because of bloodsuckers, small filmy black worms that stuck between your toes, sharp rocks and chunks of broken glass that could cut your feet. There was swimming in the creek, but not here. "Somebody could come along," I called after my cousins, splashing ahead of me, "and spring your traps. So the animals wouldn't get hurt." Luke called back, "Oh, yeah? Somebody hadn't better or she'll get her skinny ass warmed." Jake, incensed, said, "Get her skinny ass *broke*." "How would you know who did it?" I said, taunting. "You wouldn't know." The boys located their next trap and discovered that the jaws were sprung, the bait eaten—but no prey. "Shit," Luke said. "Fuck*er*," Jake said, swearing like a grown man. I said, excited, "He got away! He's too smart for you." My face throbbed with heat, I was strangely excited as if this were a game. It seemed to me an accomplishment if my cousins took note of me, glared at me. Especially Luke. I watched him examining the trap as if it had deceived him, lifting and turning it in his grimy hands. His lank, sun-bleached hair fell into his face so that he was continually pushing it back. I saw a flash of kinky brown hair in his armpit, his tight-muscled arms, his skin tanned like stained wood, and the nipples of his chest darker, like berries. Why did men and boys have those things, I wondered, if they didn't nurse babies? My cousins were sweating, giving off a rank animal odor. My mother teased my father, saying that his country Wolpert relatives bathed only once a week—"Whether they need to or not." It was true you could sometimes see a film of grime on the backs of their hands, often on their necks like a grainy shadow. Grandpa Wolpert was like that. The dirt was most noticeable when rivulets of sweat trailed through it, like those streaking my cousins' bare, tanned backs. There was a scattering of pimples on Luke's back, some of them big as boils and some like little red berries that looked as if they'd be hot to touch.

It was at the next trap, on a higher embankment, that I heard the boys murmur in surprise, and I pushed forward to see what they'd found— another limp furry body caught between the jaws' teeth, a muskrat, its swollen belly slashed, and bloody, and a sac of wriggling hairless things no longer than my thumb inside. Was it slugs? Worms? Tiny babies? I didn't scream but I made a sound, and Luke and Jake turned to look at me with odd, half-shamed expressions, and Luke quickly dropped the furry body into the sack, crushed it beneath his foot, and laughed harshly. "Shouldn't look, you. Shouldn't be seeing such things," Luke said. His manner was strangely prim, his face flushed with blood. But Jake was giggling, "Yeah, you! You *shouldn't.*" Jake reached out and grabbed at my arm and left a smear of slimy blood on it. I screamed.

Jake laughed, chasing me up the hill. We were scrambling in loosened dirt, pebbles. Luke yelled for him to leave me alone but a minute later he came running after us, through a field, wild rose briars cutting at us like living claws, the boys were shouting and laughing, chasing me into a corn-field, I screamed in excitement, it was like tag, like hide-and-seek in the rows of tall cornstalks, like pom-pom-pull-away when one of the boys grabbed at my arm and the other grabbed at my hair but I managed to wriggle free, laughing, a vein beating in my throat. The boys picked up dried clods of earth and tossed them at me and at each other. They were yelling, laughing. Even Luke. I saw his shirtless figure rushing through the rows of cornstalks, I saw his head turn, he'd sighted me, I half-crawled on my hands and knees to escape, there came Jake almost colliding with Luke, Luke shouted, "Watch your ass, asshole!" giving his brother a shove that made him yelp in pain and stagger backward to fall to the ground landing, hard as a sack of laundry, on his rear. Funny! I was shrieking with laughter, and Luke was shrieking with laughter, turning to chase me, clapping his hands in pursuit—"Shoo! Shoo!" Sharp cornstalk blades cut against my face as I ran, soft-silky tassels of corncobs brushed against my face, between the rows of corn there were tall weeds, and the sky overhead a bright hazy blue in skidding patches, black flapping wings that frightened me rising on all sides and a harsh caw-cawing like angry scolding. I turned and ran to the right, then to the left, zigzagging by instinct, this was a game like tag, a game like hide-and-seek I played with my sister and brothers, an innocent game like pom-pom-pull-away in the schoolyard. My face was burning, bits of dirt and grit stuck to it like ticks. From out of nowhere in front of me, there was my cousin Luke. He'd run ahead of me to cut me off, chunky yellowish teeth bared in a dog's grin, but I scrambled sideways, I was quick and crazed as a wild, hunted animal, but behind me there was another boy—shirtless, his skinny dark chest sleek with sweat, and for a moment I believed this was a third boy, a stranger, not Jake, my cousin Jake, but of course it was Jake, though his dirty grinning face wasn't a face I seemed to recognize, and his clownish pop-eyes. And there was Luke's flushed face, his laughing teeth, his angry teeth, why was he angry, and that sharp frown between his eyebrows like a knife blade the way an adult man might frown, the way my father frowned when one of his children displeased him, that staring frown of wrath. Luke grabbed at me but was able to catch only my T-shirt, the neck and the sleeve of my T-shirt he ripped, I was swinging my fists at his middle, at his chest, we were on the ground wrestling, crashing against the brittle cornstalks, dried corncobs hard and hurting beneath my back, my bottom, Luke grunted, cursing me, straddling me, holding me tight as a vise with his thighs, he was tickling me with something hard and scratchy, something his fingers had closed over, and Jake was crouched over us panting, cursing, yet happy, tugging at one of my ankles, tugging at my shorts which he managed to yank down only a few inches before his way was stopped by Luke's tight-pressed knee. I smelled the strong animal sweat on their bodies, I smelled my own suddenly released hot pee, I screamed and kicked Jake in the belly, between the legs so he whimpered with pain, Luke was laughing wildly, tickling-poking at me with that hard scratchy object, I didn't see it, I don't believe I saw it, only the confused recollection afterward of an object consisting of hundreds of tiny eyes, except the crows had pecked away most of the eyes, there were rows of tiny gouged-out eyes, it was hurting me, under my arms, my tummy, between my legs, between the cheeks of my buttocks where I was tender, where I could bleed, I was kicking, squealing, except Luke had pressed his salty-sweaty palm over my mouth to shut me up, his face was strained like a fist clenched tight, his jaws were clenched tight, I saw his eyes rolling white and I screamed through the hard hurting flat of his hand, and in that instant the earth opened up, it was a black soft-melting pit into which I fell, like falling asleep in church, my head pitching forward suddenly, the cornfield was still bright with light, dazzling and blinding with light, and the patches of sky overhead, but I wasn't there to see, my boy cousins grunting and cursing but I wasn't there to hear.

★   ★   ★

OF THE FAIRY TALES of my childhood in a brightly illustrated book I read practically to shreds, the one I most feared was "Sleeping Beauty." I stared with grim fascination at the enchanted princess on her bed in the forest and thought how such a thing could happen to any little girl, it could happen to me. Snow White had fallen asleep in one of the dwarves' beds but that was all right, she wasn't under an evil spell, she woke up when the dwarves came home. Goldilocks, too, was wakened when the three bears discovered her in the littlest bear's bed. But Sleeping Beauty was under a spell cast by an ugly old woman fairy and she slept for years because no one could wake her, and then she was wakened only by a special prince and would never have wakened without him. I hated the story of "Sleeping Beauty." Yet I read it, and reread it, and stared at the illustration of the beautiful blond-haired princess who looked as if she were floating in her bed in the forest. No other fairy tale was so awful. Because it could happen, I thought. Every time you went to bed at night, or lay down for a nap—it could happen. You could fall asleep and never wake up. For not all girls would attract a prince to wake them. Most of us would sleep, sleep, and sleep forever with no kiss to revive us.

"HEY. Wake up. C'mon."

"Come *on*."

They were hunched over me, and now they weren't laughing. My boy cousins. Luke was lightly slapping my cheeks, he'd splashed water onto my burning skin, brushed my hair off my forehead. Such comfort I took in those hands. I wanted to cry. I might have been crying. Jake was resting back on his heels, he looked scared, his own face smeared with dirt, sweat, blood from where he'd been wiping it roughly with his arm. I saw the filmy no-color sky behind Luke's head but I didn't know where I was. Not in the cornfield, they must have carried me out of the cornfield, down to the creek bank where Luke was muttering to himself, splashing water onto my face, begging me to wake up, *wake up*. I'd never heard such urgency in a boy's voice before. Luke was trying clumsily to wash me—face, arms, legs. As if I were a baby, even a doll, lying motionless on her back. The ground was pebbly beneath me and hurt. But much of my body was numb. My belly, between my legs. I had the confused idea they'd gotten big chunks of ice from Grandma's icebox and pressed them against me so I couldn't feel anything. Behind Luke, Jake was sniffling and whining,

"She's gonna tell them, what if she tells them, we're gonna get hell," and Luke cursed his brother without turning, "Asshole, shut *up*." Luke was hunched over me, shaking me gently, the way you'd shake a deep-sleeping child to wake her. "Hey, c'mon, wake up, you're OK. You fell asleep up there. You got tired running, and the sun—it's like heatstroke. Your face is all hot. Your skin's burning. You had a nap. You're OK now. OK? You just fell asleep."

I was trying to wake up. But it was like swimming to the surface of the water, the weight of the water pressing against my chest, and my eyelids heavy.

How long, I would not know. Probably not more than ten or fifteen minutes. *She's gonna tell* the one voice intoned and the other *Wake up, hey, c'mon, you're OK.* My shirt was damp and smeared with dirt from the cornfield, my shorts and panties—I'd wet my panties, and Luke didn't act disgusted but splashed water onto me there, to disguise the smell. For otherwise I would be so ashamed. Ten years old, wetting my panties. I would say I'd fallen into the creek, I'd been wading, following after my cousins, and I'd fallen into the creek, that was why I was so wet, and maybe I'd hurt myself on the rocks, the sharp edges of rocks in the creek bed. And the boys would say yes, that was what happened. I should not have been following after them as they checked their trapline, that was what happened.

I was sitting up, I was confused and dazed but I was awake, and I was all right. Luke grinned at me, as if he'd performed a miracle. I wasn't crying, and I wasn't bleeding. Or if I'd been crying, now I'd stopped. For I still wanted them to like me—I wanted these older boys not to hate me. If I'd been bleeding, now I'd stopped. It was a sharp rock I'd fallen on, those outcroppings of slate like knife blades. But I might not have been bleeding, it might have been blood from the dead or dying animal that Jake had gotten onto his hands and wiped on me. Even if I seemed to remember, I could not know. For just to remember something is not to know if it really happened. That is a primary fact of the inner life, the most difficult fact with which we must live.

4. *The Bull Jumps the Fence*

Why did Grandma Wolpert hate me? I was thirty-nine years old and my mother was saying, her eyes fixed on mine with a look of utter sincerity, "Why, it wasn't you that woman hated; where did you get that idea? It was your grandfather. Your grandfather was so fond of you, so to get back at him, rankle him, the way those two were forever poking and prodding each other, Grandma Wolpert was sometimes a little—mean, maybe— harsh with you. Sometimes. And you did so well in school, all A's, and she couldn't even read—you know, she never learned. None of the girls in her family learned to read, can you imagine? At first it was ignorance, simple backcountry ignorance, then it was her pride. That woman was *proud*. But you're exaggerating, I think. The way you do. That 'social psychology' work of yours—you take an idea and fuss with it instead of some other idea, and emphasize it so—but of course what do I know, listen to me. Except about Grandma: yes, she could be sort of sarcastic, mean, I suppose, but not just to you, to all of us, even Dad she was so partial to. But see, hon—" my mother was saying, smiling, in a sudden glow of an idea, "—it was never anything personal directed against *you*. Not ever."

I smiled at my mother. I was grateful that my father was out of the room. "Well. That's good to know."

My mother. At the edge of elderly. In her eighth decade. Yet seated poised on the sofa like someone at the edge of a stream of rushing, churning, noisy water, foam-flecked water, water that will bear her away to oblivion, smiling as she advances a toe to test its temperature, as if she'll have the choice to step into that stream or remain safe on the bank. Saying, "It IS good to know, I think. But I've been telling you all along, haven't I? Like the other night, on the phone. Scaring us half to death, the way you looked on TV. All that 'back there' is ancient history. Nobody ever talks of those days anymore. Not around here. We've got plenty to talk about, your dad and me! The grandchildren—our property tax being hiked up again—"

"But why was Grandma Wolpert so angry? At Grandpa, I mean."

"*I* don't know," my mother said evasively, with a hurt, pouty expression as if she were about to cry. "Why always ask *me*? That woman has been dead for twenty years. That woman wasn't my mother, thank God."

I might have wished to say, No. *You were my mother.*

A strange logic. A riddle. But what point to such a riddle, after so many years?

This was in the old house in Ransomville, following Aunt Dell's funeral. The old house actually looks rather new from the road, matte-white aluminum siding, a six-foot plate-glass window overlooking the enormous front lawn, a new carport my father built himself. The suburban lawn he keeps neatly trimmed on his deafening John Deere mower ridden high in the saddle like a tractor. As soon as we returned to the house, my mother removed her purplish-black silk jacket and kicked off her black patent leather pumps with a sigh while Dad went to change into old, comfortable work clothes that fitted him like pajamas. As if to say *Well, that's it. Another funeral. Till the next one.*

I hadn't intended to come home for Aunt Dell's funeral, of course; the timing was coincidental.

After the incident at Lincoln Center, when I seem to have upset my parents, I thought I'd better come home for a few days. I'd felt a powerful, childish urge to come home. For just a few days.

Tell me you love me. Always, you'd loved me.

You didn't know. If you'd known . . .

. . . you would have protected me. You and dad.

Not that I was anxious or unwell. I'd immediately returned to work the following day. Work has always been my strategy. For the sleep fugue, the incident backstage, was nothing, really nothing; I'd already forgotten it. My agitated night and the incoherent journal entry I'd scribbled for hours and a few days later tossed out in bemused disgust—I'd already forgotten.

I visit my parents two or three times a year. They never leave Ransomville. In their generation, in the Chautauqua Valley, no one is comfortable traveling more than short distances by car. Airports are too confusing, airplanes too "dangerous." Things are "nice and quiet, peaceful" right at home.

Mom had assured me that Dad and his older sister Dell had "made it up" at the end, but that seemed doubtful to me judging from Dad's stiffness with Dell's family. And the slow grudging greetings they'd bestowed on me. The mood of the funeral had been leaden and melancholy, tinged with bitterness rather than grieving. For Aunt Dell had been a difficult woman in her old age and she'd been sick for a long time. Seventy-seven at the time of her death, she'd looked (as relatives murmured pityingly) "so much older, poor thing." It was perceived to be a "blessing at last" that she'd died, and was at peace.

At the margins of such funerals there are invariably certain individuals, usually young people, in-laws, or older, disaffected male relatives, in whose strained or expressionless faces you can detect an air of resentment simply at having to be there, at a depressing church service, in a dripping-wet cemetery, at all. I took note of these individuals but I did not align myself with them, I was the Wolpert daughter who'd left the valley, gone away, and made what you'd call a career for herself somehow. The Wolpert girl whose parents complained they rarely saw her but of whom they were proud nonetheless. *She has her own life, she always has. Always independent. Who she takes after, we don't know.*

At the reception at the funeral home yesterday evening, Dad had surprised me, and unsettled me a little, with his blustery, grimly humorous manner. Maybe he hadn't hated Dell, maybe he'd loved Dell, or a girl he remembered as Dell a lifetime ago when they'd both been young, sassy, and good-looking. Dad had been drinking and was working his mouth wetly in that way he's developed; possibly it has to do with imperfectly fitting dentures, possibly it's just a mannerism—I must take care not to imitate it for I'm susceptible to such contagion from people with whom I'm close. There he was nudging the funeral director, a man of youngish middle-age, saying in a lowered voice, "You sizing me up for one of these, eh, friend?"—meaning the shiny black casket containing his sister's body. "Well, not just yet, friend, *I'm still kickin'.*" And he laughed, a startled wheezing laugh at the look on the younger man's face.

There was my cousin Joe whom I hadn't seen in decades, a bulky, balding, aging man with a cane who'd once looked like Eddie Fisher. He shook my hand in a way that indicated he wasn't accustomed to shaking women's hands, with a quizzical half-smile—"Saw your name and photo in some magazine a while back, maybe *Time?* In the doctor's office." Luke wasn't there. Nor was Jake, who'd died in a gun accident (in Alaska, where he'd moved in his late twenties). Where was Luke, people were inquiring, and it wasn't certain: he'd been living in Pittsburgh for a while but might've moved after his divorce, it was hard on Dell that he'd lost contact with the family. It was Joe who had the most recent news of him, but that was three years ago at least when he "hadn't been well, had some health complications." What these complications were, I didn't learn. I perceived in my Wolpert relatives' eyes an eagerness to change the subject.

"Luke was always my favorite cousin of the boys," I said. "He was quiet. He didn't tease. He—" But I couldn't say, *His touch had been gentle, not rough, waking me.* I couldn't say, *The other one, Jake, might've killed me, I think. Maybe I'm exaggerating. But that's what I've always thought. But not Luke. Never Luke.*

Of course, over the years, visiting Ransomville, I'd made inquiries about my cousins, as one might expect of me. Always discreetly, circuitously asking after the girls first and then after Joe, Luke, and Jake, equal emphasis upon all, in a casual tone. Once, a dozen years ago, my father remarked philosophically that Luke had done pretty well for himself considering, and immediately I asked what did that mean, *considering*, and my father said vaguely, "Well, you know he'd gotten in some trouble after he was discharged from the navy. Before he married that girl from Watertown. You remember that." "No, Daddy," I said casually, "I didn't know. What kind of trouble?" Sucking at his lips, not meeting my eye, Dad said, "Well, I don't know, exactly. Old Dell and me, we don't exactly communicate." I let this remark pass; as if there weren't plenty of Wolperts and others to circulate news, particularly bad news. I just smiled at Dad, innocently perplexed. And then, later during that visit, Dad said, as if just remembering, "Your cousin Luke, you know—he got in some trouble with a young girl, it was said. At Olcott Beach. Not that there was a trial, or anything in the paper." "How young was the girl?" I asked. Dad sucked at his lips, seeming not to know, and Mother in the kitchen leaned out and said, "They can make any kind of accusation, you know. High school girls. There'd been one right here in Ransomville, remember? I had my doubts about that." "A girl accusing Luke?" I asked. "When was this?" Annoyed, Dad said, "He was just in high school himself, for God's sake." Mother said, "What difference does that make? You never know who to believe, you can't trust a certain kind of girl." "Yes, but Luke did pretty well for himself, I always say," Dad said, raising his voice to discourage Mother from arguing, "the only boy of that family I ever liked. Give him credit. He'd been a good husband and father, people said." Mother disappeared back into the kitchen, and Dad winked at me good-naturedly, saying, "Of course people will say any kind of bullshit, and some of it even true, you've got to suppose. Sometimes." The wink was to assure me that he and I had an understanding that excluded poor Mother, yes?

Now, after Aunt Dell's funeral, Dad came into the living room yawning and stretching. He'd been overhearing part of my conversation with Mother and said, "That Grandpa of yours. 'The bull jumps the fence.'" He laughed, and I asked what did that mean—"The bull jumps the fence." He said, "Just what it says. A bull will jump a fence if he can, or he'll break a fence if he can, if he has to—to get to mate with a cow. That was old Hiram." He laughed again, as Mother made a signal of disgust. "He had a woman friend? He was unfaithful to Grandma?" I asked. "Hell, he had *women*. And I don't mean *friends*." Rising from the sofa, Mother said, "I don't care to hear this, frankly. It's ancient history and none too pleasant." "That was why Grandma was angry with him? He was unfaithful to her?" I asked. "*Unfaithful*—you wouldn't use a word like that to apply to old Hiram," Dad said, vastly amused. "Not to him or any of the men in his family." Mother said, smiling at me, "Honey? You come out into the kitchen with me, we'll start dinner. Come *on*." She tugged at my hands as if I was a little girl, and like a little girl I leapt to my feet to follow her into the kitchen.

What comfort, even at the age of thirty-nine, in a mother's soft-grasping, firm hands. What comfort to be called, after so much time apart, "honey."

FOR THIS IS a fact I've learned that has surprised me a little: we come to love our parents more as we grow older together, in a kind of jolting lock-step. Realizing at the midpoint of our lives, looking at them looking anxiously at us, *My God. We're all in this together.*

5. An Alternative Ending

THE STRANGEST IDEAS in my head, sometimes when I'm partly asleep, but sometimes when I'm fully awake, I've shared with no one.

Such as: I've been operated on in secret, the lower part of my body anesthetized, and my insides ingeniously arranged. Or, so vivid in my memory I must have dreamed it more than once, there's a sac of slippery hairless wriggling little creatures inside me.

If I shared fantasies. But I don't share fantasies.

And I don't confuse fantasies with reality. In my profession, in order to help others—and helping others is the point of my profession—you learn to separate fantasy from reality in your own life as well as in the lives of others.

My cousins are in Grandma's kitchen gulping down glasses of ice water, bare-chested, sweaty, crowding each other at the sink, and Grandma says in that scolding way of hers you couldn't always judge was it only just scolding or was it part-affectionate, as close to affection as the woman could bring herself with human beings as with animals including the very animals she butchered, Enough now, you two, go on out, and I'm at the round bare-board kitchen table helping Grandma prepare that special dessert of hers where you fry big thin round pancakes in a heavy iron skillet in butter and fill them with sugared black cherries and sour cream and bake them on cookie sheets, and the boys run out letting the screen door slam and I ask, Where are they going, Grandma? *and Grandma says,* Never mind, you stay here with me. You don't want to be tramping around the fields with those big boys, *and so I stay in the kitchen with Grandma helping her bake. All afternoon.*

It might have happened that way. Maybe it was meant to happen that way. But then, what would have been my life?

SECRET, SILENT

$\mathcal{H}$e was telling me he couldn't drive me to the interview after all. Saying, "I know I promised, honey. But I don't see how, things being what they are, this can be." And I hear these words but can't at first believe them. For I'm hurt as a child is hurt, slapped with no warning in the face, and I'm hurt as a seventeen-year-old is hurt, in my pride. Wanting to cry, *You promised! You can't do this! I thought you loved me.*

It was an evening in April. We were in one of the rooms of the upstairs house as we called it. And we were having this conversation that would alter my life, anyway Dad was having it, informing me on Thursday evening that he couldn't after all drive me three hundred twenty miles across the daunting breadth of New York state for an interview at Albany State University where I'd been awarded something called a Founders' Scholarship for tuition, room, and board provided I completed my application with an interview on campus—which interview had been scheduled, after numerous telephone calls, for Saturday morning at eleven o'clock. To arrive at the university by that time we would have had to leave home no later than four o'clock in the morning. Yet now Dad was telling me he'd have to work on Saturday morning; his foreman at the tool shop wanted him, for time-and-a-half wages, which couldn't be turned down. *Things being what they are* meaning he needed the money, our family needed the money, he hadn't any choice.

Nor could my mother drive me. "You know I can't be away from Grandma for so many hours."

I told Mom yes, I knew.

"Please look at me! I'm talking to you."

I told Mom yes, I knew she was talking to me.

"I know you're disappointed, but it can't be helped. When you're older you'll understand, things happen to us that can't be helped. Poor Grandma—"

I wasn't listening. At the time I didn't understand how my mother was terrified of her own mother's dying, though Grandma was eighty years old and had been ill for years; how despite all circumstances, and some of them grim, there's a profound distinction between being a woman who still has her mother and being a woman who does not. What I heard of my mother's plea was *Things happen. Can't be helped. When you're older you'll understand.* That deadly refrain. That litany of defeat. My young heart beat hard in defiance, *Oh no I won't, not me!*

"I'VE FIGURED OUT a way I can get to Albany, without Daddy driving me. By Greyhound bus."

"So far? Alone?"

"I won't be alone, Mom. There's another girl in my class—" with ease I supplied the name, an acquaintance, not a friend, a name my mother might recognize, "—who's going to be interviewed, too. I asked around at school today. Her father can't drive her, either."

All that day I'd planned this, these very words. To be spoken without reproach or rancor, simply a statement of fact. *There are other fathers who can't help their daughters at such crucial times. It's an ordinary matter to be remedied in ordinary, practical ways.* I'd called the Greyhound station: there was an overnight bus that left Port Oriskany at 11:10 P.M. that night, made numerous stops along the Thruway and arrived in Albany at 7:50 A.M. tomorrow. Presumably, passengers slept on the bus.

My mother stared at me, I was so effervescent, so happy, all smiles; so very different from the way I'd been the previous evening, and from my truest most secret self. I expected her to object to such an adventure, my traveling such a distance, overnight, meeting with strangers in a city where we knew no one, had no relatives, and in fact Mom did object, but weakly, saying she didn't think it was a good idea for young girls to be traveling by themselves, but Dad shrugged and declared it was fine with him—"Hell, the girl's no fool, she can take care of herself." He was relieved, obviously. He needn't feel any guilt now. Fondly he squeezed my shoulder, he called me "sweetheart."

In this way, it was decided.

2

DAD DROVE ME to the Greyhound station that night. The bus, which looked massive, spouting exhaust in a bluish cloud, was already boarding when we arrived at eleven o'clock. Dad had been drinking after supper and his handsome, ravaged face was flushed but he was nowhere near drunk, only in good spirits; he'd probably be dropping by one of his taverns before returning home. First, he saw his daughter off for her interview, gave me a big hug and a wet kiss on the side of my face and told me, "Take care, sweetheart! See you tomorrow." There was no sign of my classmate, whoever she was supposed to be, but Dad wasn't suspicious as Mom would have been. He seemed to believe me when I pretended to be pointing out someone on the bus, waving happily to her—"There's Barbara. She's saving me a seat."

Most of the passengers were men traveling by themselves, but there were several women, among them, hurrying late to board, a striking young woman who might have been in her mid-twenties, with crimped auburn hair and thin arched eyebrows and a very red, moist mouth. She called out, "Driver, wait for me, *please!*" This was intended as a flirtatious joke, for the bus driver wasn't about to leave just yet; he laughed and assured the young woman she'd gotten there in time, and did she need help with her suitcase?

I was several passengers ahead of this woman, making my way along the bus aisle, but I observed through the windows that, as she hurried past my father out on the pavement, the two of them glanced searchingly at each other. Their gazes held for a long moment as if they were waiting to recall that they knew each other. So the young woman in staccato high heels climbed up into the bus, breathless, with an air of entering a space in readiness for her, like a stage; she took for granted that people would be looking at her, women and men both, and was careful to make eye contact with no one. By this time most of the single seats had been taken. I'd found one of the last ones, toward the rear of the bus; I glanced back at the auburn-haired young woman hoping she'd follow me and sit with me, but she didn't notice me, and took a seat with one of the better-dressed men passengers who'd risen gallantly to give her the window seat.

They were three seats ahead of me on the other side of the aisle. I would hear them talking together for the next forty minutes as the Greyhound heaved its way through Port Oriskany streets and out to the Thruway. The man's voice was indistinct but persistent; he did most of the talking; the young woman's responses were few, and punctuated by nervous laughter. I wondered how it was possible to fall so quickly into conversation with a stranger; there was something thrilling in it, risky and dramatic.

I'd brought with me *The Plays of Eugene O'Neill* and was midway into that strange, surreal play *The Hairy Ape* which was so very different from the other O'Neill plays I'd struggled through, and fascinating to me, for I believed I would like to write plays someday; but my attention was drawn repeatedly to the couple several seats ahead, particularly to the auburn-haired young woman. Who was she? Why was she traveling alone on an overnight bus to—where? The bus's final destination was New York City. I wanted to think she was headed there. She had the looks and style (I thought) to be an actress or a showgirl of some kind. I'd had an impression of a fine-boned profile, a delicate nose, wavy shoulder-length hair, and the sharp gleam of gold earrings. She'd been wearing a dark blue raincoat shot with iridescent threads which she'd removed with some ceremony when she took her seat, folding it and placing it in the overhead rack with her bags. Around her neck she'd knotted a stylish silk scarf, crimson peonies on a cream-colored background. I was curious to know what her companion was saying to her so earnestly, but there was too much noise from the bus's motor; it was like trying to hear my parents' murmurous voices through a wall, mysterious and teasing. I had the idea that the man was offering the young woman a drink from a bottle or flask in a paper bag and that she'd declined more than once. (Alcohol was forbidden on the bus.) My heart pounded with a sudden thrill of excitement. I'd deceived my parents, and they would never know. I would escape their plans for me, whatever those plans were, or were not: my mother had several times said plaintively that it was too bad my scholarship at Albany couldn't be "cashed in"—we could certainly use the money to help pay my grandmother's medical bills.

Most of the other passengers had settled in to sleep by midnight; only a few, like me, had switched on overhead lights to read. The auburn-haired young woman and her companion sat in semidarkness. I'd begun to lose interest in them when I heard a woman's voice sharply raised—"No, *sir.*" A man said, "Eh? What's wrong?" trying to laugh. But already the young woman was out of her seat, determined to leave. "Go to hell, mister." She grabbed her coat and the smaller of her bags from the overhead rack and, incensed, began to make her way toward the rear of the bus. Behind her the man stood, protesting, "Hey wait, hey c'mon—I was only kidding. Don't go away mad." The bus had begun to slow; up front, the driver must have been watching through his rearview mirror, ready to intervene. The young woman stood beside my seat panting and glaring at me. "D'you mind?" she demanded, and before I could tell her no, of course not, she swung into the seat heavily. "That bastard. That *son of a bitch.*" She ignored the scrutiny of others close about her as, charged with outrage as with static electricity, she ignored me. Her oversized handbag of simulated lizard skin was crowding against my legs and her clumsily bunched coat was pressed against me. I'd moved over toward the window as far as I could. I was flattered she'd come to sit with me, even if she hadn't exactly chosen me, and hardly dared speak to her for fear of being rebuffed. Finally, seeing that the man in the seat up ahead had given up, she stood, folded her coat and placed it in the overhead rack, smoothed the long sexy angora sweater she was wearing down over her hips, and sat down again. Her movements were fussy, showy, self-dramatizing. She said, with a side-long glance at me and a tight smile, "Thanks! I appreciate it. That bastard mistook me for someone I'm *not.*"

"I'm sorry."

"*I'm* not sorry. These damned buses!"

I was somewhat overwhelmed by her. Close up, she was beautiful. Her smooth creamy skin that seemed poreless, unlike my own; her thick-lashed mascaraed eyes; that glistening of female indignation of a kind I could never express except in mimicry or parody. "I don't know why I expect anything better on a damned *bus,*" she was saying. "It's not exactly first-class travel accommodations on the New York Central Pullman. You'd think by now I'd *know.*" I was tempted to tell her that she hadn't needed to sit with that man, or with any man at all. Instead I said again that I was sorry she was upset, but probably he'd let her alone now. "I'm not *upset, I'm disgusted,*" she said quickly. "I can take care of myself, thank you." But this wasn't a rebuff, evidently, for a moment later she asked, "What's that you're reading?" I showed her the opened pages and she frowned at the small print as if nearsighted. " 'Hairy *Ape*'? Jesus. Never heard of that, what's it about?" I tried to explain, so far as I knew, which wasn't very far, that it was a play set on an ocean liner and there was a fierce, muscular man named Yank Smith who worked with the furnaces and he was proud of himself as a man who made the ship go until—"He turns into an ape, huh? Sure! There's been a movie of that, I bet. I've seen it. I've seen *him*. Don't tell *me*," the woman said, laughing. I had to laugh with her. Amid a scent of talcum and warm flesh there was a mild sourness as of whiskey lifting from her. "My name's Karla with a 'K.' What's your name?" I'd drawn back the heavy book that seemed embarrassing to me now. "I'm Kathryn. With a 'K.' " She said, "I'm going to Albany, what about you?" I said, "I'm going to Albany, too." She said, "I've got important business in Albany, what about you?" I said, "I guess I do, too." She asked where I lived and I told her, and I asked where she lived and she said, stiffly, she was between cities—"But not Albany. That's for damned sure." She added, loud enough for her ex-companion to hear if he was listening, "We should sleep then, best we can, and not let any assholes trouble us." Without waiting for my reply Karla reached up and switched out the overhead lights.

I'd shut the book anyway. I wouldn't have been able to concentrate.

THE ROMANCE OF night travel by bus. When you're alone, and no one. The thrill of such aloneness. The strange headachey insomniac nights of such aloneness. I tried to sleep, my eyes shutting upon a kaleidoscope of broken, bright images. I thought—My head is a doll's head, my eyes are glass eyes that open and shut but not with my volition. Through my eyelashes I saw headlights appearing and disappearing like lone comets on the mostly deserted Thruway. Outside was a steeply hilly landscape, dimly visible by clouded moonlight. Living in such a landscape, as I'd done since birth, you don't need to see it to know it's there. *How happy I am. How scared, and how happy.*

It was 3:10 A.M. when the Greyhound lumbered off the Thruway to stop at an all-night service station and restaurant. Karla, who'd been sleeping, woke and poked me in the arm with unexpected sisterly solicitude. "You awake? C'mon, we got ten minutes." There was a parched taste like dried glue at the back of my mouth. It was a relief to be fully awake and on my feet. Only a few other passengers climbed out of the bus with us, most remained sleeping. Outside, the air was a shock, so damp and cold. Though this was the last week in April, a fine gritty sleet was being blown across the pavement. Beyond the dull-glaring fluorescent lights on their tall poles illuminating the service station and the restaurant there was nothing, as in a stage set. Neither Karla nor I had troubled to put on a coat and we ran shivering toward the restaurant. I saw that Karla was barely my height in her impractical high-heeled ankle-strap shoes. Her coral-pink angora sweater fitted her slender body snugly at her breasts and hips; to emphasize her small waist, she wore a tightly cinched shiny black belt; her skirt, not quite reaching her knees, was some shimmery synthetic fashion, dark crimson. "*Don't* look at asshole, he's poison," Karla warned me out of the side of her mouth, like a tough girl in the movies. The man she'd been sitting with had gotten to the restaurant entrance before us and was standing by the door holding it open for us, staring at Karla with doggy reproachful eyes. I supposed he was drunk, he had that look. But it wasn't possible for me to ignore him as Karla did; I couldn't be rude. "Thank you," I murmured as Karla and I slipped inside.

The man's lips moved. His face remained expressionless. I didn't exactly hear what he murmured after me—*Don't bounce your tits, honey.*

I didn't acknowledge this. So maybe I hadn't heard. I was grateful that Karla hadn't.

The restaurant was nearly empty, only a single section was open for service, and a single counterman in a soiled white uniform. Karla ordered "decaf"—"and make sure it's decaf, man, not coffee, OK?"—and a large jelly doughnut covered in powdered sugar which she insisted I share with her—"I certainly don't intend to eat this thing all by *myself*." Consuming the jelly doughnut with the counterman and other customers looking on was a performance of some hilarity. I wasn't hungry but managed, with Karla's encouragement, to swallow a few mouthfuls, which tasted like mashed dough laced with sweet, vile chemicals. Close by at the counter, the youngish bus driver in his Greyhound uniform observed us smilingly. And other men observed us. "This night!" Karla exclaimed. Though speaking to me, she was speaking to be overheard. Yet she seemed sincere, her smooth forehead creased for the moment. Drinking hot coffee, even decaffeinated, diluted with cream and sugar, seemed to enliven her; her eyes, which were a hazy green-brown, were widened and oddly dilated. "Jesus God, Kathryn! I have crucial business in Albany and already it's 3:20

A.M. Feels like I been awake and going for *days*." Sitting on a stool at the counter, legs crossed, sheer black stockings giving a sexy glisten to her shapely legs, Karla turned in restless half-circles. She fell into a spirited conversation with the bus driver, who seemed to have known her from somewhere, and the counterman, a taffy-skinned young black or Hispanic with deep circles beneath his eyes but an infectious laugh. In the joking and laughter that followed—what was funny exactly, I didn't know—espe-cially with the dour doggy man from the bus, Karla's ex-seatmate, sitting on a stool at the edge of our hilarity—the counterman asked me if I was Karla's kid sister and what were "you girls" doing in the middle of the night in the middle of Nowhere, USA? He made an eloquent gesture with his hand to indicate the bleak, tacky expanse of the restaurant, all Formica and plastic surfaces, a space large as a warehouse but semidarkened now and nearly empty of customers. Near the bright-lit entrance to the rest rooms a lone cleaning woman was mopping. What if this is all the world adds up to finally, I thought: a lone woman mopping a grimy floor in the middle of the night in the middle of Nowhere. I felt the horror of this vision but heard myself laugh in Karla's bright way. I said, "We have secret business, don't we, Karla? We can't tell." It was a clumsy, blushing flirta-tion. I might have been thirteen years old. Karla didn't help me, saying with a frown as if distancing herself from a reckless younger sister, "*I* can't tell. I sure as hell can't see into the future that's black as *ink*."

I remembered a line I'd written in my journal, copied from a library book; the author was Thomas Mann (of whom I'd only just heard, had never read) and this was taken from a letter to his son. *The secret and almost silent adventures in life are the finest.*

"D'YOU MIND?"

Back on the bus Karla climbed luxuriously into the seat beside the win-dow that had been mine, and curled up to sleep. Of course I didn't mind, and wouldn't have spoken if I had.

The remainder of the night passed in dreamy jolts and blurs. Karla slept like a cat; breathed deeply and evenly, low as a cat's purr; before long she nudged her head against my shoulder; I was stirred that a stranger should so trust herself with me. On the floor was the lizard skin bag pressing against my legs. I would have liked to look inside. In the women's room back at the restaurant I'd caught a glimpse inside the bag of a jumble of items including a plastic makeup kit, a bottle of red nail polish, the metallic handle of what might have been a knife but was probably a cheap hair-brush. And there was Karla's wallet, thick with snapshots and a wad of bills.

In the stark solitude of the night I could hear the snores and occasional mutterings of strangers. Earlier I'd told Karla where I was going, hoping to impress her, but now I was beginning to feel anxiety about my plan. An interview that would decide my college career (for so I thought at that time) after a night spent like a vagrant on a bus; without even a change of clothes, because I hadn't wanted to carry so much. I planned to use the women's room at the Greyhound station in Albany to "freshen up"—my mother's term. I'd remembered to bring a stick of deodorant, but didn't have a toothbrush. Even if my nerves kept me alert and awake I was certain to be exhausted by eleven o'clock in the morning after virtually no sleep the night before. *This is madness. Why did they let me do this. Did they know—I'd fail. Want me to fail. What a fool. Like the Hairy Ape.* I missed my step on stairs, cried out as I fell. Someone was poking my shoulder, hard. "Hey, Kathryn. Wake up." It was Karla. I was groggy, confused. Somehow, it was morning: a bleak gray dawn beyond the bus's rain-splotched windows. We'd left the Thruway and were passing through the outskirts of a city I guessed must be Albany. I murmured I was sorry, embarrassed; I hadn't thought I was asleep. "You were grinding your back teeth," Karla said. "Like you were having a bad dream."

AT THE GREYHOUND STATION in downtown Albany I felt another wave of panic. I stood on the pavement not knowing where to go next. Karla too was looking quickly about as if in dread of seeing someone she knew. On the bus she'd powdered her face and fluffed out her hair; despite the rocky night, she seemed alert and enlivened. She was carrying a light-weight polyester suitcase as well as her lizard-skin bag. "Say, Kathryn— I've got this place I'm going to, you could come with me, OK? Like if you wanted to wash up or whatever." Though I didn't think this was a practical idea I wasn't sure how to decline. Karla said, as if impulsively, "Y'know what—I'll make breakfast for us. I could get some things." Still I hesitated. Karla seemed almost to be pleading with me. She added, with a nervous giggle, "This early in the morning, I don't like to be alone with my thoughts. The rest of the day's like a goddamn *desert*." "Thanks," I said awkwardly, edging away, "—I guess I can't." Karla must have stared after me as I hurried away, almost colliding with people, to search out a rest-room. I knew I was behaving strangely. I was desperate to splash cold water onto my eyes, which ached as if I'd been crying (maybe in fact I had been crying), and I badly needed to use a toilet; my stomach churned with tension. I'd been overwhelmed by Karla's powerful personality and wanted only to escape her.

Yet, when I emerged shakily from a toilet stall a few minutes later, there was Karla in the rest room waiting for me, briskly washing her hands at a sink and smiling happily at me through the clouded mirror like a kindly older sister. Had I agreed to go with her after all? "We'll take a cab, Kathryn. You're looking pale. This job interview or whatever it is—what time is it? Not till eleven? You need to be *fed*."

WHY I WENT with Karla whom I didn't know when it was my adamant wish not to go with her, I could not have said. In the cab I nervously studied a city map the admissions office had mailed me on which I'd marked in red ink the locations of the Greyhound station and the university campus, which appeared to be some distance away. Karla seemed annoyed that I was looking at the map. "*I'll* take you there. It's only a mile or so from my place. You have plenty of time." She was speaking brightly and rapidly and tapping at my wrist with her red-polished nails, which were uneven, some of the nails much longer than others. When I told her worriedly that I couldn't seem to match the streets we were passing with street names on the map she laughed, took the map from me, and folded it carelessly and shoved it into her coat pocket. "There! No need to fret. *I* don't like to be alone with my thoughts, either." This made no sense but I wasn't in a mood to object. My hands were tingling warmly: I was thinking of how in the bus station rest room after I'd washed and dried my hands on a coarse paper towel, Karla had seized both my hands in hers, her hands that were startlingly soft, and rubbed Jergen's lotion into them so that now my hands were fresh and fragrant as Karla's though nowhere near as soft. Fall and winter I'd played basket-ball at school or practiced shots whenever I could, I wasn't the most competitive girl player at school but there was something fascinating about sinking the ball through the hoop, dashing toward the basket and shooting, or shooting from the foul line, something deeply satisfying even as it was clearly pointless. But the palms of my hands were calloused from gripping the ball. Compared with Karla's hands they hardly seemed like a girl's hands at all.

WHY I WENT with Karla, and why I found myself a half-hour later ringing the doorbell of a house, Karla's place as she called it, while Karla remained in the cab idling at the curb not in front of the shabby brownstone rowhouse but a few doors down; why I was with this woman I didn't know, obeying her without question; I could not have said for my head was a doll's head rattling-empty and finely cracked beneath the hair. As I slid out of the rear of the cab Karla impulsively looped her silk scarf around my neck. "This will keep you warm, Kathryn!" I smiled at Karla not knowing what the gesture meant—if the scarf was a gift I'd certainly return it for I couldn't accept such an expensive gift from her but maybe it wasn't a gift exactly and in any case how could I hurt Karla's feelings?

Yet on the sidewalk I'd hesitated, staring at the brownstone house with its four front windows in which blinds had been yanked to differing levels, a weatherworn row house in a block of similar homes, and Karla leaned out the car door—"Just go ring the doorbell, Kathryn. Just to make sure. Nobody's home, I promise." I asked who might be home and Karla said emphatically, "Nobody! But we need to be certain."

The narrow front yard was grassless and rutted and the front stoop listed to one side yet I found myself bounding up to the door buoyant and daring in my ballerina flats wanting simply to please Karla, not thinking, *Where am I, why am I here? Who is this woman?* The morning was raw and scintillating, patches of bright blue sky overhead and a rising sun so fierce it made my eyes water. Everywhere the pavement was wet and glistening. I rang the doorbell and heard the buzzer inside and it was an extension of the morning's raw scintillating mood. I was nervous but not frightened exactly. In my good-girl shoes and nylon stockings that were beginning to run and my plain blue raincoat and Karla's silk scarf around my neck, the long ends fluttering in the wind, the most beautiful scarf I'd ever worn. A scarf that seemed to confer upon me a new, strange, mysterious power, an invulnerability to harm or even distress. Though conceding that there was—there might be—an element of risk in what I seemed to be doing. A second time and a third I rang the doorbell and there was no sound from inside the house; so narrow a house I imagined that I could stretch my arms across the entire facade. In the adjoining brownstone a dog had begun to bark hysterically. Claws scratching against a windowpane.

Karla hurried up the walk behind me and gave me a quick hug. "Good girl! You're my heart." It would occur to me later that by this time, in her state of excitement, Karla had forgotten my name. Her eyes were widened and despite the morning sunshine oddly dilated, there was a feverish glow to her skin. She seemed to me more beautiful than ever. She'd had the presence of mind to take from the cab both our bags and her polyester suitcase and she was brandishing on a strip of red wool yarn a key with which she unlocked the door and drew me breathlessly inside with her. We were confronted by cold stale air that seemed to rush at us, an underlying odor of something rotted, mustiness like damp newspaper. "Hello? Hello? Hello? He*llo?*" Karla cried, as a guest might call out stepping into a house whose front door is open. Except for the dog barking frantically next door there was silence. Yet the interior looked lived-in, and recently—a pair of men's boots in the narrow hallway at the foot of the stairs, a plaid shirt tossed onto a chair, in the living room a space heater, unplugged. In a glass bowl on a table, floating on the surface of scummy water, was a black-striped goldfish which upset Karla so she hid her eyes. Her lips moved almost inaudibly—"Bas*tard*."

In her staccato high heels, still carrying her bags, Karla marched back to the kitchen, where a faucet was dripping loudly, jeeringly; here the odor of rot was stronger. She threw open the refrigerator door and recoiled with a curse from the stink. I didn't want to look inside; in that instant I was beginning to feel nauseated; exhaustion was catching up with me; through a crudely taped-together windowpane above the unspeakably filthy sink I could see into the small backyard grassless as the front, and littered. *A space the size of a large grave.* By this time the sun was more fiercely blazing and the April day would rapidly warm except in the foul-smelling house where the air was still cold ehough for our quickened breaths to vaporize. Yet even now not thinking, at least not thinking coherently, *Why am I here? And where am I?* For Karla gave me no time to think. Scarcely time to breathe. I glanced worriedly at my wristwatch, seeing with alarm that it was already past nine o'clock and Karla noticed, pinching my wrist, saying, "I promised I'd get you to wherever, didn't I? Stop obsessing. You're getting on my nerves." Karla led me upstairs, my heart beat with anticipation. *You could be trapped: up these stairs and no other way out.* In a dim-lit bedroom smelling of soiled clothes and mildew and stale cigarette smoke Karla dropped her suitcase onto an unmade bed and opened it and began tossing in items from a bureau drawer, and from a closet, articles of clothing. "C'mon, hon, don't just stand there, *help me,* huh?" So I helped, clumsy and hurried, my hands shaking. The bedroom was small and would have been depressing except for its lilac wallpaper, inexpertly laid on the walls (my father had wallpapered much of our house, which my grandmother owned, and I knew well how difficult it was to paper walls even if you know what you're doing), and cream-colored organdy curtains on the back windows. The front-window curtains had been yanked down, it seemed, curtains and curtain rods on the floor as if they'd been tossed there in a rage; these I kept tripping over. Karla said, whistling, "Jesus God! Look here." She was holding a lacy red nightgown against herself; the front had been ripped nearly in two. She stared down at the nightgown smiling a peculiar smile as if the nightgown were her own mutilated self. By this time I was anxious to use a bathroom. My bladder ached, there was a loose hot rumbling in the pit of my belly, a threat of diarrhea like scorn. *You'll miss the interview. Fail the interview. To erase this shame you'll have to kill yourself.* Karla decided to laugh at the torn nightgown and ripped it further and threw it to the floor.

From the top shelf of the closet Karla took a small but heavy cardboard box and handed it to me to dump into the suitcase. A cascade of loose snapshots, printed documents, and letters. One of the snapshots fluttered to the floor, I reached for it and glancing up saw a man standing in the bedroom doorway. He was just standing there.

Though I was staring directly at this man and though he was surely aware of me only a few feet away he didn't seem to see me at all. He was watching Karla. And he was smiling.

A good-looking man in his mid-thirties compact and muscled as a middleweight, not tall, with dirt-colored oily hair curving over his ears and thinning at the crown of his head, and a glittery stubble of beard on his jaws; his eyes were coppery as a stove's coils, heated. This was a man who looked as if, if you made the mistake of touching him, your fingers would burn. Karla came out of the bathroom adjoining the bedroom with an armful of toiletries and when she saw this man she gave a little scream like a kicked cat, and dropped the toiletries, and the man said to me out of the side of his mouth without so much as glancing at me, "Get out of here, you. This is between her and me." Karla cried to me, "Don't leave me!" and I stammered I would not, even as the man pushed past me to grab Karla's arm, and Karla was screaming, shoving at him, he gripped her shoulders in both hands and shook her and she punched and kicked and used her elbows against him as in a clumsy violent dance. I picked up one of the curtain rods from the floor and swung it at Karla's attacker, striking him on the side of the head; he turned to curse me and in desperation I swung the rod back this time striking him on the neck, and he grabbed the rod and tossed it aside, the torn curtains still dragging with it as in a comic cinematic sequence, and as I stood paralyzed he punched me with his right fist, a blow to my jaw that knocked me backward, legs dissolving beneath me, and I fell heavily to the floor. There I lay unable to move, I'd been knocked unconscious, concussed, like a boxer who's been struck a blow he has seen flying at him yet hasn't comprehended, and now he's out though his eyes are open and he's staring blankly not seeing anything not even the proverbial black lights that mimic death; and by the time vision and comprehension return you understand that a very long time has passed in your life, if only a few seconds by the clock.

Always afterward recalling, *How close to brain-death, extinction. The snap of a finger more and you'd be gone.*

And what would they have done with my body, Karla and the man who was her ex-husband, or husband? I've never wanted to speculate.

But this happened instead: as the man turned to me, Karla drew out of her lizard-skin bag a knife, a steel-handled eight-inch steak knife, and in a fury began stabbing at him, and the astonished man backed off saying, "Jesus, Karla! Give that to me!" He was actually laughing, or trying to laugh. As if he thought it might be a joke. And there was something comical about Karla's rage, the awkward way she wielded the knife, as a child might, the handle gripped tight in her fist and her blows overhand like a windmill's blades; so that the man, quick on his feet, shrewd and strong, had reason to think he could take the knife from her without being cut even as, trying to wrest it from her by the blade, he was being cut; blood ran down both his hands in quick eager bright streams. They were shouting accusations at each other. Cursing each other. Karla had the man backed against the edge of the bed; the flashing blade struck him in the shoulder, in the upper chest; he fell clumsily onto the bed and yet more clumsily onto the opened suitcase, trying to shield his head with his arms and pleading for her to stop as blood spilled like a garish crimson blossom down his chest, darkening his shirt and unzipped suede jacket. "See how you like it! See how you like it! I hate you! I'll kill you! Why are you here! You're not supposed to be here! You have no right to be here!" Karla cried. But seeing then what she'd done, she threw down the bloody knife;

in an instant her fury changed to horror and repentance. "Arnie, no—I didn't mean it. Arnie—" She knelt beside the bed, now desperate, asking was he all right? saying he'd made her do it, she was sorry, don't die on me Karla was begging, don't bleed to death Karla was sobbing. By this time I'd managed to get to my feet though reeling with dizziness; I leaned over coughing, and a thin scalding stream of vomit issued from my mouth. When I could speak, I told Karla I'd call an ambulance and went to a phone on a bedside table, began to dial 911 when the wounded man Arnie told Karla, "Take that fucking thing from her," and Karla stumbled to me, one of her high-heeled shoes on and the other off, and snatched the receiver out of my hand, fixing me with her widened blackly dilated eyes. "He's all right! He isn't going to die! We can take care of him ourselves!"

And so we did.

KARLA COMMANDED ME to help her and I obeyed. Afterward I would conclude I'd been in a state of shock. And I would wonder at the logic of bringing a badly bleeding man into the bathroom as he'd insisted, as I would wonder at the logic of not calling an ambulance. I would wonder, *Did he live?—or did he die? Was I a witness to manslaughter? Was I an accessory?* Stumbling and swaying like drunks, Karla and I walked the wounded man into the bathroom. Each of us grasped him around the waist and how heavy he was, how his terrible weight pulled me down. My head and jaw were pounding from the blow I'd taken, the left side of my face beginning already to swell. Karla was saying in a dazed voice, "You'll be all right. Honey, you'll be all right. It's just flesh wounds, I think. *You'll be all right.*" Her face looked coarse, makeup streaked in unflattering rivulets, mascara smeared beneath her eyes like ink; I saw that Karla wasn't a young woman only a few years older than me but well into her thirties and now looking her age. In the dank, ill-smelling bathroom with no window and a single bare lightbulb overhead the wounded man sat down heavily on the rim of a bathtub, whimpering and cursing with pain. He was panting, yet couldn't seem to take his injuries seriously, impatient with himself for being weakened and slowed down. I would never know if this man, Arnie, was Karla's ex-husband or still her husband but it seemed they'd been married; there may even have been a child involved, and this child may even have died—from what they said, elliptically, and in fragments, and from what I was able in my distracted state to comprehend, this seemed to be the case. Clearly they were lovers even if they'd wanted to hurt each other badly; clearly Karla was appalled at what she'd done to him, the dozen shallow wounds on his hands, forearms, and neck and the deeper wounds in his chest and shoulder. Karla commanded, "Don't just stand there, help us, for God's sake." I fetched towels, pillowcases, even soiled sheets from the bed. Clumsily we made bandages, thick wads of cloth to stanch the bleeding, or to try to stanch it; for blood soaked through the makeshift bandages within seconds, glistening on our hands and splattering onto our legs. Star-bursts of blood collected on the tile floor. The wounded man demanded cold-water compresses, which may have helped a little. His impatience with his bleeding wounds reminded me of my father's angry impatience with his own infrequent illnesses and gave me a sense of the man's personality. I would never know more about him. I would never know Karla's last name. Though involved in this terrible episode, like sisters baptized in another's blood, I would never see Karla or hear of her after that morning.

The wounded Arnie was deathly pale but insisted to Karla for Christ's sake he was all right, she hadn't struck deep with the fucking knife and he'd had worse than this happen to him, he'd been shot for Christ's sake and it hadn't killed him. He gave her a wincing grin, saying, "So you did it, eh? Got guts, eh?"—which made Karla cry harder. She was crouched beside him with her arms around him and her forehead pressed against his. I stood in the doorway not knowing what to do. Next door, the maddened dog was barking furiously at us through the plasterboard wall, only a few feet away. The wounded man at last squinted at me, asking Karla who I was, and Karla said, "Nobody. A friend," and the man asked, "A friend *who?*" and Karla said, "I don't know! Nobody." Karla didn't so much as glance at me. The wounded man was panting, scowling; he stared at me for a long moment before saying, "*You,* you better leave. Don't make any fucking calls, just *go.*" So I did.

On the bedroom floor amid the wreckage of the curtains I discovered Karla's beautiful silk scarf, which I carried away with me. *I deserve this,* I thought.

3

AS IN A NIGHTMARE it was 11:25 A.M. when I finally arrived for the interview.

I'd had to run several blocks after leaving the brownstone to find a pay phone in a drugstore so that I could call a taxi, and I'd waited with mounting anxiety for a taxi to arrive, and the ride itself seemed to take forever, and at the university I had to ask directions to the admissions office, and once in that building at the top of a steep hill I had to spend frantic minutes in a women's room in a state of physical distress, afterward trying to make myself presentable for meeting the associate dean of admissions who would be interviewing me: for the front of my raincoat was stained with both vomit and a stranger's blood, and there was a wide, wet stain on the skirt of my navy blue wool suit, which I cleverly disguised by shifting the front of the skirt to the side and covering the stain with my raincoat, which I'd carefully folded so that the stain didn't show and hung over my arm. It looked quite natural, didn't it, for me to be carrying my coat over my arm, on a warm April morning? Of course I had to wash my hands and my face; without removing my nylon stockings (which were now marred by runs) I managed to lighten the bloodstains on my legs. The left side of my face was swollen so that I looked as if I had mumps on just that side, and there was an ugly bruise taking shape but this too I disguised, or believed I disguised, by looping Karla's long scarf around my neck and tying it in a bow at my jawline. In the mirror I saw an unnaturally pale girl with stark, shadowed, blood-veined eyes and windblown hair and a look about the mouth that might have been desperation or triumph. *I'm here. I'm here!*

I'd missed my appointment of course. The dean was interviewing other students. His receptionist advised me to reschedule my interview for the following Saturday but I said that wasn't possible—"I'll wait." Staring at my swollen jaw and rumpled clothes the receptionist tried to discourage me but I said I couldn't come back to Albany another time—"I'm here *now.*" I must have spoken sharply, for the woman pursed her lips and said nothing more.

You can't deny me, I've come so far.

Waiting in the dean's outer office as other students my age, glancing at me curiously, came and went. Pacing in the corridor outside. And more than once retreating to a women's rest room to stare at my reflection, which seemed to waver in the glass. A ghastly radiance shone in my skin. My eyes resembled Karla's—glittery and dilated. And the silk scarf with the crimson peonies was so beautiful, the most beautiful item of clothing I'd ever worn.

Not until 1:20 P.M. would the associate dean have time to "fit me in." And then I was allowed to know it was something of a special favor. The man's name was Werner—I was careful to address him as "Dr. Werner," perceiving him as one of a sequence of adults in my adolescent life who must be judiciously courted, placated, seduced. This man was frowning yet kindly, with deep dents and fissures in his middle-aged, claylike face; he'd have been willing to forgive me for being late if only I might have explained myself, yet I couldn't seem to explain myself except to say tersely that I'd come from Port Oriskany on the Greyhound bus and had been unavoidably detained. " 'Unavoidably'—? You didn't have an accident, did you, Miss—" he peered through bifocals at documents on his desk and pronounced my tricky ethnic name with elaborate care. *Tell him yes! Arouse the bastard's sympathy*. This was a reckless voice not my own, which I ignored. I thanked Dr. Werner politely and told him no, I was fine. "Is this your first visit to Albany?" he asked, as if such a fact might help to explain me, and I murmured yes it was. I believed I was speaking normally despite the stiffness in my jaw and a fiery ache that ran along my gumline as if every tooth there were abscessed. Dr. Werner shuffled through documents in my folder, now and then making notations with a pen. Though I knew there were bookshelves in his office it seemed that my vision was narrowed as if by blinders and I could see only Dr. Werner clearly. I was very tired suddenly and yearned to rest my arms on the edge of his desk and my heavy head upon my arms for only just a moment. I saw the man's fleshy lips move before I heard his question—"Why do you believe you would make a good, dedicated teacher, Kathryn?" But I didn't recall having said I wanted to be a teacher or that this subject was the purpose of our conversation. *Tell the man something. Out of pride, you must not fail.* So I spoke. Falteringly at first and then with more confidence. I saw that Dr. Werner stared at me, my dilated eyes and swollen jaw, but I'd long been an articulate child and though I might stammer under pressure, words rarely failed me; especially adult words of a lofty, abstract nature. I spoke of what my own education had meant to me so far, how it had "saved my life by giving purpose to my life"; I spoke of how my grandparents, Hungarian immigrants, hadn't had the opportunity to be educated beyond grade school and were barely literate in English; I spoke of my parents, growing up during the Depression, who hadn't graduated from high school—"I want to be part of the world beyond that. A world of the intellect and of the spirit." Tears stung my eyes, these words so moved me; even as, offering them to a stranger as I was, in the hope of winning his approval, I felt deeply ashamed. Dr. Werner was nodding, and frowning.

Perhaps he was moved, too. Or embarrassed for me. His wide dark nostrils pinched. *He's sniffing you. Smells blood. Menstrual blood, he'd think. Oh, shame!*

My voice, stricken, trailed off into silence. The ache in my jaw was fierce. Mistaking my hesitation for shyness, and liking shyness in a girl, Dr. Werner was deciding he liked me; he concluded the interview by praising my scholastic record, which was spread out before him on his desk like the innards of a dissected creature—and my teachers' "glowing" letters of rec-ommendation—and assured me that I was exactly the kind of dedicated young person the university hoped for as Founders' Scholars. The inter-view was over: Dr. Werner had heaved himself up from his swivel chair, a shorter and stockier man than I'd believed; he was smiling, showing an expanse of pinkish gum, and congratulated me on the scholarship which was, he hoped I knew, highly competitive, awarded to no more than twenty students out of an entering class of eleven hundred; my final acceptance forms would arrive at my home within a few weeks. I said, stammering, "Dr. Werner, it might not be absolutely true—that I want to be a teacher. That I know what I want to do with my life." Dr. Werner snorted with laughter as if I were joking, or he wished to think I was jok-ing. He repeated that the final acceptance forms would arrive within a few weeks and he hoped I'd have a good return trip home. I said, "Then I am—admitted? I'm *in?*" I felt a stab of dismay. Was my life decided? Had I agreed to this? Dr. Werner said, with just perceptible impatience, "Yes, of course. Our interview is only a formality." He extended his hand for a brisk, firm handshake and sent me on my way.

Hurrying down a flight of vertiginous stairs—so like the stairs in my dream of the previous night!—I realized that there might have been blood on my hand, still; that I hadn't been able to scrub every stain off. I could envision Dr. Werner, his claylike face creased in revulsion, contemplating his own blood-sticky hand.

4

But I won't come back here. Not here.

Returning to Port Oriskany on the 5:35 P.M. bus I was sitting alone, my head slumped against a window. My face was throbbing with pain but it was pain at a distance, for I'd swallowed a handful of aspirins to numb it. Much of that day would be lost to me in cloudy amnesiac patches like strips of paper torn from a wall. How I would explain the silk scarf to my mother I didn't yet know, but I wasn't much worried. I was in a state of exhilaration. A state of certitude. On the mammoth lumbering bus like a prehistoric creature vibrating with energy. I wanted to sleep yet my eyes wouldn't close. Far to the west as if at the end of the Thruway, there was a horizon seething with red like the flames of an open furnace.

The countryside darkens by rapid degrees, I begin to see my face reflected in the steamy window. A face-to-come, the face of my adulthood. And beyond it my parents' faces subtly distorted as if in water. For the first time I realize that my parents are a man, a woman; individuals who'd loved each other before they'd ever loved me. And they do love me, only they can't protect me; nor do they know me. I realize that I will leave home soon. In fact, I've already left.

Part Three

A MANHATTAN ROMANCE

*Y*our Daddy loves you, that's the one true thing.
Never forget, Princess: that's the one true thing in your life of mostly lies.

That wild day! I'd woken before it was even dawn; I seemed to know that a terrible happiness was in store.

I was five years old; I was feverish with excitement; when Daddy came to pick me up for our *Saturday adventure* as he called it, it had just begun to snow; Momma and I were standing at the tall windows of our eighteenth-floor apartment looking out across Central Park when the doorman rang; Momma whispered in my ear, "If you said you were sick, you wouldn't have to go with—him." For she could not utter the word *Daddy*, and even the words *your father* made her mouth twist. I said, "Momma, I'm not sick! I'm not." So the doorman sent Daddy up. Momma kept me with her at the window, her hands that sometimes trembled firm on my shoulders and her chin resting on the top of my head so I wanted to squirm away but did not dare, not wanting to hurt Momma's feelings or make her angry. So we stood watching the snowflakes—a thousand million snowflakes drifting downward out of the sky glinting like mica in the thin sunshine of early December. I was pointing and laughing; I was excited by the snow, and by Daddy coming for me. Momma said, "Just look! Isn't it beautiful! The first snow of the season." Most of the tall trees had lost their leaves, the wind had blown away their leaves that only a few days before had been such bright, beautiful colors, and you could see clearly now the roads curving and dipping through the park; you could see the streams of traffic—yellow taxis, cars, delivery vans, horse-drawn carriages, bicyclists; you could see the skaters at Wollman Rink, and you could see the outdoor cages of the Children's Zoo, which was closed now; you could see the outcroppings of rock like miniature mountains; you could see the ponds glittering like mirrors laid flat; the park was still green, and seemed to go on forever; you could see to the very end at 110th Street (Momma told me the name of this distant street, which I had never seen close up); you could see the gleaming cross on the dome of the Cathedral of St. John the Divine (Momma told me the name of this great cathedral, which I had never seen close up); our new apartment building was at 31 Central Park South and so we could see the Hudson River to the left, and the East River to the right; the sun appeared from the right, above the East River; the sun vanished to the left, below the Hudson River; we were floating above the street seven-teen floors below; we were floating in the sky, Momma said; we were floating above Manhattan, Momma said; we were safe here, Momma said, and could not come to harm. But Momma was saying now in her sad angry voice, "I wish you didn't have to go with—him. You won't cry, will you? You won't miss your momma too much, will you?" I was staring at the thousand million snowflakes; I was excited waiting for Daddy to ring the bell at our front door; I was confused by Momma's questions because wasn't Momma me? so didn't Momma know? the answer to any question of Momma's, didn't Momma already know? "I wish you didn't have to leave me, darling, but it's the terms of the agreement—it's the law." These bitter words *It's the law* fell from Momma's lips each Saturday morning like something dropped in the apartment overhead! I waited to hear them, and I always did hear them. And then Momma leaned over me and kissed me; I loved Momma's sweet perfume and her soft-shining hair but I wanted to push away from her; I wanted to run to the door, to open it just as Daddy rang the bell; I wanted to surprise Daddy, who took such happiness in being surprised; I wanted to say to Momma, *I love Daddy better than I love you, let me go!* Because Momma was me, but Daddy was someone so different.

The doorball rang. I ran to answer it. Momma remained in the front room at the window. Daddy hoisted me into his arms, "How's my

Princess? How's my baby-love?" and Daddy called out politely to Momma, whom he could not see, in the other room, "We're going to the Bronx Zoo, and we'll be back promptly at 5:30 P.M. as agreed." And Momma, who was very dignified, made no reply. Daddy called out, "Goodbye! Remember us!" which was like Daddy, to say mysterious things, things to make you smile, and to make you wonder; things to make you confused, as if maybe you hadn't heard correctly but didn't want to ask. And Momma never asked. And in the elevator going down Daddy hugged me again saying how happy we were, just the two of us. He was the King, I was the Little Princess. Sometimes I was the Fairy Princess. Momma was the Ice Queen who never laughed. Daddy was saying this could be the happiest day of our lives if we had courage. A light shone in Daddy's eyes; there would never be a man so handsome and radiant as Daddy.

"NOT THE BRONX, after all. Not today, I don't think."

Our driver that day was an Asian man in a smart visored cap, a neat dark uniform, and gloves. The limousine was shiny black and larger than last week's and the windows were dark-tinted so you could see *out* (but it was strange, a scary twilight even in the sun) but no one could see *in*. "No plebeians knowing our business!" Daddy said, winking at me. "No spies." When we passed traffic policemen Daddy made faces at them, waggled his fingers at his ears and stuck out his tongue though they were only a few yards away; I giggled frightened Daddy would be seen and arrested, but he couldn't be seen, of course—"We're invisible, Princess! Don't worry."

Daddy liked me to smile and laugh, not to worry; not ever, ever to cry. He'd had enough of crying, he said. He'd had it up to here (drawing a forefinger across his throat, like a knife blade) with crying, he said. He had older children, grown-up children I'd never met; I was his Little Princess, his Baby-Love, the only one of his children he did love, he said. Snatching my hand and kissing it, kiss-tickling so I'd squeal with laughter.

Now Daddy no longer drove his own car, it was a time of rented cars. His enemies had taken *his driver's license* from him to humiliate him, he said. For they could not defeat him in any way that mattered. For he was too strong for them, and too smart.

It was a time of sudden reversals, changes of mind. I had been looking forward to the zoo; now we weren't going to the zoo but doing something else—"You'll like it just as much." Other Saturdays, we'd driven through the park; the park had many surprises; the park went on forever; we would stop, and walk, run, play in the park; we'd fed the ducks and geese swimming on the ponds; we'd had lunch outdoors at Tavern on the Green; we'd had lunch outdoors at the boat-house; on a windy March day, Daddy had helped me fly a kite (which we'd lost—it broke, and blew away in shreds); there was the promise of skating at Wollman Rink sometime soon. Other Saturdays we'd driven north on Riverside Drive to the George Washington Bridge, and across the bridge, and back; we'd driven north to the Cloisters; we'd driven south to the very end of the island as Daddy called it—"The great doomed island, Manhattan." We'd crossed Manhattan Bridge into Brooklyn, we'd crossed the Brooklyn Bridge. We'd gazed up at the Statue of Liberty. We'd gone on a ferry ride in bouncy, choppy water. We'd had lunch at the top of the World Trade Center, which was Daddy's favorite restaurant—"Dining in the clouds! In heaven." We'd gone to Radio City Music Hall, we'd seen "Beauty and the Beast" on Broadway; we'd seen the Big Apple Circus at Lincoln Center; we'd seen, the year before, the Christmas Spectacular at Radio City Music Hall. Our *Saturday adventures* left me dazed, giddy; one day I would realize that's what *intoxicated, high, drunk* means—I'd been drunk with happiness, with Daddy.

But no other *drunk,* ever afterward, could come near.

"Today, Princess, we'll buy presents. That's what we'll do—'store up riches.' "

Christmas presents? I asked.

"Sure. Christmas presents, any kind of presents. For you, and for me. Because we're special, you know." Daddy smiled at me, and I waited for him to wink because sometimes (when he was on the car phone, for instance) he'd wink at me to indicate he was joking; for Daddy often joked; Daddy was a man who loved to laugh, as he described himself, and there wasn't enough to laugh at, unless he invented it. "You know we are special, Princess, don't you? And all your life you'll remember your Daddy loves you?—that's the one true thing."

Yes Daddy, I said. For of course it was so.

I SHOULD RECORD how Daddy spoke on the phone, in the backseats of our hired cars.

How precise his words, how he enunciated his words, polite and cold and harsh; how, though he spoke calmly, his handsome face creased like a vase that has been cracked; his eyes squinted almost shut, and had no focus; a raw flush like sunburn rose from his throat. Then he would remember where he was, and remember *me.* And smile at me, winking and nodding, whispering to *me;* even as he continued his conversation with whoever was at the other end of the line. And after a time Daddy would say abruptly, "That's enough!" or simply, "Goodbye!" and break the connection; Daddy would replace the phone receiver, and the conversation would have ended, with no warning. So that I basked in the knowledge that any one of Daddy's conversations, entered into with such urgency, would nonetheless come to an abrupt ending with the magic words "That's enough!" or "Goodbye!" and these words I awaited in the knowledge that, then, Daddy would turn smiling to *me.*

That wild day! Breakfast at the Plaza, and shopping at the Trump Tower, and a visit to the Museum of Modern Art where Daddy took me to see a painting precious to him, he said . . . We had been in the café at the Plaza before but this time Daddy couldn't get the table he requested, and something else was wrong—it wasn't clear to me what; I was nervous, and giggly; Daddy gave our orders to the waiter, but disappeared (to make another phone call? to use the men's room?—if you asked Daddy where he went he'd say with a wink, That's for me to know, darlin', and you to find out); a big plate of scrambled eggs and bacon was brought for me; eggs Benedict was brought for Daddy; a stack of blueberry pancakes with warm syrup was brought for us to share; the silver pastry cart was pushed to our table; there were tiny jars of jams, jellies, marmalade for us to open; there were people at nearby tables observing us; I was accustomed, in Daddy's company, to being observed by strangers; I took such attention as my due, as Daddy's daughter; Daddy whispered, "Let them get an eyeful, Princess." Daddy ate quickly, hungrily; Daddy ate with a napkin tucked beneath his chin; Daddy saw that I wasn't eating much and asked was there something wrong with my breakfast; I told Daddy I wasn't hungry; Daddy asked if "she" had made me eat, before he'd arrived; I told him no; I said I felt a little sickish; Daddy said, "That's one of the Ice Queen's tactics—'sickish.' " So I tried to eat, tiny pieces of pancakes that weren't soaked in syrup, and Daddy leaned his elbows on the table and watched me, saying, "And what if this is the last breakfast you'll ever have with your father, what then? Shame on you!" Waiters hovered near in their dazzling white uniforms. The maitre d' was attentive, smiling. A call came for Daddy and he was gone for some time and when he returned flush-faced and distracted, his necktie loosened at his throat, it seemed that breakfast was over; hurriedly Daddy scattered $20 bills across the table, and hurriedly we left the café as everyone smiled and stared after us; we left the Plaza by the side entrance, on 58th Street, where the limousine awaited us; the silent Asian driver standing at the curb with the rear door open for Daddy to bundle me inside, and climb inside himself. We had hardly a block to go, to the elegant Trump Tower on Fifth Avenue; there we took escalators to the highest floor, where Daddy's eyes glistened with tears, everywhere he looked was so beautiful. Have I said my Daddy was smooth-shaven this morning, and smelled of a wintergreen cologne; he was wearing amber-tinted sunglasses, new to me; he was wearing a dark pinstriped double-breasted Armani suit and over it an Armani camel's-hair coat with shoulders that made him appear more muscular than he was; he was wearing shiny black Italian shoes with a heel that made him appear taller than he was; Daddy's hair had been styled and blown dry so that it lifted from his head like something whipped, not lying flat, and not a dull flattish white as it had been but tinted now a pale russet color; how handsome Daddy was! In the boutiques of Trump Tower Daddy bought me a dark blue velvet coat, and a pale blue angora cloche hat; Daddy bought me pale blue angora gloves; my old coat, my old gloves were discarded—"Toss 'em, please!" Daddy commanded the saleswomen. Daddy bought me a beautiful silk Hermès scarf to wrap around my neck, and Daddy bought me a beautiful white-gold wristwatch studded with tiny emeralds, that had to be made smaller, much smaller, to fit my wrist; Daddy bought me a "keepsake" gold heart on a thin gold chain, a necklace; Daddy bought for himself a half-dozen beautiful silk neckties imported from Italy, and a kidskin wallet; Daddy bought a cashmere vest sweater for himself, imported from Scotland; Daddy bought an umbrella, an attaché case, a handsome suitcase, imported from England, all of which he ordered to be delivered to an address in New Jersey; and other items Daddy bought for himself, and for me. For all these wonderful presents Daddy paid in cash; in bills of large denominations; Daddy no longer used credit cards, he said; he refused to be a cog in the network of government surveillance, he said; they would not catch him in their net; he would not play their ridiculous games. In the Trump Tower there was a café beside a waterfall and Daddy had a glass of wine there, though he chose not to sit down at a table; he was too restless, he said, to sit down at a table; he was in too much of a hurry. Descending then the escalators to the ground floor, where a cool breeze lifted to touch our heated faces; I was terribly excited in my lovely new clothes, and wearing my lovely jewelry; except for Daddy gripping my hand—"Care-ful, Princess!"—I would have stumbled at the foot of the escalator. And outside on Fifth Avenue there were so many people, tall rushing rude people who took no notice of me even in my new velvet coat and angora hat, I would have been knocked down on the sidewalk except for Daddy gripping my hand, protecting me. Next we went—we walked, and the limousine followed—to the Museum of Modern Art, where again there was a crowd, again I was breathless riding escalators, I was trapped behind tall people seeing legs, the backs of coats, swinging arms; Daddy lifted me to his shoulder and carried me, and brought me into a large, airy room; a room of unusual proportions; a room not so crowded as the others; there were tears in Daddy's eyes as he held me in his arms—his arms that trembled just slightly—to gaze at an enormous painting—several paintings—broad beautiful dreamy-blue paintings of a pond, and water lilies; Daddy told me that these paintings were by a very great French artist named "Mon-ay" and that there was magic in them; he told me that these paintings made him comprehend his own soul, or what his soul had been meant to be; for as soon as you left the presence of such beauty, you were lost in the crowd; you were devoured by the crowd; it would be charged against you that it was your own fault but in fact—"They don't let you be good, Princess. The more you have, the more they want from you. They eat you alive. Cannibals."

When we left the museum, the snowflakes had ceased to fall. In the busy Manhattan streets there was no memory of them now. A bright harsh sun shone down almost vertically between the tall buildings but everywhere else was shadow, without color, and cold.

By late afternoon Daddy and I had shopped at Tiffany & Co., and Bergdorf Goodman, and Saks, and Bloomingdale's; we had purchased beautiful expensive items to be delivered to us at an address in New Jersey—"On the far side of the River Styx." One purchase, at Steuben on Fifth Avenue, was a foot-high glass sculpture that might have been a woman, or an angel, or a wide-winged bird; it shone with light, so that you could almost not see it; Daddy laughed, saying, "The Ice Queen!—exactly"; and so this present was sent to Momma at 31 Central Park South. As we walked through the great glittering stores Daddy held my hand so that I would not be lost from him; these great stores, Daddy said, were the cathedrals of America; they were the shrines and reliquaries and catacombs of America; if you could not be happy in such stores, you could not be happy anywhere; you could not be a true American. And Daddy recited stories to me, some of these were fairy tales he'd read to me when I'd been a little little girl, a baby; when Daddy had lived with Momma and me, the three of us in a brownstone house with our own front door, and no doorman and no elevators; on our ground-floor windows there were curving iron bars, so that no one could break in; there were electronic devices of all kinds, so that no one could break in; our house had two trees at the curb, and these, too, were protected by curving iron bars; we lived in a narrow, quiet street a half-block from a huge, important building—the Metropolitan Museum of Art; when Daddy had been on television sometimes, and his photograph in the papers; they would say I knew nothing about this, I was too young to know, but I did; I knew. Just as I knew it was strange for Daddy to be paying for our presents with cash from his wallet, and out of thick-stuffed envelopes in his inside coat pockets; it was strange, for no one else paid in such a way; and others stared at him; stared at him as if memorizing him—the vigor of his voice and his shining face and his knowledge that he, and I, who was his daughter, were set off from the dull, dreary ordinariness of the rest of the world; they stared, they were envious of us, though smiling, always smiling, if Daddy glanced at them, or spoke with them. For such was Daddy's power.

I was dazed with exhaustion; I was feverish; I could not have said how long Daddy and I had been shopping, on our *Saturday adventure;* yet I loved it, that strangers observed us, and remarked how pretty I was; and to Daddy sometimes they would say, *Your face is familiar, are you on TV?* But Daddy just laughed and kept moving, for there was no time to spare that day.

OUT ON THE STREET, one of the wide, windy avenues, Daddy hailed a cab like any other pedestrian. When had he dismissed the limousine?—I couldn't remember.

It was a bumpy, jolting ride. The rear seat was torn. There was no heat. In the rearview mirror a pair of liquidy black eyes regarded Daddy with silent contempt. Daddy fumbled paying the fare, a $50 bill slipped from his fingers—"Keep the change, driver, and thanks!" Yet even then the eyes did not smile at us; these were not eyes to be purchased.

We were in a dark, tiny wine cellar on 47th Street near Seventh

Avenue where Daddy ordered a carafe of red wine for himself and a soft
drink for me and where he could make telephone calls in a private room at
the rear; I fell asleep, and when I woke up there was Daddy standing by
our table, too restless to sit; his face was rubbery and looked stretched; his
hair had fallen and lay in damp strands against his forehead; globules of
sweat like oily pearls ran down his cheeks. He smiled with his mouth, saying, "There you are, Princess! Up and at 'em." For already it was time to
leave, and more than time. Daddy had learned from an aide the bad news,
the news he'd been expecting. But shielding me from it of course. For only
much later—years later—would I learn that, that afternoon, a warrant for
Daddy's arrest had been issued by the Manhattan district attorney's office;
by some of the very people for whom, until a few months ago, Daddy had
worked. It would be charged against him that as a prosecuting attorney
Daddy had misused the powers of his office, he had solicited and accepted
bribes, he had committed perjury upon numerous occasions, he had falsely
informed upon certain persons under investigation by the district attorney's office, he had blackmailed others, he had embezzled funds . . . such
charges were made against Daddy, such lies concocted by his enemies who
had been jealous of him for many years and wanted him defeated,
destroyed. One day I would learn that New York City police detectives
had come to Daddy's apartment (on East 92nd Street and First Avenue) to
arrest him and of course hadn't found him; they'd gone to 31 Central Park
South and of course hadn't found him; Momma told them Daddy had
taken me to the Bronx Zoo, or in any case that had been his plan; Momma
told them that Daddy would be bringing me back home at 5:30 P.M., or in
any case he'd promised to do so; if they waited for him in the lobby downstairs would they please please not arrest him in front of his daughter,
Momma begged. Yet policemen were sent to the Bronx Zoo to search for
Daddy there; a manhunt for Daddy at the Bronx Zoo!—how Daddy
would have laughed. And now an alert was out in Manhattan for Daddy,
he was a "wanted" man, but already Daddy had shrewdly purchased a new
coat in Saks, a London Fog trench coat the shade of damp stone, and made
arrangements for the store to deliver his camel's-hair coat to the New Jersey address; already Daddy had purchased a gray fedora hat, and he'd
exchanged his amber-tinted sunglasses for darker glasses, with heavy black
plastic frames; he'd purchased a knotty gnarled cane, imported from Australia, and walked now with a limp—I stared at him, almost I didn't recognize him, and Daddy laughed at me. In the Shamrock Pub on Ninth

Avenue and 39th Street he'd engaged a youngish blond woman with hair braided in cornrows to accompany us while he made several other stops; the blond woman had a glaring-bright face like a billboard; her eyes were ringed in black and lingered on me—"What a sweet, pretty little girl! And what a pretty coat and hat!"—but she knew not to ask questions. She walked with me gripping my hand in the angora glove pretending she was my momma and I was her little girl, and Daddy behind hobbling on his cane; shrewdly a few yards behind so it would not have seemed (if anyone was watching) that Daddy was with us; this was a game we were playing, Daddy said; it was a game that made me excited, and nervous; I was laughing and couldn't stop; the blond woman scolded me—"Shhh! Your Daddy will be angry." And a little later the blond woman was gone.

Always in Manhattan, on the street I wonder if I'll see her again. *Excuse me* I will cry out *do you remember? That day, that hour?* But it's been years.

SO EXHAUSTED! Daddy scolded me carrying me out of the taxi, into the lobby of the Hotel Pierre; a beautiful old hotel on Fifth Avenue and 61st Street, across from Central Park; Daddy booked a suite for us on the sixteenth floor; you could look from a window to see the apartment building on Central Park South where Momma and I lived; but none of that was very real to me now; it wasn't real to me that I had a Momma, but only real that I had a Daddy. And once we were inside the suite Daddy bolted the door and slid the chain lock in place. There were two TVs and Daddy turned them both on. He turned on the ventilator fans in all the rooms. He took the telephone receivers off their hooks. With a tiny key he unlocked the minibar and broke open a little bottle of whiskey and poured it into a glass and quickly drank. He was breathing hard, his eyes moving swiftly in their sockets yet without focus. "Princess! Get up *please*. Don't disappoint your Daddy *please*." I was lying on the floor, rolling my head from side to side. But I wasn't crying. Daddy found a can of sweetened apple juice in the minibar and poured it into a glass and added something from another little bottle and gave it to me saying, "Princess, this is a magic potion. Drink!" I touched my lips to the glass but there was a bitter taste. Daddy said, "Princess, you must obey your Daddy." And so I did. A hot hurting sensation spread in my mouth and throat and I started to choke and Daddy pressed the palm of his hand over my mouth to quiet me; it was then I remembered how long ago when I'd been a silly little baby Daddy had pressed the palm of his hand over my mouth to quiet me.

I was sickish now, and I was frightened; but I was happy, too; I was drunk with happiness from all we'd done that day, Daddy and me; for I had never had so many presents before; I had never understood how special I was, before; and afterward when they asked if I'd been afraid of my Daddy I would say no! no I hadn't been! not for a minute! I love my Daddy I would say, and my Daddy loves me. Daddy was sitting on the edge of the big bed, drinking; his head lowered almost to his knees. He was muttering to himself as if he were alone—"Fuckers! Wouldn't let me be good. Now you want to eat my heart. But not *me*." Later I was wakened to something loud on the TV. Except it was a pounding at the door. And men's voices calling "Police! Open up, Mr.—"—saying Daddy's name as I'd never heard it before. And Daddy was on his feet, Daddy had his arm around me. Daddy was excited and angry and he had a gun in his hand—I knew it was a gun, I'd seen pictures of guns—this was bluish-black and shiny, with a short barrel—and he was waving the gun as if the men on the other side of the door could see him; there was a film of sweat on his face catching the light, like facets of diamonds; I had never seen my Daddy so furious calling to the policemen—"I've got my little girl here, my daughter—and I've got a gun." But they were pounding at the door; they were breaking down the door; Daddy fired the gun into the air and pulled me into another room where the TV was loud but there were no lights; Daddy pushed me down, panting; the two of us on the carpet, panting. I was too scared to cry, and I started to wet my pants; in the other room the policemen were calling to Daddy to surrender his weapon, not to hurt anyone but to surrender his weapon and come with them now; and Daddy was sobbing shouting— "I'll use it, I'm not afraid—I'm not going to prison—I can't!—I can't do it!—I've got my little girl here, you understand?"—and the policemen were on the other side of the doorway but wouldn't show themselves saying to Daddy he didn't want to hurt his daughter, of course he didn't want to hurt his daughter; he didn't want to hurt himself, or anyone; he should surrender his weapon now, and come along quietly with the officers; he would speak with his lawyer; he would be all right; and Daddy was cursing, and Daddy was crying, and Daddy was crawling on his hands and knees on the carpet trying to hold me, and the gun; we were crouched in the farthest darkest corner of the room by the heating unit; the ventilator fan was throbbing; Daddy was hugging me and crying, his breath was hot on my face; I tried to push out of Daddy's arms but Daddy was too strong calling me Princess! Little Princess! saying I knew he loved me didn't I.

The magic potion had made me sleepy and sickish, it was hard for me to stay awake. By now I had wet my panties, my legs were damp and chafed. A man was talking to Daddy in a loud clear voice like a TV voice and Daddy was listening or seemed to be listening and sometimes Daddy would reply and sometimes not; how much time passed like this, how many hours—I didn't know; not until years later would I learn it had been an hour and twelve minutes but at the time I hadn't any idea, I wasn't always awake. The voices kept on and on; men's voices; one of them saying repeatedly, "Mr.—, surrender your weapon, will you? Toss it where we can see it, will you?" and Daddy wiped his face on his shirt sleeve, Daddy's face was streaked with tears like something melting set too near a fire, and still the voice said, calmly, so loud it seemed to come from everywhere at once, "Mr.—, you're not a man to harm a little girl, we know you, you're a good man, you're not a man to harm anyone," and suddenly Daddy said, "Yes! Yes that's right." And Daddy kissed me on the side of the face and said, "Good-bye, Princess!" in a high, happy voice; and pushed me away from him; and Daddy placed the barrel of the gun deep inside his mouth. And Daddy pulled the trigger.

SO IT ENDED. It always ends. But don't tell me there isn't happiness. It exists, it's there. You just have to find it, and you have to keep it, if you can. It won't last, but it's there.

MURDER-TWO

his, he swore.

He'd returned to the townhouse on East End Avenue after 11 P.M. and found the front door unlocked and, inside, his mother lying in a pool of squid ink on the hardwood floor at the foot of the stairs. She'd apparently fallen down the steep length of the stairs and broken her neck, judging from her twisted upper body. She'd also been bludgeoned to death, the back of her skull caved in, with one of her own golf clubs, a two-iron, but he hadn't seemed to see that, immediately.

Squid ink?—well, the blood had looked black in the dim foyer light. It was a trick his eyes played on his brain sometimes when he'd been study-ing too hard, getting too little sleep. An *optic tic.* Meaning you see some-thing clearly, but it registers surreally in the brain as something else. Like in your neurological programming there's an occasional bleep.

In the case of Derek Peck, Jr., confronted with the crumpled, lifeless body of his mother, this was an obvious symptom of trauma. Shock, the visceral numbness that blocks immediate grief—the unsayable, the unknowable. He'd last seen his mother, in that same buttercup-yellow quilted satin robe that had given her the look of an upright, bulky Easter toy, early that morning, before he'd left for school. He'd been away all day.

And this abrupt, weird transition—from differential calculus to the body on the floor, from the anxiety-driven jokes of his Math Club friends (a hard core of them were meeting late, weekdays, preparing for upcoming SAT exams) to the profound and terrible silence of the townhouse that had seemed to him, even as he'd pushed open the mysteriously unlocked front door, a hostile silence, a silence that vibrated with dread.

He crouched over the body, staring in disbelief. "Mother? Mo*ther!*"

As if it were he, Derek, who'd done something bad, he the one to be punished.

He couldn't catch his breath. Hyperventilating! His heart beating so wildly he almost fainted. Too confused to think *Maybe they're still here? upstairs* for in his dazed state he seemed to lack even an animal's instinct for self-preservation.

Yes, and he felt to blame, somehow. Hadn't she instilled in him a reflex of guilt? If something was wrong in the household, it could probably be traced back to *him.* From the age of thirteen (when his father Derek, Sr., had divorced his mother Lucille, same as divorcing *him*) he'd been expected by his mother to behave like a second adult in the household, growing tall, lank, and anxious as if to accommodate that expectation, and his sand-colored body hair sprouting, and a fevered grimness about the eyes. Fifty-three percent of Derek's classmates, girls and boys, at the Mayhew Academy were from "families of divorce" and most agreed that the worst of it is you have to learn to behave like an adult yet at the same time a lesser adult, one deprived of his or her full civil rights. That wasn't easy even for stoic streetwise Derek Peck with an IQ of, what was it?—158, at age fifteen. (He was seventeen now.) So his precarious adolescent sense of himself was seriously askew: not just his *body image* (his mother had allowed him to become overweight as a small child; they say that remains with you forever irremediably imprinted in the earliest brain cells) but more crucially his *social identity.* For one minute she'd be treating him like an infant, calling him her baby, her baby-boy, and the next minute she was hurt, reproachful, accusing him of failing, like his father, to uphold his *moral responsibility* to her.

This *moral responsibility* was a backpack loaded with rocks. He could feel it, first fucking thing in the morning, exerting gravity even before he swung his legs out of bed.

Crouched over her now badly trembling, shaking as in a cold wind, whispering, "Mommy?—can't you wake up? Mom-*my* don't be—" balking at the word "dead" for it would hurt and incense Lucille like the word "old," not that she'd been a vain or frivolous or self-conscious woman for Lucille Peck was anything but, a woman of dignity it was said of her admiringly by women who would not have wished to be her and by men who would not have wished to be married to her. *Mommy don't be old!* Derek would never have murmured aloud, of course. Though possibly to himself frequently this past year or so seeing her wan, big-boned and brave face in harsh frontal sunshine when they happened to descend the front steps together in the morning, or at that eerie position in the kitchen where the overhead inset lights converged in such a way as to cruelly shadow her face downward, bruising the eye sockets and the soft fleshy tucks in her cheeks. Two summers ago when he'd been away for six weeks at Lake Placid and she'd driven to Kennedy to pick him up, so eager to see him again, and he'd stared appalled at the harsh lines bracketing her mouth and her smile too happy and what he felt was pity, and this too made him feel guilty. *You don't pity your own mother, asshole.*

If he'd come home immediately after school. By 4 P.M. Instead of a quick call from his friend Andy's across the park, guilty mumbled excuse left on the answering tape *Mother? I'm sorry guess I won't make dinner tonight OK?—Math Club—study group—calculus—don't wait up for me please.* How relieved he'd been, midway in his message she hadn't picked up the phone.

Had she been alive, when he'd called? Or already . . . dead?

Last time you saw your mother alive, Derek? they'd ask and he'd have to invent for he hadn't seen her, exactly. No eye contact.

And what had he *said.* A rushed schoolday morning, a Thursday. Nothing special about it. No premonition! Cold and windy and winter-glaring and he'd been restless to get out of the house, snatched a Diet Coke from the refrigerator so freezing his teeth ached. A blurred reproachful look of Mother in the kitchen billowing in her buttercup-yellow quilted robe as he'd backed off smiling, *'Bye Mom!*

Sure she'd been hurt, her only son avoiding her. She'd been a lonely woman even in her pride. Even with her activities that meant so much to her: Women's Art League, East Side Planned Parenthood Volunteers, HealthStyle Fitness Center, tennis and golf in East Hampton in the summer, subscription tickets to Lincoln Center. And her friends: most of them divorced middle-aged women, mothers like herself with high school or college-age kids. Lucille *was* lonely; how was that his fault?—as if, his senior year in prep school, he'd become a fanatic about grades obsessed with early admission to Harvard, Yale, Brown, Berkeley, just to avoid his mother at that raw, unmediated time of day that was breakfast.

But, God, how he'd loved her! He had. Planning to make it up to her for sure, SAT scores in the highest percentile he'd take her to the Stanhope for the champagne brunch then across the street to the museum for a mother-son Sunday excursion of a kind they hadn't had in years.

How still she was lying. He didn't dare touch her. His breathing was short, ragged. The squid-inky black beneath her twisted head had seeped and coagulated into the cracks of the floor. Her left arm was flung out in an attitude of exasperated appeal, the sleeve stained with red, her hand lying palm up and the fingers curled like angry talons. He might have noted that her Movado watch was missing, her rings gone except Grandma's antique opal with the fluted gold setting—the thief, or thieves, hadn't been able to yank it off her swollen finger? He might have noted that her eyes were rolled up asymmetrically in her head, the right iris nearly vanished and the left leering like a drunken crescent-moon. He might have noted that the back of her skull was smashed soft and pulpy as a melon but there are some things about your mother out of tact and delicacy you don't acknowledge seeing. *Mother's hair, though*—it was her only remaining good feature, she'd said. A pale silvery-brown, slightly coarse, a natural color like Wheaties. The mothers of his classmates all hoped to be youthful and glamorous with bleached or dyed hair but not Lucille Peck, she wasn't the type. You expected her cheeks to be ruddy without makeup and on her good days they were.

By this time of night Lucille's hair should have been dry from the shower of so many hours ago Derek vaguely recalled she'd had, the upstairs bathroom filled with steam. The mirrors. Shortness of breath! Tickets for some concert or ballet that night at Lincoln Center?—Lucille and a woman friend. But Derek didn't know about that. Or if he'd known he'd forgotten. Like about the golf club, the two-iron. Which closet? Upstairs, or down? The drawers of Lucille's bedroom bureau ransacked, *his* new Macintosh carried from his desk then dropped onto the floor by the doorway as if—what? They'd changed their minds about bothering with it. Looking for quick cash, for drugs. That's the motive!

What's Booger up to, now? What's going down with Booger, you hear?

He touched her—at last. Groping for that big artery in the throat—

cat*eroid?*—car*toid?* Should have been pulsing but wasn't. And her skin clammy-cool. His hand leaped back as if he'd been burnt.

Jesus fucking Christ, was it possible—Lucille was *dead?*

And *he'd* be to blame?

That Booger, man! One wild dude.

His nostrils flared, his eyes leaked tears. He was in a state of panic, had to get help. It was time! But he wouldn't have noticed the time, would he?—11:48 P.M. His watch was a sleek black-faced Omega he'd bought with his own cash but he wouldn't be conscious of the time exactly. By now he'd have dialed 911. Except thinking confused the phone was ripped out? (*Was* the phone ripped out?) Or one of them, his mother's killers, waiting in the darkened kitchen by the phone? Waiting to kill *him?*

He panicked, he freaked. Running back to the front door stumbling and shouting into the street where a taxi was slowing to let out an elderly couple, neighbors from the adjoining brownstone and they and the driver stared at this chalk-faced grief-stricken boy in an unbuttoned duffel coat, bareheaded, running into the street screaming, "Help us! Help us! Somebody's killed my mother!"

EAST SIDE WOMAN KILLED
ROBBERY BELIEVED MOTIVE

In a late edition of Friday's *New York Times,* the golf club bludgeoning death of Lucille Peck, whom Marina Dyer had known as Lucy Siddons, was prominently featured on the front page of the Metro section. Marina's quick eye, skimming the page, fastened at once upon the face (middle-aged, fleshy yet unmistakable) of her old Finch classmate.

"Lucy! *No.*"

You understood that this must be a *death photo:* the positioning on the page, upper center; the celebration of a private individual of no evident civic or cultural significance, or beauty. For *Times* readers the news value lay in the victim's address, close by the mayor's residence. The subtext being, *Even here, among the sequestered wealthy, such a brutal fate is possible.*

In a state of shock, though with professional interest, for Marina Dyer was a criminal defense attorney, Marina read the article, continued on an inner page and disappointing in its brevity. It was so familiar as to resemble a ballad. *One of us* (Caucasian, middle-aged, law-abiding, unarmed) surprised and savagely murdered in the very sanctity of her home; an instrument of class privilege, a golf club, snatched up by the killer as the murder weapon. The intruder or intruders, police said, were probably looking for quick cash, drug money. It was a careless, crude, cruel crime; a "senseless" crime; one of a number of unsolved break-ins on the east side since last September, though it was the first to involve murder. The teenage son of Lucille Peck had returned home to find the front door unlocked and his mother dead, at about 11 P.M., at which time she'd been dead approximately five hours. Neighbors spoke of having heard no unusual sounds from the Peck residence but several did speak of "suspicious" strangers in the neighborhood. Police were "investigating."

Poor Lucy!

Marina noted that her former classmate was forty-four years old, a year (most likely, part of a year) older than Marina; that she'd been divorced since 1991 from Derek Peck, an insurance executive now living in Boston; that she was survived by just the one child, Derek Peck, Jr., a sister, and two brothers. What an end for Lucy Siddons, who shone in Marina's memory as if beaming with life: unstoppable Lucy, indefatigable Lucy, good-hearted Lucy: Lucy who was twice president of the Finch class of 1970, and a dedicated alumnus: Lucy whom all the girls had admired, if not adored: Lucy who'd been so kind to shy stammering wall-eyed Marina Dyer.

Though they'd both been living in Manhattan all these years, Marina in a townhouse of her own on West 76th Street, very near Central Park, it had been five years since she'd seen Lucy, at their twentieth class reunion; even longer since the two had spoken together at length, earnestly. Or maybe they never had.

The son did it, Marina thought, folding up the newspaper. It wasn't an altogether serious thought but one that suited her professional skepticism.

Boogerman! Fucking fan-tas-tic.

Where'd he come from?—the hot molten core of the universe. At the instant of the big bang. Before which there was *nothing* and after which there would be *everything:* cosmic cum. For all sentient beings derive from a single source and that source long vanished, extinct.

The more you contemplated of origins the less you knew. He'd studied Wittgenstein—*Whereof one cannot speak, thereof one must be silent.* (A photocopied handout for Communication Arts class, the instructor a cool youngish guy with a Princeton Ph.D.) Yet he believed he could recall the circumstances of his birth. In 1978, in Barbados where his parents were vacationing, one week in late December. He was premature by five weeks and lucky to be alive and though Barbados was an accident yet seventeen years later he saw in his dreams a cobalt-blue sky, rows of royal palms shedding their bark like scales, shrieking bright-feathered tropical birds; a fat white moon drooping in the sky like his mother's big belly, sharks' dorsal fins cresting the waves like the Death Raiders video game he'd been hooked on in junior high. Wild hurricane-nights kept him from sleeping a normal sleep.

He was into Metallica, Urge Overkill, Soul Asylum. His heroes were heavy-metal punks who'd never made it to the Top Ten or if they did make it fell right back again. He admired losers who killed themselves ODing like dying's a joke, one final FUCK YOU! to the world. But he was innocent of doing what they'd claimed he'd done to his mother, for God's sake. Absolutely unbelieving fucking fantastic, *he, Derek Peck, Jr.,* had been arrested and would be tried for a crime perpetrated upon his own mother he'd loved! Perpetrated by animals (he could guess the color of their skin) who would've smashed his skull in, too, like cracking an egg, if he'd walked in that door five hours earlier.

SHE WASN'T PREPARED to fall in love, wasn't the type to fall in love with any client yet here is what happened: just seeing him, his strange tawny-yearning eyes lifting to her face *Help me! save me!*—that was it:

Derek Peck, Jr., was a Botticelli angel partly erased and crudely painted over by Eric Fischl. His thick stiffly moussed unwashed hair lifted in two flaring symmetrical wings that framed his elegantly bony, long-jawed face. His limbs were monkey-long and twitchy. His shoulders were narrow and high; his chest was perceptibly concave. He might have been fourteen, or twenty-five. He was of a generation as distant from Marina Dyer's as another species. He wore a T-shirt stamped Soul Asylum beneath a rumpled Armani jacket of the color of steel filings, and pinstriped Ralph Lauren fleece trousers stained at the crotch, and size-twelve Nikes. Mad blue veins thrummed at his temples. He was a preppy cokehead who'd managed until now to stay out of trouble, Marina had been warned by Derek Peck, Sr.'s, attorney who'd arranged, through Marina's discreet urging, for her to interview for the boy's counsel: a probable psychopath-matricide who not only claimed complete innocence but seemed actually to believe it. He gave off a complex odor of the ripely organic and the chemical. His skin appeared heated, of the color and texture of singed oatmeal. His nostrils were rimmed in red like nascent fire and his eyes were a pale acetylene yellow-green, flammable. You would not want to bring a match too close to those eyes, still less would you want to look too deeply into those eyes.

When Marina Dyer was introduced to Derek Peck the boy stared at her hungrily. Yet he didn't get to his feet like the other men in the room. He leaned forward in his chair, the tendons standing out in his neck and the strain of *seeing, thinking* visible in his young face. His handshake was fumbling at first then suddenly strong, assured as an adult man's, hurtful. Unsmiling, the boy shook hair out of his eyes like a horse rearing its beautiful brute head and a painful sensation ran through Marina Dyer like an electric shock. She had not experienced such a sensation in a long time.

In her soft contralto voice that gave nothing away, Marina said, "Derek, *hi*."

IT WAS IN the 1980s, in an era of celebrity-scandal trials, that Marina Dyer made her reputation as a "brilliant" criminal defense lawyer; by being in fact brilliant, and by working very hard, and by playing against type. There was the audacity of drama in her positioning of herself in a male-dominated courtroom. There was the startling fact of her physical size: she was a "petite" size five, self-effacing, shy-seeming, a woman easy to overlook though it would not be to your advantage to overlook her. She was meticulously and unglamorously groomed in a way to suggest a lofty indifference to fashion, an air of timelessness. She wore her sparrow-colored hair in a French twist, ballerina-style; her favored suits were Chanels in subdued harvest colors and soft dark cashmere wools, the jackets giving some bulk to her narrow frame, the skirts always primly to mid-calf. Her shoes, handbags, briefcases were of exquisite Italian leather, expensive but understated. When an item began to show signs of wear, Marina replaced it with an identical item from the same Madison Avenue shop. Her slightly askew left eye, which some in fact had found charming, she'd long ago had corrected with surgery. Her eyes were now direct, sharply focused. A perpetually moist, shiny dark-brown, with a look of fanaticism at times, but an exclusively professional fanaticism, a fanaticism in the service of her clients, whom she defended with a legendary fervor.

A small woman, Marina acquired size and authority in public arenas. In a courtroom, her normally reedy, indistinct voice acquired volume, timbre. Her passion seemed to be aroused in direct proportion to the challenge of presenting a client as "not guilty" to reasonable jurors and there were times (her admiring fellow professionals joked about this) that her plain, ascetic face shone with the luminosity of Bernini's Saint Teresa in her ecstasy. Her clients were martyrs, their prosecutors persecutors. There was a spiritual urgency to Marina Dyer's cases impossible for jurors to explain afterward, when their verdicts were sometimes questioned. *You would have had to be there, to hear her, to know.*

Marina's first highly publicized case was her successful defense of a U.S. congressman from Manhattan who'd been charged with criminal extortion and witness tampering; her second was the successful if controversial defense of a black performance artist charged with rape and assault of a druggie fan who'd come uninvited to his suite at the Four Seasons. There had been a prominent, photogenic Wall Street trader charged with embezzlement, fraud, obstruction of justice; there had been a woman journalist charged with attempted murder in the shooting and wounding of a married lover; there had been lesser known but still meritorious cases, rich with challenge. Marina's clients were not invariably acquitted but their sentences, given their probable guilt, were considered lenient. Sometimes they spent no time in prison at all, only in halfway houses; they paid fines, did community service. Even as Marina Dyer shunned publicity, she reaped it. After each victory, her fees rose. Yet she was not avaricious, or even apparently ambitious. Her life was her work, and her work her life. Of course, she'd been dealt a few defeats, in her early career when she'd sometimes defended innocent or quasi-innocent people, for modest fees. With the innocent you risk emotions, breakdown, stammering at crucial moments on the witness stand. You risk the eruption of rage, despair. With accomplished liars, you know you can depend upon a performance. Psychopaths are best: they lie fluently, but they believe.

Marina's initial interview with Derek Peck, Jr., lasted for several hours and was intense, exhausting. If she took him on, this would be her first murder trial; this seventeen-year-old boy her first accused murderer. And what a brutal murder: matricide. Never had she spoken with, in such intimate quarters, a client like Derek Peck. Never had she gazed into, for long wordless moments, any eyes like his. The vehemence with which he stated his innocence was compelling. The fury that his innocence should be doubted was mesmerizing. *Had* this boy killed, in such a way?—"trans-gressed"?—violated the law, which was Marina Dyer's very life, as if it were of no more consequence than a paper bag to be crumpled in the hand and tossed away? The back of Lucille Peck's head had literally been smashed in by an estimated twenty or more blows of the golf club. Inside her bathrobe, her soft naked-flaccid body had been pummeled, bruised, bloodied; her genitals furiously lacerated. An unspeakable crime, a crime in violation of taboo. A tabloid crime, thrilling even at second or third hand.

In her new Chanel suit of such a purplish-plum wool it appeared black as a nun's habit, in her crisp chignon that gave to her profile an Avedon-lupine sharpness, Marina Dyer gazed upon the boy who was Lucy Siddons's son. It excited her more than she would have wished to acknowledge. Thinking, *I* am unassailable, *I* am untouched. It was the perfect revenge.

Lucy Siddons. My best friend, I'd loved her. Leaving a birthday card and a red silk square scarf in her locker and it was days before she remembered to thank me though it was a warm thank-you, a big-toothed genuine smile. Lucy Siddons who was so popular, so at ease and emulated among the snobbish girls at Finch. Despite the blemished skin, buckteeth, hefty thighs, and waddling-duck walk for which she was teased, so lovingly teased. The secret was, Lucy had *personality.* That mysterious X factor which, if you lack it, you can never acquire. If you have to ponder it, it's out of your reach forever. And Lucy was *good, good-hearted.* A practicing Christian from a wealthy Manhattan Episcopal family famous for their good works. Waving to Marina Dyer to come sit with her and her friends in the cafeteria, while her friends sat stonily smiling; choosing scrawny Marina Dyer for her basketball team in gym class, while the others groaned. But Lucy was good, so good. Charity and pity for the despised girls of Finch spilled like coins from her pockets.

Did I love Lucy Siddons those three years of my life, yes I loved Lucy Siddons like no one since. But it was a pure, chaste love. A wholly one-sided love.

HIS BAIL had been set at $350,000, the bond paid by his distraught father. Since the recent Republican election-sweep it appeared that capital punishment would soon be reinstated in New York State but at the present time there was no murder-one charge, only murder-two for even the most brutal or premeditated crimes. Like the murder of Lucille Peck about which there was, regrettably, so much local publicity in newspapers, magazines, on television and radio, Marina Dyer began to doubt her client could receive a fair trial in the New York City area. Derek was hurt, incredulous: "Look, why would *I* kill her, *I* was the one who loved her!" he whined in a childish voice, lighting up another cigarette out of his mashed pack of Camels, "—*I was the only fucking one who loved her in the fucking universe!*" Each time Derek met with Marina he made this declaration, or a variant. His eyes flamed with tears of indignation, moral outrage. Strangers had entered his house and killed his mother and *he* was being blamed! Could you believe it! His life and his father's life torn up, disrupted as if a tornado had blown through! Derek wept angrily, opening himself to Marina as if he'd slashed his breastbone to expose his raging palpitating heart.

Profound and terrible moments that left Marina shaken for hours afterward.

Marina noted, though, that Derek never spoke of Lucille Peck as *my mother* or *Mother* but only as *her, she.* When she'd happened to mention to him that she'd known Lucille, years ago in school, the boy hadn't seemed to hear. He'd been frowning, scratching at his neck. Marina repeated gently, "Lucille was an outstanding presence at Finch. A dear friend." But still Derek hadn't seemed to hear.

Lucy Siddons's son who bore virtually no resemblance to her. His glaring eyes, the angular face, the hard-chiseled mouth. Sexuality reeked about him like unwashed hair, soiled T-shirt, and jeans. Nor did Derek resemble Derek Peck, Sr., so far as Marina could see.

In the Finch yearbook for 1970 there were numerous photos of Lucy Siddons and the other popular girls of the class, the activities beneath their smiling faces extensive, impressive; beneath Marina Dyer's single picture, the caption was brief. She'd been an honors student of course, but she had not been a popular girl no matter what her effort. Consoling herself, *I am biding my time. I can wait.*

And so it turned out to be, as in a fairy tale of rewards and punishments.

Rapidly and vacantly Derek Peck recited his story, his "alibi," as he'd recited it to the authorities numerous times. His voice resembled one simulated by computer. Specific times, addresses; names of friends who would "swear to it, I was with them every minute"; the precise route he'd taken by taxi, through Central Park, on his way back to East End Avenue; the shock of discovering *the body* at the foot of the stairs just off the foyer. Marina listened, fascinated. She did not want to think that this was a tale invented in a cocaine high, indelibly imprinted in the boy's reptile-brain. Unshakable. It failed to accommodate embarrassing details, enumerated in the investigating detectives' report: Derek's socks speckled with Lucille Peck's blood tossed down a laundry chute, wadded underwear on Derek's bathroom floor still damp at midnight from a shower he claimed to have taken at 7 A.M. but had more plausibly taken at 7 P.M. before applying gel to his hair and dressing in punk-Gap style for a manic evening downtown with certain of his heavy-metal friends. And the smears of Lucille Peck's blood on the very tiles of Derek's shower stall he hadn't noticed, hadn't wiped off. And the telephone call on Lucille's answering tape explaining he wouldn't be home for dinner he claimed to have made at about 4 P.M. but had very possibly made as late as 10 P.M., from a SoHo club.

These contradictions, and others, infuriated Derek rather than troubled him, as if they represented glitches in the fabric of the universe for which he could hardly be held responsible. He had a child's conviction that all things must yield to his wish, his insistence. *What he truly believed, how could it not be so?* Of course, as Marina Dyer argued, it *was* possible that the true killer of Lucille Peck had deliberately stained Derek's socks with blood, and tossed them down the laundry chute to incriminate him; the killer, or killers, had taken time to shower in Derek's shower and left Derek's own wet, wadded underwear behind. And there was no absolute, unshakable proof that the answering tape always recorded calls in the precise chronological order in which they came in, not one hundred percent of the time, how could that be proved? (There were five calls on Lucille's answering tape for the day of her death, scattered throughout the day; Derek's was the last.)

The assistant district attorney who was prosecuting the case charged that Derek Peck, Jr.'s, motive for killing his mother was a simple one: money. His $500 monthly allowance hadn't been enough to cover his expenses, evidently. Mrs. Peck had canceled her son's Visa account in January, after he'd run up a bill of over $6,000; relatives reported "tension" between mother and son; certain of Derek's classmates said there were rumors he was in debt to drug dealers and terrified of being murdered.

And Derek had wanted a Jeep Wrangler for his eighteenth birthday, he'd told friends. By killing his mother he might expect to inherit as much as $4 million and there was a $100,000 life insurance policy naming him beneficiary, there was the handsome four-story East End townhouse worth as much as $2.5 million, there was a property in East Hampton, there were valuable possessions. In the five days between Lucille Peck's death and Derek's arrest he'd run up over $2,000 in bills—he'd gone on a manic buying spree, subsequently attributed to grief. Derek was hardly the model preppy student he claimed to be, either: he'd been expelled from the Mayhew Academy for two weeks in January for "disruptive behavior" and it was generally known that he and another boy had cheated on a battery of IQ exams in ninth grade. He was currently failing all his subjects except a course in postmodernist aesthetics in which films and comics of Superman, Batman, Dracula, and Star Trek were meticulously deconstructed under the tutelage of a Princeton-trained instructor. There was a Math Club whose meetings Derek had attended sporadically, but he hadn't been there the evening of his mother's death.

Why would his classmates lie about him?—Derek was aggrieved, wounded. His closest friend Andy turning against him!

Marina had to admire her young client's response to the detectives' damning report: he simply denied it. His hot-flamed eyes brimmed with tears of innocence, disbelief. The prosecution was the enemy, and the enemy's case was just something thrown together, to blame an unsolved murder on him because he was a kid, and vulnerable. So he was into heavy metal, and he'd experimented with a few drugs, like everyone he knew for God's sake. *He had not murdered his mother, and he didn't know who had.*

Marina tried to be detached, objective. She was certain that no one, including Derek himself, knew of her feelings for him. Her behavior was unfailingly professional, and would be. Yet she thought of him constantly, obsessively; he'd become the emotional center of her life, as if she were somehow pregnant with him, his anguished, angry spirit inside her. *Help me! save me!* She'd forgotten the subtle, circuitous ways in which she'd brought her name to the attention of Derek Peck, Sr.'s attorney and began to think that Derek, Jr., had himself chosen her. Very likely, Lucille had spoken of her to him: her old classmate and close friend Marina Dyer, now a prominent defense attorney. And perhaps he'd seen her photograph somewhere. It was more than coincidence, after all. She knew!

She filed her motions, she interviewed Lucille Peck's relatives, neighbors, friends; she began to assemble a voluminous case, with the aid of two assistants; she basked in the excitement of the upcoming trial, through which she would lead, like a warrior-woman, like Joan of Arc, her beleaguered client. They would be dissected in the press, they would be martyred. Yet they would triumph, she was sure.

Was Derek guilty? And if guilty, of what? If truly he could not recall his actions, was *he* guilty? Marina thought, *If I put him on the witness stand, if he presents himself to the court as he presents himself to me . . . how could the jury deny him?*

It was five weeks, six weeks, now ten weeks after the death of Lucille Peck and already the death, like all deaths, was rapidly receding. A late-summer date had been set for the trial to begin and it hovered at the horizon teasing, tantalizing as the opening night of a play already in rehearsal. Marina had of course entered a plea of *not guilty* on behalf of her client, who had refused to consider any other option. Since he was innocent, he *could not* plead guilty to a lesser charge—first-degree, or second-degree, manslaughter, for instance. In Manhattan criminal law circles it was believed that going to trial with this case was, for Marina Dyer, an egregious error, but Marina refused to discuss any other alternative; she was as adamant as her client, she would enter into no negotiations. Her primary defense would be a systematic refutation of the prosecution's case, a denial *seriatim* of the "evidence"; passionate reiterations of Derek Peck's absolute innocence, in which, on the witness stand, he would be the star performer; a charge of police bungling and incompetence in failing to find the true killer, or killers, who had broken into other homes on the East Side; a hope of enlisting the jurors' sympathy. For Marina had learned long ago that the sympathy of jurors is a deep, deep well. You would not want to call these average Americans fools exactly but they were strangely, almost magically impressionable, at times susceptible as children. They were, or would like to be, "good" people; decent, generous, forgiving, kind; not "condemning," not "cruel." They looked for reasons not to convict, especially in Manhattan where the reputation of the police was clouded, and a good defense lawyer provides those reasons. Especially, they would not want to convict, of a charge of second-degree murder, a young, attractive, and now motherless boy like Derek Peck, Jr.

Jurors are easily confused, and it was Marina Dyer's genius to confuse them to her advantage. For wanting to be *good,* in defiance of justice, is one of mankind's greatest weaknesses.

⋆　　⋆　　⋆

"HEY: you don't believe me, do you?"

He'd paused in his compulsive pacing of her office, a cigarette burning in his fingers. He eyed her suspiciously.

Marina looked up startled to see Derek hovering rather close beside her desk, giving off his hot citrus-acetylene smell. She'd been taking notes even as a tape recorder played. "Derek, it doesn't matter what I believe. As your attorney, I speak for you. Your best legal—"

Derek said pettishly, "No! You have to believe me—*I didn't kill her.*"

It was an awkward moment, a moment of exquisite tension in which there were numerous narrative possibilities. Marina Dyer and the son of her old, now deceased friend Lucy Siddons shut away in Marina's office on a late, thundery-dark afternoon; only a revolving tape cassette bearing witness. Marina had reason to know that the boy was drinking, these long days before his trial; he was living in the townhouse, with his father, free on bail but not "free." He'd allowed her to know that he was clean of all drugs, absolutely. He was following her advice, her instructions. But did she believe him?

Marina said, again carefully, meeting the boy's glaring gaze, "Of course I believe you, Derek," as if it were the most natural thing in the world, and he naive to have doubted, "Now please sit down, and let's continue. You were telling me about your parents' divorce . . ."

" 'Cause if you don't believe me," Derek said, pushing out his lower lip so it showed fleshy-red as a skinned tomato, "—I'll find a fucking lawyer who *does.*"

"Yes, but I do. Now sit down, please."

"You *do?* You *believe*—?"

"Derek, what have I been saying! Now sit down."

The boy loomed above her, staring. For an instant, his expression showed fear. Then he groped his way backward, to his chair. His young, corroded face was flushed and he gazed at her, greeny-tawny eyes, with yearning, adoration.

Don't touch me! Marina murmured in her sleep, cresting with emotion. *I couldn't bear it.*

Marina Dyer. Strangers stared at her in public places. Whispered together pointing her out. Her name and now her face had become medi-sanctioned, iconic. In restaurants, in hotel lobbies, at professional gatherings. At the New York City Ballet, for instance, which Marina attended with a friend . . . for it had been a performance of this ballet troupe Lucille Peck had been scheduled to attend the night of her death. *Is that woman the lawyer? the one who . . . ? that boy who killed his mother with the golf club . . . Peck?*

They were becoming famous together.

HIS STREET NAME, his name in the downtown clubs, Fez, Duke's, Mandible, was "Booger." He'd been pissed at first then decided it was affection not mockery. A pretty white uptown boy, had to pay his dues. Had to buy respect, authority. It was a tough crowd, took a fucking lot to impress them—money, and more than money. A certain attitude. Laughing at him, *Oh you Boogerman!*—*one wild dude. But now they were impressed. Whacked his old lady? No shit! That Booger, man! One wild dude.*

Never dreamed of *it*. Nor of Mother, who was gone from the house as if traveling. Except not calling home, not checking on him. No more disappointing Mother.

Never dreamed of any kind of violence, that wasn't his thing. He believed in *passive-ism*. There was the great Indian leader, a saint. *Gandy.* Taught the ethic of *passive-ism*, triumphed over the racist-British enemies. Except the movie was too long.

Didn't sleep at night but weird times during the day. At night watching TV, playing the computer, "Myst" his favorite he could lose himself in for hours. Avoided violent games, his stomach still queasy. Avoided calculus, even the thought of it: the betrayal. For he hadn't graduated, Class of '95 moving on without him, fuckers. His friends were never home when he called. Even girls who'd been crazy for him, never home. Never returned his calls. *Him, Derek Peck! Boooogerman.* It was as if a microchip had been inserted in his brain, he had these pathological reactions. Not being able to sleep for, say, forty-eight hours. Then crashing, dead. Then waking how many hours later, mouth dry and heart hammering, lying sideways on his churned-up bed, his head over the edge and Doc Martens combat boots on his feet he's kicking like crazy as though somebody or something has hold of his ankles and he's gripping with both hands an invisible rod, or baseball bat, or club—swinging it in his sleep, and his muscles twitched and spasmed and veins swelled in his head close to bursting. *Swinging swinging swinging!*—and in his pants, in his Calvin Klein jockey shorts, he'd *come.*

WHEN HE WENT OUT he wore dark, very dark glasses even at night. His long hair tied back rat-tail style and a Mets cap, reversed, on his head. He'd be getting his hair cut for the trial but just not yet, wasn't that like . . . giving in, surrendering . . . ? In the neighborhood pizzeria, in a place on Second Avenue he'd ducked into alone, signing napkins for some giggling girls, once a father and son about eight years old, another time two old women in their forties, fifties staring as if he were Son of Sam, sure OK! signing *Derek Peck, Jr.,* and dating it. His signature an extravagant red-ink scrawl. *Thank you!* and he knows they're watching him walk away, thrilled. Their one contact with fame.

His old man and especially his lady-lawyer would give him hell if they knew but they didn't need to know everything. He was free on fucking bail wasn't he?

IN THE AFTERMATH of a love affair in her early thirties, the last such affair of her life, Marina Dyer had taken a strenuous "ecological" field trip to the Galápagos Islands; one of those desperate trips we take at crucial times in our lives, reasoning that the experience will cauterize the emotional wound, make of its very misery something trivial, negligible. The trip was indeed strenuous, and cauterizing. There in the infamous Galápagos, in the vast Pacific Ocean due west of Equador and a mere ten miles south of the Equator, Marina had come to certain life-conclusions. She'd decided not to kill herself, for one thing. For why kill one*self,* when nature is so very eager to do it for you, and to gobble you up? The islands were rock-bound, storm-lashed, barren. Inhabited by reptiles, giant tortoises. There was little vegetation. Shrieking seabirds like damned souls except it was not possible to believe in "souls" here. *In no world but a fallen one could such lands exist* Herman Melville had written of the Galápagos, which he'd called also the Enchanted Isles.

When she returned from her week's trip to hell, as she fondly spoke of it, Marina Dyer was observed to devote herself more passionately than ever, more single-mindedly than ever, to her profession. Practicing law would be her life, and she meant to make of her life a quantifiable and unmistakable success. What of "life" that was not consumed by law would be inconsequential. The law was only a game, of course: it had very little to do with justice or morality, "right" or "wrong," "common" sense. But the law was the only game in which she, Marina Dyer, could be a serious player. The only game in which, now and then, Marina Dyer might win.

THERE WAS Marina's brother-in-law who had never liked her but, until now, had been cordial, respectful. Staring at her as if he'd never seen her before. "How the hell can you defend that vicious little punk? How do you justify yourself, morally? He killed his *mother,* for God's sake!" Marina felt the shock of this unexpected assault as if she'd been struck in the face. Others in the room, including her sister, looked on, appalled. Marina said carefully, trying to control her voice, "But, Ben, you don't believe that only the obviously 'innocent' deserve legal counsel, do you?" It was an answer she had made numerous times, to such a question; the answer all lawyers make, reasonably, convincingly.

"Of course not. But people like you go too far."

" 'Too far'? 'People like me'—?"

"You know what I mean. Don't play dumb."

"But I don't. I don't know what you mean."

Her brother-in-law was by nature a courteous man, however strong his opinions. Yet how rudely he turned away from Marina, with a dismissive gesture. Marina called after him, stricken, "Ben, I don't know what you mean. Derek *is* innocent, I'm sure. The case against him is only circumstantial. The media—" Her pleading voice trailed off; he'd walked out of the room.

Marina?—don't cry.

They don't mean it, Marina. Don't feel bad, please!

Hiding in the locker-room lavatory after the humiliation of gym class. How many times. Even Lucy, one of the team captains, didn't want her: that was obvious. Marina Dyer and the other last choices, a fat girl or two, myopic girls, uncoordinated clumsy asthmatic girls laughingly divided between the red team and the gold. *Then, the nightmare of the game itself.* Trying to avoid being struck by thundering hooves, crashing bodies. Yells, piercing laughter. Swinging flailing arms, muscular thighs. How hard the gleaming floor when you fell! The giant girls (Lucy Siddons among them, glaring, fierce) ran over her if she didn't step aside; she had no existence for them. Marina, made by the gym teacher, so absurdly, a "guard." *You must play, Marina. You must try. Don't be silly. It's only a game. These are all just games. Get out there with your team!* But if the ball was thrown directly at her it would strike her chest and ricochet out of her hands and into the hands of another. If the ball sailed toward her head she was incapable of ducking but stood stupidly helpless, paralyzed. Her glasses flying. Her scream a child's scream, laughable. It was all laughable. Yet it was her life.

Lucy, good-hearted repentant Lucy, sought her out where she hid in a locked toilet stall, sobbing in fury, a bloodstained tissue pressed against her nose. *Marina?—don't cry. They don't mean it, they like you, come on back, what's wrong?* Good-hearted Lucy Siddons she'd hated the most.

ON THE AFTERNOON of the Friday before the Monday that would be the start of his trial, Derek Peck, Jr., broke down in Marina Dyer's office.

Marina had known something was wrong; the boy reeked of alcohol. He'd come with his father, but had told his father to wait outside; he insisted that Marina's assistant leave the room.

He began to cry, and to babble. To Marina's astonishment he fell hard onto his knees on her burgundy carpet, began banging his forehead against the glass-topped edge of her desk. He laughed, he wept. Saying in an anguished choking voice how sorry he was he'd forgotten his mother's last birthday he hadn't known would be her last and how hurt she'd been like he'd forgotten just to spite her and that wasn't true, Jesus he loved her! the only person in the fucking universe who loved her! And then at Thanksgiving this wild scene, she'd quarreled with the relatives so it was just her and him for Thanksgiving she insisted upon preparing a full Thanksgiving dinner for just two people and he said it was crazy but she insisted, no stopping her when her mind was made up and he'd known there would be trouble, that morning in the kitchen she'd started drinking early and he was up in his room smoking dope and his Walkman plugged in knowing there was no escape. And it wasn't even a turkey she roasted for the two of them, you needed at least a twenty-pound turkey otherwise the meat dried out she said so she bought two ducks, yes *two dead ducks* from this game shop on Lexington and 66th and that might've been OK except she was drinking red wine and laughing kind of hysterical talking on the phone preparing this fancy stuffing she made every year, wild rice and mushrooms, olives, and also baked yams, plum sauce, cornbread, and chocolate-tapioca pudding that was supposed to be one of his favorite desserts from when he was little that just the smell of it made him feel like puking. *He* stayed out of it upstairs until finally she called him around 4 P.M. and he came down knowing it was going to be a true bummer but not knowing how bad, she was swaying-drunk and her eyes smeared and they were eating in the dining room with the chandelier lit, all the fancy Irish linens and Grandma's old china and silver and she insisted *he* carve the ducks, he tried to get out of it but couldn't and Jesus! what happens!—he pushes the knife in the duck breast and there's actual blood squirting out of it!— and a big sticky clot of blood inside so he dropped the knife and ran out of the room gagging, it'd just completely freaked him in the midst of being stoned he couldn't take it running out into the street and almost hit by a car and her screaming after him *Derek come back! Derek come back don't leave me!* but he split from that scene and didn't come back for a day and a half. And ever after that she was drinking more and saying weird things to him like he was her baby, she'd felt him kick and shudder in her belly, under her heart, she'd talk to him inside her belly for months before he was born she'd lie down on the bed and stroke him, his head, through her skin and they'd talk together she said, it was the closest she'd ever been with any living creature and he was embarrassed not knowing what to say except *he* didn't remember, it was so long ago, and she'd say yes oh yes in your heart you remember in your heart you're still my baby boy *you do remember* and he was getting pissed saying *fuck it, no: he didn't remember* any of it. And there was only one way to stop her from loving him he began to understand, but he hadn't wanted to, he'd asked could he transfer to school in Boston or somewhere living with his dad but she went crazy, *no no no* he wasn't going, she'd never allow it, she tried to hold him, hug and kiss him so he had to lock his door and barricade it practically and she'd be waiting for him half-naked just coming out of her bathroom pretending she'd been taking a shower and clutching at him and that night finally he must've freaked, something snapped in his head and he went for the two-iron, she hadn't had time even to scream it happened so fast and merciful, him running up behind her so she didn't see him exactly—"It was the only way to stop her loving me."

Marina stared at the boy's aggrieved, tear-stained face. Mucus leaked alarmingly from his nose. What had he said? He had said . . . *what?*

Yet even now a part of Marina's mind remained detached, calculating. She was shocked by Derek's confession, but was she *surprised?* A lawyer is never surprised.

She said, quickly, "Your mother Lucille was a strong, domineering woman. I know, I knew her. As a girl, twenty-five years ago, she'd rush into a room and all the oxygen was sucked up. She'd rush into a room and it was like a wind had blown out all the windows!" Marina hardly knew what she was saying, only that words tumbled from her; radiance played about her face like a flame. "Lucille was a smothering presence in your life. She wasn't a normal mother. What you've told me only confirms what I'd suspected. I've seen other victims of psychic incest—I know! She hypnotized you, you were fighting for your life. It was your own life you were defending." Derek remained kneeling on the carpet, staring vacantly at Marina. Tight little beads of blood had formed on his reddened forehead, his snaky-greasy hair drooped into his eyes. All his energy was spent. He looked to Marina now, like an animal who hears, not words from his mistress, but sounds; the consolation of certain cadences, rhythms. Marina was saying, urgently, "That night, you lost control. Whatever happened, Derek, it wasn't you. *You are the victim*. She drove you to it! Your father, too, abrogated his responsibility to you—left you with *her*, alone with *her*, at the age of thirteen. Thirteen! That's what you've been denying all these months. That's the secret you haven't acknowledged. You had no thoughts of your own, did you? For years? Your thoughts were *hers*, in *her* voice." Derek nodded mutely. Marina had taken a tissue from the burnished-leather box on her desk and tenderly dabbed at his face. He lifted his face to her, shutting his eyes. As if this sudden closeness, this intimacy, was not new to them but somehow familiar. Marina saw the boy in the courtroom, her Derek: transformed: his face fresh-scrubbed and his hair neatly cut, gleaming with health; his head uplifted, without guile or subterfuge. *It was the only way to stop her loving me.* He wore a navy blue blazer bearing the elegant understated monogram of the Mayhew Academy. A white shirt, blue-striped tie. His hands clasped together in an attitude of Buddhistic calm. A boy, immature for his age. Emotional, susceptible. *Not guilty by reason of temporary insanity*. It was a transcendent vision and Marina knew she would realize it and that all who gazed upon Derek Peck, Jr., and heard him testify would realize it.

Derek leaned against Marina who crouched over him, he'd hidden his wet, hot face against her legs as she held him, comforted him. What a rank animal heat quivered from him, what animal terror, urgency. He was sobbing, babbling incoherently, "—save me? Don't let them hurt me? Can I have immunity, if I confess? If I say what happened, if I tell the truth—"

Marina embraced him, her fingers at the nape of his neck. She said, "Of course I'll save you, Derek. That's why you came to me."

THE VIGIL

hy be ashamed? I'm not ashamed.

    You, passing judgment? The hell with you.

    Pretending to think people don't do things like this, not people like yourself ending up like this. And this not even the end, yet.

Not jealous but he might've been lonely. So he drove past the house in the early evening. Her house that had been his until the divorce. And she had custody of their daughter except for precisely scheduled visits with Daddy. *Whatever you want,* he'd said, *if you want it so badly.* He wasn't jealous of her new life (of which he heard from friends, without inquiring), hey look: he had a new life, too. He wasn't angry, not by nature an angry man, but he was a man you wouldn't want to provoke, like his uncle in Minnesota of whom it was said with a bemused shake of the head you wouldn't want to make an enemy of him, if you could avoid it.

Just it felt necessary some nights to get into his car and drive past the house. Not every night (he had his own life!) but two or three times a week maybe. Along Ridge Road to the cul-de-sac a mile or so beyond the house, turning and driving back casually at a time of evening when his car was one of numerous cars of no special distinction, as he knew himself a man of no special distinction, not young, not old, might've been any husband-father-homeowner in the neighborhood returning to what's called *home*. For in fact he was one of these men; he belonged here. Some nights driving past 11 Ridge Road in the early evening and seeing no lights, or just a kitchen light; or lights in most of the house meaning they were certainly home, the bluish flicker of the TV like water rippling behind glass, seeing her car (white, compact) in the carport and if not her car, the baby-sitter's car (dark green) in the driveway meaning she wasn't home yet from work, sometimes he'd glimpse both her car and the baby-sitter's car and a third car intrusive and jarring to his eye, a new-model Lexus belonging to no one R__ knew, and he would know he'd be returning later that night, around midnight when all lights at 11 Ridge Road should be out, and there was just the single (white) car in the carport; and he would park his car on the road at the foot of the driveway and sit there quietly in the darkened car thinking, *I am protecting them*. The rifle he'd bring with him only at night, late. Never in the early evening.

Eventually, the Lexus was there most nights. Remaining in the driveway later and later.

So the vigil began by chance it seemed to R__. He hadn't intended it. He wasn't a man of premeditation. He wasn't a man who sought revenge. He might've been (he was discovering) a man who sought justice. *My right. Protecting them.* He was of that brotherhood of the once-loved, now unloved. That brotherhood of the dispossessed. Learning to shave without meeting his own eyes in the mirror. Avoiding his reflection in shiny surfaces. Not an angry man but numbed. The wound so deep it hadn't bled. In his car in the night dreaming of such things losing track of time (he had a day life, a work life, of which he had no need to think) though always awake and alert and prepared to protect himself, and the woman and the child in the darkened house. *They know Daddy's here. Where else?*

Not often but occasionally another car would pass his parked car. Headlights glaring up in the rearview mirror, blinding, then gone. He'd find he was gripping the rifle without knowing what he did, low on the seat beside him so that the passing driver couldn't see. For just to hold any weapon is calming.

He remained there in his parked car on Ridge Road until he felt it was time to leave, it was safe for him to drive away. *How when I know, do I know? I don't.* In the early hours of the morning his thoughts came to him jumbled like popcorn in a popper. How he knew what he wanted to do, needed to do, what was required of him as a man even as he was acting, without thinking beforehand. Possibly this was instinct? Those venomous speckled-gray spiders of the Amazonian rain forest he'd seen on TV, big as a woman's fist yet graceful, swift, swifter than an eye-blink leaping onto their prey (mostly other insects but also newborn mice, toads, even snakes), the lightest brushing of the spider's hairy body, its sensitive cilia, and the spider *leaps*. If asked how can he distinguish prey from not-prey, edible from inedible, helpless prey from fellow predator, the spider would say *How when I know, do I know? I don't. I act.*

R__ WAS an American boy, a rural Minnesota boy; he'd grown up with guns. Rifles, shotguns. Never handguns, which were "concealed weapons" and for purposes other than hunting. He'd grown up in a hunting community though his own father, a public school principal, hadn't been a hunter. He'd gone deer hunting with his cousins and their dads, as a boy. He'd liked to tramp the woods and fields with a common purpose though he hadn't been a very good shot and probably not a very devoted hunter. His uncle admonished him *You have to want to kill, to hunt.* The truth was he'd wanted to impress the other men and boys but he hadn't much wanted to kill. He couldn't now remember that he'd killed though he'd shot his rifle and he'd been in the presence of killing. Frantically shot, thrashing, bleeding deer. He'd wanted to shut his eyes but there he was running with the others, shouting. Running with his borrowed rifle held close against his body, the long barrel pointed skyward. He'd never felt comfortable with the weapon. He'd said he wanted to buy his own, but he'd never really pressed his father. What he most remembered was the vigil of the hunt, the dreamy silence of the woods before the shooting began, isolated birds' cries overhead, his steaming breath and quickened heartbeat. *Just to be there. One of them.* These were vivid happy memories though in fact he hadn't hunted more than three or four times, always with a Springfield deer-hunting rifle lent to him by his father's younger brother. He was R__ but it hadn't truly mattered which one of them he was, only that he'd been there.

In Axton County, seventy miles northwest of Minneapolis. In the years of his growing up. But he'd never owned a rifle. Not as a boy and not as an adult man. Until now, newly divorced, he felt the necessity. He bought a Springfield target rifle, a .22, in a distant part of the state. But only a single box of bullets.

The salesclerk remarked, *You're starting off modest, eh?*

★   ★   ★

HIS WIFE HAD hated hunting on principle. Moral principle, for she was a moral person. *Killing for sport* she called it. Those damning words *Killing for sport!* Spoken with disdain, derision. R__ who was no hunter and who'd never killed in the Minnesota woods found himself defending the sport as if defending his and his family's pride. As if hunting was only just that, a sport; a game for boys; not something profound and mysterious. *Hey, listen, it isn't like that at all. What it's like . . .* His wife listened, or pretended to listen. That flamelike conviction in her, which had always daunted him, of being right, and knowing she was right. In her fierce smiling way saying yes, but how can you justify hunting, shooting helpless creatures, terrorizing animals, and he'd shrugged like a boy who meant no harm though harm might come of his actions. His wife then asked if there'd been any gun accidents in his family, a question that took him by surprise. He told her no. No "gun accidents." Thinking afterward, offended, *We don't do careless things. Nothing by accident.*

WHEN IT WAS time to drive away he drove away. When it was time to leave the road above the city and return to the place he'd moved into but could not bring himself to call *home.* When it was time, when he was released from his vigil. When it became clear to him that *whatever was going to happen would not happen that night* and he would place the rifle in the back of the car, on the floor. It wasn't a concealed weapon. It wasn't an illegal weapon. (He had a permit.) *Not that night* and this realization might come after an hour or after two hours or after a shorter interlude, forty minutes perhaps; and if a car passed by (driven by an ex-neighbor on Ridge Road?) he might quickly depart, not wanting a police patrol car to be summoned.

He wasn't worried he'd be recognized by ex-neighbors. He'd bought a new car, very different from the old one, around the time he'd bought the rifle.

Not that he was afraid of being arrested by a police officer, because he wasn't breaking any law. What he was afraid of was killing a police officer.

When the vigil was over for the night he returned to this place in which he found himself living. Not *home.* Never to be *home.* It was only a ten-minute drive at night when the roads were clear. Often he forgot this place in which he lived when he was away from it. A rented place, interchangeable with countless others. Anonymous rooms. Anonymous furnishings. Sometimes, sleeping there, in a bed newly purchased, box springs, mattress, headboard, in his confused dreams he wandered not knowing where he was, or how old; on foot in a childhood memory of Minnesota, or on Ridge Road above the city, or on a road meant to resemble it. That disturbing way of dreams that seem to be of people, places, incidents already known to us and yet wrongly assembled. Even R__ in these dreams was not R__ as he knew himself. Sometimes, in fact, in such dreams he saw R__ at a distance, as if he were split in two: the physical being R__ and the R__ who observed him. Oh, but where was he? Why had this happened, R__ so alone? This woman he loved, and who loved him— where had she gone? And the little girl they'd told him was his daughter. *You have a daughter, a baby girl. Congratulations!* He'd thought his heart would burst with happiness, he'd never again be unhappy, one of those men other men envied, but the clock continued ticking, hours days weeks months and finally years, the baby girl was now six years old, and he'd become older, not R__ the father of an infant but R__ the banished husband-father-homeowner. And he would wake groaning from his sweaty ignoble sleep. And he would wake alone in damp, twisted sheets. In a place of shame. In a bed smelling of his body, yet of newness. Cheap-bargain newness. He would wake in this barely furnished apartment on the tenth floor of a newly built building beside a slate-colored river. Across the river were apartment buildings like mock mirror-reflections of this building. R__ was the inhabitant of approximately four rooms smelling of fresh paint and plasterboard and newly laid wall-to-wall carpeting he could not recall having chosen, a dull wet-sand hue, the very color of grime. Not *home* but a temporary set of rooms. As his life too was temporary. A continuous vigil.

You have to want to kill, to hunt.

Still, he liked the view from the tenth floor. He liked his freedom, he declared. Not waiting to be asked, for those remaining friends would not have wished to ask him, any more than they would have wished to ask how he could endure living without his wife, his daughter, his home. (For wasn't that house on Ridge Road his *home*? Of course it was.) Questions you can't ask of a man. Questions a man can't answer. So he was quick to declare that he liked the view from his new place, he liked the freedom the view promised. He liked the kinds of people who visited him in this new freedom. Girls he brought back with him. They were of the age of adult women yet were unmistakably girls. Leaning over the rail of his miniature balcony admiring the view of the river below. Praising R__ for the view as if it was a considerable accomplishment of R__'s. He said little in response. Perhaps he wasn't listening. Not wanting to scream, *Get away from me! I don't need this.* Not wanting to plead, *Hey: love me? I'm a deserving guy.* In this temporary life on the tenth floor of a high-rise apartment building he seemed often not to know what words meant. As if he'd wakened in a foreign country in which words resembling English words were spoken, but were not words he knew or could mimic. Thinking how those years he'd been married he'd spoken without needing to ponder the meanings of words and now he wasn't married, in this strange freedom he could barely speak. Asked how he was, and this was a question put to him frequently, like buckshot spraying him from all angles, he could not think of a reply except *Fine!* which came immediately to his lips. *How're you?* Like a desperately sick person asked to give his temperature, his white blood cell count, the rate of his heartbeat. Making love to a naked laughing blond girl with a forehead prematurely lined like pie dough across which a fork's prongs have been drawn he'd said suddenly, seriously, *Hey: you don't have to do this. It isn't going to make any difference in your life.*

Another time, guilty at a girl's quick warmth and overnight devotion he'd said, *Whatever you want from me, I don't have. It's gone.*

Yet even these words, uttered spontaneously, without premeditation, weren't authentic. Just words. Spoken by R__ as an actor might speak lines from a script he'd never seen before, and would not read through to the end.

> *If we're so unhappy maybe we should both die.*
> *No but I'm not unhappy. Hell no!*
> *More company than I can handle. Telephone ringing.*
> *It was for the best. A mutual decision. A long time coming. Amicable divorce.*
> *No contest. She has custody. The mother of course.*
> *Bitter? Not me.*
> *No time to be lonely. Freedom! I'd been suffocating.*
> *The three of us, I mean. If we're so unhappy.*

WHEN IT WAS time to drive away he drove away. When it was time to return he returned. In a jacket, dark trousers, and gloves and sometimes if he remembered clean-shaven, though more often not, and his hair damp-combed, grown long behind his ears. In the early evening he came without the rifle, driving in no haste and yet not conspicuously slowly along the semirural road of shadowy houses set back behind stands of pine and deciduous trees and wooden fences. His own house, the house that had been his, was the fourth house on the left after you turned onto Ridge Road, and the left-hand side of the road was on higher ground than the right, for this rural-suburban area had been built on the side of a massive hill locally known as a mountain, though nothing more than a massive glacier hill rising above the city. This route he'd memorized. Living here at 11 Ridge Road for seven years of the twelve. And the earlier years of the marriage faded like a movie seen long ago. For the earlier years had preceded the baby girl's birth. Driving along the road he'd memorized sometimes drifting into a dream. A dream of homecoming. Coming home. Like the other husbands-fathers-homeowners of Ridge Road. As lights were coming on, at dusk and after. And the headlights of vehicles. He was a driver who held off switching on lights, didn't want to hurry dusk, or the coming of night. Thinking as he drove past his house (not pausing to stare, only glancing up the driveway to see: the white car, the green car, the Lexus) how strange it was, you lived in one of these houses and no other; that's to say, you didn't live in one of these houses, and no other; and years ago when you'd lived here if you'd made a mistake and turned into any driveway except the fourth (on the left) you'd have been out of place; you'd have been not-home; you'd have been experienced not as a husband-father-homeowner but as a stranger, an intruder; if you persisted, entering the house that was not-home, you'd be a dangerous man, a criminal. It was such simple logic it might be overlooked.

Now the owner of the Lexus turned up that driveway at dusk, as if he had the right. A man unknown to R__, who had too much pride to make inquiries of him. An intruder, an adversary. This man with whom R__'s wife was what you'd call involved. *Sleeping with him. Fucking him.* A man glimpsed at a distance, in a suit and tie, or in a leather coat, now entering R__'s house as if he had the right, parking his car in the driveway behind the white car in the carport as if he had the right, and this insult was astonishing to R__ who believed himself a reasonable and honorable man and who could not assimilate it into what he knew. For wasn't it a fact that only a year ago if this stranger had turned into the driveway at 11 Ridge Road, and R__ and his wife and daughter were inside, he'd have been an intruder; it would have been R__'s duty to refuse him entry, to use force if required. When R__ had lived in that house, though, he hadn't owned the rifle. *A homeowner is justified. Protecting his home, his family. Yes, he had a permit!* That was why the correct driveway and the correct house were so crucial.

Always, turning onto Ridge Road, R__ looked for the mailbox. It was on the opposite side of the road from the driveway for 11 Ridge Road. All the mailboxes were on that side. His eye glided along until he saw the mailbox, his mailbox. Plain weathered black and utilitarian and marked with only a luminous white 11, no name. He knew that mailbox. He'd bought that mailbox at Kmart seven years ago and he'd pounded the post for that mailbox into stony soil and his fingers and arms still ached from the memory but it was a good sensation. *If she didn't want this, didn't want me, she'd have changed the mailbox.*

ONE NIGHT a few weeks ago he'd returned to the apartment on the tenth floor of the high-rise by the river and listened to her voice on his answering machine.

Please don't whatever you are doing please
Don't make me get a court order injunction don't please
I thought you'd agreed I thought why are you
This isn't the kind of man you are I thought
Are you?

Her voice in this new, echoing place. Her voice so strangely here where girls' voices were shrill and flat as cartoon voices. Her voice he replayed to listen to again, again. Her voice he'd come to hate. No he'd come to love. But in a new way as you'd come to love the voice, the single voice, you might hear through a pipe if you were buried underground and this pipe to the outer world was your only salvation. He replayed it, until it was more than memorized. He wondered if she'd planned her words beforehand or if she'd only just spoken, trusting to instinct. He wondered if the man, the stranger, had been present; possibly holding her hand. (Actually, he doubted this.) Her voice so reasonable. Her voice so wary, frightened. (Of R__? Her husband? Too bad she hadn't thought of that earlier.) In the end he'd erased the tape. He had no urge to call her back and he recognized that as a good sign. There'd been a time he'd called her back, left messages on her machine and his lawyer had told him what an error, she'll save them, of course she's saved them, use against you in a court of law, please be prudent and if you can't trust yourself to be prudent don't contact the woman at all.

It was a usage that rang oddly in R__'s ears. *The woman.* As if his wife, now his ex-wife, was, from the perspective of a neutral observer, simply *the woman.*

Woman, a specimen. Of a species.

He'd ceased driving along the Ridge Road. He'd ceased parking at the end of the driveway. In the early evening and later at night. He'd kept the rifle at home, in safekeeping in a closet. He had not contacted her but he'd immediately obeyed her, he'd granted the woman that power over him, knowing she would rejoice in it. She would tell her lover, *I think it's all right now. I don't want to file a complaint.* In the meantime R__ bought a car very different from the previous car, as that car had been very different from the car he'd driven when he'd lived in the house at 11 Ridge Road.

Have to want to kill, to hunt. It was another month now, a new season. He'd returned to his vigil and was feeling good. Driving along the Ridge Road at dusk, as lights came on. That quickening of the pulse when lights begin to come on. He had only to glance to the left as he passed the black mail-box (on his right) to see, brazen in the driveway, the new-model metallic-gray Lexus. And her car, a white compact of no special distinction, in the carport. And the baby-sitter's car gone. *He's there for dinner with them. And then?* R__ continued to drive along the suburban road not too fast or con-spicuously slowly, passing homes like his own, ranch-style, wood-frame and stucco and brick, sliding glass doors and redwood decks and "cathe-dral" ceilings and asphalt driveways and carports and tall pines and decidu-ous trees on two-acre lots. This paradise from which R__ had been expelled like one infected with rabies.

Please, she'd begged, *let's remember each other as we used to be. Can't we?*

Stroking the rifle he felt calmed, reassured. He cared for it with a methodical tenderness. Oil gleamed on the metal parts like a film of per-spiration, a smell he liked. And the smell of the maple stock he'd polished until it shone with pride. Afterward putting on tight-fitting leather gloves and carefully cleaning the rifle of all fingerprints and smudges.

Just to be certain, he'd wiped it down twice.

Please, she'd begged. R__ whispered, *Yes.*

Driving now to the cul-de-sac a mile beyond 11 Ridge Road and returning and passing the house seeing that lights were on in most of the rooms. That warm domestic glow through sliding glass doors and plate-glass windows partly hidden from the road by trees. He drove on. Returned to the high-rise building on the river with the name *Riverview*

Tower affixed. And hours later emerging again in dark clothes, a dark cap pulled down onto his forehead. Returning to his car this time with the rifle carried inside a garment bag to be removed from the bag in the privacy of his car.

Now he'd returned to his vigil it was late November and a bright-bone moon shone above the tall trees of Ridge Road. The visible world was bathed in chill moonlight drained of color as in a black-and-white photograph. There was the Lexus still parked in the driveway! For neighbors and passers-by to see. And the white car, her car, diminutive in the carport. Most of the house lights were darkened but the kitchen light and the lights above the carport were still on.

Maybe it's a game you're playing. But not me.

If she'd wanted R__ to go away forever, she'd have changed the mailbox when he'd moved out. There was that understanding between them.

R__ cut his lights and made a U-turn in the road. He parked a short distance from the driveway of 11 Ridge Road, not where he'd parked last time but at a curve in the road, where his car was partly obscured by a redwood fence and shrubs. He parked facing the driveway. He was counting on the owner of the Lexus not staying the night. For if his wife's lover dared to remain until dawn, and the suburban world coming alive, R__ couldn't last his vigil; he'd have to leave, before he was noticed; but the lover, the adversary, usually left by 2 A.M., for R__'s wife seemed not to want the man in her bed all night, out of consideration for their daughter possibly, wanting to spare the six-year-old seeing another man in Daddy's bed; or possibly R__'s wife simply wanted her new lover gone. She'd make use of him as women make use of men and expel him, poor bastard, as she'd expelled R__ when she was finished with him.

So he waited.

Waited in a trance, eyes open but unseeing. Head against the headrest and one gloved hand, his right, laid upon the stock of the rifle. It was about 2:20 A.M. he heard voices, and a car door slamming, and there were the rear red lights of the Lexus, and the car being backed out of the driveway. *It's time. At last!* R__ felt relief like a man who'd been swimming underwater now surfacing to the air to fill his lungs with oxygen. Not switching on his ignition until the Lexus was a block away and not switching on his headlights until the Lexus was turning off Ridge Road onto a larger road, a state highway.

R__ followed the metallic-silver car down toward the city, and the river. Empty streets, empty intersections. The Lexus moved in the direction of a bridge, R__ a distance of about a city block behind. Easy to keep his adversary in sight. Easy to contemplate what he should do. Following the man to his home *and then? then what?* He wasn't certain. When he knew, he would know. He wasn't a man to shrink from doing what had to be done though for the past year or more he'd been in a kind of waking trance, behaving in a way he seemed to know was the "way" to behave like an actor stumbling through his role, yet not believing in it. *But I have you now. Poor bastard.* They were the only two crossing the bridge, which was a high, humped, double-span bridge in the moonlight, a mesh of crossed steel trusses supported by massive girders and thick stone pillars like ancient towers. The bridge was maybe fifty feet above the river at its highest point. By day an ordinary bridge, weatherworn and sooty, in need of repair; by night a strange fantastical structure that looked, as you moved onto it, like a launching pad. R__ felt a stab of excitement. His hunter's instinct! Keeping the red lights of the car in front of him in sight, matching his speed exactly with his adversary's speed: 40 mph.

Strange, he was smiling. R__ who since the catastrophe so rarely smiled.

I deserve this! Deserve something.

Recalling how as a boy he'd be struck by weird flashes of happiness for no apparent reason. Alone, at such times. Once, crossing a footbridge beside a railroad trestle, above this same river in wind-driven wet snow; another time, in a movie house, astonished at the ease with which the camera slipped from the consciousness of a man desperately driving a car to a head-on shot of the car seen approaching and to an aerial shot of the same speeding car. So easy! To get out of yourself.

Except it wasn't. That was mankind's curse.

R__ had been feeling relief that his adversary didn't live in his own neighborhood. What if, in R__'s very building? And their cars in the same parking garage? But he lived on the far side of the river, R__ was following him now along an elevated riverside highway, seeing in the corner of his eye his own high-rise apartment building across the river, mostly darkened, though here and there riddled with light; he'd left his own lights on, tenth-floor lights visible at this distance. The other, the adversary in the silver-metallic car, lived 2.2 miles from the bridge in a renovated riverfront area where condominium "villages" had been fashioned out of derelict warehouses and factories, aged granite and brick refurbished with sleek facades, vaulting plate-glass windows, decks and balconies overlooking the river. The place was called Riverside Heights. It was one of those R__ had considered at the time of his separation.

The way we live now. Some of us.

R__ parked in a shadowy drive, headlights off, observing his adversary parking the Lexus on the second floor of a well-lighted parking garage. The garage was adjacent to a row of two-story townhouses. These residences were mostly darkened and there appeared to be no one in the vicinity. Emptied trash containers at a curb. The time was 2:55 A.M. If a shot were fired in such a place, the gunman would have to flee immediately; possibly there'd be time for a second shot, but he wouldn't be able to examine his victim up close. In R__'s gloved hands was the Springfield rifle, the safety lock now off. The drama of that *click!* R__ had lowered the window beside him and was leaning out, aiming the barrel at his target, liking the feel of the weapon in his hands, its weight and heft. Pull the trigger or don't pull, it's your choice. A way of calming your thoughts. *A gun in your hand, you're not bullshitting anybody including yourself.*

R__ wasn't used to the scope, turning the focusing ring until abruptly he saw his target, his adversary, up close, from a distance of only a few feet. Oblivious of R__ the man was locking the door of his Lexus. His face in the crosshairs of R__'s scope. R__'s mouth had gone dry; his heart was beginning to pound. It was a good sensation. *Have to want to hunt, to kill. Or was it kill, to hunt.* He saw that his wife's lover, his adversary, was about R__'s age, not younger as he'd believed. The man wore a russet-brown leather coat, he was hatless, hair the color of ditch-water and thinning at the crown. His skin was slightly coarse, the cartilage in his nose appeared just slightly twisted. His forehead was lined. It was late, he was tired, possibly his parting words with R__'s wife troubled him, for a woman's words lingering in the mind are always troubling. R__ didn't want to think, *Divorced, poor bastard, like me.* Calmly R__ was following his target through the scope, the crosshairs tremulous on his adversary's face, his throat, the carotid artery, now the side of his head, his left ear, now the back of the head, his back in the leather coat. So strange, R__'s adversary had no awareness of him. As wild creatures, hunted, seem always to have a sense of being watched, lifting their heads alertly, their eyes moving, ears pricked for the slightest sound and their nostrils twitching. *Man is the only animal oblivious of death, is that it?* R__ allowed his adversary to move behind a concrete post, knowing he'd reappear at the exit ramp. There was only one way for the man to come, to get to the row of townhouses. R__ was thinking how, once he pulled the trigger, his vigil would end. Once he pulled the trigger and his adversary fell, whether dead or wounded, or dying, once the sound of the shot rang out in this quiet, he, R_, would be propelled into action. The first thing, escape. He was certain he'd have no trouble getting out of the Riverside Heights complex. A few seconds, his headlights off, trusting to street lights and the waning moon, he'd be gone. It was his plan to dispose of the rifle (this rifle that was possibly the only thing he owned that he truly valued), drop it in the river on his way back, and his gloves smelling of gun powder. And his vigil would end.

That would be the hard part. The vigil ended.

He would be a prime suspect in the stranger's death. A man not known personally to R__ but of course his wife, that's to say his ex-wife, would tell the police. R__'s life that was so intensely private and secret would become a public life, at least for a while. Yet R__ had faith in himself, he would never be charged with the "crime." He wouldn't even hire a lawyer; he hated lawyers living off the misery of others. What would shame him would be having to lie to other men. Not being able to tell other men, men like himself, *Sure I killed the bastard fucking my wife.* For he knew (any man knew) it was a necessary act, a just act. But he'd be forced to lie. Forced to make himself into another man, an inferior man, a man who lied. And his vigil, that had come to be his life, would end.

His finger strained against the trigger; he was prepared. Seeing the man in the leather coat was exiting the parking garage exactly as R__ had anticipated. Now about thirty feet away from R_, and walking with purpose. The paved area through which the adversary moved was well-lighted, like the area around R__'s high-rise building; ironically, to deter crime, for these renovated areas near the river were bracketed by poor ghetto neighborhoods with high crime rates, and a flourishing drug trade; but R__ was hidden in shadow. If the adversary glanced toward R__ he would see maybe the front bumper, the chrome grill of a parked car and no more. R__ was watching his adversary through the scope, centering the delicate crosshairs on the man's forehead. *Why should you live if I can't?* Fire on an intake of breath. Or was it an exhalation of breath. But what was his adversary doing?—instead of heading for one of the townhouses, turning his back so that R__ could fire at the heart, he'd gone to the trash cans on the curb, and was stooping to drag two of them clumsily with him. Yellow plastic trash containers like R__'s own.

Fuck! Can't kill a man at such a time.

The All-Nite Bridge Diner. R__ had seen the diner glinting like cheap tin beyond the bridge ramp. He parked and locked his car and went inside. Lights bright as a dentist's office, booths with ripped vinyl seats and Formica-topped tables and full-color plastic photos of giant cheeseburgers with french fries, hotdogs and pie. R__ was dying of thirst. R__ was hungry, ravenous. There was a roaring in R__'s ears like a waterfall or possibly rock music from a radio. R__ sat at the counter. Elbows on the damp counter. Adrenaline flooded his veins like liquid flame leaving him shaking and sweaty but now beginning to fade like water down a stopped-up drain, slow but inevitable. It was 3:17 A.M. and he'd been awake for a long time. He was still wearing his gloves, which meant (he believed) it hadn't happened yet. R__ and his adversary were both (still) alive. Or had it happened, and that was why his blood beat so strangely? Why he was so hungry?—as if he hadn't eaten (and maybe he hadn't) for a day or more. In one of the torn vinyl booths a young couple paused in their conversation to look at R__. On a stool at the counter a middle-aged black man in a security guard's uniform regarded R__ sidelong with a wary expression. In a foggy mirror behind the counter was a male face, fierce and heated. The skin was waxy but flushed in patches as if he'd been slapped. The eyes were bloodshot and dilated. A man in his mid- or late thirties in a canvas jacket open at the throat, hadn't shaved in some time so his beard was pushing out like barbed wire glinting gray. In the rifle scope he'd seen the other's face clean-shaven, that look of hope. Damp-combing hair that's thinning, rubbing and slapping a face to bring a little life to it. *Hey: love me? I'm a deserving guy.*

Behind the counter was a brass-haired waitress of about forty with a red-lipstick smile determined to be friendly and welcoming to R__ who was a stranger in the All-Nite Bridge Diner and in a state of unnatural exaltation that might've been, but didn't appear to be, alcohol- or drug-induced. The woman handed R__ a stained menu saying, "How're you this evening, mister?" R__ was wiping his face with a napkin. Reasoning that, if he was here, allowing these witnesses to take note of him, and if he was still wearing the gloves, his rifle would still be in the rear of the car, zipped up safely in the garment bag. *Hasn't happened yet. The vigil not over. Not yet!* R__ said, smiling at the woman, "Ma'am, I'm the happiest I've been in my life."

WE WERE WORRIED ABOUT YOU

*D*ad was driving the family home from church in the shining new 1949 Packard Admiral when the hitchhiker appeared suddenly at the side of the road. As if, out of the tar-splotched weeds, the bleach of Sunday sun, the man had leaped up. And his strange staring eyes, and his gray wisps of beard like an aged dog's muzzle. And his bib overalls, and his greasy red bandanna around his neck. A man of no age you could guess except not young, with a smudged face, a look of being familiar yet—who was he?

"Oh!—should we stop? He looks so sad," Mom cried.

Dad was already slowing the Packard so's to see the hitchhiker's face more clearly. Often, these country highways and dirt-gravel roads, it's a neighboring farmer's "handyman" or somebody's old hermit-uncle it would be bad manners to pass by though the smell of him would pervade your car.

Dad, driving the new Packard. Four-door, cushioned seats. Heavy as a tank and of the hue and pride of something military—the sheen of the finish, a muted silver-grape, and the splendid chrome trim, front, rear, and sides, aflame in the Sunday sun. You can't imagine the joy! You can try but it's gone, it's lost and you can't retrieve it: pretty Mom in the front passenger's seat trying to smile at Dad's teasing (Dad is good-natured, but his humor has barbs) these ten or so minutes since leaving the weathered-gray shingleboard Methodist church in Haggertsville where once again the new minister Reverend Bogard wept during his sermon speaking of the suffering of Jesus Christ Our Savior and of humankind's (and his own) failings each of which is yet another spike in Christ's bleeding hands and feet, another thorn lacerating His tender forehead. Reverend Bogard's emotional outbursts stirred the women of the congregation to sympathy, tears, even pain but frankly embarrassed the men, and Dad was an impatient man, any display of weakness made him squirm. Mom smiled at his words of criticism but rarely contradicted, not quick or bold enough, to match wits with him. As with careful fingers she removed several long hatpins from her glazed-straw navy blue pillbox hat and her curled brunette hair, removing then the hat and placing it on her lap beside her navy blue straw purse and her spotless white lace gloves she'd worn into church, and out, then peeled off in the privacy of the Packard, like the other wives and mothers of the congregation in cars manned by husbands—no one wore white Sunday gloves for one minute longer than necessary!

And in the rear of the Packard, pigtailed Ann-Sharon, aged eight; and Baby Bimmy, aged three.

Then, so abruptly, the hitchhiker. On the Haggertsville Road, Route 33, approximately halfway home. How tall he seemed!—like a walking scarecrow. Eyes lifting to the oncoming car creased and narrowed as if the Packard were ablaze, blinding like a fiery chariot, and standing to peer over Mom's shoulder Baby Bimmy saw the hitchhiker raise his arm tentatively, gesture with his thumb, a mute appeal—*Help me? Whoever you are?*

But Dad was saying, "Nobody we know."

Mom said softly, "But he looks so—sad!"

"He might be dangerous," Dad said. "Might be a drinker. And he'd surely smell."

Already we were passing the hitchhiker, already the rush of air in the Packard's wake was shaking his beard, ruffling his red bandanna. In a firm, slightly chiding voice, meant only for Mom to hear, Dad said, "Anyway, dear, as you can see—there's no room for somebody else."

AND ANOTHER Sunday after church, Dad was driving his family into Yewville for dinner at Grandma's, Sunday dinner it's called though served promptly at 1 P.M., and this time—"Oh, look!—is that a *woman?*" Mom's voice lifted more in faint astonishment than in dismay or disapproval as out of a patch of tall thistles by the elevated train tracks a disheveled figure in trousers, a torn plaid shirt, a man's unlaced shoes staggered into the road blinking and raising her arm, jerking her thumb in a gesture almost rude, or obscene, indicating she wanted a ride into town. She had a red-roughened face, carroty-frizzy matted hair.

And those eyes!—glittering like coal chunks sunk in flesh.

Bim thought, trembling, *She sees me.*

"Should we stop, dear?—she must be desperate," Mom said uncertainly. "She might be ill, or . . ."

Dad was braking the Packard, though not to a full stop. The hitchhiker was in the road and he would have to drive around her.

Years had passed and the Packard was less new. But manned with no less pride by Dad who kept it in "A-1 condition" lovingly washing and polishing with chamois cloths the elegant silver-grape chassis, keeping the windshields clean despite the hundreds—thousands?—of flying insects that mangled and smeared themselves on the glass. His boy Bim was thrilled to assist him, dreamy Saturday mornings, as, over the car radio turned up high, a baseball game—St. Louis Cardinals! Chicago Cubs! New York Yankees! Brooklyn Dodgers! Cincinnati Reds!—was so vividly broadcast Bim would swear, thirty years later, his Dad had actually taken him to the ballpark and they'd witnessed with their own eyes such spectacles as a ninth-inning bases-loaded home run by Stan Musial, a similar ecstatic home run by Joe DiMaggio, they'd joined in the frenzied cheers for Jackie Robinson loping like a panther past first, past second, past third, and HOME! This Sunday, in an August heat-haze, the interior of the little shingled church was so airless even Reverend Bogard, face greasy with perspiration, seemed eager to hurry the service to its conclusion. One less hymn sung than usual. "A Mighty Fortress Is Our God" pumped out on the organ and the white-haired organist's ruffled pink rayon blouse stained across the back in the shocking shape of a bat with outspread wings, so the congregation was released early to the glimmering August sky, families hurrying to their cars and all windows cranked down to allow air to rush inside, once in motion, with a deceptive feel of coolness. As the Packard accelerated Mom laughed, breathless, pressing her hands (bare hands, she'd quickly peeled off her gloves) against her whipping hair. In the backseat, Ann-Sharon and Bim giddy with heat in starched Sunday clothes bounced on the cushions, "Drive faster, Daddy!—faster!"

"You kids settle down back there," Dad said, a note of surprise in his voice, and his eyes searching for them in the rearview mirror, "—it's too hot to fool around."

Bim thought, *Fool around!*

Fool around!—fool around! That's what people *do.*

Those years, how many?—until he was thirteen, at least—Bim saw so vividly a magnificent black stallion galloping by the roadside, keeping pace with the car, though often a little in the lead, flowing black mane and tail, flashing hooves, he had to pinch himself to realize the stallion was *not real*; and no one else, not even nosy Ann-Sharon, could see it.

That Sunday too the stallion was galloping alongside Dad's car, oblivious of Dad, and Dad oblivious of him, when, at the outskirts of Yewville, in the slummy shantytown area by the train yard, the female hitchhiker appeared. By this time Dad had slowed the car because the speed limit was thirty miles an hour, and the black stallion had faded, vanished even as Bim forgot him, the way, waking, we lose our dreams not to daylight but to consciousness. Dad peered at the woman through the windshield, and the woman peered at Dad with a peculiar grin, a jack-o'-lantern grin, too wide for her face.

"A shameful sight," said Dad stiffly, "—a female drunk—and at this hour of the day—Sunday!"

"Drunk? Oh, what a pity," Mom said, staring, "—oh, then we can't— mustn't—"

"Of course we can't," Dad said, steering the car around the swaying figure in the road, "—don't be silly!"

Ann-Sharon and Bim cringed as the Packard passed so close by the woman she might have leaned in the rear window and touched them. And when the car was past her, how awful that she began yelling at them, shaking her fist, her ugly face distended like putty and her mouth a furious O wide and gaping as a fish's so scary to see!—Ann-Sharon would dream of that mouth for years, black flying-darting things issued from it, hurtled in the direction of the fleeing car bearing Dad, Mom, Ann-Sharon, and Bim to Grandma's white clapboard house on Prospect Street where, arriving for Sunday dinner, or for Thanksgiving dinner, or for Easter dinner, no sooner did you step into the vestibule with its frosted-glass windows than the warm delicious aroma of a roasting chicken, or turkey, or ham, or beef, would fill your nostrils and cause your mouth to water so you were giddy crying, "Grandma! Oh, Grandma!—WE'RE HERE!"

⋆   ⋆   ⋆

ANOTHER TIME. The following summer. That day Mom was driving the Packard, and not Dad. Mom, Ann-Sharon in the front seat, Bim in the back with the groceries from Loblaw's, staring out at the black stallion galloping through the fields, leaping ditches, lanes, though when Mom drove the black stallion's speed was lessened, and at the Elk Creek bridge (when Mom drove, she took the long way home from Yewville: the fast-moving traffic on Route 31 made her nervous) there was a hitchhiking couple!—a scruffy bearded young man and a long-haired young woman with a filthy khaki bundle (a baby?) slung over the man's back. There they stood, bold as daylight, by the bridge's steep ramp, and as Mom approached the man shot out his thumb staring into Mom's face as she eased the bulky car past, "Hey lady, how's about a ride? Where ya goin' lady?" but Mom paid him no heed, nor glanced at his defiant companion. The man, fierce-eyed up close, sunburned, with rotted teeth, made an obscene gesture and leaned over grinning to spit onto the car's roof—but Mom, stiff with fear, simply kept driving, crossing the single-lane plank bridge at four miles an hour which was her normal speed for crossing such bridges, whether in the presence of danger or not. Poor Mom!—Bim saw how her face was dead-white and the creases and lines in her forehead were exposed, she was panting, her jaw trembling yet resolutely, stubbornly she stared straight ahead, bearing her children to safety.

Saying, afterward, when she could catch her breath, "We won't tell your dad about this. Not a word!"

SUNDAY AFTERNOON DRIVES. Just Mom, Ann-Sharon, and Bim. Dad never took the family for Sunday drives, he'd had enough of driving five days a week to Yewville to work, nine miles in and nine miles back, plant manager at Woolrich's Masonite, Inc., and after his first heart attack, the "silent" one as it was called, Dad took Sundays easy, stopped going to church, too. But Mom loved Sunday drives, even on overcast or sultry days, long dreamy looping drives through the countryside of her girlhood along Elk Creek to Lake Nautauga and a stop there for refreshments at the Tastee Freeze then across the bridge and home along the Canal Road. Or along the Chautauqua River to Milburn or Tintern Falls, over the bridge and home again on the other side of the river. Ann-Sharon rode quietly listening to Mom speak of the old days, of who lived in which house, whose farm that used to be, which girlfriend of hers from grade school had married and lived where, but Bim was an excitable child with odd, unpredictable worries—what if they got lost? ran out of gas? Mom laughed frowning at him, "Bim, don't be silly!"

Later saying, as they neared home, as if Mom could read Bim's innermost thoughts, of which he, a nine-year-old, was unaware, "Now you know, children—your dad isn't exactly his old self yet, but he will be, soon."

THAT SUNDAY THEN in May, when on the way home after the Tastee Freeze Mom decided to park in the weedy drive of an old collapsed farmhouse where a family she'd known had once lived, and she and Ann-Sharon and Bim poked about the ruins, and loaded their arms with wild lilac (rich, deep purple and white lilac, grown to a height of fifteen feet, so fragrant!), turning then amazed to see a stranger, a woman, near the car—a swarthy-skinned thick-bodied woman of no age you could guess, and there was a skinny child with her, about four years old, a little boy, the woman's eyes were slow and dull and her stained-looking face was a maze of wrinkles and her words clotted as if there were pebbles in her mouth, "Ridemizzus?" she seemed to say, and Mom stared at her and said quickly, politely, "I'm sorry, my husband doesn't allow me to pick up hitchhikers," and the woman blinked and grinned and repeated what sounded like, "Ridemizzus?—eh?" and Mom took Ann-Sharon's and Bim's hands to lead them to the car parked at the top of the driveway, as the woman stared at them flat-footed in the cinders where they'd dropped the lavish sprays of lilac they'd been picking. "Come along, come along, children," Mom whispered, her eyes bright, her fingers squeezing theirs icy-cold and strong, and the woman stared after them, and the little boy gap-toothed and spiky-haired dark like an Eskimo stared too. "Ridemizzus?" the woman was whining now, gesturing at the car, as Mom, Ann-Sharon, and Bim hurriedly got inside, Ann-Sharon in the passenger's seat, Bim in back, and Mom started the car after two tries when the engine turned over and went dead and now the woman took a step toward them, and another, raising her voice saying what sounded like "Gimme ridemizzus?—hey!"— but at last the Packard was in motion, tires flinging up cinders out of the weedy drive and this time too, headed home, Mom didn't so much as glance back.

*   *   *

HOW THINGS END!—the last time, rarely can you guess it will be the last time. For that afternoon, the day of the lilac-picking, was to be the last Sunday drive that Ann-Sharon went on, grown bored with the memorized landscape and wanting to be with her friends. And soon, too, Bim decided he had other things he'd rather do, boys to play with he preferred to the Sunday drives, so Mom's feelings were hurt and sometimes she went alone but not far, and not with much enthusiasm, and eventually the Sunday drives ceased. And at last too the old Packard was traded in for a new 1958 Studebaker, four-door, canary yellow, and one December evening driving home from work in Yewville Dad was alone and braked for a red light at the Transit Street intersection by the trainyard and out of the shadows how suddenly, unexpectedly a figure appeared!—a gaunt ragged man whose face Dad wasn't to see clearly, he was wearing a dark wool-knit cap low on his forehead, a vagrant pleading for a ride, and Dad said, "Sorry, no," and the man repeated his request, and now it was a demand, "Mister, I need a ride! hey mister gimme a ride!" but Dad said, louder, "Sorry—*no*." The light changed to green and he pressed down on the gas pedal and exactly at this moment the man grabbed the handle of the passenger's door, opened it, and Dad yelled at him leaning over to yank the door shut, and there was a struggle, and the man cursed and struck at Dad but the car leaped forward lurching and Dad kept his foot on the gas to accelerate so his attacker was thrown off and Dad escaped driving in a fury nine miles home with the passenger's door bumping and rattling, this was the night of Dad's second heart attack which was a serious one and so that spring he retired from Woolrich's and never again would he be completely well, tired easily and prone to melancholy moods never again *his old self* though Mom continued to wait faithfully for this *old self* to reappear and Dad would live to be eighty-three years old to die one snowy afternoon napping on the sofa.

THERE WAS pretty Ann-Sharon who grew up and married out of high school and had four children within the space of six years and lived in Yewville all her life. And Bim who went away to college where his professors knew him by another name though his closest friends called him Bim. And returning home for Thanksgiving his senior year driving ten hours in the rain, in the gathering dark, a foolhardy thing to do in a car borrowed from a roommate, Bim was late and so was speeding on Route 31 taking the underpass by the new shopping mall at fifty miles an hour, sheets of water spraying out winglike from the car's tires when Bim saw someone, or thought he saw, a figure hunched and huddled there in the underpass, all his life he would recall a fleeting impression of something crinkled and shiny (a cheap plastic raincoat?) and a pale startled grimacing face lifting in the car's bright beams then somehow, it made no sense how, there was a *thunk!* and the car lurched, there was a muffled cry, unless Bim imagined it, but already the car had righted itself and was speeding up out of the underpass, back into the pelting rain, onto a stretch of deserted country highway, and gone.

Twelve minutes later entering the house, his home, shaky and smiling and an aroma of roasting turkey making his mouth water, and they're waiting for him crowding to embrace him, Dad rising from his leather chair by the TV, "Bim, thank God!—we were worried about you."

THE STALKER

*A**fter it happens*. She will quit her job, and perhaps her profession. She will move away from Detroit and she will break off relations with her colleagues and even her friends who will speak of her for years afterward pityingly, wonderingly, *Does anyone ever hear from Matilde?* and *What has happened to Matilde, do you know?* and *We warned her, didn't we? We did!* As soon as she recovers from the episode, she will put her aunt's house on the market (after eight years of occupancy she still thinks of the brownstone at 289 Springwood, Mittelburg Park, as her deceased aunt's and not her own) and accept the first offer any buyer makes no matter how low. Because she isn't a woman to care much about money. Nor is she a sentimental woman. *After it happens* she will never be inclined to sentimentality again; she will have earned that distinction.

The handgun. She'd already had the permit, issued by the county, when she went to the Liberty Gun Shop on North Woodward—a cream-colored stucco building in a mini-mall between Adult X-Rated Videos & Supplies and *House of Wong* Restaurant & Carry-Out. Liberty Gun Shop advertised handguns and long guns, new and used, sales and purchases. The manager's name was Ted, call me Ted OK? but Matilde did not call him anything except a cool murmured schoolgirl *sir* once or twice. His eyes lighting on her, the tall poised height of her. Her forward-tilting head, slender neck, eyes that pebbly-gray gaze her first lover, twenty years ago, had called the hue of infinite regret, though possibly he'd said infinite *regress*, it had been something of a joke. (Between Matilde and her lovers there had always been odd, awkward, ongoing jokes she'd never quite got, though like a good sport she'd laughed on cue.) The gun shop owner pressed Matilde to consider high-capacity semiautomatic pistols, but Matilde insisted on considering only the most conventional and economic handguns. A used .38-caliber Smith & Wesson was what she wanted, ex-police issue and good enough for her purposes. Ted was disappointed, she could see. And when she took up the gun in her hand, and found it heavier than she'd anticipated, and her hand shook until she steadied it with the other, Ted expressed doubt he should sell the gun to her at all—it went against his "code of ethics" to sell any weapon to anyone who might not be capable of using it. Because a gun can be taken from you and used against you. Because to freeze with a gun in your hand can be a worse predicament than to be caught unarmed. Because you have to be prepared not just to shoot but *to kill*—and she didn't look like she'd be tough enough. But this, too, was a joke—of course. Matilde had her checkbook in hand. There was never any doubt that she, who believed in a total ban of firearms to private citizens, would be sold the revolver of her choice in the Liberty Gun Shop on North Woodward: a medium-barreled, six-shot, second-hand .38-caliber Smith & Wesson. And a small box of ammunition, two dozen bullets. Though Matilde knows, if she uses the gun at all, she will use it only once.

The heartbeat is her own, of course. Yet so frequently now she seems to be hearing it, feeling it, at a distance. Like the myriad unnamed noises of the city, ceaseless grinding-thumping, ceaseless drilling you hear without listening, planes passing high overhead in the night, invisible contrails of sound, ceaseless. *I can feel your heartbeat!—Jesus.* And then he'd laughed, she didn't know why, doesn't know why. Was he laughing at her, or in sympathy with her. She has thought of it, of him, obsessively. But she doesn't know.

The heartbeat is her own, of course. Yet it's his, too. *Look, my name is—* what sounded to her ear like *Bowe, Bowie—I'd like to see you, soon. Tomor-*

row? Tonight? Lying in this bed with its bone-hard mattress (Matilde has had a tricky back for the past several years) her eyes shut tight and sticky sweat-pearls glistening on her face, *I see him:* the rain-splattered blue Volvo with a frayed Clinton/Gore sticker on the rear bumper, he's behind the wheel parked at the entrance to the high-rise garage where Matilde parks her car while she's at work and she sees him then quickly *not-seeing* hurrying to the elevator to take her to C-level, to her car. And his telephone messages, *Matilde, Please call*—his home number, office number (he's a lawyer, a litigator, does volunteer work for Legal Aid)—which Matilde replays and erases. *Not ever again, please God. I can't.* She sees the Volvo slowly passing the brownstone at 289 Springwood with its wine-dark, slightly corroded facade, its single splendid bay window, she isn't watching, still less is she waiting, but she sees. What does he want of her, what is the connection between them, their blood commingled, she guesses *Bowe, Bowie?*—first name *Jay,* or was it the initial *J?*—he's married, she'd caught a glimpse of a ring on his left hand. He'd been breathing quickly, she felt the heat rise from him. *No. Not ever again. I can't.*

Fate. Why, Matilde Searle has often wondered, do we so crave romantic love as if it were our destiny—our private, secret, individual fate? As if romantic love, yes let's be candid and call it sexual love, the real thing, might define us in a way nothing else (our families, our hard-won careers) can define us. *I've never known who I am except when I've been in love,* Matilde has said, *and I haven't recognized that self and I haven't admired that self and I can't bear being that self again.*

Vital statistics. Born November 11, 1953. Ypsilanti, Michigan. First daughter, second child of a Roman Catholic family that would burgeon—the word "burgeon" is Matilde's, she'd used it perhaps one thousand times while growing up to speak with fond contempt of her parents and their restricted, to her restrictive, world—to six siblings. Six! people say, smiling. Your parents must have liked babies! and Matilde used to roll her eyes and say, dryly, I think it just took my mother that long to figure out what was causing it. (Now she's an adult, and her mother has been dead for three years, Matilde never jokes like that. She rarely jokes about *family* at all.) But the unexamined and wholly unquestioned Roman Catholicism of her parents and grandparents was a heavy, tacky wool overcoat that never fitted *her,* she's proud of having given up even the pretense of belief at the age of twelve. Went to Ypsilanti public schools, graduated *summa cum laude* from Michigan State University, 1976 (B.A., American history, politics), received a master's degree from the University of Michigan, 1978 (social work). Positions in East Lansing with the Michigan State Bureau of Youth and Family Service (1978–1982) and in Detroit with the Wayne County Clinic of Counseling of the State of Michigan (1982–present). At the Wayne County Clinic, one of the state's most massive and bureaucratized agencies, Matilde Searle is an assistant supervisor for Family Services, but she is also "on the floor"—she has a caseload of never less than twenty families, involving never less than one hundred individuals, and frequently twice that number. Her annual salary, determined by the Michigan legislature's budget allotment, is $41,000 and she has not had a raise in two years. There is no medically recorded "nervous breakdown" in the file on Matilde Searle, nor do rumors circulate among her colleagues that she has tried to commit suicide, as certain of her colleagues, over the years, have: the Clinic is notorious for burning out its social-services staff, female and male, but mostly female, on the sixth floor of the ancient buff-brick Wayne County Agencies building at Gratiot and Stockton where Matilde Searle has a corner-window office shared with another social worker with a master's degree from Ann Arbor, also female, five years older than Matilde, but black-Hispanic. *She* is Caucasian, a distinct minority in the city of Detroit.

The stalker. Matilde is awake yet the fevered pulse of her body suggests sleep, the paralysis of sleep. A soft, urgent, quickening heartbeat. She'd felt it—*his*. She has kicked off the quilted-satin bedspread sometime during the night and is covered now only partly by a sheet damply clinging to her lower body leaving exposed her sweat-slick chest, her small girlish-hard breasts, painfully prominent collarbone, shoulders . . . Is she naked? Where's her nightgown? She is not a woman who waits yet night is a time of waiting, sleep and bed and nakedness a time of waiting, inescapable. The .38-caliber revolver is inches away in the drawer of the bedside table and the drawer is ajar perhaps an inch. *Because you have to be prepared not just to shoot but to kill.* She's naked, sweating in her bed listening to the myriad sounds of the nighttime city and to the closer, mysterious sounds of her aunt's house and to the soft urgent quickening heartbeat she understands is her own and not another's *and yet she sees him, hears him.* She knew he'd been stalking her for weeks, she even knew his name, Ramos, Hector

Ramos, he's the estranged husband of one of her battered women clients, a woman she'd arranged to be admitted to the Wayne County Women's and Children's Shelter and for this he is furious with her, he hates her, wishes her grief, death—oh, Matilde knows. Briefly Hector Ramos had been her client too, the previous year, but whatever was thrumming along his veins—alcohol, coke, manic juices—had been too much, too intense, he hadn't been able to sit in the chair facing Matilde for more than three minutes without squirming and jumping up, and he hadn't been able to speak coherently, his eyes glistening, his lips sparked with spittle, still less had he been in a mood to fill out forms for the county, produce identification, sign his name *Hector Ramos* except in a grandiose, unintelligible scrawl. He's a short, lean-muscled man of thirty-one, unemployed carpenter, a single conviction aged nineteen ("assault"—for which he'd served a brief eighteen months in Michigan State Prison), with stark-staring black eyes, black oily-kinky hair. His forehead is deeply, tragically creased. That baffled, ravaged look, that look of ancient desperation Matilde sees in so many of her (male) clients, in so many men on the streets, Detroit's citizens. *Think I can't read, eh?—think I don't know words, eh?*—throwing the forms down on Matilde's desk. She sees him now, fierce, betrayed Hector Ramos, approaching her, something metallic and glinting in his right hand which is pressed low against his thigh. He's wearing a simulated leather jacket like vinyl, trousers with a tear in one knee, high-top sneakers like the black street kids. Swift and silent as a snake, no yelled curse to warn her, a gleam of damp teeth, then he's on her. They are in a crowded place, the outer foyer of the Wayne County Building and Ramos hasn't passed through the metal detector, which is farther into the interior, nor has he been sighted by the pair of sheriff's deputies who are on guard, Matilde Searle will not have seen him until he's on her.

Terror of death. In the abstract, it's absurd. Has not Matilde argued so, many times? Where there's no consciousness there can be no pain, no sorrow, no humiliation, no loss, no regret, no terror. Where no consciousness, no memory. Where no memory, no humanity. You, no longer living, are not you. Yet, warding off the slashing, jabbing knife blade wielded by the madman, pain so swift, intense, unexpected it seems to be a phenomenon of the very place, the air, like deafening noise. And the woman's cry, childlike, terrified—*No! Don't! Help me! I don't want to die!*

★   ★   ★

Vital statistics. Nineteen years old, a sophomore at Michigan State, when she'd lost her virginity. Odd, archaic language: *lost.* Lost what, precisely? Later, her first intense, serious love affair, yes then she'd lost something more tangible, if undefinable: her heart? her independence? her control of, definition of, *self*? That first true loss, the furious bafflement of it. And never again quite so assured, confident. Never again quite so certain, *Yes I know what I am doing, for God's sake leave me alone.*

What if: she has taken not one of the elevators that open out onto the front foyer, but the stairs at the rear of the building. Which she has done, occasionally: five flights down. Exiting then by the rear doors, guarded also by Wayne County Sheriff's men, out onto Stockton. And so she'll avoid him. For that day. How many days she's been *not seeing* him. The lone figure in the periphery of her vision. Footsteps echoing hers to her car in the high-rise parking garage, slow angry smile as she drives past him she's *not seeing* because she's calm, resolute. Determined not to be intimidated, still less terrorized. Long before Hector Ramos there had been threats against Matilde Searle's life, and there had been stalkers in her life, before even the term "stalker" came into general usage. *Look, I'm a professional woman. I can take care of myself.*

What if: she has taken not one of the elevators that open out onto the front foyer, but the stairs at the rear of the building. And so she would not be assaulted that day by a madman wielding a ten-inch carving knife newly purchased at Kmart. And so *he* would not step forward to intervene, even before he hears her screaming, and the screams and shouts of others around her. *He,* having legal business that day with the Child Protection Department, but otherwise infrequently in the county building, would not seize hold of Hector Ramos taking a knife-slash in the face, a stab in the forearm, wrestling the knife from Ramos before the sheriff's deputies have even drawn their guns.

So human! So absurd!—to make of a purely random incident, an event of no greater significance than the the encounter of microbes, or molecules, or subatomic particles, an event charged *with meaning.*

So human! so absurd!—to make of a man's desire for her anything more significant and more profound than a man's desire for a woman, any woman.

Because he'd intervened, and her blood was on him, in streaks on the front of his coat, and on his hands; her blood, and his own. Afterward insisting, *Look, we've got to see each other, Matilde—you know that, don't you? That's your name, Matilde?*

The heartbeat is her own, of course. Even when making love, grasping a lover's shoulders, the small of the back, the buttocks, moving her body with his, her loins against his, the smooth heated skin, mouths sucking mouths, even then she had known which heartbeat is her own, which his. But it has been so long.

Fear of death?—*not fear of death* but fear of sudden helplessness, violence. A shattering of glass downstairs and the breaking-in of a door (it will be the rear, kitchen door: this, the door forced open two years ago by an unknown burglar or burglars who trashed Matilde's kitchen, living room, study before taking away what could be carried of Matilde's valuable possessions which, in fact, added up to very little) and the sound of rapid footsteps. How many times in the night before even the assault by Hector Ramos has she wakened dry-mouthed to hear sounds downstairs like a rough-rocking dark tide rising to drown her. How many times waking, her body quivering taut as a bow from which an arrow will fly. Then, she'd had no handgun in her bedside table. She had wanted no gun, no weapon. She would rise swiftly and lock the door of her room, and she would dial the emergency number 911 if the sounds persisted and if she was truly awake and not dreaming which in fact so often even before the assault by Hector Ramos, she was. And so there was no need, for there was no danger. For when the house had indeed been broken into, she hadn't been home. (Though she'd left lights on, a radio turned up high.) And when Hector Ramos had so carelessly stalked her those several weeks, late September through October, into November, it was always in the vicinity of the Wayne County Clinic or in the high-rise garage in which she parked and she'd never been really alone, not really alone, as now, in her bed, upstairs in the elegant old crumbling brownstone at 289 Springwood she'd inherited from her aunt, she is.

Naked woman. She throws off the damp sheet that smells of her body though she'd showered and washed her hair before going to bed. Rises from bed, unsteady on her legs, she's a thin-legged bird like a flamingo, or an ostrich. Corrective lenses required for driving, especially night driving. When depths flatten to the thickness of playing cards and even bright, primary colors are drained of their brilliance. She's in excellent physical condition except for occasional migraine headaches, bouts of insomnia, irregular and painful menstrual periods. She drives forty miles to be examined by a (woman) gynecologist in Oakland County, north of the city. She has no internist in the city since the doctor she'd been seeing was shot to death in his office near Wayne State University by black youths demanding drugs and cash, a year ago last Christmas. No prescription drugs now, not even birth-control pills. There are other methods of contraception if contraception is required . . . She's staring at something on the floor. She knows what it is, only the sweat-soaked nightgown she'd yanked off over her head and tossed away. She knows what it is, a puddle of cloth; still she stares.

Infinite regret. Infinite regress. There's something about a naked woman, one of Matilde's lovers whom she has not seen, nor spoken with, since 1981, once said. A naked woman in a man's close proximity always appears so . . . unexpected somehow. Fleshy, overpowering. Too big. *Even,* he'd said thoughtfully, *when you're not.*

How many years ago in another city before Matilde's life was her own. In the grip of an obsession, sexual love making of her body a vessel of yearning, of hunger, *This is not me! Not Matilde Searle,* she'd driven slowly and methodically past the home of her (married, law professor) lover, at dusk, and at midnight, one mad, desperate, lonely time at dawn, not truly wishing to see the man (with whom, shortly, she would break) and still less wishing to be seen (for what shame to be seen! So exposed! Where her lover fantasized twenty-seven-year-old Matilde, mysterious, elusive, too young and too idealistic for him, to be so exposed!) but simply to be in physical proximity to him who at that time in her life had seemed to Matilde Searle the very center of her life, her life's radiant core. Which is why we say *I can't live without you* meaning *your life gives life to me, who am otherwise an empty vessel, nameless.*

Is she a feminist, yet thinks such thoughts?—but Matilde Searle does not think such thoughts, nor express such thoughts, no one of her acquaintance has ever heard such thoughts, certainly no one of her female clients whose lives, ensnarled with men who mistreat them, has ever heard such thoughts articulated by Matilde Searle. In her aloneness is her strength.

White bitch, scumbag cunt! Only after the bloody carving knife has been wrenched from him, when he's been pounded to his knees by the man named Bowe, Bowie, does Hector Ramos begin to scream at Matilde Searle. *Bitch! Cunt! I kill you!*—she's too surprised, too stunned to register what has happened, why she's bleeding from cuts on her hands, a three-inch slash on her left forearm, why she's staggering on the verge of fainting and strangers' hands, arms are holding her up—suddenly such a commotion, an outcry, the sheriff's deputies rushing with their guns drawn—why, what has happened, why has someone wanted to injure *her?* The man in the camel's-hair coat splattered with blood—his own, hers—is holding Matilde up, supporting her head, strong fingers gripping the back of her head. Her handbag stuffed with wallet, wadded Kleenex, notebook, papers, comb, plastic drugstore compact has fallen to the dirty foyer floor, someone takes it up and passes it quickly to the man comforting Matilde, here, here's the lady's purse, watch out it don't get stolen, and afterward Matilde will hear this murmured solicitude, a gray-haired black man's voice, she'll hear and be touched to the heart, *Here's the lady's purse, watch out it don't get stolen.* Her assailant who had? hadn't? intended to actually kill her is being handcuffed by the deputies, on his knees struggling with them shouting obscenities and lunging to escape, and his face is more youthful than Matilde recalls, it would be a handsome face except it's distorted with rage and pain as the deputies clamp on the cuffs and, police-style, yank the man's arms up behind his back so he's screaming in agony, begging *No! no! no!*—To all this Matilde Searle is a witness but she isn't capable of comprehending. She is calm enough, her pride won't let her give in to hysteria or even tears in this public place and in any case it's impossible for certain individuals—liberal, educated, idealists by temperament and training, their lives dedicated to "helping humanity"—to believe that anyone knowing them might wish them harm. Impossible!

The handgun. She has not practiced. Not once firing the gun though it's fully loaded: six bullets in the oiled revolving chambers. She has not cashed in her coupon from the Liberty Gun Shop redeemable at the Crossroads

Indoor Firing Range on North Dexter, in the suburb of Ferndale, which would give her a free hour's session with a "licensed" firearms instructor. From time to time during the past several days and nights she has removed the gun from the bedside table drawer, she has weighed it in her hand *ugly thing! ugly!* with the air of one weighing a profound and inexpressible yearning. The .38-caliber Smith & Wesson is a dull metallic blue, cool to the touch. Its surface, presumably once smooth, is covered with minute scratches, tiny near-invisible figures like hieroglyphics. The gun has its secrets—how many times has it been fired, how many bullets flying into flesh, how many deaths. There's a wholly objective statistical "life" of Matilde Searle's handgun inaccessible to her. *Because you must be prepared not just to shoot but to kill.* She won't be able to do it, when he comes for her. If he comes for her. He, or his brothers, cousins . . . there are so many of them, and time is on their side: any night, so many nights, she's alone, she's waiting. Better not to think of such possibilities. A gun heavy in your hands, you don't think. Except it's always heavier than you expect, which is a thought.

She has told no one about the gun, her shameful purchase, her purchase of shameful expediency. Not any brother or sister, not any of her friends who have so frequently expressed concern for her, worry that she continues to live in Mittelburg Park surrounded by encroaching "urban decay." Not her colleague Mariana with whom she shares an office and who has a handgun of her own—a compact, snub-nosed .45-caliber automatic with a pretty mother-of-pearl handle. Not the man who intervened to save her life, the man whose name she doesn't quite know, Bowe, Bowie . . . the man whose telephone calls she doesn't return, the man of whom she is not going to think. She lifts the gun glancing up shy and bemused seeing her reflection in her aunt's mahogany-framed mirror a few feet away—amid the faint, cloying fragrance of talcum, and a faint whiff of cedar and mothballs from the aunt's capacious step-in cedar closet. Matilde Searle, a deadly weapon in her hands, barrel upright and slanted across her breasts. *Is this me? Is this the person I've become?* She has told no one, and will not.

Sucking. Lifting the gun, Matilde feels a sharp sensation of faintness rising from the pit of her belly. Frightening, and delicious. Upward-flowing like water, a dark undertow. It's a familiar sensation but Matilde can't recall it, then suddenly she remembers: this is the way she used to feel, many years ago, when a boy or a young man first touched her, when they first kissed, the remarkable sensation of another's mouth on hers, another's tongue prodding hers. So suddenly, the gesture of intimacy irrevocable. And Matilde, young, dazed in delight and revulsion, excitement, dread, relief—sucking on the kiss, a stranger's tongue, as if there were no other nourishment she craved.

I can feel your heartbeat!—Jesus. In the front seat of the Volvo, awkward, the man's arms around her, gripping her tight. They'd been treated for their wounds, stitched, bandaged in the emergency room of the Detroit Medical Center. And he was driving her, not home as he thought wisest, but back to her car in the parking garage—as Matilde said, she'd need her car, she was going back to work the next day. The man who'd intervened to save her life, the man whose name was Bowe, or Bowie, said, concerned, maybe you'd better not, you're obviously upset, for Christ's sake *I'm* upset and that maniac wasn't trying to kill *me*. He was a lawyer, a litigator. And he was articulate, though shaken as Matilde was, and excited; a man she understood was accustomed to attentiveness, respect. You didn't contradict this man if you wanted to live in peace with him, but Matilde was firm, Matilde insisted no, thank you very much, you've been very kind but no, I'm all right. Trying not to look at his face more than she needed to, the square patch of gauze beneath his left eye; trying not to meet his eyes. That locking of the eyes—no. There was already a palpable tension between them and Matilde put her hand on the passenger's door to open it and she winced with pain, slashes in the palm of her hand that had seemed to be numb but now she winced with pain, and in the Volvo parked on Stockton Street at the rear of the county building she lost her composure at last, suddenly choking, crying, her stiff face crumpling like tissue paper. *Don't touch me!* she might have cried but the man touched her. Put his arms around her. Matilde, it's going to be OK, it's over now—his breath coming quickly, he was sexually aroused Matilde could tell, adrenaline pumping his veins. Then, I can feel your heartbeat!—Jesus. And he held her, and Matilde clutched at him, she could not control her choked breathless crying which was a wild laughter too but when the man tried to kiss her Matilde wrenched away. *No.*

★   ★   ★

Not a victim! She has been strongly advised to take at least two weeks' leave from the Clinic and to see one of the staff trauma counselors but she has declined. Apart from the wounds, which are only flesh wounds, and not infected, Matilde is certain she hasn't been traumatized. And Hector Ramos is still in custody and no one, so far, has posted bail for him ($2,500 bond on $25,000 bail)—Matilde calls the Detroit House of Detention daily, she knows how quickly even murder suspects are released back to the streets in Detroit. Back to their victims, but *I am not a victim: I can protect myself.*

A fever. She's awake for hours, then sleeping fitfully, kicking at the bed-clothes. Sees again the flying flashing knife which she tries again to deflect with her bare hands, forearms. If that man—that stranger—had not intervened perhaps she would be dead. And if then dead—where? Through the window beside the bed a tattered luminescent night sky, moonlit clouds like rock fissures. A harsh whining November wind. It's only 3:20 A.M. If she can make it through the night. *And the next night?—and the next.* She isn't going to quit the job for which she's been trained, the profession to which she's given her youth, her passion, her unmediated heart. She isn't going to move from her aunt's house. But hearing, with a stab of panic, a car at the curb, or is it in her driveway: *his* car: the Volvo. *Matilde?—I want to see you.* Matilde stands cautiously beside the window looking down, sees no car in the driveway, or at the curb; goes to the other windows, looks out and sees nothing; hears nothing. (Except the wind flinging leaves against the windows. And the myriad ceaseless noises of the city.) Thinking, but he wouldn't come here. Uninvited. At this time of night. That's absurd. That's madness. Of course. I know. Yet unable to return to bed for some time, staring at the street, the windswept trees, the sky marbled with light—a scene weirdly dilated as if, violently shaken, it hasn't yet settled back into place, into its normal proportions.

A case of nerves. That morning at eight-fifteen, leaving her car parked on C-level of the high-rise garage, Matilde experienced a sudden jolt of panic—ridiculous!—as a coffee cup, Styrofoam, glaring-white, blown by the wind, rolled clattering in her direction. And every time the phone rings, and it's a man's voice. And a late-afternoon call from one of the women counselors at the shelter, a call having nothing to do with Mrs. Ramos, and Matilde steeled herself expecting to hear that Ramos had been released and had murdered his wife. Steeling herself waiting to hear what was not told her even as, gripping the telephone receiver tight, oblivious of the pain of her scabby-stitched flesh wounds, she believed she was actually hearing what was not told her amid the pounding in her head, the *beat! beat! beat!* of her brain. The madman. Ramos. *Now coming for you, Matilde.* And tonight as previous nights the telephone rang several times—at nine, at eleven, again at eleven-thirty. Matilde has shut off her answering machine; she knows who it is. *Let's just see each other, let's talk. Matilde?—I'm not going to give up.* Methodically Matilde has shredded his notes left for her at the Clinic as, that first evening, her wounds still smarting with pain, she'd thrown away the printed card he'd given her. *No. I can't. I won't.*

Wounds. A dozen cuts of varying degrees of depth, severity on her palms, knuckles, wrists, forearms. All but two were not deep enough to require stitches. Where the angry man had slashed her on the left side of her neck there's a burnlike scab of about three inches—it looks like a birthmark, or a pursed mouth. Matilde contemplates it frequently, noting the progress of its healing. How lucky you were, they told her at the hospital, your scarf (she was wearing a thin cotton-knit scarf tied casually about her neck) blunted the knife blade, an artery might have been cut. Matilde caresses the crusted scab with her fingertips, prods it into pain, scratches it gently when it itches. A fact: there's a quickened, feverish heartbeat inside the wound.

Infinite regret, regress. It's only 4:10 A.M.! Flattened on her bed, on the rock-hard mattress, a hand on her burning, slightly sunken stomach, another hand, the back of her hand, on her burning forehead. She had felt his heartbeat, too. His mouth, the heat of his breath, the adrenaline charge. Yes I want you, but what does that mean: *want*. A woman wants a man, it's a mouth wanting to be filled. No but I don't want you, I don't want *it*. Her eyeballs glaring up out of the dark mute ignominy, anonymity of desire. *I want, I want, I want.* Turning her head, her stiff neck, to see the time: only 4:11 A.M.!

The stalker. Headlights trail across the ceiling, thin and fleeting as another's thoughts. She hears footsteps below her window, on the narrow asphalt drive between her house and her neighbor's. She has been asleep—a jagged, serrated sleep like wind buffeting sails—on the bedside table a bottle of red wine, an empty glass. The house is locked and the door to the bedroom locked and the .38-caliber Smith & Wesson revolver is in the drawer of the bedside table only a few inches from her hand. Now in fact—as in a film suddenly speeded up, to indicate not just the swiftness of time's passing but the insubstantial nature of time—the revolver is in her hand. She winces with pain but it's a wakeful, tonic pain. *Not just to shoot, but to kill.*

The heartbeat. Unbearable. Pulsing everywhere like the air charged to bursting before an electrical storm. Matilde, in a state beyond fear, in a sleepwalker's calm beyond panic, has thrown on her white terrycloth bathrobe and she's barefoot, advancing to the top of the darkened stairs, the revolver in her hand: her right hand, shaky but steadied by her left. Scabbed cuts on both hands now throbbing, but Matilde doesn't notice. The *beat! beat!* in her eyes so pronounced that her vision is blotched, wavy as if she's undersea. As if the air's choppy vibrations have become visible, tactile. Beneath the sound of the wind she has heard a sound of footsteps at the rear of her house, a sound of breaking glass. It is 5:15 A.M. and the moon is gone, layered over in cloud. After the Detroit riot of 1967 Matilde's aunt had installed a burglar alarm but the system gradually broke down, the fierce frantic din was triggered by wind, or the slamming of a door, or squirrels in the attic; it rang in the night and it rang in the day and it rang when no one was in the house, nor even near it, and the police rarely responded to any homeowners' alarms in Mittelburg Park because they were always going off. And so when Matilde moved into the house she never replaced the burglar alarm system which would now be ringing as the kitchen door is being forced. Matilde at the top of the stairs descends slowly, the .38-caliber Smith & Wesson in her hand, aimed at an invisible target in midair. She calls out, *Who's here? Who are you? I've got a gun.* She believes that she is utterly in control, composed as one who has rehearsed a scene many times, yet her voice is oddly faint and shrill, shrunken like a child's piping voice, a doll's voice, a dream-voice. She speaks louder, *Is someone there? Go away! Get out! I've got a gun.* These words echoing as if they are not Matilde's but another's, mocking—*gun, gun, gun.* Someone has broken into Matilde's house, and he's heard her. An intruder, or intruders. As if Matilde can see through the door at the rear of the hall that runs the length of the house, from the front vestibule back to the rear door, the door that's been forced, she knows that the intruder or intruders are deliberating what to do: to escape, or continue. They are strangers to her, or they know her—*Matilde Searle*—very well. Her body is covered in a rank animal sweat and prickly beads of moisture have formed on her forehead but Matilde is utterly calm, as a sleepwalker is calm, never in her life so keenly awake! so alert! her slender bones bright-brittle as glass! She has positioned herself on the stairs in such a way that, crouching, aiming the gun through the bannister's rails, if the swinging door that separates the front hall from the rear is pushed open, nudged even an inch, she will fire.

The wind. The November wind, flinging leaves, bits of grit, scraps of paper, blowing the clouds in tatters across the sky that, over the industrial stretches along I-75 downriver and west of the city is a faint flamey-red through the night, has confused her: so Matilde tells herself. Barefoot and shivering at the rear of the house, finally daring to investigate, switching on lights, making of herself a bold, white-glaring target should anyone be outside watching, she sees to her embarrassed relief that the door has not been forced, after all: but a pane of glass measuring about five inches square has been shattered. Maybe a would-be intruder had smashed it, maybe it had been cracked and the wind broke it; Matilde shines a flashlight out into the backyard where tree limbs, debris have fallen, the tunnel-like swath of light quivers, she darts it quickly about the leaf-strewn browned grass but sees nothing, no one.

Dawn. At 7:05 the telephone begins to ring. Matilde has not gone back to bed but has showered, shampooed her hair; she emerges from the fragrant steamy warmth of the bathroom as the phone rings, rings. A harsh glaring-gray light porous as moisture is pressing against the bedroom windows. The wind has subsided to fitful gusts, another day of Detroit no-weather, dull blank vacuity as if the sky has sunk beneath its polluted weight and it's a joyless world of cloud, fog. As if the catastrophe has already happened, it's over and now another day rolling from the horizon. Matilde winces at the light, there's a tall narrow window beside her bed where the blind is broken, months ago the damned thing snapped up to the very top of the window frame and Matilde hasn't replaced it, countless items in the old house she should replace or repair but the thought of making an inventory leaves her dazed, exhausted. It's 7:05 A.M. and the telephone is ringing and whoever is calling Matilde at this hour must have something crucial to tell her unless of course it's a wrong number. Always the possibility, having steeled herself to hear his voice, the voice she doesn't want to hear, she will not in fact hear it. *Matilde?—I'm not going to give up.* At 7:05 A.M. taking pride she's made it through the night—another night. The gun returned to the drawer of the bedside table and the drawer shut tight. Matilde wonders, would it be easier, believing in God? At 7:05 A.M. of this November morning, which in fact is the morning of her fortieth birthday, this is a thought that strikes her as urgent. She lifts the receiver of the ringing phone believing that whoever it is on the line, wanting to speak to her, or to someone, will have the answer.

THE VAMPIRE

Through the rifle scope the woman's head silhouetted by light drifts like a wayward balloon.

Staring into darkness. Into him.

No. She can't see. The part-shuttered windowpanes, the bright-lit room behind her, would reflect light.

Seeing her own face, her fleshy torso.

Seeing her eclipsed eyes. Seeing nothing.

Now she's sighted through the rifle scope from the rear of the tall narrow house where there's a shallow ridge of grassy earth.

Through the rifle scope hair-fine lines crossing to indicate that lethal spot at the very base of the skull.

His forefinger on the trigger. Squeezing.

Except now seen at an angle, in fact barely seen, through the rifle scope as she moves through the kitchen into that alcove off the kitchen, what is it—the pantry. She's in the pantry. Where there's a second, waist-high refrigerator and a freezer.

That freezer stocked with venison. One of Carlin's fans brought it. Just a token of my esteem. My admiration for your good work. Bless you.

Through the rifle scope the woman's eyes glisten.

Through the rifle scope she's seen now from beneath. Not twelve feet away. Yet (there's music playing inside the house, loud) she hasn't heard a sound, no footstep. His quickened breath, a faint steaming breath in the just-freezing air she hasn't seen and will not see.

No moon tonight. Yes, a moon, a crescent moon (he's checked the newspaper, the weather box) but massed cumulus clouds, gusty autumn and no moonlight to expose him. In his night clothes. Night camouflage. Hooded canvas jacket purchased for this night. The color of night.

Beneath the side window, spongy leafy earth. He knows he's leaving footprints which is why he'd purchased, at a Sears in Morgantown, not the same store in which he'd purchased the jacket, a pair of rubber boots two sizes larger than his own.

Which he'll dispose of hundreds of miles away from the house in which the dead woman will be discovered, encircled by footprints in spongy leafy earth.

Through the rifle scope—is the woman smiling? Smiling!

She's speaking on a cellular phone tucked into the crook of her neck. That slow sensuous smile. Greedy gloating smile. Incisors damply glistening.

Through the rifle scope, the crosshairs, that fleshy face, smiling.

Through the rifle scope moving about idly as she speaks on the phone. Unconsciously caressing her breasts. Smiling, and laughing. Speaking to a lover. One of the widow's lovers. *Since your death. Since she's begun to feed.*

Through the rifle scope the woman's head large as a dinner plate. He wonders will it shatter like a dinner plate. He wonders whether anyone will hear the shattering.

In Buckhannon, West Virginia. On a moon-shrouded autumn night.

How many months, now it's been more than a year, since Carlin Ritchie's death he isn't sure. He'd count on his fingers except his forefinger is in use.

But his arms ache! This heavy rifle he isn't used to, the long barrel. Purchased especially for tonight. His arms, his shoulders, his backbone, and his wrists ache. His jaws ache from that fixed grimace he isn't conscious of; next time he sees his face, examines his stubbled face in a mirror (in a motel near Easton, Pennsylvania) he'll see the creases etched in the skin as with a knife blade. How he's aged.

Through the rifle scope, a woman's torso. Shapely breasts, shoulders. He'd caressed them, once: he knows. In layers of clothing, gypsy-clothing Carlin called it, admiring, lovesick, velvets and silks and Indian muslin, long gauzy skirts swishing against the floor. Even at home, by herself, she's in costume. Through the rifle scope laughing like a girl, eager, shrewd, wetting her lips; unconsciously stroking her breasts. Through the rifle scope on display as if she knows (but of course she can't know) she's observed.

On TV it looked as if she'd dyed her hair a darker, richer red. Tincture of purple. Yet streaks of silvery-white, theatrical as bars of paint. *How does it feel? Widow? His name, his memory. Dedicating her life.*

Through the rifle scope, that life. Will it shatter, like crockery? Will any neighbors hear?

But the nearest neighbors are at least a quarter-mile away. And this wind tonight. A low rumbling, a sound of thunder in the mountains. No one will hear.

Through the rifle scope she's moving toward the stairs. Still talking on the phone. Slow hip-swaying walk. She's gained how many pounds since becoming a widow, twenty pounds, twenty-five, not a fat woman but fleshy, ample. Solid. Those solid breasts. Skin that exudes heat. Burning to the touch. He knows!

His finger on the trigger. For in another minute she'll have climbed the stairs. In another minute she'll be out of the rifle sight. He's anxious, on the veranda. Peering through a side window. Risking being seen. Boots trailing mud. Nudging the barrel of the rifle against the very glass. This wide, old-fashioned veranda on which Carlin lay. *Don't want to die. Yes but I'm ready. I want to be brave. I'm a coward, I want to be brave. Help me.* On this moonward side of the house if there were a moon this October night which there isn't. *Like God watching over me* Carlin said *if there's a God but I guess there is not.*

Which is why, through the rifle scope, or not, we die.

2

IT MIGHT BE that I know of a murder soon to be committed, and it might be that I don't. I mean—I don't know if the murder will be committed, if the murderer is serious. (Though he surely seems serious.) Does this make me an accessory? Am I involved, whether I wish to be or not? I don't mean just legally, I mean morally. What's the right thing to do here? Say I make a call to the potential victim, what do I say? "Ma'am, you don't know me, but your life is in danger. You're hated, and you're wanted dead." The woman would say, "Is this some kind of joke? Who are you?" I'd say, "It doesn't matter who I am. Your life is in danger." She'd be getting upset, maybe hysterical, and what could I tell her, really? How could I save her, if the man who wants to kill her is determined to kill her? I surely couldn't give her his name. Even if that makes me an accessory. And I surely couldn't inform the police, any police. And anyway—does such a woman deserve to be saved?

My cousin Rafe has said, *There are folks who deserve to die because they don't deserve to live, it's that simple. They must be stopped in their paths of destruction.*

I've known about this murder, this potential murder, for less than a week. Never did I ask for such knowledge. I'm not a man who thinks obsessively, I mean I'm not a man who broods. I'm a tool and die designer, I'm skilled at my job, working with my brains and my hands and when I'm working I'm focused like a laser beam—I put in an eight-hour day, we're on computers now doing three-dimensional design and when I'm through for the day, I'm through. Like, wiped out. And now knowing of this murder-to-be, I'm having trouble concentrating at work. I'm having trouble driving my car. Even eating. Trying to listen to my wife, to tune in to something besides my thoughts. *She is one of these, an emissary of Satan. A vampire. Must be stopped.* My life at home is a quiet life; we've been married a long time and neither of us will surprise the other except if my wife knew my thoughts she'd be surprised, shocked. Last night was the worst yet. Trying to sleep. Kicking at the bedclothes like they're something trying to smother me and grinding my molars (a habit I'd gotten into when our two boys were young teenagers making our lives hell, but I hadn't done for years) so my wife wakes me, frightened—"Honey, what is it? What's wrong?" She switches on the light to look at me and I try to hide my face. I know what she's thinking—I might be having a heart attack; her father died of a heart attack at around my age, forty-four. That's young, but not too young. My own father had a saying—*You're never too young to die.* And it's true, my heart is pounding so hard you can feel the bed shake and I'm covered in cold sweat and shivering and for a minute I don't even know where I am. I'd had a few drinks before going to bed and my mind's like cobwebs. I tell her, "Nothing! Nothing is wrong. Leave me alone."

What the hell can I tell my wife, who loves me, and whom I love, that when she woke me up I was crouched in the dark outside some house I've never seen before, in some place I'd never been, peeking at a woman inside the house through a long-range rifle scope? A woman who's a total stranger to me? And my finger on the trigger of the rifle? Me, Harrison Healy, who's never even touched a gun in his life, let alone aimed it at another human being?

3

I NEVER ASKED for such knowledge, God knows. It was my cousin Rafe spilled it into me the way you'd tip something poisonous into a stream.

There I was at the county courthouse. Kind of anxious and self-conscious, first time I'd been summoned for jury duty in my life. And practically the first person I see in this big drafty windowless room in the basement where we're told to wait is my cousin Rafe. Rafe Healy. Who's two years younger than me, at least three inches taller, and thirty pounds heavier—a tall, husky, sort of shuffling man in overalls, a gingery beard and thinning hair sticking up around his head so he looks like (my wife used to say when we saw Rafe, which hasn't been lately) an accident getting ready to happen. Rafe commands attention in any situation because of his height and girth and his mode of dress and that look in his face like a beacon turned on high—his pebbly eyes sort of shining out. He's always looked younger than his age, even with that scruffy beard and hair and the hard-drinking life he's led. And the drugs. Rafe's an artist, you'd have to call him, he does clay pots, ceramics, latch hook rugs and quilts. He's been written up in magazines and has had exhibits in museums, even in New York. You don't think of a man making quilts but Rafe Healy is said to be one of the leading quilters in the United States. Nobody in the family knows what to make of him. Mostly, the family is sort of embarrassed. You could be switching TV channels seeing what's on and there on PBS there's Rafe Healy's broad earnest sunburned face; he's being interviewed standing in front of a quilt that looks like a constellation in the night sky, saying something weird like, *I need to talk to myself when I'm working. Otherwise I'd disappear into my hands, I'd cease to exist.* My wife disapproves of Rafe for a number of reasons and I can't argue she's wrong. Mainly it has to do with Rafe and drugs. Maybe ten, twelve years ago we were on friendly terms and we'd have Rafe over for dinner and he'd think nothing of taking out a pipe, smoking some sweetish-stale-smelling weed right in our living room, and looking surprised when Rosalind got upset and told him to put it out. Another time he showed up for dinner bringing a woman with him, an Amazon-type "sculptress" in soiled overalls just like Rafe's, loud and sassy. You just don't behave that way if you have any manners, Rosalind says. She's possibly a little jealous of Rafe and me, for we'd grown up like brothers when Rafe's father who was my dad's younger brother was killed (in a car crash) and Rafe's mother wasn't well enough (mentally) to keep him so he came to live, aged four, with my family. I was older than Rafe and so felt protective of him until he passed me by physically and in other ways, already in junior high school. And in high school he ran with a wild crowd, had a reputation for being hot-tempered and already a drinker, quick to get into fights. Nobody would've figured him for an artist in those years, except that Rafe always had a strange imagination, a sort of impassioned exaggerated attitude, as likely to burst into tears if something made him sad as he was to lash out with his fists, face boiling up like a tomato ready to burst, if something made him angry. By sixteen he'd been arrested more than once for brawling, usually with older guys in some tavern or another, and my parents couldn't handle him though they loved him, we all loved him—it was just that Rafe was too much for any ordinary family to deal with. So he moved out. Left town. Bummed around for years, up into Canada, Alaska, Oregon, and California and back to the East and somehow he wins a scholarship to the Shenandoah School of the Arts, in Virginia, when he hadn't even graduated from high school!—so that was a real surprise, and nobody in the family knew how to take it except possibly me. I told Rafe when he visited I was proud of him and Rafe said, I remember his words, clear as if he'd uttered them just yesterday and not twenty years ago, "Hell, pride's a risky thing. It 'goeth before a fall.' " And he glowered at me as if I'd said the wrong thing, making him think worried thoughts.

The past fifteen years or so, Rafe's been living just outside town. On a run-down forty-acre farm, beautiful hilly countryside we've been told (we've never visited), with people coming and going, fellow artists, so it's said that Rafe Healy is living in some sort of hippie-style commune, which I frankly doubt—Rafe was never one to tolerate anybody's bullshit. He's a hard worker, maybe a little obsessed. For an artist, as I see it, is one who works nonstop—nobody's paying him for an eight-hour day. You'd have to be a little crazy to work so hard, or maybe it's the hard work that makes you a little crazy. What's sad is that I'm living in town, a half-hour's drive from Rafe's place, and we never see each other, who'd once been so close. About five years ago there was a TV documentary about the famous West Virginia artist Carlin Ritchie who had some sort of wasting disease, and it was a surprise to see my cousin Rafe included in a segment on Ritchie's generation of "crafts" artists, and to see that Rafe was apparently a friend of Ritchie's; they'd all been at the Shenandoah School together. It made me a little dazed to think of something you could call "history" (if only "art history") and Rafe Healy included in it (if only in a brief segment). I called for Rosalind to come and see this on TV, but by the time she got there the part about Rafe was over. I said, "I don't care what you think of Rafe, I'm proud of him. He's my cousin." And Rosalind who's got this sweet, prim little face and placid eyes but never misses a beat says, "Makes no difference whose cousin he is. Even if he was mine. He's a loose, careless, dangerous man of no true morals and he isn't welcome in this house, if that's what you're edging toward." And back in April, just this year, there was Rafe Healy honored at the White House! And this is on network TV, and a big spread on the front page of our local paper so Rosalind, like everybody else in the vicinity, can't ignore it. But she says, "There were fifty other 'artists' honored at the ceremony, it couldn't have been too selective. Don't tell me there are fifty great artists like Rembrandt or Picasso living in the United States at one time. And there's absolutely no morals at the White House. So Rafe Healy would fit in just fine." I can't argue my wife is wrong but a few weeks ago for her birthday I brought home a sea-green ceramic bowl purchased at a crafts store in town, she's blinking back tears lifting it from the wrapping paper saying, "Oh, Harrison—I never saw anything so beautiful." And she looks at me surprised like I could select something so beautiful for her, and kisses me. How many times she's admired this bowl, and showed it off to visitors, and examined it, running her fingers over the potter's initials on the bottom, 𝒜ℋ, she's never caught on whose work it is. And I'm surely never going to tell her.

All this was passing swiftly through my head when I saw Rafe in the jury selection room, a big tall fattish man with gingery hair and beard, bib overalls splattered with what looked like paint or manure, and the other potential jurors, and the brisk efficient ladies who run the jury selection, looking at him as though he's either a freak or somebody of local renown, or both. He'd sighted me, and came excitedly over to me, shaking my hand so hard I couldn't help wincing, and if I hadn't blocked him he would've hugged me, cracking a rib or two, with everybody in the room gaping at us. Rafe was so happy to see me he was practically crying. His big bulgy pebble-colored eyes shining with tears. We went out into the corridor and before we'd even exchanged greetings, caught up on news, Rafe was leading me out of earshot of others, puffing hard, saying, "Oh, Jesus. Harrison. This place is like a prison. A morgue. I'm scared here. It's a bad sign I'm here. I don't want to be here." I said, "Well, I don't want to be here, either. Nobody does. It's called 'jury duty.'" Rafe just kept on, in a voice more hoarse and cracked than I remembered, but in that same intense manner, as if he's in his head so much, and you're inside his head, too, so he doesn't need to listen to anything you might actually say, "Harrison, listen. I was up all night. My brain is about to explode. I need to work, I need to use my hands—I work in the morning from six-thirty till noon and I couldn't work this morning worrying about coming here, I didn't even know if I could find the courthouse, it's not even 9 A.M. and we have to be here until 5 P.M. and I'm scared I'm going to explode, all week it's going to be like this, and if I'm seated on a jury it could be longer, I'm not a man who belongs on a jury, not at this time in my life. Oh, Jesus." He whimpered as though he felt actual pain. Here I hadn't seen Rafe in years and already I was feeling that mixture of impatience and affection he used to stir in me, that feeling that, in whatever intense mental state he's in, if you can get him to listen to you, which he will sometimes do, you can have a calming effect on him, so it makes you want to try. I said, "Rafe, it isn't the end of the world, for God's sake. Chances are you won't be seated on a jury, there's two hundred ninety of us and they won't be needing any more than seventy, somebody said." Rafe was gripping my upper arm, he'd walked me to the far end of the corridor which was just a dead end, an EMERGENCY EXIT ONLY door with warning red light DO NOT OPEN ALARM WILL SOUND. He was saying, puffing, his eyes swerving in their sockets, "I tried to get another postponement but I failed. I tried to get an exemption, I pleaded 'I can't be a juror, I believe in *Judge not lest ye be judged*—I believe in *Let he who is without sin cast the first stone.*' But all I could get when I called the number was a recorded message! I never spoke to a living human being! And that lady who's in charge, she warns me I'll be in contempt of court if I address any judge like that, and if I walk out of here like I'm thinking of doing. I don't mind paying the $500 fine but there's a chance I'd be 'incarcerated,' too. Harrison, I feel like I'm going to burst." Rafe's face was heavy with blood; a nerve or artery was twitching on his forehead; his eyes were blinking in virtual panic. I didn't know whether to laugh at him or take him seriously. That was the way of Rafe Healy, of artists, I suppose—they draw you into their moods no matter how extreme, you can see something's truly possessing them, they're in pain and you want to help. I said, leading Rafe back toward the jury selection room the way you'd lead a dazed, upright bear back to his cage (we'd been summoned inside, though I doubt Rafe noticed), "Come on, Rafe. If I can do it, you can do it. Just calm down. Can't you make some sketches while you're waiting? Work on your art?" As if I'd insulted him Rafe said, "Work on my *art?* In a place like this? Where I'm being detained against my will? Fuck you, Harrison. I thought you were my friend."

But he allowed me to lead him back inside the jury selection room where we picked up plastic JUROR badges to pin to our shirts. I was JUROR 121 and Rafe was JUROR 93. We sat in uncomfortable folding chairs and watched, or anyway looked at, a fifteen-minute TV documentary on the justice system in the county which must've been prepared for junior high kids, and then we were made to listen to a forty-minute monotone recitation on jury selection by a middle-aged female court officer who looked as if she'd been living in this windowless musty-smelling underground space most of her life, and then we were told to wait "until such time as your jury panel is called." A TV set was turned on loud, to what appeared to be a morning talk show. All this while Rafe was breathing quickly, wiping at his damp face with a wadded tissue, sighing and squirming in his seat. He reminded me of one of those hyperactive children no one knows how to treat except to dose with drugs. As Rafe said, he seemed about to burst. What if he had a stroke? A heart attack? He was making me anxious. I'd brought along the morning paper, and tried to read it, and an old back issue of *Time* someone had discarded, but couldn't help glancing sidelong at my poor cousin, with concern. The twitchy nerve or artery in his forehead was throbbing. I wondered if he was on a drug; but, no—if he'd taken any drug it would've been one to calm him down. And he hadn't been drinking, he was stone cold sober. That was the problem, I thought. Whatever was troubling Rafe (which had to be more than just jury duty) was pure and unalloyed, as real to him as a fever burning in his veins.

Every ten minutes or so Rafe would jump up, excuse himself to the court officer to use the men's room, or get a drink from a fountain in the corridor, or just pace out there like a trapped beast. I'd see him glance through the doorway at me, and I knew he wanted me to join him, but I stayed where I was. I'd been nerved-up well into my twenties but I was grown up now, or God knows I tried to be.

If you've ever been drafted for jury duty, and if the procedure is like that of Huron County, New York, you know that what you do, as the lady told us, is wait. You sit, or you stand, and you wait. You're relaxed, or you're restless, but you wait. You wait until you're officially discharged for the day. Somewhere in the courthouse there are judges preparing for trials, at least in theory, and an army of potential jurors has to be in readiness for their use; a juror is a disposable unit, just a badge and a number. In fact, the judges are hearing motions, talking and arguing with their fellow lawyers; prosecuting and defense attorneys are trying to work out pleas and settlements in order to avoid trials. Guilt or innocence doesn't much matter, except to the defendant. Everyone else is a lawyer, and the lawyers are drawing salaries. The court system is a factory that works most efficiently when what happens today is exactly what happened yesterday. I suppose I sound cynical and I'm not a cynical man but this is the wisdom I came away with after my week of jury duty and it's been confirmed by others who've had the identical experience, though nobody who hasn't had it can comprehend—"But it must be exciting, to be on a jury. At a trial." That's what everybody says who doesn't know better. The truth is, most potential jurors are never seated on a jury and don't get within fifty feet of any trial. A trial means that a deal between the lawyers couldn't be worked out. If things moved smoothly in the justice system, there would be no trials. But as it is, potential jurors are summoned, hundreds of us, made to sit like zombies in rows and wait hour after hour, day after day, until the week of jury duty is concluded, and we're sent back home with phony thanks and the promise that our payment will be mailed to us within six weeks—a salary of $5 per day.

Maybe if Rafe had understood this, and hadn't exaggerated the likelihood of being a juror at an actual trial, he wouldn't have confessed to me what he did; and I'd have been spared these miserable hours, a roaring in my ears and my stomach in knots. For in my soul I'm like a newborn baby *not knowing what to do*. It's as if my conscience is a sheet of transparent glass and I can't figure out if it's there or not, if it exists. How do I know what's the right thing to do? But even if I do nothing I will have done something. *I'm trapped.*

4

AT 1:10 P.M. our panel of jurors was released for a forty-minute lunch, with severe warnings from the court officer to return on time, and Rafe and I were about the first out of the courthouse; Rafe might've looked like a shambling bear in those overalls, and his facial expression sort of dazed and glassy-eyed, but like a bear the man could move fast when motivated. In the open air he laughed wildly. "Freedom! We can breathe! Let's celebrate, man." I didn't think it was a wise idea to drink right then, but as when we were kids I found myself going along with Rafe, Rafe's enthusiasm, so we ended up in a tavern a block from the courthouse. Rafe downed his first beer straight from the can, rubbed his knuckles over his bloodshot eyes and said, lowering his voice so no one else could hear, "Harrison. It's meant for me to tell you. I've got to tell somebody. I'm going to explode if I don't." I asked Rafe what was it, feeling a tinge of alarm, and Rafe leaned over the table toward me and said with a grimace, as of pain, "I'm being forced to—kill someone. I think. I don't have a choice."

I wasn't sure I'd heard right. I laughed. I wiped my mouth. Moisture glistened in my cousin's beard, which was threaded with gray. I heard myself asking, "Rafe, what?" and he didn't reply for so long I thought he'd decided not to tell me; then he said, his eyes fixed on mine with that look of his of profound sadness, yet with excitement glimmering beneath, that I remembered from when we were kids, and struck a spark of excitement in me, despite my good judgment, "There are folks who deserve to die because they don't deserve to live. It's that simple. They must be stopped in their paths of destruction."

"Folks?—what folks?"

"From the beginning of time they must've lived. Victimizing the innocent. Do you believe in Satan?"

"Satan?"

"I'm not sure if I believe in Satan myself. Probably I don't. You know how we were brought up—your mom would take us to that Lutheran church, and the minister talked of 'Satan' but you had the idea he didn't really mean it. Like a man speaks of 'death'—'dying'—but has no idea what he's saying. But I do believe in evil. I believe that there are individuals among us who are evil, who've chosen evil, who might believe in Satan themselves and are emissaries of Satan in their hearts." Rafe was speaking quickly in his low, hoarse voice, and gripping my wrist in a way I didn't like as if to keep me where I was, in the booth listening to him. A waitress brought us more beers, set down plates before us, and Rafe scarcely noticed. He said, breathing quickly, "I believe in vampires."

"Rafe, what? *Vampires*—?"

"What the hell's wrong with you? Everything I say you repeat like a parrot! Not actual vampires, of course—mortal men, and women, who are vampires. Who destroy others. Suck away their lives. And even after their deaths—their victims' deaths—a vampire can continue. A man's work, a man's reputation—he can't protect it if he's dead. I'm thinking of a man, a good man, a man who was a great artist, a man who was my friend, who trusted me, a man now dead who can't protect himself, whom I must protect." These were like prepared words, uttered with passion. I didn't know how to reply. I felt like an empty vessel waiting to be filled.

So Rafe began telling me about Carlin Ritchie who'd died the previous summer (I guess I knew that Ritchie had died; there'd been tributes to him in the media), at his mountain place in West Virginia that his second wife had made into a shrine for him; he'd died in "suspicious circumstances" and since his death his widow was stealing his art, his reputation, claiming the two of them had been "collaborators" on the important work Ritchie had been doing the last five or six years of his life; she'd hidden away a dozen silk screens—"Carlin's Appalachia series, some of the best work he'd ever done"—that Carlin had designated in his will should go to Rafe Healy. "She's taken from me! Stolen from me! Who was a friend of Carlin's, who loved him like a brother! Not just me but other old friends of his, she'd prevented from seeing him the last months of his life, this vicious woman, this vampire, sucking a helpless man's blood, and it goes on and on after his death—'Janessa Ritchie' she calls herself. I've tried to reason with her, Harrison. I'm not the only one, there's Carlin's first wife, and his grown children, relatives of his—she's cut us all out. She wants him for herself. Herself alone. A great American artist, an artist people loved, now he's dead and can't protect himself—it's killing me, tearing me apart. I have to stop her."

"Stop her—how?"

"A gun, I think. Rifle. I'm not a man of violence, no more than Carlin was, but—it's like there's a cancer inside me, eating me up. The vampire has got to be *stopped.*"

I was astonished. I was shocked. My cousin Rafe telling me such things! I saw he was serious, dead serious; and I didn't know what to say. There was this queer tawny light coming up in his eyes I'd never seen before. I didn't have much appetite for lunch but sat there staring as Rafe devoured his, a sandwich and french fries doused with ketchup, ducking his head toward his plate, turning it slightly to one side, his incisors tearing at the thick crust of a roll, slices of rare roast beef.

5

THIS IS WHAT Rafe told me, piecemeal over the course of the next three days.

"The last time I saw Carlin Ritchie, at his place in Buckhannon, West Virginia, that she'd made into a tourist shrine before he even died, it was eight weeks before she killed him, I swear he pleaded with his eyes—*I'm not ready to die. Rafe, don't abandon me!* Putting out his hand to me. His good hand, the left. Squeezing my fingers. Jesus, I loved that man! Even when I don't remember too clearly, I know I've been dreaming about him. Like last night. And the night before. *Rafe? Rafe? Don't abandon me, O.K.?*"

"How I knew he'd died, a friend called. Mutual friend. 'Carlin's dead, she's killed him,' my friend was screaming. I made calls, I turned on the TV but there was nothing, got a copy of the *New York Times* and there was the obituary across the full top of the page—CARLIN RITCHIE, 49, 'PRIMITIVE' ARTIST, DIES IN WEST VIRGINIA. Now I saw it was real, I started sobbing like a baby.

"That's bullshit that Carlin was a 'primitive' artist. He was a born talent, no one could capture the human face, eyes, soul, like Carlin, but he'd trained himself, too; there was a phase, when he was in his twenties, he turned out these ugly, wrenching silk screens modeled after Goya. At the Shenandoah school, we were just kids then, Carlin was the 'classicist'— 'You can't overcome the past unless you know it.' And he'd quote Blake— 'Drive your cart over the bones of the dead.'

"Yeah. The last lines of an obituary tell you who the survivors are.

Carlin's first wife was named, and his three grown kids. Then—'Janessa Ritchie, his widow.' *His murderer.*

"'Janessa'?—that isn't even her name, her name's something like Agnes, Adelaide—and she'd been married at least once before, and wasn't so young as everybody thought. I found this out later. I never did tell Carlin. He was crazy in love with her, enthralled by her—wouldn't listen to a word against her even from his old friends. Even from his kids. They're the ones who're hurting—she'd gotten him to change his will, leaving her mostly everything and naming her the executor of his estate. Carlin never spent much, money didn't seem to mean anything to him except as a means of buying art supplies, but we're talking millions of dollars here. And the way she's marketing him—we're talking double-digit millions. She's gonna suck that name for all it's worth.

"Sure I knew Carlin's first wife, his family, not intimately but I knew them and counted myself a friend. Carlin had married his high school sweetheart, both of them just kids when they started having babies. They were together for twenty-six years. Nobody could believe they'd broken up, Carlin was living with another woman—'That just can't be. Carlin isn't that type' was what everybody said. And it was true, Carlin wasn't. But *she* was—the vampire, I mean. Just took him over. Like she'd put her hand, her nail-polished talons, on the man's living heart.

"No, I don't cast any blame on Carlin. I believe he was enthralled—enchanted. Like under an evil spell. He'd been sick with MS—that's multiple sclerosis, in case you don't know. 'Mucho shit' Carlin called it—struck him down when he was twenty-nine, just starting to sell his work, make a name for himself, win prizes—and he's in a wheelchair, like that. Except he gets better, he's in remission for a while, then struck down again, can't use his legs, then he's into some holistic health regimen and actually improves—back in remission is what they call it, though in fact, as Carlin said, nobody knows what MS actually is, it's like a syndrome, what works for one person doesn't work for another, one person shrivels away and dies in five years and another person can be on his feet, walking and healthy for twenty years: 'It can't be calculated. Like life.' But Carlin was lucky, I think it had to do with his attitude, his heart—he just wasn't going to let that disease eat him away.

"First time any of us knew about 'Janessa,' it was a summer arts festival in Virginia, and there was Carlin Ritchie, a guest of honor, without his wife—surrounded by admirers, one of them this strange-looking young woman, this slender sort of snaky-sexy girl, with a constant, nervous smile, showing her gums and white, slightly protruding teeth; enormous dark eyes, you'd have to call them beautiful eyes though they were sort of weird, with bluish, hooded lids, and a way of staring like she was memorizing you. Carlin was embarrassed being with her, that shamed, lovesick look in his face, but he introduced us, saying Janessa's a photographer from New York, very talented, and I thought Oh yeah? and didn't say much. The girl looked about twenty. (In fact, she was over thirty.) She wasn't embarrassed in the slightest. Her eyes hooked onto mine, and her skin gave off a musky heat. She pushed her hand into mine like a squirmy little creature, and there's the pink tip of her tongue between her teeth—Jesus! Did I feel a charge. She said, 'Rafe Healy! I'm sure honored to meet *you*.' Like there was some immediate understanding between us and even Carlin was out of it. I was disgusted by her, but I have to admit sort of intrigued, at that time it wasn't altogether clear how serious Carlin was about her, whether they were a couple, or just together in Virginia. Nobody would've predicted Carlin would leave Laurette for her, after all they'd been through together, and Carlin making money now, famous. I watched Carlin and the girl for the rest of the week, keeping my distance, so Carlin would get the message I didn't approve, not that I'm a puritan or anything, not that I even take marriage all that seriously, most marriages at least—you make vows to be broken, is my experience. But the last night of the festival I got drunk and spoke to Janessa in private, I said, 'You know, Carlin Ritchie is a married man, a devoted family man, he hasn't been well and his wife has taken care of him and before he began to make money she supported him for years, and they've got three kids—keep that in mind.' And Janessa says, all eager and girlish, wide-eyed, laying her hand on my arm and giving me goose bumps, 'Oh Rafe, I know!' like she knew me, she'd been calling me 'Rafe' for years, '—Carlin has told me all about that wonderful woman, "My first love" he calls her.' Janessa lowered her eyes, and made this simpering face like she knew she was being naughty, flirtatious and naughty, but couldn't help it, '—but I'm thinking, Rafe, y'know?—I'd rather be Carlin Ritchie's last love than his first.'

"With his medication, Carlin wasn't supposed to be drinking. He'd had a whole life practically before he got sick when he drank—serious drinking. Without Laurette around he'd relapse, and in this situation he was drinking, and people were worried about him, but not Janessa—I watched the two of them walk off together, from a party, it was late, past 3 A.M., Carlin was leaning on the girl, and she had her arm around his waist, she was skinny but strong, practically holding him up, and Carlin was a tight-packed, heavy little guy, those muscular shoulders and torso, but Janessa supported him walking up this hill to the cabin Carlin was staying in, a white-birch log cabin, and I stood in the shadows watching, I don't believe I was drunk but stone cold sober, watching after those two, after they'd gone inside the cabin, and the cabin lights were off.

"Next thing we knew, Carlin was separated from Laurette. He was living with Janessa in New York, going to parties, gallery openings, being photographed by Avedon for *The New Yorker*—Carlin's haggard-homely face, like a kid's, yet he was beautiful in his way, his unique way, like his 'Appalachian Faces' silk screens that made him famous—there's something about faces like that, that touch you deep in the heart. A few of Carlin's friends turned against him, but not me—I'd forgive him anything, almost. Also, I'm not so innocent myself, with women. I wasn't anyone to judge. I never judged *him*—only *her*. It happened pretty fast that Carlin divorced Laurette, and married Janessa, let her take over running his life, his exhibits, his correspondence, his finances; let her talk him into buying the house in Buckhannon, and renovating it, the shrine to Carlin Ritchie, having it painted lavender with purple trim, and putting up a spike fence with a gate and a little bronze plaque CARLIN RITCHIE RESIDENCE PRIVATE PLEASE so admirers could take pictures of it from the road—'Jesus, Carlin, it's like you're on display, marketing yourself, how can you tolerate it?' I asked him, I was frankly pissed, and Carlin said, embarrassed, 'It's got nothing to do with *me*. It's just the idea. Janessa says—"People love your art, so they want to love you. You can't deny them." 'Hell you can't deny them,' I said, '—you denied them in the past.' Carlin said, in a flat, sad voice, 'Well—the past is past.' We were talking over the phone; Carlin was in his studio, it was about the only way we could talk and even then Janessa was monitoring his incoming calls, lifting the receiver so you'd hear a hissing breath. Most of the time when Carlin's friends called, Janessa would answer the phone with this mock-girlish greeting, 'Oh *hel*-lo! Of course I know who you are. Of course Carlin would love to speak with you. But—' and she'd explain how it was a day Carlin had worn himself out in the studio, or a day he hadn't been able to use his legs, or focus his eyes; a day he was 'fighting the demon'—meaning the MS. More and more when we called we'd be told that Carlin 'isn't available, regretfully.'

His sons complained they were told repeatedly, the last fifteen months of their father's life, that he 'isn't available, regretfully.' Yet there was a steady stream of photographers, interviewers, TV and videotape crews traveling to the Carlin Ritchie residence in Buckhannon, from as far away as Japan and Australia, and these people, you can be sure, who never failed to include 'Janessa Ritchie' in their profiles, were always welcome.

"When Carlin left Buckhannon it wasn't ever to visit his old friends as he used to. After he married that woman, he never came to see me again. She'd take him to arts festivals, to fancy events where Carlin was the guest of honor, black-tie evenings in New York and Washington, but she'd never take him to the Shenandoah summer festival, or anywhere ordinary. Carlin went as a star, or he didn't go at all. She demanded high fees for him, and he seemed embarrassed but proud, too; he'd never forgotten his West Virginia background. He'd been born in a small town twenty miles from Buckhannon, just a crossroads, and his folks were poor; despite the Carlin Ritchie legend that's sprung up, Carlin hadn't been happy in his childhood, I happen to know—not as happy as I was, and I'd lost both parents. (But I had good, kind, generous stepparents, you could say. And even a brother close to my heart.) Janessa wouldn't ever let Carlin talk about his real home, his real folks; everything had to be pretense, sentiment. In Carlin's best work there was always a melancholy tone, like Hopper's paintings, but with more texture and subtlety than Hopper, sort of dreamy, meditative, after-the-fact—posthumous, almost. Like these Appalachian people and places were really gone, vanished. And Carlin Ritchie was remembering them. (And Janessa started taking these phony, posed pictures in West Virginia, 'companion pieces,' she called them, to Carlin's art, and when he was too sick to prevent her, and after his death, she published them side by side with his work claiming she'd been his 'collaborator' for all of their marriage. Carlin Ritchie's 'collaborator'! But that wouldn't be the worst.)

"The last time I saw Carlin in public, it was a black-tie awards ceremony at the American Academy in New York. Carlin was a member of the Academy, and I was getting an award. And some other friends of ours, from the old days at Shenandoah, the days of our youth, were there. And celebrating. But, hell, we couldn't get within twenty feet of Carlin. He'd cast sort of wistful, embarrassed looks at us—but he was in his wheelchair, and Janessa had him surrounded by rich, important people—'Carlin's privileged patrons' she called them. It would be revealed afterward that she'd been selling Carlin's work, drawing up actual contracts, before he'd created it; she was getting the poor bastard to sign contracts, naming her as agent, without knowing what he was signing—he'd always been a careless kind of guy with contracts and money, worse even than I am. We got drunk on champagne, and watched our friend Carlin in his tux that made him look embalmed, in his wheelchair that was an expensive motorized chair but guided by this white-skinned female in a black velvet gown cut so low her breasts were almost falling out, strands of pearls around her neck, looking like the real thing, not cultured, surely not West Virginia–type costume-jewelry pearls, her glossy red hair upswept on her head and her face beautiful, radiant—this was the second Mrs. Ritchie? No wonder photographers loved snapping her and poor Carlin, sunken-chested in his chair, wearing thick glasses now, and his right hand palsied, lifting his ghastly-hopeful smile and managing to shake hands with his left hand as 'privileged patrons' hovered over him. Janessa wasn't a skinny strung-out anorexic type any longer; she'd packed on serious, solid female flesh and looked good enough to eat. Her face was pale as a geisha's and made up like a cosmetic mask, flawless—crimson mouth, inky-black mascara accentuating her big eyes, flaring eyebrows that looked as if they'd been drawn on with a Crayola. She didn't look any age at all, now—like Elizabeth Taylor in those glamor photos you used to see on the covers of supermarket tabloids, generic female vamp-beauty. Totally phony, but glamorous as hell. I have to admit that Carlin looked happy enough that night, under the sharp eye of Janessa, and her shapely bust nudging the back of his head so if he was nodding off (on medication, probably) he'd wake up with a startled smile. I managed to get near enough to him to shake his hand—hell, I leaned over to hug the guy, and Carlin hugged me, hard, like a drowning man—though the second Mrs. Ritchie didn't like this at all. Carlin was saying, almost begging, 'Rafe? Where've you been? Why don't you visit me any more? Come see me! Come soon! Next week! Show me what you're doing these days, man! I'm into some new, terrific work—I'm gonna surprise you, man!' while that bitch Janessa is smiling a tight, angry smile, pushing Carlin's wheelchair away saying, 'Mr. Healy, you're overexciting my husband. He's on medication, he doesn't know what he's saying. *Excuse us.*' And she'd gotten him to an elevator, blocking me from entering with them, though there was plenty of room, and there was the artist Robert Rauschenberg in the elevator. Janessa recognized a famous name and it was like she'd been shot with pure adrenaline; her big hungry eyes glistened, her sexy mouth lost its stiffness, her breasts sort of burgeoned out, there she was cooing and cawing over Rauschenberg saying how she'd loved his 'big wild collage paintings' since she was a young girl, all the while blocking me, and pretending not to be aware of me, while Carlin looked on, confused and anxious—it would've been a comic scene on TV, but in real life, if you had to live through it, it wasn't so pleasant. Anyway, you know me, I kept pushing onto the elevator, nudging up against Janessa, her perfume in my nostrils like rotted gardenias, and I was trying to talk to Carlin, and Janessa loses control and slaps at me, actually slaps at me, and says, 'Damn you! You're harassing my husband, and you're harassing me! We don't know you! I'm going to call a security guard if you don't let us alone!' I say, 'What the fuck do you mean, you don't know me? I'm Carlin's friend—who the fuck are *you*?' So maybe I was a little drunk, and belligerent, and my black tie was coming untied, but Janessa provoked me, and I'd like to haul off and hit her, except she starts screaming, 'Help! Police!' so I back off the elevator quick, everybody's glaring at me, even Rauschenberg."

"It's then I realize that that woman, 'Janessa,' is my sworn enemy. And she's Carlin's enemy, too. Though the poor guy wasn't in any condition to know it.

"The last time I saw Carlin Ritchie in private, it was at his place in Buckhannon, West Virginia, which I'd visited only once before. This was about eight weeks before Carlin died. I'd gotten a call from him, inviting me down; he was trying to sound in good spirits on the phone, but his voice was weak, and I had the distinct idea that our conversation was being monitored by Janessa, but I was damned happy to hear from my friend, and if I figured anything I figured that Janessa was embarrassed at her treatment of me, and worried I might make trouble somehow. So she was allowing Carlin to invite me to Buckhannon. And this was more or less what it was, I think. Also she was preparing to murder him and may have believed she needed some credible witness beforehand, to testify that the poor guy was in bad shape. 'Lost the use of his legs!'—as she'd say, in this wailing breathy voice like it was a total surprise to her, or to Carlin, that he wasn't walking just then.

"So I drove to Buckhannon, grateful to be invited if it was only for overnight, and I loaded the van with some of my new quilts to show Carlin, who'd always been a strong supporter of my work, even if it was totally different from his own, and there was Janessa opening the door for me in this weird Disney-type theme house; 'West Virginia gingerbread classic-Victorian' was how she described it in interviews, 'an exact duplicate of Carlin's family home lost in the Depression'—bullshit you'd think Carlin would be ashamed of, but he had to endure it; and instead of my enemy Janessa was now my friend, or so it seemed—hugging me with her strong, fleshy arms, dazzling me with her perfume and a wet high-school-girl kiss right on the mouth. 'Rafe Healy! We've been missing you! Come *in!* How long can you *stay!*' (Like she hadn't worked it out with me that a single night was the limit.) You'd have thought the scene was being televised: here's Mrs. Carlin Ritchie the gracious hostess, in some long, floor-length, swishing Indian skirt, layers of gauze and silk, red hair tumbling down her back, welcoming an artist-friend of her husband's, a woman who'd sacrificed her professional photography career to tend to a crippled husband she adored. And Rafe's a sap, a sucker, she kisses me on the mouth and pokes me with her tongue and Jesus!—I feel such a charge I'm thinking I'll forgive this female anything. It's a total surprise to me that the mood between us is completely different from what it had been in New York, in that elevator—which I understand now is typical of a certain kind of psychopath, the most devious kind, who aren't predictable from one occasion to another but are coolly improvising, trying out different methods for deception, manipulation, and control. (This would explain what Carlin's children said of her that sometimes, when they'd spoken with their father on the phone, on the days she'd allowed it, they could hear Janessa screaming at him, or at someone, in the background; while at other times she was cooing and welcoming, saying how nice it was of them to call, how happy their father would be hearing from them—'And that makes me happy, too!')

"This visit with Carlin, this final visit, was painful to me, but very powerful, memorable—it was like I was in the presence of a saint, yet a saint who was also a good-hearted guy, a friend, with no pretensions, no sense of who he was, what stature he'd attained. Just Carlin Ritchie I'd known since we'd been kids together at Shenandoah, groping our way into our 'careers.' It shocked me to see how he'd lost more weight, and seemed to have resigned himself to the wheelchair. His legs looked shriveled; even his socks were baggy. But his mind was clear, sharp. He told me he was supposed to be taking a certain medication, Janessa would be upset if she learned he'd skipped it that day, 'But it makes my head fuzzy, and my tongue so thick I can't talk—so the hell with it, right? For now.' We spent most of the visit out on the veranda where Carlin could lie back on a wicker divan; it was a mild May evening, and it pissed Janessa off that Carlin wanted just to eat off plates, no formal dinner like she'd planned in the dining room, and no Polaroids—'Janessa is the most posterity-minded individual I've ever known,' Carlin told me, winking, '—she'd snap me on the toilet if I didn't lock the door.' Janessa laughed, hurt, and said, 'Well, somebody's got to be posterity-minded around here. This is a living archive, and you're 'Carlin Ritchie,' lest you forget. You're not *nobody*.' Looking sort of bold-provocative at me, like she's saying Rafe Healy is *nobody*. After a while Janessa got bored with us, and went inside; I'd catch glimpses of her through a curtained window, drifting around, talking on a cellular phone, simpering, laughing so it seemed to me she must have a boyfriend, sure she's got a boyfriend, a female like that, and poor Carlin a cripple. But I was grateful she'd let us alone, and I could see Carlin was, too. He'd never say a word against that woman but there was a sad-ironic tone of his, a way he'd shrug his shoulders when she said some preposterous thing, his eyes locking with mine like we were boys and some adult female was bullshitting us. But then he'd say, a few minutes later, talking about his new work, 'Rafe, I don't know how I would continue, without Janessa. She hires my assistants, she screens my calls, my business—the world.' I wanted to retort, 'Well, Laurette would know, if you don't.' But I didn't. I knew better. The vampire had her fangs in him deep; there must've been an anesthetic effect, a comforting delusion. I get drunk for more or less the same reason, maybe I shouldn't judge. We just sat out there on Carlin's veranda and talked. Must've been three hours—and Janessa fuming and stewing inside. Carlin wasn't supposed to drink, but he had a couple of beers, and I put away a six-pack at least. It was like we both knew this might be the final time we saw each other. I said, 'Carlin. I wish the fuck there was something I could do, y'know? Like donate a kidney. A spleen transplant. Hell—half my cerebral cortex.' And Carlin laughed, and said, 'I know you do, Rafe. I know.' 'It's a goddam thing. It's fate, it's unfair. Like, why *you*?' I said. My eyes were stinging with tears; I was about to bawl. Carlin groped out for me with his left, good hand and said, like he was feeling a little impatient with me, he'd worked through this logic himself and was impatient I hadn't yet, 'But my fate was to be "Carlin Ritchie" one hundred percent. It's one big package deal.' Then he started telling me how 'we'—meaning himself and Janessa—were making 'plans of expediency.' For when, finally, he got too sick. Which might be coming a little more quickly than he'd hoped. Stockpiling pills, barbiturates. It would have to be, Carlin said, without his doctors' knowing. Without anyone 'legal' knowing. No one in his family—'They're old-style Baptists, they don't hold with taking your life, let alone your death, in your own hands.' I was shocked to hear this. I said, 'Carlin, what? You're planning—what?' Carlin said, lowering his voice, 'I don't want to be a burden on Janessa. Not any more than I am. When—if—I become 'incontinent,' as it's called, I know what to do.' 'Carlin, I don't like to hear such talk. You're young, for Christ's sake—not even fifty.' 'That's the problem, man, I'm young enough to be around, in a vegetable state, for a long time.' 'You've got more work to do—lots of work to do. What the fuck are you telling me, you're thinking of pulling out?' 'Rafe, I didn't tell you what I did, I didn't share it, for you to condemn me,' Carlin says, with dignity, '—I didn't invite you even to have an opinion. I'm telling you. That's that.' So I sat there, shaking. I'm an aggressive guy, I've been told—I talk before I think—so I tried to absorb this, tried to see Carlin's logic. I could see it, I suppose. Back inside the house, which was lit up like a movie set, Janessa was watching TV and it sounded like she was still talking on the phone. Carlin said apologetically that he'd been thinking, a few years ago, of asking me to be his estate executor if something premature happened to him—'Laurette was real enthusiastic'—but now of course things were different; Janessa was to be his executor. I swallowed hard, and said OK, I could see that, I understood. Carlin said, embarrassed, 'You know how Janessa is—she loves me so. She's a little jealous of me and some of my old friends. I can't blame her, she's a hot-blooded woman, y'know? She's an artist, too. She gave up her art for me.' 'Did she.' 'She gave up the possibility of having children, she said, for me.' 'Did she.' 'She doesn't want me to suffer, she says. She's worried sick about me, it's almost more upsetting to her than to me, that I might suffer. "Interminably" as she says.' 'So you're stockpiling barbiturates for her,' I said, sort of meanly, '—you don't want her to suffer.' Carlin blinked like he didn't exactly get this, and I said, louder, 'She's rehearsing your death, is that it? She's urging you to die? Has she picked the date yet?' Carlin said quickly, 'No, no—my wife isn't urging me to do anything. It's my own best interests she has in mind. If—when—it comes time I can't walk, can't move, can't eat, can't control my bowels, I don't want to live, man.' 'But that won't be for a long time. That might be never.' 'It might be next month.' 'I might beat you to it, Carlin. It's like shooting dice.' Carlin finished his beer, or tried to—a trickle of beer ran down his chin. He said, shrugging, 'O.K., I don't want to die. Yes, but I'm ready. I want to be brave. Fuck it, I'm a coward, I want to be brave. Help me.' 'Help you? How?' But Carlin laughed, and repeated what he'd said, adding something about God watching over him—'If there's a God but I guess there is not. We've got to grow up sometime, right?' And I said, uneasy, not knowing what the subject was any longer, 'Hell, no. Not me.' And we both laughed.

"That visit in May of last year was the last time I saw Carlin Ritchie alive, though I tried to speak with him on the phone once or twice. But Janessa always answered the phone, saying in this breathy little-girl voice, 'Who? Oh—you. Well, I'm truly sorry, Rafe Healy, but my husband isn't taking calls today.' 'When do you think he will be taking calls, Mrs. Ritchie?' I asked, trying to keep my voice steady, and she said, as rehearsed as if she was being taped for posterity, 'That's in the hands of the Lord.' "

AT THIS POINT, my cousin Rafe paused. He'd come close to breaking down. And I was feeling kind of strange, myself—exhausted by Rafe's story, but excited, too. And a little suspicious just suddenly.

We weren't at the tavern near the courthouse, or in the basement corridor of the old building. As it happened, we were having a few beers in a bar called Domino's; it was early evening of the second day of jury duty, and our panel of jurors had been dismissed that afternoon still without being summoned to any courtroom. Since Rafe had begun telling me his story, though, the hours flew past, and neither of us seemed to mind our enforced idleness. I was so caught up in Rafe's words I could feel pity for Carlin Ritchie, whom I'd never known, as intense as any I'd ever felt for anyone; and I could feel hatred fermenting in my heart for that woman Janessa. I could understand why Rafe hated her so but I wouldn't have gone so far as to wish her dead—that's a pretty extreme state after all.

The evening before I'd come home late, past 7 P.M., having stopped at Domino's with Rafe, and Rosalind was waiting for me, worried—"Since when does jury duty last so long? Were you called for a trial?" I'd decided not to tell her about meeting up with Rafe at the courthouse, and I knew it was futile to pretend to this sharp-nosed woman that I hadn't stopped at a bar and had a few beers, so I told her, yes, I'd been selected for a trial, and it was a damned ugly trial, and we were forbidden to talk about it until it was over—"So don't ask me, Rosalind. Please." "A trial! You actually got chosen!" Rosalind cried. "Is it a—murder case?" "I told you, Rosalind, I can't discuss it. I'd be in contempt of court." "But, honey, who would know? *I* wouldn't tell." "I would know. I've given my word, I've sworn on the Bible to execute my duties as the law demands. So don't tease me, I'm not going to say another word about it." And I was feeling so nerved-up anyway, about the ugly story my cousin was telling me, it didn't really seem that I was lying to Rosalind; there was a deeper truth, lodged in my heart; my cousin's secret he was sharing with me, that I would never tell to another living soul.

But Rafe was shifting his shoulders in that way he'd had when he was a kid, and you knew he wasn't telling all of the truth. So I said, on a hunch, "Rafe, back up just a bit. To the last time you saw Carlin Ritchie. That visit in Buckhannon." "Why? I already told you about Buckhannon." "But was there anything more? Between you and Mrs. Ritchie, maybe?" "That's a crude accusation," Rafe said. "Fuck you, man." "Well—was there? You'd better tell me." "Tell you what, man?" Rafe was defying me, but his pebble-colored eyes were clouded and evasive, and I kept pushing, until finally he admitted yes, there was more. And he wasn't proud of it.

"ALREADY BY 11 P.M., Carlin was exhausted. Where in the old days he'd stay up much of the night talking art and ideas and drinking, now I could see he was ready for bed when Janessa came to fetch him. She wheeled him away to a specially equipped room at the rear of the house, and when she returned she said with a sigh and a sad-seeming smile, 'That poor, brave man. Thank you for making this pilgrimage, Rafe Healy.' Pilgrimage! Like I was some kind of fawning pilgrim. I thought, *Fuck you, lady,* and should've gone off to bed myself (I was staying in a guest room upstairs) except I let her talk me into having a nightcap with her—'Just one. For old time's sake. So there's no hard feelings between us.' There was this coquettish way about the woman, yet an edge of reproach, too, as if she knew full well how certain people valued her, and was defying them yet wanted them to like her, at least be attracted to her, just the same. So she pours us both bourbon. She's wearing a gauzy cream-colored dress like a nightgown, and her hair in ringlets like a little girl's, and her eyes like an owl's ringed in mascara, and there was this hungry, ugly lipstick mouth of hers I couldn't stop staring at. *Yes, I knew I should've gotten the hell out of that house. All I can say is, I was drunk, I was a fool.* Janessa slipped her arm through mine and led me around showing off the house, which had been her idea, she boasted, a 'shrine of memories' for Carlin while he was still in good enough condition to appreciate it. I said, 'Hell, he'll be in good enough condition to appreciate lots of things, for a long time,' but she wasn't even listening. This cold, sickish sensation came over me that, to her, Carlin Ritchie was already dead and she was the surviving widow, the proprietor of the shrine, keeper of the legend. Executor of the estate. Heiress. She'd been drinking earlier in the evening, too. She showed me this display-case room, a parlor, which was papered in deep purple silk wallpaper with recessed lighting in the ceiling, photos of Carlin from the time he was a baby till the present time (except there was no evidence of Carlin with his first wife or his children), an entire wall covered with framed photos of Carlin and Janessa, posed in front of his artworks, or at public ceremonies shaking hands with important people. I flattered the woman by saying, 'Is this the president of the United States?' and she said, pleased, yet a little rueful, 'Yes, it sure is. But it was Carlin he made a big fuss over, not me.' I laughed, and said, 'Janessa, the president would've made a bigger fuss over you, if it hadn't been such a public occasion,' and she laughed hard at that; she liked that kind of humor.

"After that, things got a little confused.

"I mean—I know how it ended. I sure do. But how it got to where it ended—that's confused.

"We were in the living room, which was mostly darkened. And having another bourbon. And this hot-skinned, good-looking woman is sort of pressing up against me like she doesn't know what she's doing. And I'm not supposed to catch on till it's too late. She's complaining how Carlin's family is spreading slander about her, then she's boasting how Carlin's art was fetching higher and higher prices now it was being marketed more professionally—'Thanks to my intervention. *He'd* be happy giving it away.' She's complaining, or boasting, how so many folks make the pilgrimage to Buckhannon, a lot of them bringing gifts like needlepoint-Bible pillows, glow-in-the-dark crucifixes, a hundred pounds of venison steak Carlin's too kindly or too weak to decline—'So it's jamming our freezer. Can you believe it?' 'Well, if people love him,' I mumbled, or words like that. Janessa starts saying how lonely she is amid all this commotion, and how frightened, 'like a little girl,' of the future. How painful it is, married to a man who's not really a man any longer—'My husband, but not my lover. And I'm still *young*.' There's the pink tip of her tongue between her teeth, and suddenly she's in my arms, and we're kissing, panting like dogs like we'd been waiting for this for hours, for all of our lifetimes and now there's nothing to hold us back. Except—I'm pushing her away, disgusted. The taste of her mouth was like something rotten. Like you'd imagine old, stale blood—ugh! If I'd been drunk I was stone cold sober now, on my feet and out of there, upstairs to get my duffel bag and back down again and there's this furious, shamed woman saying, 'You! God damn you! Who do you think you are, you!'—she slapped at me, shut her fist and punched like a man, I pushed her away and she lunged back like a wildcat, clawing me in the face, and I was a little scared of her, knowing she'd have loved to murder me, she'd been so insulted, but she wasn't strong enough to do any real injury, didn't have time to rush into the kitchen for a knife, shouting after me from the veranda, as I pulled away in my van, 'You fucker! You sorry excuse for a man! Don't you ever darken this house again! You're no better than he is—cripple! *Cripple!*' And a few weeks later, Carlin Ritchie was dead."

6

ON THE THIRD DAY of jury duty, which was a Wednesday, our panel of jurors was taken at last upstairs to the fifth floor, to a judge's courtroom, where there was an aggravated assault case to be tried. After a ninety-minute voir dire session, during which time neither JUROR 93 (Rafe Healy) nor JUROR 121 (Harrison Healy) was called, meaning that Rafe and I just sat, sat, sat in enforced silence, Rafe so tense I could feel him quivering, a panel of twelve jurors and two alternates was seated, and the rest of us were dismissed for lunch with a severe warning to be back in the courthouse in forty minutes. Rafe groaned in my ear thank God he hadn't been chosen, he wasn't in any mental state to be questioned by any judge.

I wanted to say, *If you're so torn up about this, maybe you shouldn't be planning to commit a murder. Maybe you're not a murderer.* But I never said a word. It was as if I didn't want to interfere with this strange, scary thing that was happening in my cousin's soul, of such magnitude and danger it could never have happened (I was certain) in mine, as if I didn't have the right, but could only be a witness.

Again we went to the tavern up the street. Again we had several quick beers, to soothe our nerves. Rafe held out his big, burly hand—"Jesus, Harrison: I got the shakes." But he only laughed. He said, "I hope you don't think too lowly of me, Harrison, for behaving like I did. With that vicious woman." I said, truthfully, "I believe you did the right thing. Getting out like you did." "I drove all night to get back home. I was so disgusted with myself! And with her, for making a fool of me like she did. Jesus, the taste of her!—it's still with me, I swear." Rafe wiped at his mouth, and ordered another beer to assuage that taste; it was almost as though I could taste something rotten and bloody-stale on my own lips.

Rafe continued with his story, and now I already knew parts of it, and could feel I'd lived through some of it myself, and was feeling tense and agitated at what was to come. It was as if I'd been with him when he opened the *New York Times* to see CARLIN RITCHIE, 49, "PRIMITIVE" ARTIST, DIES IN WEST VIRGINIA. And Carlin's photo, taken how many years before. The county coroner ruled "complications caused by multiple sclerosis" but the actual cause of death, as Rafe hadn't been surprised to learn from the Ritchie family, was that, during a siege of bad health, and depression, Carlin had "accidentally" ingested a lethal quantity of alcohol and barbiturates. "And guess what? Janessa hadn't been there. Carlin had been alone. For the first time in years, the second Mrs. Ritchie had left her husband out of her sight long enough to travel to New York."

So she'd killed him, and would get away with it. For who was to blame *her?*

"Now, the wake. Harrison, you are not going to believe the wake.

"The wake was held in the shrine-house in Buckhannon, and, Jesus!— what a mob scene. I'd been prepared for Janessa to forbid me to come, and every other old friend of Carlin's, but that wasn't the case—Janessa hired an assistant to call us, wanting to make sure that as many people came to the wake and funeral as possible. Even Carlin's first wife and children were invited. We were advised to fly into Charleston, secure a motel room, rent a car, and drive to Buckhannon, which is what most of us did. I was in a state of shock, though I'd known what was coming. I'd about written off Carlin as a doomed man, after that visit. Though the Ritchie family was claiming he hadn't been that sick, only just depressed because he hadn't been able to work for some time. 'He was too young to die. There were doctors who'd given him hope. How could Carlin do such a desperate thing?' I knew, but I wasn't going to say. I was feeling sick and guilty myself, as if I'd betrayed Carlin, left him with the vampire to die. And Janessa was the bereaved widow, with her dead-white powdered skin and black velvet gown, even a black velvet band around her throat, and her hair streaked at her temples with silver. She stood at the door greeting everyone like a hostess. Her eyes were manic-bright and her mouth crimson like a wound. Seeing me, she pressed herself into my arms with a wail, as if we were old, intimate friends. We were on camera: there was a German documentary filmmaker on the site, who'd apparently been interviewing Carlin up to a few days before his death. There were 'selected' journalists from *Vanity Fair, People,* the *New York Times;* from England, France, Japan, and Israel. The interior of the house was packed with people, most of them strangers to me. There were flowers everywhere. What appeared to be a lavish cocktail buffet had been set up in the dining room, and white-costumed caterers' assistants were serving. The shock, and I mean it was a shock, was Carlin himself—I mean, Carlin's body. It was lying, in an expensive tuxedo, on the white lace spread of a brass four-poster bed (the marital bed, carried down from upstairs) in the parlor. Dozens of candles reeking incense had been lighted. Exclusively white lilies were banked around the bed. I stood there trembling, staring at my friend who'd been made to appear younger and healthier, you could say more garish with health, than he'd looked in years. Pancake makeup skillfully disguised the hollows beneath his eyes; his sallow cheeks were rouged. 'It's like Carlin is only just sleeping, and he'll be waking any minute to say *What's going on here?*'—this remark was repeated numerous times. I said it myself. I said it seriously, and I said it as a joke. I was in that metaphysical-drunk stage where the saddest truth in the world can be the funniest. Photos were being taken of Carlin Ritchie's beautiful grieving widow, standing at the bier-bedside, her fingers linked with those of her dead husband. A tape of mournful country-and-western rock music played. Janessa was taking photos herself, avidly. From time to time she disappeared to freshen her makeup, which was elaborate and effective; at some point she changed into another black dress, low-cut, taffeta, with a startling slit up the side to mid-thigh. Later that night she called for testimonials from 'those who'd known and loved Carlin' and I was one who stood by the four-poster bed speaking of Carlin Ritchie's great talent, his great spirit, and his great courage, and tears ran down my cheeks and others wept with me, as at a gospel ceremony. Janessa pushed into my arms, embraced me hard, her talon fingernails in my neck—'Rafe Healy! I thank you in Carlin's name.' The wake continued through the night. The problem with grief is it reaches a peak, and another peak, and quickly you begin to repeat yourself. What is spontaneous becomes a performance. Repeated. More people arrived, distraught and needing to expend their shock, grief, loss. They wept in the widow's arms. Some wept in my arms. Food had fallen underfoot in the dining room, but fresh platters were being hauled in from the kitchen, and bottles of whisky, bourbon, wine. Carlin had always appreciated a good party, hadn't stinted when it came to quality, and he'd have been proud of this one. Except there was an encounter, caught on videotape, between some Ritchie relatives and Janessa, and there was an encounter between Laurette (who proudly called herself 'Laurette Ritchie') and Janessa, and harsh words were said. Carlin's twenty-seven-year-old daughter Mandy screamed and slapped Janessa— 'You stole Daddy! Like a thief! He'd be alive this minute but for you!'— and had to be carried, hysterically weeping, out of the house. The German filmmaker hurried after her. More mourners pushed into the parlor; there was a roaring of motorcycles in the drive. Near dawn, Janessa asked several old friends of Carlin's to lift him from the bed and place him in a casket beside the bed, and we were a little unsteady on our feet, shy about touching our dead, embalmed, sleeping-looking friend with the rouged cheeks and shoe-polish hair; also, Carlin was heavier than he appeared. I said under my breath, 'Man, what'd they inject you with? Lead?' My buddies laughed. We were sweating like hogs but Carlin was cold. You could feel the cold lifting from him. I believe he was sucking the heat from our hands as cold water will do. Janessa had her camera, taking flash shots of us. I muttered, 'Fuck you, you bitch, a man has died for fuck's sake, we must respect him.' My buddies muttered, 'Amen!' But Janessa chose not to hear. She gave her camera to someone so that her picture might be taken beside us, fitting Carlin into his casket, which was silver-onyx-mahogany, purchased in Charleston and shipped to Buckhannon. We were having a hard time keeping from laughing, fitting poor Carlin into the silk-cushioned casket, and everybody looking on, gaping and drinking. Carlin's toupee was askew, and Janessa hurriedly adjusted it, and I was trying to remember if I'd realized that my friend had been wearing a toupee in life but I couldn't. The funeral was scheduled for 9 A.M. but didn't take place until 10:20 A.M. Some folks, driving from the Ritchie house to the cemetery a mile away, became lost, or disappeared. Yet others appeared. A rawboned preacher from the Gospel Church of Jesus of Buckhannon, whom Carlin hadn't known, spoke at the graveside, quoting Scripture. This was 'Americana' for the foreign journalists, I suppose—Carlin hadn't belonged to any church, though he'd been baptized Baptist. I tried to interrupt the preacher to say what Carlin had said—'I believe in God but not in man believing in God'—but everybody hushed me. I was pissed, and would've left before the casket was lowered into the grave, but Janessa gripped my arm in her talon-claws and held me there. She'd been glancing at me at the graveside, using her eyes on me; I wondered if she was worried that Carlin might've told me of the plan to stockpile barbiturates, and I might tell the authorities. Sure, the woman was guilty of aiding and abetting a suicide—probably under West Virginia law she'd be vulnerable to arrest—but no one could prove her involvement; any good lawyer would've gotten her off. Anyway that wasn't her truest crime, an act of murder. And soul-murder. But what she wanted from me was that I'd stay for the funeral luncheon at the Buckhannon Inn and come back to the house that afternoon—'There's just a select few of Carlin's artist-friends I'm inviting; Heinz Muller wants to interview you and wrap up his film.'

"When I left Buckhannon that day, which was immediately following the funeral, I could not have believed that I would ever plan to return. For any purpose possible.

"Yet now I'm being called. It's Carlin calling me. He'd been the one to own firearms, as a kid. He'd been a hunter, with rifle and shotgun.

"Only a few weeks after Carlin's death, it began to happen. Her calculated acts. Not honoring Carlin's will, getting a lawyer to help her break it, contesting the provisions Carlin had made for his first wife and his children, refusing even to surrender the artworks he'd left to museums in West Virginia and to certain of his friends, like me. Those silk screens Carlin wanted me to have—from his Appalachia series—she's claiming she doesn't have. People try to excuse her—'Poor Janessa, she's devastated with grief. Cries all the time, she says.' Bullshit. But this isn't the worst.

"This behavior, it's mean, cruel, vicious, scheming—criminal. But you wouldn't wish to kill because of it. At least, I wouldn't.

"What's unforgivable in her, what's purely evil, is that she's a vampire.

She's sucking from the living, and from the dead. On TV for instance, interviewed by Barbara Walters. Network TV. And she's reminiscing about Carlin Ritchie's last years, how they collaborated together on mostly everything, Carlin had even worked from sketches she'd provided him, and suggestions; saying theirs was 'one of the great loves of the century, like Georgia O'Keeffe and Alfred Steiglitz.' Work of Carlin's he'd done years before he met her, work he'd had in his studio but hadn't shown, turns out it's 'collaborative.' Janessa Ritchie is 'co-artist.' Right there on TV, her hair dyed almost purple, with grief-streaks of silver, and the big owl-eyes brimming with tears as Barbara Walters pretends to take this bullshit seriously. There's even a journal of Carlin's Janessa reads from, conveniently not handwritten but typed, a so-called log of the final year of his life—'My heart is full! My love for Janessa and for my work is God's grace! I will die not out of sorrow or despair but out of love, in the ecstasy of pure love, knowing my soul is complete.' And her and Barbara Walters practically bawling together. I came close to kicking in my TV, I was so furious.

"Furious, and sick in my soul. For *my* soul is sure not complete!

"Now she's being invited everywhere. 'Janessa Ritchie' is as famous as Carlin, almost. Exhibits in Berlin, Paris, London. This exhibit at the Whit-ney—it's up right now. Go and see with your own eyes. Big features in glossy magazines—*The New Yorker, Mirabella,* even *Art in America* where you'd expect the editors to be more discerning. Some people in the art world have called her to protest; Carlin's ex-dealer drew up a letter which dozens of us signed, and which was sent by certified mail to her; but none of it does any good, and it won't. To stop a creature like her you must destroy her. Trying to reason with her, pleading, even threats of lawsuits—none of that will work. This exhibit at the Whitney—that did it, for me. Tipped me over. It's more of this 'collaborative' bullshit except this time Janessa has dared to put her name to art that was Carlin's, that he hadn't finished and signed. The title of the exhibit is 'The Ritchies'—like she, the woman who killed him, the vampire, is an equal of her victim! It's a night-mare. It's like the media knows what's happening but goes along with it—Janessa's a glamorous woman, they can champion 'an exemplary female artist' as she's been called.

"I wasn't invited to the champagne opening at the Whitney, of course. But I got in anyway. I saw what was on the walls, and walked right up to her, the bitch, the thief, the 'grieving widow,' she's lovey-dovey with this

guy who's Carlin's new dealer at a wealthy uptown gallery, and she's
dressed in sexy black silk, spike-heeled shoes and textured black stockings,
she's put on more weight, in her bust and hips, fleshy but not fat, and sexy,
though her skin is powdered dead-white and looks bloated like a corpse
that's been in water. And that crimson mouth that's wider than ever, thick
with greasy lipstick. *Ugh!—I remember the taste of her.* She sights me coming
at her and I see the guilty panic in her eyes, though right away she puts on
this pose of innocence so I'm the one who comes off badly. I say, 'God
damn you, woman, what do you mean claiming this work is yours? It's
Carlin's and you know it,' and she says to her companion in this scared
little-girl voice, 'He's a deranged man! I don't know who he is! He's been
threatening me for months!' and I say, 'Don't know who I am! I'm Carlin's
friend. I'm here to speak for him. To tell the world that you are thieving
from him, and betraying him. Jesus, woman, didn't you love that man at
all?' But by this time two security guards are on me and I'm being hustled
out onto the street—Madison Avenue. And I know better than to stick
around and get arrested by some real cops.

"So what'd I do—drove home here. Sick in my heart. Wanting to
commit a murder right then if only I had the power. I saw Carlin on
that veranda, as dusk came on, wrapped in a flimsy blanket, shivering,
trying to smile at me, pleading. *I don't want to die. Yes but I'm ready. Help
me.*"

We were still in the tavern, but it was almost time to return to the
courthouse. Rafe had showed me a newspaper photo of "Janessa Ritchie"
and she looked just as he'd said: glamorous, fleshy, with hungry eyes and
mouth. I felt my heart beating hard and heavy, Rafe's hot, angry blood
streaming through my veins. He said, "Every day it gets worse. It's hanging over me always. Can't sleep, can't work. And this week of jury
duty—at the courthouse, in that atmosphere—it's like somebody is fucking with me, y'know?—mocking me. Every defendant who's on trial had
the courage to do what he needed to do—there's that way of thinking.
But Rafe Healy doesn't have the courage, so far, to do what I need
to do."

I could see how agitated he was, so I paid the bill for both of us, and got
him out of there, walking in the sunshine and trying to talk to him, reason
with him. It was as if we'd been imprisoned together in a small cell that,
even though we were in the open air now, and in the eyes of observers
free, unconfined men, continued to press in upon us. I said, "Maybe it's a

sign, Rafe? If you don't have the 'courage'? That you shouldn't do it? That you should just forget about it? Since your friend is dead anyway—"

Rafe stopped on the sidewalk, glared at me as if I were his mortal enemy. "Fuck you, man, what're you saying? Carlin's *dead,* that means— what? I should abandon him?"

"No, Rafe. Only just that—"

"She's a vicious, evil woman. I swear, an emissary of Satan. That's more and more clear to me, Harrison. Last night I was in my studio, trying to work, drinking and trying to work, and my hands shook so badly I couldn't do a thing—I heard her laughing at me, and saw those eyes, I tasted that mouth sort of nuzzling at me, teasing. She's moving onto me, now. The vampire's moving onto me."

"Rafe, that isn't right. You know that isn't right. Listen to you."

At the courthouse steps, Rafe wiped his face on his sleeve, tried to compose himself. Just since Monday, I believe he'd lost some weight. There were knifelike vertical creases in his cheeks. He said, "I believe you're right. I can hear my own voice, and it's become a deranged voice. I'm not me—I'm a deranged man. And it's that woman who's to blame. So long as she lives, I am her victim."

7

You could rent a car. Two cars. In sequence. The first you'd rent at an airport, perhaps in New Jersey. You'd leave your van in a parking lot. The second car you'd rent in Pennsylvania. And drive to Buckhannon, West Virginia, to arrive there by first dark. Because you would need to seek your target in a lighted house, yourself hidden in darkness. But wait: before this, at a Sears or Kmart in any large mall (some distance from your home) you could purchase a dark jacket with a hood. Rubber boots a size or two larger than your own. Gloves. But wait: before this, you will need to buy the rifle. The rifle with the scope. Ammunition. You're going deer hunting you'll tell the salesclerk. You'll purchase the rifle upstate where hunting is common, and you'll need to practice shooting at a target. Somewhere private. Maybe we could practice together. I don't mean that I'd be coming with you to West Virginia. I could not do that. But I could help you. I could buy the rifle, possibly. I could give you moral support. I can see you are in need of moral support. I'm your cousin but we're closer than most cousins. You could say I'm your lost brother. And I'm lonely.

Rosalind woke me, gently. Telling me I'd been grinding my teeth.

A bad dream? she asked, and I said, No. Not a bad dream. Not at all.

8

THURSDAY AFTERNOON AT 2:25 P.M., Rafe's luck runs out. Juror 93 is called to take his seat in a jury box—our panel of jurors was sent up to a sixth-floor courtroom where there's a murder case scheduled, a nasty case it looks to be, burly black man with a downlooking, gnarled face accused of having killed his wife. Rafe shudders and gives my arm a quick scared squeeze as he stumbles out of his seat to step forward. Poor Rafe: everybody's staring at him, he's unsteady on his feet as a sleepwalker (or a drunk: he'd had at least six beers at lunch, in spite of my telling him to go easy), the tallest of all the jurors and, judging by the look in his mottled face, the shyest. He's wearing his bib overalls which look as if he's been sleeping in them (I wouldn't doubt he has) and his beard and hair are scruffy. I'm worried that my cousin will get into trouble if it's discovered he's been drinking while on jury duty: does that mean contempt of court? I'd been drinking, too, but not as much as Rafe, and I believe I'm fully sober.

This trial will be for first-degree murder. Which is to say, it's a capital case. A few years ago, New York state reinstated the death penalty, by lethal injection.

As Rafe Healy passes by the defense counsel's table, the defendant turns to stare at him. It's the first time in the approximately ninety minutes we've been in this courtroom that the defendant, a muscular, near-bald man of about fifty, has roused himself to take such an interest. But Rafe, a vague dazed smile on his face, or a grimace of the lips that might be mistaken for a smile, makes it a point not to look at him.

Not many jurors, Caucasians or persons of color (as we're told they wish now to be called), are anxious to be assigned to this case. Downstairs the rumor circulated that it could last for weeks. And there's a death-penalty trial that follows, if the verdict is guilty. I swear Rafe was actually praying, moving his lips during the voir dire as potential jurors were questioned one by one, a few retained in the jury box but most dismissed. Now Juror 93 is seated in the box being asked occupation? ("self-employed craftsman"—which makes a few people smile) and whether he's associated in any way with the case, heard anything about it or believes he might be in any way disqualified to remain on the jury, and Rafe is staring pained at the judge, moving his lips but not speaking. I'm feeling, Jesus!—just so excruciatingly embarrassed for my cousin, and anxious for him; I'm worried as hell what he's going to say. *I can't sit in judgment of any murderer. I am not the man.* The way Rafe and I've worked it through, these past few days, less than a week but if feels like we've been together for a long, long time, there are times when murdering another human being isn't just not-wrong but morally and ethically right. The law just can't cover that. The judge rephrases his question, and again Rafe tries to answer, but can't seem to speak; his face is mottled now like he's got a sudden case of measles, and his eyes are glassy. "Mr. Healy, is something wrong? Mr. Healy?" the judge inquires, concerned; he's a middle-aged man, friendly-seming most of the time though he's been a little impatient with some of the jurors who'd clearly wanted to be dismissed, and now with Rafe he doesn't know how to proceed. Is this juror just being difficult, to be excused; or is there something really wrong with him? I raise my hand like a kid in school and say, "Excuse me? Your honor? That man is my cousin and he's kind of a—nervous type? He's on medication, I think—probably he shouldn't be here." Now everybody's staring at *me.*

But it's O.K. It's the right, inspired thing. The judge contemplates me for a minute, frowning; then thanks me for the information, and calls Rafe over to speak with him in private. After a few minutes' consultation (I'm watching Rafe's earnest face and hoping to hell he isn't uttering any sort of blunt truth, only just improvising a reasonable excuse to get him out of here) Juror 93 is formally dismissed for the day.

In fact, it will be for the rest of the week. Rafe Healy is finished with jury duty, probably forever.

For me, the remainder of the voir dire passes in a blur. I keep waiting for my number to be called, but it isn't. By 5:20 P.M. the jury box is finally filled, twelve jurors and two alternates, and the rest of us are dismissed for the day.

I'd been wondering if Rafe would be downstairs waiting for me, but he isn't. But he's in the parking lot, leaning against the fender of my car. "Jesus, Harrison! You saved me up there. Man, I'm grateful." Rafe actually hugs me, it's that weird. But I know I did the right, shrewd thing. It just seems as if my brain's been revved up lately, like a machine working faster and more efficiently. Things falling into place.

9

IT'S PAST 8 P.M. by the time I get home, Thursday night. Should've called Rosalind from the bar but forgot. And the woman's in my face as soon as I get in the door asking how's the trial? and I say, Trial? What trial? (Goddamn, I'd kind of forgotten what I'd told her the other day) then—"Oh, that. It's pretty ugly stuff like I said. I'll be glad when it's over." Rosalind says, with that blinking little frown of hers that isn't an accusation, but means to make you think along those lines, "I looked everywhere in the paper but I didn't find anything. About any trial that sounded like yours." I say, beginning to get pissed at her, "Look, Rosalind, I explained to you I can't discuss it. Didn't I explain to you I can't discuss it?" and she says, "It's got to be something terrible, for you to get drunk every night on the way home, like you haven't done for twelve years," and I say, "What? You've been counting?" as if it's a joke, or I'm willing to grant her the possibility that it's a joke. I'm an hour late for supper, but what the fuck, I get a beer from the refrigerator and Rosalind's pulling at my arm in that way I don't like, and she knows I don't like, saying, "Don't be ridiculous, Harrison, you can hint about it, can't you? Is it a murder case? Some kind of murder case?" I'm drinking from the can saying nothing trying to walk away and the woman keeps pushing, "Is it a woman killed, and a man on trial? Is it some pervert? It isn't a child killed, is it? And some disgusting pervert on trial? Just wink your left eye, honey, and give me a clue," and I'm beginning to lose it, I say, "Look, we could both be in trouble if I breathe a word of this trial to anyone, including even my fellow jurors, before the judge gives permission, didn't I explain that to you? Can't you comprehend? Violating the judge's order is called contempt of court and you can be jailed," and she's in my face persisting, in the way that she used to do with the boys, and that pisses me for sure, saying, "Harrison? Come *on.* Just wink your left eye if—" And I shove her back against the edge of the kitchen table, and she gives a little scream of pain and surprise and I'm out of the kitchen, I'm slamming out of the goddamn room, I'm shaking, muttering to myself words I've never heard myself speak aloud in this house, in such a voice, I'm thinking I've never touched my wife, or any woman, in anger in my life, never in anger like this, like flame, never until now and it feels right, it feels good, it feels goddamned good.

TUSK

*A*s the knife fitted into Tusk's hand, an idea fitted into his head.

Look at me! Goddamn here I am.

Exactly what he'd do, he'd make up when he got to the place it would be done in. Like a quick cut in a movie, you get to the place where something's going to happen. Or when he saw the person, or persons, it would be done to. Like jazz, what's it called, you make it up at the piano not toiling away for hours practicing scales and arpeggios and shitty Czerny exercises like he'd been made to do by his dad in the grim dead days before he was Tusk—*improvisation* it was called.

That's what Tusk was famous for, or would be famous for: *improvisation.* Forever afterward at East Park they'd be saying of Tusk, *That Tusk! Man, he's one cool dude!* And over in the high school they'd be saying it, too.

Exactly why they'd be saying this, shaking their heads in that way meaning *no shit,* blinking and staring at each other lost in wonderment, Tusk didn't yet know. But he would.

IT WAS his dad's knife. Out of his dad's desk drawer. A souvenir from 'Nam. You had to wonder how many gooks the knife had killed, right?

Tusk grinned, contemplating such freakiness. *They did the DNA and it's more blood types than they can figure. Wei-ird!*

Probably it was going to happen at school, or after school. He was headed for school. His mom calling anxiously after him but he hadn't heard, on his way out fast, like his new Nikes were carrying him. He'd been waking through the night charged with electricity like sex and it felt good. Liking how it was just an ordinary weekday, a Tuesday. Couldn't remember the calendar month—April? May? It was all a background blur. It was just the pretext for what came next. On the TV news, that was what they'd be saying. *Just an ordinary weekday, a Tuesday. At East Park Junior High in the small suburban community of Sheridan Heights. Thirteen-year-old Tusk Landrau is a ninth-grader here.* Tusk hoped they wouldn't get into the honors-student shit, anything to do with old Roland. Anyway he wasn't going to plan much. He had faith the knife would guide him. When he'd been Roland junior for twelve fucking years he'd planned every fucking thing ahead of time. Laid out school clothes the night before, even socks. Socks! Homework had to be perfect. Brushing his teeth, never less than ten vigorous brushings to each part of the mouth. Until the gums bled. Going down a flight of stairs he was compelled to hit each stair at the identical spot. Setting up the chess board to play with his friend Darian (when they'd been friends), he'd been compelled to set his pieces up from the back row forward as his dad had always done, always king and queen first. And his game planned as far as he could see it, until mist obscured his vision. Even wiping his tender ass with a prescribed length of toilet paper one two three four *five* rhythmic swipes. But no more! Now he was Tusk and Tusk moved in one direction only: fast-forward. He'd left every dork friend (like Darian) behind. His brain worked in quick leaps. Like Terminator III. Rapid fire and stop. Rapid fire and stop. Reload and *pop!* and stop. His brain was wired. His brain was fried. He didn't have to smoke dope or pop pills (though sometimes for the hell of it Tusk did) to get to that place. His head was quick starts and stops and reloads and pops and *bam! bam! bam!* and stop. Tusk was a new master of the video arcade. The older guys admired him. One cool dude! That strung-out look, dilated eyes. Certain of the girls thought him sexy-looking. Wild. Hours rushed by in this state. It was an OK state. If he stepped sideways out of it he'd feel like shit enveloped his entire soul, so why? One direction only: fast-forward. *Bam! bam! bam!* and *blip!* on the screen. And the sweet explosion that follows.

Now you see Tusk, now you don't.
Goddamn here I AM.

WEIRD THAT a souvenir from 'Nam had been manufactured in Taiwan. Stainless steel with a seven-inch blade and an aluminum grip of some strange burnished metal or possibly mineral with a greenish glow. Tusk told kids his old man had fought in Vietnam but in fact his old man had been in intelligence probably just sitting on his ass until it was time to fly home again. He'd bought the knife probably from some dumb fuck who'd actually "seen action." Tusk tested the blade by running it along his throat and wasn't sure it was sharp as it needed to be. You get your chance you don't want to fuck up, right? There was a fancy knife sharpener in the kitchen but better not. If his mom discovered him? A weekday morning? On his way to school? *Why, Roland, what's that in your hand?* (Jesus, maybe he'd stick *her!*)

So no way, Tusk's out of here.

Dad's knife shoved in his backpack with his homework.

IF THIS were a movie they'd pick up next on Tusk pushing into school like any other morning. A pack of round-head kids, muffin-face kids, kids looking more grade school than junior high. Tusk is the barracuda here. Not tall but slouched, lean like a knife blade, fawn-colored hair in flamey wings lifting from his face and that glistening in his skin like he's got a fever. And shadowy hawk eyes that are greeny glow-in-the-dark like the Assassin in his new favorite video game XXX-RATED. He's high but it's a natural high. He's a ticking time bomb but there's no defusing. There are only a few cool dudes in the junior high like Tusk and they're dressed hip-hop style in baggy T-shirts, baggy jeans and the cuffs dragging the floor, but Tusk's mom won't allow him to dress like a savage like some black ghetto gangster she says so he's in just a regular T-shirt, regular but hole-pocked jeans and his flashy new Nikes. No ear studs, no nose ring. (Which the school dress code doesn't allow anyway.) No punk streaked hair. That isn't Tusk's style. Tusk isn't a goth or a freak, he's the *X in the equation.*

But shit, when there's no camera you're invisible.

Tusk uses his elbows pushing some kids out of his way, you'd think the little jerk-offs would know to steer clear of him by now. Tusk says loudly, "It's a damn good thing there's no metal detectors in this school." And some girls giggle like this is a joke?

★   ★   ★

AT HIS LOCKER Tusk couldn't remember the fucking combination and so banged and kicked the fucking door. You can ask one of the nigger janitors but he'd done that just last week, and a few times before. So fuck that. Tusk was thinking almost he wishes there *were* metal detectors in the school like in some serious big-city school. He'd figure out some ingenious way to smuggle the blade in. That'd be the lead-in for the TV news that night: *Despite metal detectors at East Park Junior High, a ninth-grader named Tusk Landrau succeeded in*—After that, his mind goes blank as in a slow soundless explosion.

Talking with some kids, and he's sighting Alyse Renke down the corridor, there she is and it comes to him in a flash *Stick Alyse. In her sweet cunt.* Alyse is Tusk's girl or had been or was gonna be, there's been a kind of understanding between them off and on all this year. Alyse is fifteen years old, she'd been held back a year and Tusk is thirteen, he'd been promoted a year (back in grade school) which his mom hadn't thought was a good idea but his dad pushed for. But Tusk is taller than Alyse and he knows he's sexy in her eyes because she'd all but told him once. Alyse is, for sure, *sex-y.* What guys in high school call a *cock-tease,* and she hangs out with them so they should know.

Fondling the knife through the nylon fabric of the backpack like it's Tusk's secret prick.

Was a time he'd been Roland junior. Only twelve months ago but can't remember old Roland except to know the guy was a nork, a dorf, a nerd, a geek, a jerk-off. That asshole Roland who busted his balls for his old man getting high grades the old man examined like something stuck to his shoe. Son, you know, and I know, this isn't the best you can do.

Baptized himself Tusk. Where this name came from, he didn't know. Only a few kids called him Tusk but one day they all would. And his teachers too. (Alyse called him Tusk now. Wrapped her pink tongue around "Tusk" like it's his sweet cock she's sucking.)

Staring at his skinny rib cage in the mirror still steamed up from his shower (Roland had a habit of hiding in the shower, water as hot as he could stand it, running it for ten minutes or more believing himself safe there, the door locked and you can't hear voices in the shower unless they're voices in your head and his mom wasn't so likely to knock on the bathroom door if she heard the shower though of course she would if he hid in there too long) contemptuous of his puke-pale white-boy skin and the nipples that looked like raspberries and skinny as he was a little potbelly (visible if he stood sideways to the mirror and puffed it out in disgust) and dangling from peach-fuzz reddish hair at his groin a skinned-looking little penis maybe two inches long he'd try to hide from the other guys changing for swim class which he hated. *Rol-lie! Wowee! Let's see what Rollie's got!*

But all this was before Tusk. In that totally weird space when he'd been Roland junior. And Roland senior had been what's called *alive*.

BUZZER SOUNDS for homeroom. Everybody slams their lockers and it's tramp off to homeroom. Tusk slouches into his seat and lets the backpack fall gently. His usual posture and deadpan style. Miss Zimbrig reading announcements. Tusk is nervous. Tusk is excited. Tusk is sweating. Tusk is picking his nose. Needing to stoop to touch the knife hidden inside the backpack. Taking a chance maybe. He's twitchy, compulsive. If Zimbrig calls out, *Roland, what d'you have there? Please bring that backpack here.* Checking for drugs and the nosy bitch is gonna get stuck like a pig in front of twenty-seven bug-eyed ninth-graders.

Wow, you heard? Tusk Landrau whacked Zimbrig in homeroom this morning, I mean totally wasted the bitch, slitting her from throat to gizzard. His old man's combat knife from 'Nam. Yeah, that Tusk is one bad dude!

Except Zimbrig doesn't notice Tusk. Or, noticing, wisely decides not to call him on the backpack. Zimbrig never knew Roland junior, through ninth grade it's been Tusk and for sure she knows not to mess with *him*. Not even to joke with him like she does with some of the other cool dudes flashing skull tattoos on their biceps. (Tattoos are in violation of the East Park public school's dress code. But these are just vegetable-dye tattoos, not the real thing done with needles which is the only kind of tattoo Tusk would wish for himself. None of that chickenshit for *him!*) Could be, Tusk runs into Zimbrig in the parking lot behind school, he'd get the signal *Her! Stick her! She's the one.* But Tusk doubts he can get it up for an old bag his mother's age. (Though Tusk is vague about his mom's actual age. Makes him squirm, he's fucking *embarrassed*. He'd read in the obituary that Roland Landrau Sr., investment attorney, had been forty-one when he'd bought the farm last year.) Tusk crouches down to check out the knife through the canvas fabric another time, man it's *there*.

PA announcements. Blahblahblah. Amazing to Tusk how shit-faced ordinary this day *is*. Not knowing he's squirming in his seat like he's got to go pee and picking his nose and there's Zimbrig casting him dirty looks, an old nervous habit of his, of Roland's, his mom scolded him in her anxious-hurt way for bad manners as she called it, and his dad slapped him for a dirty habit as he called it—*Dis-gusting, Roland! Stop that at once.* As if picking his nose till sometimes it bleeds was nerdy Roland's dirtiest habit. And there's Zimbrig definitely eyeing him through her black plastic glasses. Fuck, where's he gonna wipe the snot? The bitch glaring at him so he wipes it on his jeans at the knee where it sort of splotches in with the other greenish stains and crud.

Buzzer sounds. First period. Tusk wakes out of a dream and it's like XXX-RATED *bam pop* rapid fire and stop! and *pop!* and he's grinning like not knowing where the fuck he is. But on his feet, and the backpack heaved up and hugged to his chest and filing out of homeroom slouched and oily hair swinging in his face Tusk has to pass Miss Zimbrig's desk and the bitch smirks murmuring, "Here, Roland. Be my guest." Handing him a Kleenex out of the box on her desk. And kids looking on giggle. And Tusk winces, his face burns but he's been so fucking brainwashed to be polite to adults he actually mumbles, "Thanks, Miss Zimbrig."

And takes the Kleenex!

Bitch is gonna pay. Nobody laughs at Tusk. Nobody fucks with Tusk. The hour of reckoning is near!

ROLAND LANDRAU SR. he can hardly remember. He hadn't known him all that well when the guy'd been his dad. Like the screen is zigzags and blurs and instead of rock music there's static. Like through a telescope he can see the three of them at the dining room table where the father had to discipline the son and took pleasure in the task, leaning forward on his elbows with an almost boyish eagerness so the tablecloth bunched and pulled toward him, and the father not noticing, quietly reprimanding little Roland (three years old? four?) for eating his food too quickly, or maybe too slowly pushing it around his plate, or for whispering to his mother instead of speaking to both his parents, or for chattering when he should have been silent because Daddy was trying to talk, or for sitting silent, his head bowed and sulky, picking at his food when he should have been talking. Roland junior who never seemed to learn (dumb-ass kid! it's hard to feel sorry for such a shithead) that he must look Daddy in the eye and not shrink or cringe or burst into tears which really infuriated Daddy for implying that Daddy was "some kind of bully who'd pick on a small kid" and next thing you knew Roland junior was shrieking because he'd been slapped, or shaken by the shoulder like a beanbag, or what scared the most though it didn't hurt the most, his plump round face gripped in Daddy's big fingers so Daddy could lean within an inch to shout at him. (And where was Mom, Mom was at the table white-faced, worried, biting her lower lip until the lipstick was eaten off, Mom was such a pretty mommy and her hair so beautifully styled it was a puzzle why little Roland grew up not to trust her for there was a time when Mom would say these episodes at the dining room table didn't happen because they could not have happened explaining to Roland, *Much of what you think has happened in a lifetime never did.*) And there was the time when Roland was six years old and no longer a baby and he'd run from the table when his dad began to discipline him and his dad had caught him on the stairs and yanked him back down and shook him till his teeth and his brains rattled in his head and Roland drew breath to scream but could not scream for the scream was trapped inside him like partly chewed food and his reddened face puffed up like a balloon to bursting and his eyes bulged in their sockets and he fainted and next thing he knew he was being wakened by someone he'd never seen before, in a place whitely glaring with light he'd never seen before, not wanting to breathe but forced to breathe, eyes rolled back in his head not wanting to focus normally but forced to focus normally and that was the occasion as his parents would afterward describe it in grave hushed voices of their son's first *asthma attack.*

THIS OLD SHIT, Tusk mostly can't remember. Like it did happen to another kid, some pathetic little nerd, now *gone.*

"HIIIII TUSK."

"Hi 'lyse."

"How's it goin'?"

Tusk shrugs eloquently. "You?"

Alyse Renke shrugs, too. In tight blue jeans and purple cotton-knit Gap sweater displaying her pear-sized little breasts. Alyse wears six glinting ear studs on her left ear and her broom-colored hair has zebra streaks of black and her flirty eyes are outlined in black mascara deliberate as crayon and she's making a kissy-pouty mouth rolling her eyes at Tusk like it's a movie close-up. Saying in a growl, "Sort of OK. But kinda pissy too, you really want to know."

Before Tusk can rack his brain for a clever reply Alyse moves on swinging her hot little ass so Tusk stares after her with *bad intentions* on his sweaty face like neon. At the door to her classroom Alyse will glance back at Tusk but Tusk has already shoved on, hugging his soiled backpack to his chest and blinking dazed into space.

Like, Alyse Renke *is* the one, maybe? And Tusk isn't gonna have any choice about it?

NEXT PERIOD, study hall in the school library, Tusk guesses he's calling attention to himself the way he's squatting for long minutes by the *World Book, Encyclopaedia Britannica,* and other reference books nobody ever looks at unless there's an assignment. Tusk is making faces to himself paging through *Human Biology* and there comes Mrs. Kottler the librarian to say, "What are you looking for, Roland? Maybe I can help you." But Tusk won't meet her eye. Shrugs and mumbles what sounds like *Nah, I'm OK.*

At last he found what he was looking for: a cartoon drawing of a human being with bones, organs, arteries, and nerves highlighted. The heart is lower in the chest than you'd think, Tusk sees. And there's bone protecting it, sort of. The neck? Those deep-blue blood vessels. *Carotid arteries supplying blood to the brain.* Instinctively Tusk locates a hot pulsing artery in his own neck, below the jawline. The carotid artery is his best bet, probably. He'd only need to slash once, twice, maybe saw the blade back and forth. If his victim is Alyse Renke, she'll be easy to overpower, no taller than he is. If his victim is somebody bigger, like an adult, Tusk will be more challenged but *You want to bet Tusk can't do it?*

For all he needs is positioning and leverage. And the right timing. As in XXX-RATED. Strike by surprise! Rapid fire and stop and *pop pop pop! Game over.*

IT WAS *pop! game over!* for Roland's dad. One minute he'd been talking on the phone and the next he was slumped sideways in his swivel chair behind his desk like a man surprised in an earthquake and paralyzed in the posture of that first second's terrible jolt. Had Mr. Landrau been arguing over the phone with a business associate?—had his son, Roland, twelve, upstairs in his room at his computer doing algebra homework heard his dad's voice lifting in pain and terror like a wounded animal? *Had the son heard his stricken father call to him for help?*

The business associate would afterward claim he'd assumed that Mr. Landrau had just hung up. Without saying good-bye. Not that Mr. Landrau was rude but he had ways of showing his impatience or moral indignation or disgust, and hanging up without saying good-bye or tossing the receiver down, off the hook, was one of them.

It was bad luck for Mr. Landrau that no one else (except his son) was home at the time of the emergency. For possibly he might have been saved. If an ambulance had been summoned, if he'd been rushed into neurosurgery, just maybe. This would be a subject for the grieving widow and the deceased man's relatives to ponder. But Mrs. Landrau was shopping at Lord & Taylor and the Puerto Rican woman who cleaned house so capably for the Landraus had gone home an hour before. And the door to Roland junior's room was shut. For since seventh grade the boy had begun to insist upon his right to privacy. So it was plausible *I didn't hear Dad. I didn't hear anything. I didn't!*

What popped in Mr. Landrau's brain was a weakened blood vessel. An *aneurysm*. An often undetectable and frequently fatal *abnormal dilatation of a blood vessel* in a brain. Roland Landrau Sr. would have ceased breathing by the time his wife returned home to discover him slumped in his swivel chair in his study, telephone receiver on the floor and his dead-white face so contorted as to be hardly recognizable. Mouth gaping open and eyes staring like a doll's eyes too round and shiny to be real.

Upstairs hunched over his computer keyboard Roland junior heard his mom begin to scream. A sound like tearing silk inside his skull he'll hear through his lifetime. He knows.

"Y'KNOW WHO I'd like to whack someday? Fuckface Snyder."

"Wow, Tusk! Cool."

"This knife of my dad's I told you about, this thing like a dagger practically, already bloodstains on it, y'know?—from 'Nam?—that's what I'd use. Because a gun, even if I had a fucking gun, would make too much fucking noise, y'know?"

"Cool, Tusk! Rii-ight."

But these assholes don't take Tusk seriously, he can tell. In the locker room fourth period. Tusk is slow and sullen changing his clothes, fucking resents fucking gym class. Today it's outdoor track and jumping he's lousy at, no more coordinated than when he'd been Roland junior shy and blinking at the guys yelling in a pack around him like hyenas. What Tusk hates is anything regimented like you're in the goddamn fucking army or something. "Butch" Snyder clapping his ham-hands and puffing his cheeks and faggot eyes twinkling shouting like it's good news he's bringing them *All rii-ight, boys! Let's go, boys! Three times around the track to warm up, boys! C'mon, let's GET IT ON!* You'd think Tusk Landrau might be a runner, he's got that lean runner's frame, long slender arms and legs, but the poor kid gets breathless in five minutes, only the fat kids run slower, there's something wrong with his nasal passages or his sinuses, he's had asthma. Coach Snyder who's one of the popular teachers at East Park tries to sympathize. Tries to disguise his contempt for certain of these soft suburban kids. Spoiled rich men's sons he can tolerate if they're athletes who follow his instructions but the rest of them, sissies, punks, and fuck-offs he's got no use for, like this "Tusk" pretending to be a cool dude grimacing and working his mouth like a schizo arguing with himself, and his baby-face oily with sweat like he's running a fever. "Roland, see me in my office, OK? Before you shower and change."

Tusk is scared. But laughing and telling the guys it's been a year since he's had a shower at school, what's Fuckface Snyder think, everybody's a faggot like himself?

In Coach's glass-brick cubicle office off the gym, with no window except opening onto the gym, Tusk grips the backpack on his knees. Christ, he is scared. Sweating and shivering and his teeth practically chattering. *He's going to stick Snyder. In the gut because Snyder's growing a gut and it serves the fucker right. Wild!* He's fumbling unzipping the pocket, slips his hand inside and there's the knife blade he touches first, it feels pretty sharp though maybe not razor-sharp, then he grips the handle, clutches it in his sweaty palm. But Coach breezes in and taps his shoulder, "OK, Roland, how's it going?" like Coach is Tusk's big brother or a different kind of a dad and before Tusk can handle it there's tears in his eyes, fucking tears spilling over and running like hot acid down his cheeks. Coach blushes pretending not to see this though for sure he's embarrassed as hell. Repeating, "How's it going?" in a kindly way that makes Tusk lose it even more so Tusk is on his feet wild-eyed stammering, "L-Leave me alone! You don't know anything about me! *Fuck you don't touch me, leave me alone!*" Tusk would yank out the knife from 'Nam, his right hand is actually shoved inside the pocket gripping the smooth handle (and this Coach will recall, speaking of the episode) but fuck it he's crying too hard, hasn't cried like this since he was a little kid, you forget how crying *hurts*. Coach is on his feet surprised saying, "Roland, hey wait—" but Tusk has already rushed out of the office hugging the backpack against his chest, can't see where the fuck he's going, choking for air, he'll hide out in a toilet stall in the lavatory off the storage room until the buzzer sounds for fifth period and the coast is clear and Coach figures he knows better than to follow a distraught adolescent.

What I'd do I thought was give the poor kid some slack; I could see he was upset but didn't think it was more than that; sometimes I don't involve anybody else at school to keep it off the kid's record. What I figured was, I'd give Mrs. Landrau a call at home that evening.

Yes. I knew the father was dead.

WHEN THE ANEURYSM went *pop!* there was Roland junior upstairs in his room almost directly overhead. Yes he'd heard his dad screaming. Not for him, or for help—just screaming. Like a hurt, terrified animal. Yet, hunched at his computer concentrating on his algebra homework Roland junior who was a nervous twelve-year-old sort of didn't hear. Or if he'd heard, he hadn't understood. Dad had a TV in his study sometimes he'd switch it on to watch news in the evening, so maybe that was it—the strangulated scream. *Yes I heard. I heard something. Yes I knew it was Dad. Yes I knew something had happened to him. Heart attack, I thought. Or somehow, I don't know how, like in a movie or something—his clothes were on fire. Always had a weird imagination, I guess! Actually I'm kidding, I didn't hear anything from downstairs. My room isn't over Dad's study really. Dad's study is at the corner of the house. I stayed with the computer doing my homework. It was like I was paralyzed I guess. From downstairs there was nothing. No TV noises. I didn't hear anything until Mom came home and started screaming.*

Then Roland junior ran into the bathroom connected to his room and locked the door and switched on the fan and even flushed the toilet pressing the sweaty palms of his hands against his ears framing his head like a vise.

No! no! no! I didn't hear a fucking thing!

RED-EYED TUSK IS skipping fifth-period math. Hanging in the hall outside Alyse Renke's social studies class. Framing his narrow paste-colored face in the door window so that Alyse can see him through her clotted eyelashes. He's excited, he knows that guys from gym class are talking and laughing about him. He knows exactly who they are. And there's Darian Fenner, his ex-friend now his enemy, who wasn't in that gym class but is a friend of a guy who was and in the corridor just now changing classes Tusk sighted Darian and this kid laughing together at Darian's locker and smiling in Tusk's direction. *There's baaad Tusk, sweated through his clothes unless some of that damp is he's peed his pants?* Just chance that Darian is in Alyse's class, Tusk doesn't want to be distracted by thoughts of Darian right now though his ex-friend has betrayed him and deserves to die—Tusk could drift into an open-eyed dream seeing this in slow motion—he'd corner Darian in the lavatory and saw the blade across Darian's throat until Darian's dorky head was severed from Darian's dorky-pudgy body and he'd position the head—eyes open—in the toilet so that's how they would discover Darian Fenner—*That Tusk! That cruel dude! You heard what he did to dorky Darian Fenner? Wi-ild!*

They wouldn't show the head on TV, though. Just photos of Darian when he'd been alive.

That's what happens, you mess with Tusk Landrau.

Tusk is hugging his backpack to his chest grinning and not seeing Alyse Renke till she's practically in his face. Breathless and cutting her eyes at him saying she'd asked to be excused to use the rest room, how's about they get out of this dump?—"Just leave by the side door by the cafeteria, nobody's gonna notice."

HE'S HEARD his mom whining on the phone she didn't know what to do with him this past year, Roland isn't himself any longer and I don't know who he *is*, whining and sniffling and if he'd walk into a room with her she'd blink at him like she was scared of him and why the fuck did the pathetic bitch imagine she could "do" anything with him, like you'd "do" something with a dog or something, fuck it what's she think? "Like it's some choice of hers! Like, she'd better *learn*."

Alyse says, coughing as she smokes, waving smoke out of her face with her stubby fingers, maroon-polished talon nails, "Fuck *yes*. Same with my mom. And my dad, too, there's two of them constantly in my face. You ever thought about—y'know—" Alyse makes a slashing gesture across her throat with her fore-finger, giggling. "—offing them?"

"Huh? *Who?*"

"Like, your mom and dad."

Tusk grins at Alyse sort of blank, dazed. Like he hasn't heard just right. "Uh, my dad's actually, like, dead. He's dead."

Alyse's pink-lipsticked mouth opens. Her mascaraed eyes widen. She touches Tusk's bare forearm with her talon nails, and every hair stirs. "Jeez! I forgot."

"That's OK."

"Tusk, I'm sorry. Jeez I knew that, I just forgot."

Tusk is embarrassed, shrugging. "Yeah, it's OK. It's cool."

"I mean—shit. I should *know*."

"Hell, it's no big deal, y'know? It was over a year ago it happened."

Tusk is surprised, and moved, that Alyse Renke is so apologetic and sincere-seeming, nudging close to him like she's his girl as they make their way along the edge of the school playing field and into a marshy wooded area sloping down to railroad tracks and a viaduct. This isn't the way Tusk walks home from school but he knows the terrain from bicycling, it's a no-man's-land except on the two-lane asphalt road East End but even on this road there isn't much traffic. In a movie, Tusk is thinking, excited and nervous, there'd be a long shot of the two of them walking here, sliding and stumbling downhill through litter drifted like seaweed against the stubby trees and bushes greening up, bursting with tawny buds in the unexpectedly bright spring sunshine. And the sky overhead is filmy patches of cloud and hard blue sky like something painted. There'd be a way the camera would zoom up to them to signal *something's gonna happen!* For every moment on the screen is charged with electricity—and with meaning—not like real life that's a fucking downer. Alyse is entertaining Tusk in that bright sharp way of hers complaining again of her parents, especially her mom "who if you ask me is morbidly jealous of her own daughter for Christ's sake" and of Mr. Thibadeau her social studies teacher who's practically harassing her "grading me so goddamn low like I'm a moron or something," and Tusk thinks he's never seen a girl close-up so sexy as Alyse Renke with her pouty lower lip and slip-sliding green eyes and a habit of sighing hard, drawing her breath in deep so her hard little breasts stand out in her plum-purple sweater *and actually nudging against him* like he's seen her do with older guys, high school guys Alyse dates on the basis (as Tusk has heard) of whether they have cars they can drive—and know how to use condoms. In school, in the cafeteria where sometimes a gang of them hangs out, if other kids are around Alyse is flirty and loud-laughing and sarcastic, and Tusk isn't too good with trading wisecracks and gets pissed off, and he never knows whether Alyse is putting him on like he never knows whether he's crazy about her, crazy in love with her, or whether he actually despises her, she's a cheap flirt and not too bright. (There's been a rumor in their class since seventh-grade testing that a number of kids tested out with IQs below 100—and Alyse Renke is one of these. Roland Landrau Jr. tested out at 139 which was a moderate disappointment to Roland senior who'd had reason to expect his only son would score higher, as he did at that age.)

Tusk murmurs, "Y'know—my old man?—I let him die, sort of."

Alyse maybe hears this or maybe doesn't, she's blinking and squinting nearsightedly across the highway. There's a 7-Eleven store not far away but they'll have to tramp through a marshy vacant lot and get their feet wet probably. But if they walk around the longer way, on pavement, that's twice as far, a bummer. "Yeah, what? That's cool. I mean—too bad," Alyse says vaguely. She's leading the way, must be they're going to tramp through the field. On this damply sunny day there are insects everywhere, droning and buzzing and fluttering, tiny flies, clouds of gnats, from out of puddles an eager trilling sound like castanets that's maybe—peepers? Alyse has said she's thirsty, dying for a diet Coke, she drinks maybe a dozen diet Cokes a day, smiling sidelong at Tusk who's staring at her with his fever-eyes saying it's how she keeps her weight down, lifting her sweater and tugging down her tight-fitting jeans just a bit so Tusk can see her warm smooth pale midriff and the glass-ruby stud glittering in her belly button, Alyse is vain about being thin but not *skinny,* not one of these *anorexics,* guys get turned off by that. Also, she's running out of cigarettes and he hasn't got any, has he?—and it's shitty, this state law, or maybe it's federal law—"You can't buy cigarettes if you're a fucking *minor.* Like that's supposed to stop you from *smoking,*" she says with withering sarcasm.

Seeing that little glass-ruby stud in Alyse Renke's belly button—oh, man. *Like, Tusk is turned on. Man, Tusk is TURNED ON.* It's got to be a signal, right? Alyse Renke has brought Tusk Landrau out here back of school because she wants to make out with him, right? She's done it with lots of guys, Tusk has heard—Jakey Mandell, Derek Etchinson, Buddy Watts as long ago as seventh grade, and older guys in high school, must be she's giving Tusk Landrau the high sign she wants him to fuck her, right? It's his turn! It's his time! He's scared, and excited, hears himself saying sort of choked up, his voice a weird croak, "Uh, 'lyse?—let's go over this way, OK? C'mon." Tusk is pointing toward the viaduct where there's a pedestrian tunnel beneath the railroad tracks, a rarely used tunnel strewn with debris and puddles glittering like glass, graffiti scrawled on the walls like shouts, and Alyse squints and wrinkles her nose, "Huh? Why? I want a Coke, I said." Her lipstick-pink lower lip is swollen, pouting. You can see she's a girl accustomed to getting her way, with no delay. There's a pimpled rash at her hairline where the black zebra stripes begin. Tusk says, choked, "Yeah. C'mon. OK?" Alyse shakes her head no, pettishly, but sees in Tusk's looming face, in his heated pasty skin and red-rimmed eyes, eyes like he's been crying, old-young eyes, *eyes like you'd never see in any boy his age I swear,* a promise of something interesting, something sexy, for a thirteen-year-old kid who'd been an honor-roll nerd only the year before, you have to grant Tusk Landrau is *cool.* So impulsively Alyse leans over and kisses Tusk—kisses him!—his first kiss from a girl, ever—on his parched lips light as a butterfly brushing against him and murmurs suggestively, "OK, maybe afterward. After the Coke and some chips, OK?" and nudges against him so the blank-staring boy gets her meaning, her left breast hard as a green pear against his electrified arm. Man, this is it. Tusk hears a roaring in his ears. Tusk is having trouble breathing. Fucking asthma! No, he's never had asthma, he's OK. He's always been OK. They tried to make a freak out of him but he's OK. He's got a hard-on like a knife. His hard-on *is* a knife. He'll drag this slut into the tunnel and fuck her till her brains fall out and he'll stick her with his dad's 'Nam knife like it was meant to do and the strength of this will carry him in his new Nikes flying a mile and a half to the five-bedroom green-shuttered white colonial on Pheasant Hill Lane where he'll stick his mom with the same instrument from 'Nam. It's time! It's his turn! *To put my mom out of her mercy, I mean misery, not like I hated her or anything, shit I loved her I guess—she was my mom, y'know?* Tusk will have to work out coherently what he's gonna tell the police and his lawyer, his statement for TV and the press, he's anxious he won't get a second chance, it will have to go down perfectly the first time. "Hey Tusk? You spaced out or what? Come *on!*"—flirty Alyse Renke giggling at him and he's staring at her seeing her pink lips move but can't hear what she's actually saying. *Alyse was my girl. I warned her from the first I would not share her with anybody! I would not be disrespected.* Tusk is hugging the nylon backpack against his chest wondering if this sounds OK. He thinks so. Maybe. Is it plausible? He is sort of crazy about Alyse, to tell the truth. He'd like to kiss her and kiss her in some dark place like the Cinemax. He'd like to hang out at her house like he's heard Jakey Mandell does, Saturdays. But Jesus, his hard-on is aching, his entire cock and balls, like a metal pipe or something inside his jockey shorts—how's he gonna *walk?* His old man was embarrassed telling him about sex, sexual experimentation as his old man called it, sexual reproduction of the species which is nature's imprint you might say upon the individual, but—how's he gonna *walk?* He'd take Alyse's stubby little hand to press against his bulging fly, give the slut a good feel and she'd shriek and giggle and snatch her hand away like it was burned but she'd be impressed, too—wouldn't she?—except Alyse is running across the field squealing and cursing getting her feet wet, and Tusk hasn't any choice but to trot after her, breathless and crouched over like he's got a stomachache. "Hey, 'lyse! Wait."

Fuck, he's getting his new Nikes wet.

IN THE TACKY 7-Eleven they're the only customers. Alyse knows the store and goes directly to the rear to get her Coke. A staticky radio playing old-time rock from the seventies and behind the counter staring unsmiling at Tusk is this fattish grizzle-bearded guy like a hippie going bald and what's left of his stringy hair is totally gray, he's wearing it in a ponytail tied with a piece of yarn, a soiled Grateful Dead T-shirt straining against his beer gut and bib overalls fitting him like sausage casing and those steely eyes behind rimless bifocals are fixed on Tusk immediately. *Fucker never gave me a chance! What'd I ever do to* him? *Fucking Nazi like I'm, what?—a nigger or something.* Alyse must know the fat hippie, or anyway she's acting like she does, chattering and flirting, complaining why can't she buy a pack of Virginia Slims at least?—"Who would ever know, I mean it's just us in here, I mean—it's just common sense. Or you could give me the pack, y'know? And I could, like, pay a little more for these chips? Tusk, you got some change?" But the hippie pays Alyse no more mind than you'd pay a cloud of gnats, and Tusk doesn't hear her either, nervously prowling the aisles blinking at brightly packaged displays of Sunshine Cheez-Its, Doritos chips, Snak-Mix, Jif peanut butter, Pringles Potato Crisps, Miracle micro popcorn, Hungry Jack Bagel Bites, and at knee level ten-pound sacks of Purina Dog Chow and Kleen Kitty Litter. Tusk is a shy boy actually, hunching his shoulders like he wants to disappear, his chest practically caved in, that posture that so pissed off his old man he half expects to hear the old man's disgusted voice over the radio *Son!* Tusk is talking to himself which he never does in public only when he's alone, not audibly talking but his mouth is working, his grimacing, puckered-up baby face is close to crying. Heat prickling in his underarms like red ants. For Tusk seems to know before the hippie behind the counter speaks a single word to precipitate his doom, *This is it! He's the one I been waiting for, the fucker.* "You, kid—yeah, you!—take your punk ass out of this store and keep on moving, you hear?" the hippie says in a sharp nasal voice pressing his gut against the counter, beefy muscled guy with wiry hairs bristling up through the Grateful Dead T-shirt and Tusk says stammering, "Say— what? I'm not doing nothing," and Alyse is protesting, "Tusk isn't doing a thing! Hey he isn't! Hey c'mon, mister," and the hippie ignores her saying to Tusk in a sneering voice, "Yeah? Like the other day you and your punk pals weren't doing anything except tearing open bags, right? Right on the shelves, right? Yanking pull-tops and leaving the fucking cans to drain on the shelves while I'm waiting on fucking customers, *right?*" Tusk is hurt, Tusk is shaking his head confused, saying, "Mister, I was never in this store before. I was *never.*" This is true!—Tusk's lower lip is trembling and his eyes are misting over but the hippie is furious and unforgiving, stalking out from behind the counter waving his fatty-muscled arms, splotches of red in his face and his eyes steely-cold, "I said get out of my store, you little punk! You're a thief, you're a vandal and a thief and a punk and if I was your old man I'd blow out my brains, I want you out of this store right now before I break your skinny little—"

Suddenly then the hippie is gaping down at himself with this look of profound astonishment and wonder *where Tusk has shoved a seven-inch knife to the hilt in his guts.*

Following this, things happen swiftly.

And Tusk is watching, and Tusk is moving with it but it's like he's outside himself watching. Grinning dazed at his blood-splattered hands and jeans and he yanks the knife out of the fat man falling to his knees and stabs at him with it—"Fucker! You got no right! I got my rights! See how you like it now!" The hippie is on the floor screaming, trying to stop the blood from rushing out of his belly, Tusk is panting, triumphant, kicks himself free except he's splashed with goddamn blood—his jeans, his new Nikes—shit!—he's excited, pissed—only just a little scared— runs behind the counter to the cash register reasoning *I will need money if I go underground* but the fucking cash register is shut up tight and there's no way to open it Tusk can figure, tearing at the drawer with his hands and breaking his fingernails leaving blood-smears on the metal he knows are fingerprints to incriminate him but what's he gonna do?—it's all happening so swiftly.

This buzzing in his ears like a trapped hornet, he can't figure where it's coming from. Old-time rock music at high decibels and somebody screaming? Then Tusk remembers with a tinge almost of nostalgia as if it had all happened long ago and they're flying away from each other like the universe is said to be broken into an infinity of isolated parts rushing away from one another at nearly the speed of light: the girl with the zebra-stripe hair. Alyse Renke. Alyse who's *his girl*. Her face wizened like a monkey's contorted in rage rather than horror *What the fuck are you doing Tusk! Just what the fuck are you doing you sorry asshole!* as in a frenzy he'd stabbed the fat hippie as many times as he could draw the knife blade out and sink it into the man's flesh like blue flames were licking over his brain until practically he was coming in his pants and panting he'd turned glassy-eyed toward the furious girl and seeing his face she backed off as the situation registered upon her—the knife, the gushing blood, the adult man thrashing and groaning at Tusk's feet. And now he doesn't know where she is. " 'lyse? Hey 'lyse?" he hears himself yelling in a raw hurt voice, almost he's laughing, "—you hiding on me? *Hiding?*" But she isn't anywhere in sight. Isn't in the store. Just Tusk in the store, and the whimpering man. Just shelves of merchandise, rows of tins and paper packages and on the farther wall a flyspecked Coors clock showing 2:25 P.M. and it flashes through Tusk's mind that school's still in session, no wonder there's no kids hanging out at the 7-Eleven. The fat hippie, lying on his back, gasping and twitching his left leg in a pool of neon-glistening liquid like varnish is all that Tusk can see and then Tusk sees the girl outside, running toward the road and possibly she's screaming. Alyse has left him? Alyse Renke his girl running from *him?* when she'd been kissing him just a few minutes ago? and he'd done this for *her?* to show her how serious he is, how serious about *her?* Tusk runs to the door and calls plaintively, " 'lyse! Hey come back! Hey—" but Alyse doesn't hear, she's waving her arms running and stumbling in the road now and there's a station wagon approaching and it's going to stop, Tusk knows.

WHERE THEY FIND him only a few minutes later, it wasn't where he might've planned to be. Or at this abrupt time, either.

Back of the 7-Eleven, behind the smelly overflowing Dumpster. The slippery knife in his fingers as he's groping for the artery, what is it, carotid artery, in his throat. His fingers are clumsy, anxious. *I never heard him calling me. Never heard him scream. I didn't!* Hearing now a faint train whistle. A dog's forlorn persistent barking in the distance. A siren. A siren coming closer? He's got to hurry. Doesn't want to fuck up like he's fucked up just about everything else today but he's got to hurry. There's no going back because he could not live this day again or any other day recalling what he'd learned in science class of how the sun is promised to continue shining for five billion more years before at last swelling and vaporizing the entire solar system but Tusk could not endure even one more day. Not one more! Drawing the knife across the artery he's located pulsing hot beneath his jawbone, a sharp burning sensation and at once he's bleeding but the cut isn't deep enough so he tries again, holding his right hand steady with his left and pressing with his remaining strength, on his knees swaying, gasping for air, choking on something hot and liquid. Shit, he's dropped the knife, can't see to pick it up, groping amid wet newspaper on the pavement, crinkly yellow Doritos wrapper, but there's the knife, the blood-glistening knife that's his only consolation, he picks it up and tightens his fist around it and tries again.

THE HIGH SCHOOL SWEETHEART:
A MYSTERY

*T*here was an intensely private man whose fate was to become, as year followed year, something of a public figure and a model for others. Nothing astonished R___ more, and alarmed him! Relatively young, he'd achieved renown as a writer of popular, yet literary novels; his field was the psychological suspense mystery, a genre in which he excelled, perhaps because he respected the tradition and took infinite care in composition. These were terse, minimally plotted but psychologically knotty novels written, as R___ said in interviews, sentence by sentence, and so they must be read sentence by sentence, with attention; as one might perform steps in a difficult dance. R___ was himself both choreographer and dancer. And sometimes, even after decades of effort, R___ lost his way, and despaired. For there was something of horror in the lifelong contemplation of *mystery;* a sick, visceral helplessness that must be transformed into control, and *mastery.* And so R___ never gave up any challenge, no matter how difficult. "To give up is to confess you're mortal, and must die."

R___ was one of those admired persons who remain mysterious even to old friends. By degrees, imperceptibly as it seemed to him, he became an elder, and respected; perhaps because his appearance inspired confidence. He had fair, fine, sand-colored hair that floated about his head, and a high forehead, and startlingly frank blue eyes; he was well over six feet tall, and lean as a knifeblade, with long loose limbs and a boyish energy. He seemed never to grow older, or even mature, but to retain a dreamy Nordic youthfulness with a glistening of something chill and soulless in his eyes; as if, inwardly, he gazed upon a tundra of terrifying, featureless white, and the utterly blank, vacuous Arctic sky above. One of the prevailing mysteries about R__ was his marriage, for none of us had ever glimpsed his wife of four decades, let alone been introduced to her; it was assumed that her name began with "B," for each of R__'s eleven novels was dedicated, simply, to "B," and it was believed that R__ had married, very young, a girl who'd been his high school sweetheart in a small town in northern Michigan, that she wasn't at all literary or even interested in his career, and that they had no children.

In one of his reluctant interviews R__ once admitted, enigmatically, that, no, he and his wife had no children. "*That,* I haven't committed."

How proud we were of R__, as one of the heralded patricians in the field! When he spoke to you, smiled and shook hands, like a big, animated doll, you felt privileged, if only just slightly uneasy at the remote, Arctic gleam in those blue, blue eyes.

R__ WAS OFTEN NOMINATED to run for office in professional organizations to which he belonged, yet always he declined out of modesty, or self-doubt: "R__ isn't the man you want, truly!" But finally at the age of sixty, he gave in, and was elected by a large majority as president of the American Mystery Writers, a fact that seemed to both deeply move him and fill him with apprehension. Repeatedly he called members of the executive board to ask if truly R__ was the man we wanted; and repeatedly we assured him, yes, certainly, R__ was.

On the occasion of his induction as president, R__ meant to entertain us, he promised, with a new mystery story written especially for that evening; not a lengthy, rambling speech interlarded with lame jokes, like certain of his predecessors. (Of course there was immediate laughter at this remark. For our outgoing president, an old friend of R__'s and of most of us in the audience, was a well-liked but garrulous gentleman not known for brevity.)

Almost shyly, however, R__ took the podium, and stood before an audience of perhaps five hundred mystery writers and their guests, straight-backed and handsome in his detached, pale, Nordic way, a fine figure of a man in an elegant tuxedo, white silk shirt, and gleaming gold cuff links. R__'s hair was more silvery than we recalled, but floated airily about his head; his forehead appeared higher, a prominent ridge of bone at the hairline. Well back into the audience, you could see those remarkable blue eyes. In a beautifully modulated, rather musical voice, R__ thanked us for the honor of electing him president, thanked outgoing officers of the organization, and alluded with regret to the fact that "unforeseen circumstances" had prevented his wife from attending that evening. "As you know, my friends, I did not campaign to be elected your president, it's an honor, as the saying goes, that has been thrust upon me. But I do feel that I am a kinsman of all of you, and I hope I will be worthy of your confidence. I hope you will like the story I've written for you!" Almost, R__'s voice quavered when he said these words, and he had to pause for a moment before beginning to read, in a dramatic voice, from what appeared to be a handwritten manuscript of about fifteen pages.

The High School Sweetheart: A Mystery

There was an intensely private man whose fate was to become, as year followed year, something of a public figure and a model for others. Nothing astonished R__ more, and alarmed him! Relatively young, he'd achieved renown as a writer of popular, yet literary novels; his field was the psychological suspense mystery, a genre in which he excelled, perhaps because he respected the tradition and took infinite care in composition. These were terse, minimally plotted but psychologically knotty novels written, as R__ said in interviews, sentence by sentence, and so they must be read sentence by sentence, with attention; as one might perform steps in a difficult dance. R__ was himself both choreographer and dancer. And sometimes, even after decades of effort, R__ lost his way, and despaired. For there was something of horror in the lifelong contemplation of *mystery;* a sick, visceral helplessness that must be transformed into control, and *mastery.* And so R__ never gave up any challenge, no matter how difficult. "To give up is to confess you're moral, and must die."

At this apparent misstatement R__ paused in confusion, peering at his manuscript as if it had deceived or betrayed him; but a moment later he regained his composure, and continued—

"To give up is to confess you're *mortal,* and must die."

Forty-five years ago! I wasn't yet R__ but rather a fifteen-year-old named Roland, whom no one called Rollie, skinny, gawky, self-conscious, with a straight-A average and pimples like hot little beads of red pepper scattered across my forehead and back, lost in helpless erotic dreams of my high school sweetheart, a beautiful, popular blond senior named Barbara, whom everyone at Indian River High School called Babs. Now that I am no longer this boy I can contemplate him without the self-loathing he'd felt for himself at the time; almost, I can feel a measure of pity for him, and sympathy, if not tenderness. Or forgiveness.

My high school sweetheart was two years older than I, and, I'm ashamed to confess, didn't realize that she was my high school sweet-heart. She had a boyfriend her own age, and numerous other friends besides, and had no idea how I secretly observed her, and with what yearning. The name "Babs"—unremarkable, yet so American and some-how wholesome, makes me feel faint, still, with hope and longing.

In high school, I came to dread mirrors as I dreaded the frank assess-ing stares of my classmates, for these confronted me with a truth too painful to acknowledge. Like many intellectually gifted adoelscents I was precocious academically and retarded socially. In my dreams, I was freed of my clumsy body and often glided along the ground, or soared, swift as thought; I felt myself purely a mind, a questing spirit; it was my own body I fled, my base, obsessive sexual yearning. In actual life I was both shy and haughty; I carried myself stiffly, conscious of being a doctor's son in predominantly working-class Indian River, even as I saw with painful clarity how my classmates were only polite with me when required, their mouths smiling in easy deference even as their eyes drifted past me. *Yes, you're Roland the doctor's son, you live in one of the big brick houses on Church Street, and your father drives a new, shiny black Lincoln, but we don't care for you anyway.* Already in grade school I'd learned the crucial distinction between being envied and being liked. Where there was laughter, and the magical joy and release of laughter, there, Roland the doctor's son was excluded. Of course, I had one or two friends, even rather close friends, boys like myself, brainy and lonely, and given to irony, though we were too young to grasp the meaning of *irony:* where heartbreak and anger conjoin. And I had my secret dreams, which attached themselves with alarming abruptness, and a terrible fixedness, at the start of my sophomore year in high school, to beautiful blond Babs; a girl whose father, a carpenter and stonemason with a good local reputation, had worked for my father.

Why this fact filled me with shame in Babs's presence, while Babs herself took no notice of it at all, I can't explain.

Adolescence! Happiness for some, poison for others. The killer's heart is forged in adolescence. Sobering for R__ in his rented tuxedo, gold cuff links gleaming, to recall that forty-five years ago he would have eagerly exchanged his privileged life as a small-town physician's brainy, beloved son, destined to graduate *summa cum laude* from the University of Michigan, for that of Babs Hendrick's boyfriend Hal McCreagh, a good-looking football player with a C average destined to work in an Indian River lumberyard for life. *If I could be you. And no more me.* Mostly I managed to think not of Hal McCreagh but solely of Babs Hendrick, whom in fact I saw infrequently, and when I did manage to see her, in school, in passing, I was so focused upon the girl that she existed for me in a rarefied dimension, like a specimen of some beautiful creature, but-terfly, bird, tropical fish, safely under glass. I saw her mouth move but heard no sound. Even when Babs smiled in my direction and gaily mur-mured *Hi!* in the style of popular girls at Indian River High who made it a point, out of Christian charity perhaps, to ignore no one, I scarcely heard her, in a buzzing panic, and could only stammer a belated reply. Half-shutting my eyes in terror of staring at Babs too openly, her small shapely dancer-like body, her radiantly glistening pink-lipsticked lips and widened smiling eyes—for in my paranoia I was convinced that others could sense my yearning; my raw, hopeless, contemptible desire—I imagined overhearing, and often in my fever-dreams I did actually hear, voices rising in derision, "Roland? *Him?*" and cruel adolescent laughter of the kind that, decades later, reverberates through the "patrician" R__'s dreams.

For this, I cannot truly blame the girl. She knew nothing of her power over me.

Did she?

Babs was a senior; I was only a sophomore, and did not exist to her; to be in close proximity to such a girl, I had to join Drama Club, in which Babs was a prominent member, a high school star, invariably cast in student productions directed by our English teacher Mr. Seales. Onstage, Babs was a lively, very pretty, and energetic presence, one of those golden creatures at whom others gaze in helpless admiration, though to be truthful, and I mean to be truthful in this narrative, Babs Hendrick was probably only moderately talented; by the standards of Indian River, Michigan, she shone. In Drama Club, I was an eager volunteer for work no one else wanted to do, like set design and lighting; I helped Mr. Seales organize rehearsals; to the surprise of my friends, who had no idea of my infatuation with Babs, I spent more and more time with the Drama Club crowd, comfortable in my role of relative invisibility, and happy to leave the spotlight to others.

In that context, as a kind of young mascot, *Roland* became *Rollie*. What a thrill!

For Babs herself would summon me, "Rollie? Would you be a sweetheart—" (with what ease and unconscious cruelty murmuring such words to me!) "—and run out and get me a cola? Here's change." And there Rollie would go flying out of the school, and down the street a block and a half to a convenience store, to bring back a cola for Babs Hendrick, thrilled by the task. More than once I'd run to fetch something for Babs and when I returned to the rehearsal room panting like a good-natured dog, another of the actors would send me out again, and there Rollie would fly a second time, not wanting to protest, for fear of arousing suspicion.

Once, I overheard behind me Babs's musical voice: "That Rollie! I just love him."

Between Clifford Seales and certain of his girl students, particularly blond, effervescent Babs, there was a heightened electric mood during Drama Club meetings and play rehearsals; a continuous stream of bright, racy banter of the kind that left the girls pink-cheeked and breathless with giggling and Mr. Seales (though long married, and his children grown) grinning and tugging at his shirt collar. Perhaps there was nothing seriously erotic about such banter, only playfulness, but unmistakably flirtatious undercurrents wafted about us, for most of the Drama Club members were not ordinary students but students singled out for *attention;* and Mr. Seales, in his early fifties, thick-waisted, porcine, with a singed-looking face and wire-rimmed bifocals that shone when he was at his wittiest and most eloquent, was no ordinary high school teacher. He cultivated a brush-like rufous moustache and wore his hair long, past his collar. He'd been an amateur actor with the Milwaukee Players in his early twenties and he'd impressed generations of Indian River students by hinting that he'd almost had, or possibly had had, a screen test with

Twentieth-Century Fox in his youth. Babs daringly teased Mr. Seales about his wild Hollywood days when he'd been Clark Gable's double. (Mr. Seales did resemble, from certain angles of perspective and in a flattering light, a fleshier Clark Gable.)

After the tragedy, and the scandal that surrounded it, rumors would fly through Indian River that Mr. Seales was a pervert who'd insisted upon his girl and boy actors rehearsing passionate love scenes in his presence, to prepare them for acting together onstage; Mr. Seales was a pervert who rehearsed passionate love scenes with his girl students, private sessions. He'd "brushed against"—"touched"—"fondled" Babs Hendrick before witnesses, and made the girl blush fiercely. It was claimed that Mr. Seales carried, in his briefcase, a silver flask filled with vodka, and out of this flask he secretly laced coffee and soda drinks to give to unsuspecting students, to render them malleable in his pervert hands. I doubted that any of this could be true, since in the seven months I belonged to the Drama Club I'd seen no evidence of it, and so I would testify to Indian River police in Mr. Seales's defense (though my father forbade me to say anything kindly about the "pervert" and was furious with me afterward). Yet how strange: never had I witnessed Mr. Seales pouring anything into any drinks, including his own, yet somehow I was inspired to such an action myself, out of despair, out of my obsession with Babs, and out of (how can I explain, without seeming to be trying to excuse myself?) a conviction of my essential helplessness. *For never would Roland have believed himself capable of what he dreamed of committing; never would he, who believed himself a victim, have imagined himself so powerful, and lethal.*

Not vodka out of a silver flask, but a heavy dose of barbiturate from my mother's crammed medicine cabinet. It was an old prescription; I took the chance that my distracted, nervous mother would never notice.

It was not my intention to hurt my high school sweetheart. For I so adored her, I could not imagine even touching her! In my sickly, fevered dreams I "saw" her vividly, or a female figure that resembled her; beneath layers of bedclothes, as if hoping to hide myself from my father's suspicious eyes that could penetrate my bedroom walls, I groaned in anguish, and in shame, in thrall to her female beauty. *I was the victim, not the girl.* I wished to free myself from my morbid obsession, and I became desperate. For had not my father (perhaps reading my thoughts? identifying certain symptoms in my person, my behavior?) warned me with much embarrassment of the danger of "unclean practices"—"compulsive self-abuse." Had not my father turned aside from me in disgust, seeing in my frightened eyes and inflamed pimply skin an admission of guilt. And yet I could not beg him for mercy claiming *I am the victim!*

In actual life, Babs Hendrick existed in what seemed to me another dimension, inaccessible to someone like me; I might brush against her in a high school corridor, or descending a flight of stairs, or I might sit on the floor of the "green room" backstage, six inches from her feet, yet this distance was an abyss. The girl was invulnerable, immune to anything Roland might say or do. At such times I knew myself invisible, and though lowly, in a way blessed. Unlike other, older and more attractive boys, I had not a chance to compel this girl to love me, or even to notice me; thus I risked little, like a craven but faithful mongrel. Even when someone called out "Rollie!" and sent me on an errand, I felt myself invisible, and blessed. During rehearsals on the open, bare stage, which was often drafty, I liked it that Babs might send me for her sweater, or her boyfriend's jacket; I loved it that, in this place devoid of glamour, Babs yet exuded her innocent golden-girl beauty, which (I came to think) no one really appreciated but me. At such times I could crouch on the floor and gaze openly at Babs Hendrick's flawless heart-shaped face, her perky, shapely little body, for she was an "actress"; it wasn't forbidden to stare at Babs Hendrick when she was an "actress"; in fact, and this was a delicious irony not lost on Roland, Babs and the other Indian River stars were dependent upon people like Roland, an admiring audience for their self-display, or what was called "talent." And so I made myself more and more available to the Drama Club, and to the rather vain, pompous Mr. Seales, as a way of making myself liked, and trusted. How quiet Roland was, and utterly dependable! No one else in Drama Club was either, and this included Mr. Seales the faculty adviser. I was always available if, for instance, Babs needed someone patient to help her with her lines, in the green room, or in an empty classroom. ("Gosh, Rollie, what would I do without you! You're so much sweeter and a darn sight smarter than *my* kid brother.") Because she was a favorite of his, Mr. Seales had cast, or miscast, Babs as the wan, crippled, poetic Laura in Tennessee Williams's *The Glass Menagerie;* this was a plum of a role for an aspiring actress, but one for which Babs's healthy, wholesome golden-girl looks and childlike extroversion hardly suited her. Her quick, superficial facility for rote memory wasn't helping her much with the poetic language of the

Williams play, and she was continually baffled by its emotional subtext. Even Mr. Seales was beginning to be impatient with her tearful outbursts and temper tantrums, and several times spoke cuttingly to her in front of others.

These others to be shortly designated as "witnesses." Even I, who had no choice but to tell police officers all that I'd truly heard.

One of my frequent errands was to fetch quart plastic bottles of a certain diet cola, explosively carbonated and artificially sweetened, from the convenience store up the street; a vile-tasting chemical concoction that my father claimed had caused "cancerous growths" in laboratory rats, and that, though I exulted in going against my father's wishes whenever I could, I found repellent, undrinkable. Yet Babs was addicted to this drink, kept bottles in her locker and was always running out. The fact that the cola was in a quart bottle and not a can, and that I was often the person to open it, and pour cola into paper cups to pass around to the actors, gave me the idea, and an innocent idea it seemed to me, like a magical fantasy interlude in a Disney film, of mixing something in the fizzing liquid, a sleeping potion it might be romantically called, that would cause Babs Hendrick to become sleepy suddenly, and doze, for just a few precious minutes, and I alone might observe her close up, watch over and protect her; if needed, I would wake her, and walk her home.

Babs Hendrick, walked home by Roland the doctor's son.

This was a fantasy that sprang from one of my fevered erotic dreams. I both loathed these dreams as unhealthy and unclean, and craved them; I both wished to rid myself of them forever, and cherished them as one of the few authentic creations of my lonely life. Out of this paradox grew, like poisonous toadstools by night, my compulsion to write, and to write of certain subjects the world designates as morbid. Out of the tragedy of that long-ago time grew my obsession with *mystery* as the most basic, and so most profound, of all artistic visions. Out of my obsession with my high school sweetheart, the distinguished (and lucrative) career of R__, newly elected president of the American Mystery Writers! Though R__ is far from fifteen years old, he is not so very distant from the fifteen-year-old Roland secretly planning, plotting, rehearsing his deed of great daring. He seemed in his sex-obsessed naïveté to think that he could accomplish his goal without having the slightest effect upon reality, and without consequences for either himself or his victim.

Of course, fifteen-year-old Roland did not think of Babs Hendrick as a *victim*. She wielded such power!

And so it happened, as in a dream, one bleak, gunmetal-gray afternoon in March, in that limbo season poised between late winter and early spring, when the temperature seems frozen at thirty-two degrees Fahrenheit, that rehearsals for *The Glass Menagerie* broke off around five o'clock, and Mr. Seales sent everyone home except Babs, with whom he spoke in private, and twenty minutes later Babs appeared in the corridor outside the auditorium, wiping at her beautiful downcast eyes; and seeing me lurking nearby (but Babs wouldn't have thought that her friend Rollie was capable of *lurking)* eagerly she asked would I help her with her lines? just for a half-hour?

Murmured Rollie shyly, "Sure."

Babs led us back to the green room backstage. As usual, Babs stood as she recited her lines, and moved about restlessly, trying to match her gestures with Tennessee Williams's maddeningly poetic, repetitive language. She scarcely glanced at me as I read lines, or prompted her, as if she were alone; I was Laura's mother, Laura's brother, Laura's caddish gentleman caller, yet it was exclusively her own image she gazed at in the room's long horizontal mirror. Even in this fluorescent-lit, stale-smelling room with the shabby furnishings and worn linoleum tile, how beautiful Babs was! Far more beautiful than poor doomed Laura. *I loved her, and hated her. For the sake of the Lauras of the world, as well as the Rolands.*

The other day, in my leafy, affluent suburban town fifty minutes north of Grand Central Station, where I live, as the irony of circumstance has placed me, on Basking Ridge Drive, which intersects with Church Street, I was walking into the village to pick up my newspapers, as I do each day for the exercise, and I saw her: I saw Babs Hendrick: a lovely blond girl with shoulder-length wavy hair and bangs brushed low on her forehead, walking with high school classmates. I stopped in my tracks. My heart clanged like a bell. I nearly called out to her—"Babs? Is it you?" But of course, being R__, and no longer naive, I waited until I could ascertain that of course the girl wasn't my lost high school sweetheart, and didn't truly resemble her. I turned aside to hide my grief. I limped away shaken. I took solace all that day in writing this story, for I no longer have lurid, delicious erotic fantasies by night, beneath heavy bedcovers; the only fantasies that visit me now are willfully calculated, impeccably plotted contrivances of my writerly life.

I repeat: it was not my intention to hurt my high school sweetheart.

In my anxiety, I must have mixed too much of the barbiturate into the cola drink. I'd taken a number of capsules from my mother's medicine cabinet, broken them and carefully poured the white powder into a tissue; this tissue, wrapped in cellophane, I'd been carrying in my pocket for what seemed like months, but could have been only two or three weeks. I knew that my opportunity would come if I was patient, and I had no choice but to be patient. And that March afternoon, when Babs and I were alone together in the green room, and no one near, and no one knowing of us, and she sent me to her locker to fetch her opened bottle of cola while she used the girls' backstage lavatory, I knew that this was meant to be: almost, I had no choice. I siphoned the white powder into the virulent dark chemical drink, replaced the top and turned it upside down, shook it gently. Babs took no notice of the barbiturate, for she drank the cola in distracted swallows while trying to memorize her lines, and was on her feet, restless and impatient, having decided that the secret to Williams's heroine was her anger, hidden beneath layers of girlish verbiage of which the playwright himself hadn't been aware. "Cripples are always angry, I bet. *I'd* sure be, in their place."

Roland, sitting on an old worn corduroy-covered sofa, waiting anxiously for the sleeping potion to take effect, murmured yes, he guessed Babs must be right.

She continued with her lines, reciting, forgetting and needing to be prompted, remembering, reciting, moving her arms, making her face "expressive"; the more she rehearsed Laura, the more Laura eluded her, like a mocking phantom. Ten minutes passed, with excruciating slowness; I felt beads of sweat break out on my heated face, and trickle down my thin sides; fifteen minutes passed, and by slow degrees Babs appeared to be getting drowsy; then by sudden degrees she became very drowsy; murmuring she didn't know what was wrong with her, she was feeling *so tired,* couldn't keep her eyes open. She knocked the cola bottle over; what remained of the liquid spilled out onto the already stained carpet. Abruptly then she slumped down at the far end of the sofa, and within seconds was asleep.

I sat without moving, not even looking directly at her, at first, for some time. The magic had worked! It wasn't believable, yet it had happened; Roland could have no real power over a girl like Babs Hendrick, yet—this had happened. *Yes I was elated. Ecstatic! Yes I was terrified. For what I had done, the crudest of tricks, I could not undo.*

Not scrawny brainy Roland, that shy boy, but another person, calculating and almost-calm, moved at last from his position on the sofa, and
stood trembling with excitement over the sleeping girl. Beautiful when
awake and animated, Babs was yet more beautiful in sleep; waxy-
skinned, and vulnerable; she seemed much younger than seventeen; her
face was pale and slack and her lips parted, like a sleeping baby's; her arms
were limp, her legs sprawled like the legs of a rag doll. She wore a pale
yellow angora sweater with short puffy sleeves, and a charcoal-gray
pleated skirt. (This predated the era of universal blue jeans.) I whispered,
"Babs? Babs?" and she gave no sign of hearing. She was breathing in
deep, erratic, shuddering breaths and her eyelids were quivering. My fear
was that she'd wake suddenly and see me standing over her and know
what I'd done, and begin to scream; and what would happen to Roland
the doctor's son, then? I dared to touch her arm, and shook her, gently.
"Babs? What's wrong?" So far, what was happening wasn't suspicious,
exactly. (Was it?) Kids often fell asleep in school, cradling their heads on
their arms in the library, or in study hall; in boring classes nearly everyone nodded off, at times. Self-dramatizing young actors, complaining of
exhaustion and overwork, stole naps in the green room, and tales were
told of couples "sleeping" on the infamous corduroy couch when they
were assured of a few minutes' quick-snatched privacy. Babs, like her
popular friends, stayed up late, talking and laughing over the telephone,
as I'd gathered from overhearing their conversations, and she'd been anxious about the play, and sleep-deprived, so it wasn't so unlikely that, in
the midst of going over her lines with me, she might become exhausted
suddenly and fall asleep. *None of this was suspicious. Not yet!*

But Roland's behavior was beginning to be suspicious, wasn't it? For
stealthily he went to the door, which had no lock, and dragged a heavy
leather armchair in front of it, to prevent the door from being opened
suddenly. (There were likely to be a few teachers and students remaining
in the building, even past six o'clock.) He switched off all the lights in
the windowless room except one, a flickering fluorescent tube on the
verge of burning out. He spoke gently, cautiously to the deeply breathing, sleeping girl, "Babs? Babs? It's just me. Rollie." For long mesmerized
seconds he stood above her, staring. The elusive girl of his fever-dreams!
His high school sweetheart, whom his father had tried to forbid him.
Unclean. Compulsive. Self-abuse. Daringly Roland touched the girl again,
caressing her shoulder like a film lover, and her arm in the fuzzy angora

sweater, and her limp, chill fingers. He was breathing quickly now, and he'd become sticky with sweat. If he leaned closer, if he kissed her? (But how did you kiss a girl like Babs Hendrick?) Just her forehead? Would she wake suddenly, would she begin to scream? "It's just me. Rollie. *I love you*." Suddenly he wondered, with a stab of jealousy, whether Hal McCreagh had ever seen Babs like this. So deeply asleep! So beautiful! He wondered what Hal did to Babs, when they were alone together in Hal's car. Kissing? (Tongue kissing?) Touching, fondling? "Petting"? It excited Roland, and infuriated him, to imagine.

But Hal wasn't here now. Hal knew nothing of this interlude. This "rehearsal." There was no longer any Hal. There was only Roland the doctor's brainy, beloved son.

He was trembling badly now. Shaking. A powerful throbbing ache in his groin which he tried to ignore, and a rapid beating of his heart. This could not be happening, could it? How could this be happening? Bringing his lips against the girl's strangely cool, clammy forehead. It was the first true kiss of his life. Babs's silky-blond head had fallen limply back against the soiled armrest of the sofa, and her mouth had dropped open. Her eyelids were oddly bluish, and fluttering as if she wanted desperately to open them, but could not. "Babs? Don't be afraid." He kissed her cheek, he stooped to kiss her mouth, that hung open, slack, helpless, a string of saliva trailing down her chin. The taste of her mouth excited him terribly. With his tongue he licked her saliva. *Like tasting blood. Roland the vampire. That first kiss!* His brain seemed to go black. He was seized by a powerful need to grab hold of the girl, hard. To show her who was master. But he restrained himself, for Roland was not such a person; Roland was a good boy, and would never harm anyone. (Would he?) Babs Hendrick was, he knew, a good Christian girl, as he was a good Christian boy; what harm could come to them *really?* If he meant no harm, harm would not ensue. He would be protected. The girl would be protected. He'd begun to notice her strange, labored breathing, audible as a grown man's breathing in stress, and yet he did not somehow absorb the possible meaning of such a symptom though he was (but right now, *was not*) Roland the doctor's son. He was trembling with excitement. His hand, which seemed to him slightly distorted as if seen through a magnifying lens, reached out to smooth the silky blond hair, and cradle it in his fingers. He stroked the nape of the girl's neck, slowly he caressed her shoulder, her left breast, delicately touching the breast

with his fingertips, that fuzzy pale yellow angora wool that was so beautiful; he cupped his hand (but was this *his hand?*) beneath the small, shapely
breast, gently and then with more assurance he caressed, he squeezed
lightly. "Babs! I l-love you." The girl moaned in her heavy, stuporous
sleep, a sexual moan it seemed to Roland, who was himself whimpering
with excitement; but she didn't wake; his power over her, Roland's
revenge, was that she could not wake; she was at his mercy, and he
would be merciful; she was utterly helpless and vulnerable, and he would
not take advantage of her as one of the crude Indian River High boys
would have done in his place (Would he?) In even the most lurid of his
dreams he hadn't defiled his sweetheart. (At least that he'd allowed himself to remember.) In a cracked, hoarse, half-pleading voice whispering,
"Babs? Don't be afraid, I would never hurt you, *I love you.*" And the
blackness rose swooning in him a second time, annihilating his brain; and
he would not afterward recall all that happened in that dim-lit windowless room, on the shabby corduroy sofa, or was caused to happen, perceived as through a distorting lens that both magnified and reduced
vision.

When again Roland was able to see clearly, and to think, he saw to his
horror that it was nearly six-thirty. And still the stricken girl slept on the
corduroy sofa, the sound of her breathing now filling the airless room.
Her head lay at a painful angle on the soiled armrest and her arms and
legs were limp, loose as those of a rag doll. Except now her unseeing eyes
were partly open, showing a crescent of white. Anxiously he whispered,
"Babs? Wake up." He felt panic: hearing voices in the corridor beyond
the backstage area, boys' voices, perhaps basketball players leaving practice; and Hal McCreagh was among these, or might have been, for Hal
was on the team; and what would Roland do, and what would be done
to Roland, if he were discovered like this, in hiding, guilty-faced, with
Babs Hendrick sprawled on the sofa helpless in sleep, her hair disheveled
and her clothing in disarray? Hurriedly, with shaking fingers, Roland
readjusted the fuzzy angora sweater, and the pleated skirt. Whimpering,
pleading for the girl to wake up, please would she wake up, yet like
Sleeping Beauty in the Disney film, she would not wake up; she was
under a curse; she would not wake up for *him.*

    For the first time it occurred to the trembling boy that he might have
given his sweetheart too strong a dose of the drug. *What if she never woke*

up? (But what was *too strong,* he had no idea. Half the bottle of six-milligram capsules? That odorless chalky-white powder?)

Panic swept over him then. No, he wouldn't think of *that.*

On a shelf amid tattered copies of play scripts he found a frayed light-wool blanket to draw gently over Babs. He tucked the blanket beneath her damp chin, and spread her blond, wavy hair in a fan around her head. She would sleep until the drug wore off, and then she would wake; if Roland—"Rollie"—was very lucky, she wouldn't remember him; if he was unlucky, well—he wouldn't think of *that.* (And he did not.) Stealthily then he fled, and was unseen. He would leave the single fluorescent light flickering. He would slip from the green room to the darkened backstage area, and make his way out into a rear corridor, not taking the most obvious, direct route (which would have brought him into a corridor contiguous with the corridor that led to the boys' locker room), and so, breathless, he would flee the scene of the crime, which in his heart he could not (could he?) acknowledge was a crime, even into his sixty-first year, when R_ had long replaced both Roland and "Rollie." Contemplating then through the distorting lens of time the pale, calm-seeming doctor's son safe in the brick house on Church Street, and safe in his room immersed in geometry homework at eight-twenty that evening, the approximate time that Babs Hendrick's heart ceased beating.

The Glass Menagerie would not be performed that spring at Indian River High.

Clifford Seales would be suspended without salary from the school, and his contract terminated soon after, during the Indian River police investigation into the barbiturate death of Seales's seventeen-year-old student Babs Hendrick. Though not enough evidence would be gathered against Seales to justify a formal arrest, Seales would remain the prime suspect in the case, and his guilt taken for granted. Forty-five years later in Indian River if you speak of Babs Hendrick's death, you'll be told in angry disgust that the girl's English teacher, an alcoholic pervert who'd molested other girl students over the years, drugged her with barbiturates to perform despicable sexual acts upon her, and killed her in the process. You will be told that Seales managed to escape prosecution, though of course his life was ruined, and he would die, divorced and disgraced, of a massive heart attack a few years later.

Ladies and gentlemen, you will ask: had the Indian River Police no other suspects? Possibly yes. Practically speaking, no. Even today, small-town police departments are ill-equipped to undertake homicide investigations in which neither witnesses nor informants come forward. Dusting for fingerprints in the "green room" yielded a treasure trove of prints, but all of these, even Seales's, were explainable. DNA evidence (saliva, semen) would have convicted the guilty individual, but DNA evidence was unknown at that time. And the boy, the shy bespectacled doctor's son Roland, was but one of a number of high school boys, including the dead girl's boyfriend, whom the police questioned; he was not singled out for suspicion, spoke earnestly and persuasively to police officers, even defending (in his naïveté) the notorious Seales, and was never to behave in any way that might be labeled suspicious. *In a state of suspended animation. No emotion, only wonder. That I, Roland, had done such a thing. I, a victim, to have wielded such power!*

If my mother was ever to discover that a bottle of old prescription sleeping pills was missing from her medicine cabinet, she never spoke of her discovery and what it might mean.

It would be rumored (but never printed in any newspaper or uttered on radio or TV) that "sick, disgusting things" had been done to Babs Hendrick's helpless body before her death; only a "pervert" could have done such acts upon a comatose victim. But there would never be any arrest of this criminal, and therefore there was no trial. And no public revelations.

(What "sick, disgusting things" were done to my sweetheart, I don't know. Another individual must have slipped into the green room between the time Roland fled and Babs died later that evening.)

The sick horror of *mystery* that remains unsolved.

You will ask: did the killer never confess?

The superficial answer is no, the killer never confessed. For he did not (did he?) truly believe himself a killer; he was a good, Christian boy. And he was (and is) a coward, contemptible. The more complex answer is yes, the killer confessed, and has confessed many times during his long and "distinguished" career. Each work of fiction he has written has been a confession, and an exultation. For, having committed an act of *mystery* in his adolescence, he understood that he'd proved himself and need never commit another; forever afterward, he would be an elegist of mystery, and honored for his style.

Ladies and gentlemen, thank you for this new honor.

In the sudden silence, R__ self-consciously stacked his manuscript pages together to signal that "The High School Sweetheart: A Mystery" was over, as we in the audience, his friends and admirers, sat stunned, in a paralysis of shock and indecision. R__'s story had been compelling, and his delivery mesmerizing—yet, how should we applaud?

DEATH WATCH

*A*s soon as the condemned man was brought into the room by prison guards, shackled at his wrists and ankles, breathing harshly, perspiring, yet with bright glistening eyes and a look of unnerving optimism, suggesting he was another convert to Christianity just in time to die, a terrible sense of desolation swept over me. *I can't do it. Not another time.*

I was a journalist; more than a journalist, a "conscience"; my column "Death Watch" appeared in a prominent newspaper with a national distribution; my responsibility lay upon me heavy as fate. Yet as in a nightmare made familiar and even numbing through repetition I foresaw that the "press conference" would be as mediocre as a segment from a TV movie; worse yet, the execution scheduled for midnight tonight would be mediocre, stale from repetition. *It has all been performed before, by superior actors.* I had flown from New York to Birmingham in the sulphurous heat of early September and I'd rented a budget car to drive sixty-eight miles to Hartsfree State Prison for Men, a maximum security facility that looked more or less as one might imagine, dour, drab, stereotypical with a twelve-foot concrete wall surrounding it, and by midafternoon I'd had nothing to eat except an airplane lunch with unspeakable red wine, and for what? Not all my skill as a writer or my outrage at the inhumanity of state-sanctioned murder could raise this sordid tale of the death of an individual named Roy Beale Birdsall beyond cliché and into the realm of metaphor, myth, poetry. *Nothing so depressing as an execution in Alabama unless it's an execution in Alabama following a coach class airplane lunch.*

It did hurt: When my writing assignments had been higher priority than the capital punishment beat, I'd flown first-class all the time. In the early days of "Deathwatch," when my byline had sometimes appeared on the front page of the paper, to be syndicated across the country, I'd flown first-class with a double seat so that I could spread out my papers and work on the plane in a frenzy of inspiration. And I'd taken it as my due, the way a first-class journalist should be treated.

Roy Beale Birdsall! Poor guy. Not knowing that Roy Beale Birdsall was a name that could never evoke tragedy. At the most, pathos. A hokey kind of trailer-park, country-and-western pathos already overexposed in the media. Almost I could have sworn I'd already written about Birdsall's death in *the luridly bright-yellow wooden electric chair still in use after decades at Hartsfree.*

I and a few other hardy journalists were here this afternoon because the Birdsall case was "controversial." There had been irregularities in both of Birdsall's trials; above all, a question about the man's mental age, whether he'd been fully *compos mentis* in confessing to a double murder seven years ago. (The murders, crazed hackings with a long-handled ax, had been committed against neighbors of Birdsall's in Parrish, Alabama; since Birdsall had been a parolee from a state prison at the time, convicted of theft and attempted arson, it had seemed reasonable for sheriff's deputies to wake him in the middle of the night and question him. Things had gone rapidly downhill for Birdsall after that.) Birdsall had been a husky young nineteen-year-old pro wrestler just embarked upon his career at the time of his first arrest; in prison he'd metamorphosed into a fattish, hulking, hairless individual of thirty-nine with a wizened baby face like one of those hypnagogic images that rush at you when you're falling to sleep in a state of extreme strain or exhaustion. His forehead was low, and broad; his eyes were eyes I'd seen before in the faces of the condemned: puppy-bright, shiny-brown, with a desperate hope of making eye contact with his visitors, so disappointingly few today, emissaries from the outside world. (There were only five of us. The last time I'd covered an execution at Hartsfree, two years ago, there must have been twelve media people at least; and, picketing at the front gate, a brave little band of anti-execution demonstrators led by a Dominican nun named Sister Mary Bonaventure whom I'd later profiled for one of my most effective "Death Watch" columns.)

The press conference had begun. Birdsall was telling us how he'd "seen Jesus" three days before after hours of praying on his knees with Reverend Hank (Hank Harley, a popular, ebullient Baptist minister with a long string of death row conversions to his credit, whom I'd interviewed for "Deathwatch" a few years ago); Jesus had "held my aching head in His hands, and washed my face in the balm of Gilead." It was all so simple, and so sincere; you wanted to believe Birdsall, even if he was mad; his eyes clutched at mine as I tried not to see. *As if at this hour people like me, "media" people, had the power to save his life.*

". . . terrible darkness and sin in my heart . . . now there is light and love. Praise Jesus!"

A nasal Alabama twang, which not even the poetry of Homer, Shakespeare, Milton could have elevated. And how ghastly the man's smile, a lockjaw-smile, even as he shifted his rounded shoulders like a barnyard animal beset by swarms of flies.

God, this was agony.

Praise Jesus I wrote quickly on my notepad. Wanting Roy Beale Birdsall to see I was rapt with attention.

It was an old, sad, familiar tale: how Roy Beale Birdsall's court-appointed attorneys had gone through the motions for seven years—filing appeals to the Alabama state court and to the governor for commutation of sentence. At each stage there had been delays, premature glimmerings of hope, disappointments. The issue of Birdsall's possibly coerced confession, like the issue of his mental age, had been ruled out, as was the issue of his claiming not to remember any ax murders. Ruled out, too, was the likelihood of another man's having committed the crime, now long vanished. Naturally, Birdsall's claim to totally not remember any ax murders was discredited. For his final appeal, the only argument Birdsall's lawyers could come up with was the claim that death in the electric chair constituted "cruel and unusual punishment"—the most melancholy of clichés—and the presiding judge of the Alabama district court had rejected it wittily. *Electrocution may be unsightly, it may bother some folks, but I have yet to see evidence that it is cruel and unusual punishment for the person who is executed.* The governor, too, was on record as pro–capital punishment, pro–death. *You'll find here in Alabama we don't coddle murderers and perverts like you do up north. The death penalty is kind of sacred to our soil.* An ugly sentiment but a terrific quote! Unfortunately I'd already used it in "Death Watch" five years ago when I'd interviewed the governor regarding another controversial capital case.

The one mitigating factor in the Birdsall case, as my colleague Claude Dupre remarked, was that Roy Beale Birdsall was Caucasian, for a change. For the past year we'd been on a dispiriting run of black and Hispanic males, I'd lost count of how many—electrocution, lethal injection, firing squad, and gas; Virginia, Florida, Oklahoma, Utah, Georgia, California, Texas, and Nevada. I'd been hammering away in my column at the "race issue"—the disproportion of non-Caucasian males put to death in the United States—until I couldn't think of any more ways of presenting it, let alone engaging or dramatic ways. If you looked closely, however, Birdsall wasn't very Caucasian. I'd have guessed some Native American blood, maybe. His skin was sallow with a coppery tincture and his thinning hair was flat dead black where it wasn't streaked with gray.

Claude was asking questions of Roy Beale Birdsall's attorney, practically interrogating the man. They were questions I might have asked, myself; I suppose they were questions I had asked, in other pre-execution press conferences, at which Claude had been present. Claude and I were old, friendly rivals on the deathwatch beat. Years ago at Yale, as undergraduates, we'd been fairly close friends, and allies, involved in passionate meetings and demonstrations during the Vietnam War. Now, decades later, we were middle-aged brother-seamen huddling together in the same cramped life-boat. My "Death Watch" was still read by many more people than Claude's eloquent freelance pieces (which appeared frequently in *The New York Review* and *The Nation*); but in intellectual-leftist quarters Claude was famous as a beloved champion of lost causes while I seemed to lack identity, density. There's a bittersweet accumulative impression that comes from catching odd, unflattering glimpses of yourself in mirrors; so I'd come by slow degrees to understand that my hope of being famous was past, like my prevailing hope of having any significant effect upon society.

Claude Dupre retained his old youthful edginess and pushy, abrasive ways. He'd become an aging ex-hippie with a wispy beard resembling detergent froth, a ponytail straggling between his shoulder blades, and rimless John Lennon glasses with bifocal lenses. For the past fifteen years he'd been wearing the identical black leather jacket, and hiker's boots, both grown shabby. A single gold stud glittered in his left earlobe. He had broad, sloping shoulders that sagged in repose (as I'd happened to notice on the flight down) but were kept rigidly erect when he was being observed. We can't afford to give the impression of being defeated, super-annuated people, Claude had said with an angry smile.

Our press conference was faltering to an end. Claude Dupre was the only one of us to have asked more than a few perfunctory questions, pur-suing his usual line of inquiry into the condemned man's background, there to discover, like glass gems hidden in a few inches of soil, the usual depressing evidence of poverty, alcoholism, child beating, and molestation in state-run foster homes. In an Alabama mumble Birdsall was saying, eyes downcast, "—yeh I was beaten and m'lested till I couldn't hardly sit. Ran away age eleven and never looked back. And so when Jesus came into my heart just the other day—"

I took notes; it was my duty. Worthless notes! For all this had been said before by other condemned men. It's a bitter truth: In a capitalist society, truth must be marketed like any other product.

Birdsall's words ran out. There was silence. I felt a rush of panic: The poor bastard was going to be taken away, the doors shut upon him, I hadn't asked a single question so far, drawing glances of curiosity and disapproval from Claude Dupre—as if I'd betrayed him personally. So there I was rais-ing my hand, and asking a question that flew into my head that very moment, "Mr. Birdsall, what will be your meal this evening?" (How much more tactful to phrase it this way, instead of asking *What will be your last meal?*) As if I'd uttered unexpected, startling lines in a play others had assumed they knew by heart, everyone stared at me; Birdsall most eagerly, rattling his shackles as he hunched forward. As if, simply by asking this question, I'd bonded with him in some mysterious way. But Birdsall was at a loss to say anything sharp, witty, original. He mumbled in his apologetic way he'd like maybe a Big Mac double cheeseburger, home fries and grits and ketchup and Coke, and cherry pie with chocolate ice cream; in a pathetic gesture of bravado he smacked his lips, but I saw the rising terror in his eyes.

It was then inspiration came to me. A wild, impulsive gesture. I asked permission of Birdsall to order his meal myself—"Something a little more imaginative, just this once?" Claude Dupre was gaping at me; and Mr. Jesse Heaventree, the warden at Hartsfree; and most intensely, Roy Beale Birdsall. His broad, coarse face colored with embarrassment and pleasure. He said, glancing shyly at me, "—gosh, wouldna know what fork to use—" and wiped at his face and laughed; but I refused to take no for an answer, this was the poor guy's opportunity to sample a decent meal before he died, it fell to me to provide it. I've been told that I have a personality like a steamroller once I'm roused to action and purpose, and this appeared to be one of those times. Most reasonably I argued, "Now, Mr. Birdsall, you've had Big Macs and french fries all your life, why not a gourmet dinner for—for tonight? I'm not a food specialist but I do know a little about food, and Italian wine, and—" The condemned man's eyes, fixed on mine, began to go dreamy, abstract; as if he were staring through me, and through the prison walls, to the very horizon. At this point the warden Mr. Heaventree intervened, saying sourly there was no budget for fancy food, the limit was $15 and that was enough for what most inmates requested. I said, incensed, "Of course I intend to pay for Mr. Birdsall's dinner. Will you trust me with the menu, Mr. Birdsall?"

Birdsall shrugged, laughed, and mumbled what sounded like, "—well my granddaddy used to say it don't hurt none to try one thing once."

STILL, THE WARDEN had to be convinced, so I went with him into his office. He wasn't a bad fellow—warden of Hartsfree for twenty-six years—I'd interviewed him often in the past. Heaventree was belligerent to outsiders but congenial, like most southern men, when you come to know them. "The State of Alabama has never executed an innocent man," he would say, with a waggish smile; I would ask how he knew, and Heaventree would say, "Son, I *know.*"

Today, when I brought up the subject of Roy Beale Birdsall, who was probably an innocent man, Heaventree said, in a lowered voice, as if to flatter me with a confidence, "It's a principle of *sacrifice,* son. People want to know that there's punishment. If the punishment don't always go to the guilty party, 'cause we can't find the guilty party one hundred percent of the time, then the punishment goes where it fits."

Goes where if fits. I made a mental note of this.

"Why'd *you* care, son? Educated white man like you, you're not gonna wind up on death row, see? So—better leave this to us pros."

Heaventree objected to my proposal, initially. Providing a special meal for Roy Beale Birdsall might set a bad precedent, he said, for other death row inmates, of whom there were quite a few; I listened politely, and countered his logic by offering to provide him a second, identical meal, plus a bottle of Old Grand-Dad thrown in, to be delivered to the warden's office at the same time Birdsall received his in his cell on death row.

So the delicate matter was resolved; we shook hands; most generously, Heaventree allowed me to use his private office phone, for I needed to work quickly. Already, as in a nightmare, it was 3:35 P.M.; in nine hours, Roy Beale Birdsall would be a thoroughly cooked, cooling corpse.

I *was* INSPIRED. In earlier days I would have written in outraged defense of a luckless victim of the system like Roy Beale Birdsall, but now the lastmeal menu was a kind of poem; an ode and an elegy combined; a musical composition, even. I called several Birmingham restaurants before settling upon The Castle, a pricey three-star place I'd dined in once or twice (a long time ago, when the paper allowed me a considerable expense account for such trips into the American heartland); and explained the situation to the bemused chef; and worked out with him a dream last meal for Roy Beale Birdsall. No compromises, I said; no condescension; no down-homey southern cuisine; Birdsall had entrusted me with this menu and I intended to do us both proud. It's my belief as a political liberal that the "common man" can appreciate good food and wine just as he can appreciate good art, music, literature if he's properly introduced to it; if he isn't made to feel inadequate, ignorant. Since this was his last meal, Birdsall would savor each morsel; he wouldn't rush through it, as no doubt he'd rushed through most meals of his life. My one disappointment was that I couldn't talk Heaventree into allowing Birdsall even a single glass of wine . . . A ridiculous state law forbade alcohol to the condemned prisoner, like tranquilizers or sedatives of any kind.

Here is my dream menu for Roy Beale Birdsall:

Vichyssoise garnished with salmon roe and fresh chives
    (with hard-crusted French bread, lightly salted butter)
A light risotto with chopped shiitake mushrooms
Lobster à l'américaine (fresh-killed, boiled lobster)
Sautéed snow peas, button onions, julienne carrots, zucchini
Mixed green salad including arugula and Belgian endive
    (with a classic Italian dressing made with imported olive oil)
Assorted desserts—chocolate mousse, zabaglione, strawberry
    crêpes, crème brûlée

By way of my Visa account, I arranged for two such exquisite meals to be prepared, packaged, and delivered (by a Birmingham car service) to the Hartsfree facility kitchen, to be reheated in time for a 6:30 P.M. serving. The Castle was charging double what the already exorbitant meals would have cost under ordinary circumstances, since this was an emergency. I couldn't afford it, but in my excitement and euphoria I didn't give the price a second thought.

"A SHAMEFUL TIME in America," Claude Dupre said wearily. "Even as police departments across the country are being exposed as racists and extortionists, victimizing the very citizens they're paid to protect, faking evidence, lying on the witness stand, there's more and more public pressure for executions. Outrageous!"

"God, yes." I tried to sound vehement, incensed.

"Is that all you can say? 'God, yes'?"

My head was an echo chamber of words too clamorous yet indistinct to be heard. I kept glancing in dread at my watch—it was already after six! Claude and I were having drinks in the near-deserted cocktail lounge of our motel, the Hartsfree Holiday Inn; but neither of us was enjoying them much. Our drinks, our outrage, our commiseration: all had an air of déjà vu, like recycled breaths. Seeing that Claude was looking at me reproachfully, I said, "It's just that we've had this conversation before, Claude."

Claude grimaced, and plucked at his earlobe.

"We *have*? When?"

"Niles, Texas. Last Easter. Willie Joe Rathbone, remember? The three-hundred-pound boy who torched his—"

Claude turned away irritably, signaling the bartender for another beer. How many vigils of this kind we'd passed together in each other's company, drinking; how many years. Waiting for 11 P.M. and the inevitable drive to a prison for an execution we were "covering." Sometimes we ate together, more often not. (But Claude was drinking more than I remembered.) We were intimates without being friends any longer. Or maybe we'd never been friends, only frustrated idealists together.

"And another thing," Claude said, as if we'd been quarreling, frowning at me through his round priggish glasses, "I don't approve of you ordering that absurd meal for Roy Beale Birdsall. Lobster!"

"Why not? The poor man is going to die at midnight, why not send him off with a good meal for once?" I protested. "And it's lobster à l'américaine, he won't have any trouble eating it."

Claude said, disgusted, "It's obscene. He's going to *die*. And you, of all people, are celebrating his death."

My face burned as if Claude had struck me. "I'm not celebrating anything," I said. "You know how I feel about capital punishment."

"You're cooperating with the system, you're buying into it."

"I feel sorry for the poor man, where's the harm in that?"

So we quarreled, with surprising bitterness. I accused Claude of being jealous of me for having thought of buying a condemned man a last meal; Claude accused me of "bourgeois excess." I'd known that Claude was priggish about spending money on food and drink, primarily, I'd thought, because he couldn't afford it himself. Most of our fellow journalists, even the younger ones, were more obsessed with food and drink than I was, fanatics about French cuisine, Italian cuisine, vineyards; in me, the predilection had grown gradually with the years, compensation, I suppose, for the uncertainty and frequent misery of my professional life. *It's what we journalists have instead of God.* I might have joked with Claude except the man had no sense of humor.

Claude knew how to hurt me: threw a few bills down onto the bar, and stalked out. Leaving me alone with my thoughts.

IT HAD BEEN a season when many things were going wrong.

My nation. My political beliefs. My personal life. (Of course I couldn't afford the meals from The Castle, or the car service.)

Once, not too long ago, when they were relative rarities, and therefore the more outrageous, I'd covered executions and publicly protested death penalty legislation with a true sense of mission. I was twenty-five years old when I witnessed my first hanging, in Utah in 1979. I'd done freelance political-activist writing before then but I'd never written about anything so *real*. I could not have guessed that the hanging of a human being (in this case a black man convicted of armed robbery and murder), while morally and physically revolting as you would expect, could be so mesmerizing!

Or that the essay it inspired, originally printed in *Mother Jones,* would draw so much attention, and launch my career. "The Cruelest Death: Politics and Aesthetics of 'Legalized' Strangulation"—a classic.

A year later, when the Utah legislature voted to abandon their old frontier traditions of hanging and firing squad, and replace them with lethal injection, I had reason to think it was in response to my essay.

And so—I'd embarked upon my career. Almost accidentally at first, then with purpose, mission. My goal was to expose the horror of government-sanctioned barbarism, to educate the public, and to help sway fickle public sentiment. What revolutionary fervor drove me! I might lose ten, fifteen pounds in the course of investigating and writing; fueled by a passion for truth, and often by Dexedrine, I went without sleep for as long as forty-eight hours. My much-noted prose was modeled upon Jonathan Swift's elegantly corrosive prose, my touchstone being "A Modest Proposal"—that great text of savage indignation (which, I've heard, my younger colleagues with their watered-down B.A. degrees haven't even read). I was a zealot, a firebrand, a martyr in the making. The Vietnam War was over at last; what of wars at home? Horrors at home? Unbelievable to me as to numerous others, including the equally vocal Claude Dupre, that the United States alone of civilized nations would condone capital punishment!—resumed after the Supreme Court decision in the mid-seventies to give back to the states the privileges of executing persons convicted of "capital" crimes. A reversion to barbarism! And how quickly certain states began to "reform" statutes, incarcerate usually indigent inmates on death row, and execute a disproportionately high percentage of black males.

Look, I'm no sentimentalist. I know that the heart of man is sinful, capable of the most unspeakable cruelty. I know that our ancestors punished even minor crimes with death. But my point is, and has always been, not just that innocent persons might be (and have been) sent to their deaths under this system, but that the very principle of a government exerting its authority in *committing violence against any of its citizens* is in itself abhorrent.

It all seems, or seemed, self-evident.

But after my early, apparent success in Utah, I could not comprehend how, as I traveled about the country interviewing, investigating, writing my passionate stories, so many individuals in authority totally ignored me; refused to speak with me, dismissed my arguments, or gave no evidence of reading me at all. How could it be, I wondered in my youthful naïveté, that the controversial cases I wrote about, given public prominence in *The New York Times, Newsweek, The New Republic,* and even upon one occasion the mass-market *People,* nonetheless continued like gruesome clock-work—as if no one had intervened at all? After one of these miscarriages of justice, ending with the execution of a young mentally impaired black man in Oklahoma, I collapsed and was ill for months with what the nineteenth-century Russian novelists would have called "brain fever." (My marriage of three years, already shaky, collapsed, too—but that's another story.) When I recovered, however, I refused to listen to well-meaning advice from friends and family, and returned to Tulsa, to take up the very case that had devastated me. I spent twelve hours daily for weeks sifting through trial transcripts and related documents until I discovered errors committed by the defendant's court-appointed attorney (who'd neglected to vigorously cross-examine a clearly lying police informant) and by the prosecution (which had "lost" exculpatory evidence suggesting that the defendant had been nowhere near the crime scene). I turned up witnesses the defense had ignored. I came to the conclusion that the executed man had certainly been innocent. Yet, still, I couldn't get Oklahoma authorities to acknowledge my findings, still less to admit to their reckless, corrupt, and criminal behavior. But my ten-thousand-word article "Justice Denied in Oklahoma," which appeared in the *New York Times Magazine,* received much public attention and acclaim; has been several times reprinted, and won the coveted Polk Award for Journalism. There was a rumor of a Pulitzer, which came to nothing; but, not long afterward, I was offered a position, a column, at a most distinguished East Coast newspaper.

If you know me at all, recognize my name, it's because of "Death Watch." At its height of popularity, it was syndicated in forty newspapers across the country and sometimes reprinted in *The International Herald Tribune.*

"Death Watch" was launched with much fanfare at the paper. I was charged with not just presenting anti–death penalty arguments (the paper, a liberal bastion, had long been on record opposing the death penalty) but with telling the stories of death row inmates, their families and lovers, their guards, chaplains, wardens. I might interview prison psychiatrists, mothers of the condemned, an executioner or two. Anything pertaining to "Death Watch" was material for my column. It was perceived by the newspaper's socially conscious board of editors that there was, in the paper, a dearth of information about the downtrodden, the defeated, the doomed, and the despicable. Where a death row inmate was mentally incompetent, a yet more dramatic story might be forged. These were *citizens of the underclass,* the *insulted and injured* amid America's affluence. It was my duty to come up with ever new and original and "entertaining" ways of dealing with them.

For the first several months, "Death Watch" drew a barrage of letters, and delighted the editors of the paper. Here was controversy, here was "social responsibility"! But by degrees interest waned; readers dropped off, or failed to respond. Our crowning blow was the reinstitution of the death penalty in New York state, long and bravely opposed by a liberal governor and swept in by a Republican-conservative triumph at the polls—a shocking, demoralizing, and embarrassing development. The newspaper's editors were made to see how little influence they wielded; my column was discreetly shifted from the editorial page to other parts of the paper. Like a cork bobbing in choppy waters it began to turn up in the second section, or the third. At the time of the Birdsall execution in Alabama it was appearing at erratic intervals in the nether regions of the fourth section, adjacent to the obituaries. To have sunk so low!

Syndication, too, was down—by three-quarters.

Roy Beale Birdsall would be my twenty-sixth execution since I'd launched "Death Watch" only five exhausting years ago and I was close to extinction myself. *Can't do it. Not another time.*

IN THE END, the execution of Roy Beale Birdsall by the sovereign state of Alabama took place exactly as scheduled. Despite the controversial nature of the case, there was no last-minute postponement or commutation of sentence by the governor. Nor was there even any suspense, any glimmer of anticipation or hope.

I almost missed it. Drinking for hours alone in my motel room, which is a habit I'd vowed I would break, and waking dazed and panicked at 11:20 P.M.; rushing to the prison and grudgingly allowed inside, checked through by surly guards and led on a brisk hike to the death row wing at the rear of the prison where, in a windowless alcove resembling a warehouse, the electric chair was located. I could hear inmates throughout the facility shouting, stomping, banging against bars and walls, protesting the imminent execution. "Apparently they never get used to it," I said, meaning to make conversation; and the guard said, shrugging, "They like making noise, is all."

As I was ushered into the viewing room, I began to shiver; I'd broken into a cold sweat.

There were only two rows of hard-backed wooden chairs, and mine was in the first; reserved for me in the name of my newspaper, as if I had no identity otherwise. Claude Dupre was sitting behind officials, journalists. Several ravaged-looking Birdsall relatives, no mistaking they were relatives, among them a heavyset older woman whispering, or praying, to herself, and a stocky man of about fifty, bald, dirt-colored, who resembled Roy Beale Birdsall closely enough to be an elder twin. The Birdsalls were of that class of Americans for whom fate is purely bad luck. But I'd written of such people too often in the past and had exhausted my capacity for sympathy.

Everyone was sitting, staring straight ahead, through the plate-glass window, at The Chair: the peculiarly mustard-yellow Hartsfree electric chair, many times photographed and commented upon. *An aesthetic object more evocative than the human sacrifice strapped into it. The one custom-made by art, the other mass-produced by nature.* But I couldn't write that! Not for "Death Watch." This chair was both a familiar object and a monster-object; made of wood, as if by a painstaking craftsman (which, in fact, might have been the case), it exuded an air of homespun, rough-hewn, rustic-American earnestness, a Norman Rockwell innocence even as it was malevolently tricked up with straps, clamps, electrodes, and a crown-like device to fit tightly on the condemned person's head like something in a low-budget horror film of the fifties. *The Chair as iconic image.* And the brightly lit execution chamber, like a stage awaiting a solitary performer.

On this side of the glass there was silence except for husky, hoarse breathing and the throbbing pulse of a wall air conditioner. My own breath was coming thick as mucus. In the motel room I'd paced about drinking, smoking one cigarette after another, imagining myself as *a man so sensitive to another's imminent death* he can't even sit still. I'd been thinking about Roy Beale Birdsall's last meal: Had he liked it, had he even been able to eat it? Lobster à l'américaine—why had I chosen such a specialty? Birdsall had the look of a man (I loved turning such clever phrases; such phrases turned themselves in my brain without my volition) who'd never tasted lobster in his life. And salmon roe, and the risotto—my mouth watered obscenely. But what a disappointment Birdsall hadn't been allowed a single glass of wine.

At 12:01 a door to the rear of the execution chamber opened, and lanky Reverend Hank Harley entered solemn-faced and glowering with piety, carrying a conspicuous Bible; behind him came poor Roy Beale Birdsall between two guards like a man in a dream. It seemed a final insult that Birdsall should die in his prison garb—a baggy uniform the color of dishwater. His head had been brutally shaved and resembled a bowling ball. His face was puffy and flushed as if with exertion. Like a clumsy barn-yard animal he was shackled as before at his wrists and ankles. Globules of oily sweat shone on his forehead yet he was trying to smile, a ghastly *I am at peace, Christ is in my heart* stretching of the lips. I wondered if he would see me, if he would remember me? He was resolutely not looking at the bright yellow chair; his head turned toward the plate-glass window, he was frowning and squinting into the witness room. Searching out his relatives who stared at him in speechless chagrin and wonderment. And then he caught sight of me, and a light came into his glazed eyes, his smile twitched in recognition and he tried to raise a hand as if to signal OK with his thumb and forefinger. *Yes, he'd liked the meal! Fantastic meal! Surely did appreciate the meal, thank you, sir.*

Or so it seemed Roy Beale Birdsall meant to communicate.

The ritual of execution proceeded like clockwork, and swiftly. That's the horror: Once it begins it won't stop. A living man enters a room from which he will be carried a corpse. I sat transfixed and staring at the activities on the other side of the glass, scarcely twelve feet away. How could I have imagined that Birdsall's death would be routine, this execution stale from repetition? I flinched as Birdsall was forcibly seated in the chair and his shaved head fitted to the metal contraption; as leather straps were buckled at his wrists and ankles and across his chest, which had begun to heave in panic. The sleeves and pants legs of his uniform were neatly folded back to expose pale hairless flesh to which electrodes were attached. An attendant trained in the craft of electrocution prepared the "condemned man" for death as impersonally and deftly as a robot might have done. And all this while Birdsall was trying to maintain his vague strained smile as if to assure us he was still in control, his soul was his own.

Reverend Hank Harley was reciting Bible verse in a sonorous voice, asking then with grave solicitude had Roy any final statement to make?—and Birdsall was distracted and seemed not to hear so Reverend Hank repeated his formula-question and Birdsall drew a deep breath straining at the straps and murmured in his Alabama drawl a rambling nasal prayer. I would have liked him to protest his innocence and the barbarism of what was being done to him—I would have liked him to curse the state—but of course he did not. ". . . Just gonna put my faith in Jesus like I been doin amen . . ."

Next, the attendant fastened a plain black cloth over Birdsall's eager face even as the man's eyes darted about with animation, hope.

I wanted to shout, "No! Stop!"

But of course I sat silent, mute; watching through half-shut eyes; my fists clenched. For always witnesses sit silent and mute and impassive, making no move to intervene. It never seems possible that powerful currents of electricity will be sent through the body of a human being in our presence, and no one will intervene, yet that's exactly what happens when a person is executed; the wonder is that it happens every time and it happened that sulphurous-warm September night in Hartsfree, Alabama. After seven years of anticipation the end came abruptly, and rudely: Somewhere out of sight a switch was pulled, and invisible electricity coursed through the condemned man's body; the first jolt lasted a full two minutes, one hundred twenty distinct seconds, at the start the man's fists clenched and his body went rigid until consciousness drained from it and he "relaxed," slumped. For Birdsall it was over, he'd passed out of reach, but the procedure continued with more jolts, and more. The heartbeat has to be completely extinguished, the brain absolutely gone. A small spiral of smoke curled from the electrode attached to Birdsall's left leg, the flesh of which was now pinkened, flushed.

More smoke, a delicate bluish aura appeared about the motionless rigid head. Roy Beale Birdsall's departing spirit, fading even as we stared.

JUST AHEAD of me, walking briskly, a middle-aged man in a shabby leather jacket with a graying ponytail straggling between his shoulder blades, we were urged to leave the prison premises as quickly as possible and no one wished to linger. Claude Dupre sighed as I caught up with him but neither of us spoke until we reached the parking lot where, in bright beacons of light, swarms of moths and smaller insects roiled like crazed molecules. In a brotherly gesture of disgust Claude lay a heavy hand on my shoulder, muttering, "Another! Another."

Politely I shook off the hand. "No. He was like no other."

AND NEXT MORNING on an early flight to New York I am working inspired, typing furiously on my laptop. *Death is original, death is always present tense.* I will speak of the death of a man named Roy Beale Birdsall in the electric chair at Hartsfree, Alabama, in such a tone, in such a voice, with such passion, with such conviction that no one who reads my words can escape them or forget them. I am sure! For hours the night before I'd been awake in my motel room, pacing, too excited to sleep, taking notes, speaking lines aloud in a state of euphoria I haven't experienced for years.

The thought even comes to me, slantwise, sly: Now New York state has reinstituted the death penalty, I won't have to travel far to cover executions.

We are thirty thousand feet above land. The Carolinas, though invisible. Below the hurtling aircraft is an opaque mass of cloud, like frozen white-water rapids. How happy I am to be alive, and to be headed north, and to be writing with such purpose, such a mission. *A delicate bluish aura . . . about the motionless rigid head.* A few seats ahead of me in coach class sits my old classmate and rival Claude Dupre, unshaven, disheveled, shoulders slumped, staring at a window past which vaporous cloud-fragments stream, stream.

IN *COPLAND*

*I*t was last March I was almost killed in *COPLAND*.

It's June now. I'm barricaded in my house most days. I'm protected by electronic surveillance. I have my own spying devices. I applied for, but was denied, a home-owner's license for a firearm. (I have another application filed, and I'm waiting to hear.) You'd recognize my face if you saw it, which is why I keep hidden much of the time.

Possibly I'm not now, for TV viewers' memories fade quickly, but I used to be famous in northeast New Jersey. Within the orbit of WNET-TV "The People's Power Station" of Newark. I was S. of EXPOSÉ!, broadcast Wednesdays at 7 P.M. I'd been on the controversial EXPOSÉ! team for three years.

Three years is about the time most EXPOSÉ! reporters burn out. S. was just getting started.

Maybe I sound vain. I'm just being honest. My injuries don't show in my face, which remains a handsome if slightly vacuous, youthful face. The cops who beat me were careful not to injure my face.

I know—I can't prove they were actual *cops*. The thing about *COP-LAND*—I can't prove it's an actual place. Even if I could find it again, which probably I could not. Even if I left my safe house in Deer Trail Vil-

las, a private residential community in Lakeview, New Jersey, to search for
⋆COPLAND⋆ in Newark, which probably I could not for psychological as
well as medical reasons.

This is a fact: my naked, bruised body, bleeding from a "badly lacerated" anus, was found amid trash in a Dumpster in Hoboken, New Jersey,
by city sanitation workers, early in the drizzly morning of March 29. An
ambulance arrived and carried me away, unconscious.

Luckily for me, no rival TV camera crews or photojournalists were
present. My face would have been recognized immediately. Media cap-
tions would have been taunting and cruel: EXPOSÉ! REPORTER EXPOSED!

But none of it seeped into the press. I was an "anonymous" body until
my wife came to claim me. I've kept a low profile since.

Press charges? You've got to be joking.

Next time, the cops would kill me. This time, I think it was mainly for
laughs. And they left my face untouched.

Why? Not out of kindness, or mercy. It's a PR thing, I suppose.
Because facial injuries, in news photos or on TV, are so much more lurid-
looking than bruises on the body or even broken bones. Because a face is
an *individual,* and a body is *anonymous.* My attackers exercised professional
discretion.

Knowing the injuries to my genitalia and anus are "evidence" I'm not
eager to share with the public.

My wife, M., was horrified by the beating I'd received, yet strangely
thrilled, too. Staring at me as if seeing me for the first time in years. "Poor
darling. You're lucky to be alive."

The subtext being *luck. Lucky to be alive. How can you complain? What a
complainer you are!*

One truth I've learned in TV journalism, human beings have a limited
capacity for solemnity and sympathy. A few intense minutes is it. Before
EXPOSÉ! I was on the WNET-TV *Nightly News* for seven years. On camera
we'd be all glum formality but as soon as the red light clicked on, meaning
we were off, we'd grin and exchange wisecracks. The more solemnity, the
more laughs. I have to confess, S. was one of the worst. I mean, one of the
wittiest guys at the station. Witty is sexy, right? You know how hard it is to
resist saying anything if you get a few laughs. So I'm not passing any high-
brow moral judgment on other people; that's not my nature.

A while back, before my career ended, I happened to overhear my
fifteen-year-old son K. boasting of me, sprawled on his bed watching TV

with the phone receiver on his shoulder (this is how K. talks to his girl-friend for hours: he's got his own phone line of course), "My dad's OK. He's cool. There's no generation thing between us because we're, like, the same generation, y'know?"

Maybe I shouldn't be, but I'm flattered by this.

I'M A FORTY-SIX-YEAR-OLD Caucasian straight male.

Even with my disabilities, I look much younger than my age. M., my wife, who's at least forty-three (she's kept her exact age ambiguous) looks like a girl in her mid-twenties.

No one we know looks "his" or "her" age. It's as if the concept "age" no longer applies.

Impossible to guess "ages." And type-casting people? It can't be done.

Take S., for instance. I have a B.A. in classics from Princeton and an M.A. in TV journalism from N.Y.U. But my mind is mostly empty; I've forgotten most of the Greek I knew and remember only the ominous, cloudy penumbra of tragedy. I've been married to M. for eighteen years. We have two children, K. and his sister C. who's eleven, or maybe, now, twelve. M. is an executive at CitCorp Trust and I'm not sure what she does, but she does it capably. Through our investments we've accumulated somewhere beyond $2 million in property, assets, and savings. Which is about average for Deer Trail Villas, I think. One million dollars doesn't mean what it meant in my parents' generation; it's more like what $100,000 was then.

I don't know my family very well. It isn't something that upsets me, but it's a fact. When I was S., a dashing TV personality, one of the EXPOSÉ! reporters sent out undercover to investigate secrets of "graft, corruption, dishonesty and immorality in the private and public sectors"—"EXPOSÉ! in the interests of American Democracy"—my kids were proud of me, yet I was never able to interest them in person the way my TV-self S. did. S. was a kind of twin-rival: enhanced by skillful camera work, giddy helicop-ter shots, and an edgy rock-music score that kept the atmosphere tense and percussive even when nothing much was happening. In real life, where most of us live, when nothing happens, which is most of the time, you've got no background music to suggest *something is going to happen—soon!* Both K. and C. used to ply me with questions about the more sensational exposés but they got restless if I spoke beyond five minutes. Any lapse into technical vocabulary made their eyes glaze over. Even M. with her appetite for insider information and scandal became visibly bored if I went on too long. I was hurt, but joked that as S. of EXPOSÉ! I had plenty of fans who sent me messages, gifts, marriage proposals, so why didn't my own family love me more? M. laughed in that way that sounds like expensive silverware clattering and said, "Because we are your family, silly, you're supposed to love *us*."

A reply that left me stunned, for it was both senseless and profound.

In our six-bedroom fieldstone colonial at 9 Deer Trail Road, we see one another fleetingly. It's as though each of us is surfing TV channels and the others are TV images flashing by. Sometimes you pause and watch for a few seconds, or minutes; most of the time you get restless and move on, looking for something more exciting. We eat meals at different times and in different parts of the house and most evenings we're in different rooms watching TV or cruising the Internet, though the kids are supposed to be doing homework of course. My wife brings home CitCorp work but sometimes I hear TV voices in her bedroom, at least I assume they're TV voices, as late as 2 A.M. I used to know every inch of my wife's body and in the early mornings when we were young we'd make love tenderly and M. would tell me her dreams, which seemed to me the most intimate of all human gestures; but I haven't been told a dream of M.'s in years, possibly because she's stopped having them, or I've forgotten to ask. I do know that I haven't seen M. unclothed in a long time and have a mild curiosity about what she looks like. She seems not to have gained an ounce. She's so glamorous, energetic, and "young." Like S., she's experimented with her hair color, so there are no gray hairs on her head; but I can't recall whether the glossy maroon highlights were always there amid the mahogany-brown, or whether they've been added recently. I would never ask M., of course.

I would never spy on M. She knows she's perfectly safe singing to herself in her steamy bathroom after a shower, or undressing in her bedroom adjacent to my own. She knows I would never "accidentally" push open her door. She knows I would never "sleepwalk" into her bed.

After ★COPLAND★ I'm not going to sleepwalk into anybody's bed for a long, long time.

It's true, like most media people S. had a fast pulse. I'd been sexually active, sometimes a little compulsive, but rarely with a WNET colleague or anyone "serious" and much of the time with professionals, about whom

I'd have no more feeling than I have for the dental assistant girl who so avidly cleans the tartar off my teeth every six months. So there'd never been any question of personal involvement or what you'd call, strictly speaking, "marital infidelity." All my male, married friends at the station feel exactly the same way: what you do with a pro is a cash deal and nothing more, and no one's business but your own. In any case, M. assures me she prefers me "in a neutral state." That is, neuter. In the days when we visited friends' houses, after she'd had a few glasses of wine, I'd overhear her confiding she could go without sex for the rest of her life—"As long as I have my warm cuddly companion in bed."

M. means our dachshund Chop-Chop. But as long as she leaves this ambiguous, I haven't felt hurt or challenged.

MAYBE MY MISTAKE WAS, preparing for our investigation of New Jersey police, I had my brown hair bleached platinum-blond, trimmed up the back of my head and styled into long, wavy wings with a center part. Even my eyebrows and lashes—bleached, too. My left earlobe was pierced and inserted with several gold studs. At a local tanning salon I acquired a smooth roasted-almond look. (Cops are notoriously homophobic, right?) The effect was *spectacular*.

Young women who'd been seeming not to "see" me in recent years, and men who'd never given me a second glance, now gave me that second glance, and a third. My bosses at WNET, including even the billionaire owner Mister G-d (as he was fondly known), stared after me *searchingly*. An over-forty straight Caucasian male?—married, with two kids? Hard to believe.

I learned that sexual power is generated through the eye of the beholder. If you charge someone up, whether it's a *her* or a *him,* you can't help charging yourself up, too.

Not that I strayed across the gender line, even so. Though I had opportunities.

When M. first saw my new look, she was alarmed, even a little frightened. "My God, what have you done to yourself? *Is* this you?" She actually touched my face with her cool fingers, like a blind woman. I told her she could cut her hair, too, bleach it, get a tan—"Join me." Quickly she said, trying not to show the disdain she felt, "Oh no. I'd lose the respect of my colleagues. I've got a serious job."

As if my EXPOSÉ! job wasn't serious.

As if American democracy doesn't depend upon a continuous exposure of truth.

AND NOW I'm on disability leave, "convalescing."

"Did you take Chop-Chop out, at least?"—so M. asks when she returns home, never earlier than 7 P.M. weekdays, from CitCorp. Implying *I can't imagine what the hell you do all day long but I'm not going to say a word.* So I tell her yes, even if I haven't taken Chop-Chop farther than the rear of the garage, where the little dog's turds are accumulating as rapidly as the populations of third world countries.

K. is embarrassed of his dad hobbling around on crutches, whimpering on the toilet straining to produce a few rabbit-pellets every two or three days. My hair's no longer blond of course but shock-white. And thinning. My sky-blue eyes women seemed to adore are now a grubby blue like stained pebbles. My contact lenses don't fit the way they used to but irritate my eyes so that it looks as if I have a perpetual allergy, or I've been crying. (Have I been crying? The other evening I overheard C. ask her mother, "Why is Dad so sad now? Why does he *cry?*" and M. said gently, "Your father isn't sad, honey, and he isn't crying. Men rarely display their emotions. He has *allergies.*")

It depresses me to think that I might have as many as four decades remaining. If I stay out of the way of vengeful ★COPS★.

My own father, whom I've been said to resemble, though I've never seen it, is still alive "and kicking"—as he says—well into his eighties. He's delusional, yet not much more than he'd been in the prime of life.

The other day I read in the *New York Times* a startling statistic: as many as one-fifth of Caucasian males of my generation and older are "disabled" and drawing benefits. Physical, mental, vocational disabilities. We millions constitute a "potentially powerful political force" if anyone could be motivated to organize us, but who'd volunteer for such a task? Most of us don't get out of bed until after our wives leave for work and our children, if we still have children living at home, leave for their schools, and it can take as long as two hours for us to prepare and eat breakfast (in my case sugared cornflakes, skim milk, cups of Sanka, and half a pack of forbidden cigarettes) and to watch morning TV news or read the paper (in my case, the *Times* with its proliferating sections: first the obituaries, the best-written prose in the paper, then the A section which is mainly international news, then the dreary "metro" section and local New Jersey news which is petty politics and sordid crimes, then the sports section, then the business section, then the arts which is mostly movie ads and movie PR, then special sections like science, house and home, dining in and dining out, and computer news—whew!). By the time I've finished breakfast and the pages of the *Times* are scattered around me on the floor it's nearing noon, I haven't shaved or dressed yet and I feel like the melted watch in that painting of Salvator Dalí, with the black ants crawling over it.

Still, most days I force myself to go into my study and turn on this tape recorder and speak into it. Because my therapist Dr. A. has urged me to record what happened to me back in March, to alter my life forever; or, to be precise, what I believe happened to me. (Does Dr. A. believe me? At our second meeting, seeing the look of incredulity and repugnance in his face, I asked him point-blank if he believed me, and Dr. A. quickly said yes he believes that I experienced something, and it was "genuinely traumatic." Yes, Doctor, I said, but do you believe it happened as it did, and that it was *real?*—and Dr. A. repeated in his phlegmy voice that, yes, he believes I experienced something, and it was "genuinely traumatic." I walked out of the bastard's office and stayed away for two weeks, then decided to swallow my pride and return because my disability pension covers therapy, and antidepressant drugs, and seeing Dr. A. twice a week gives focus to my life the way my work once did.) On a wall in Dr. A's office is the command attributed to Socrates—*Know yourself*. It's a challenge, I figure.

So I speak into this tape recorder. I get dizzy watching the cassettes spin. Sometimes I hear my voice like a TV voice become urgent, even anxious, as I circle the trauma of my beating on March 29. *It was police who did it! Our police! Whose uniforms, firearms, and billy clubs we buy for them!* Then I'll be overcome by a fit of yawning. I rest my heavy head on the tape recorder and I wake an hour later, sharp pains in my neck and spine. Sometimes, overcome by fatigue, I stumble to the nearest sofa, where I sleep until early afternoon when hunger pains wake me as if I were an infant ravenous for the breast. When I get up for the second time, I avoid the tape recorder except to quickly switch it off.

I'll fix myself a late lunch. Cottage cheese spooned out of the container, sprinkled with wheat germ. I'm hoping to replenish some of my lost calcium. More Sanka, more cigarettes. I'm too restless to sit down. I wander the house. In each room I enter I switch on the TV so I'm not too lonely. I don't want to start talking to myself like a "tragic" figure. That old bore Oedipus at Colonus. *An outcast. In a strange land. Wrapped in rags—disgusting! Filth of years on his withered body, skin wasting away, and the flesh on his ribs. And his face, the blind sockets of his eyes. And the scraps he eats to fill his shrunken belly.*

Rainy days I stay inside. Sunny days are too bright for my eyes, even with dark glasses. I don't want to obsess about being watched. Being videotaped. Deer Trail Villas is a private residential community patrolled by security guards and obviously these rent-a-cops aren't just guarding homeowners like me but spying on some of us, too. Security guards licensed to carry firearms like ours are connected with the police; probably most of them are ex-cops in fact. Whenever I take Chop-Chop out, even if it's only to the rear of the garage and back, I experience a hallucinatory vision of such clarity!—myself seen through a rifle scope. My thin, haggard figure intersected by the killer × of the scope. I can "feel" the faceless assassin's finger on the trigger. Had S. the integrity of those tragic old Greeks, he'd turn calmly to confront death. Wouldn't grovel for mercy as I'd done in ★COPLAND★. Instead, I'm overcome by animal panic. "No! Please don't shoot!"—I'm scrambling to get back inside the house, and poor Chop-Chop is in a panic too and nearly trips me, and my crutches, and we collapse in a whimpering heap just inside the door.

WHOEVER IT IS, hasn't yet fired a shot. Even as a prank.

I'm wondering which of us will prevail: him, or me.

IT'S A FACT, yet a fact we couldn't seem to demonstrate visually on EXPOSÉ!, that New Jersey cops are larger than normal human beings. You see them in squad cars larger than normal-sized cars, more like tanks, and they hardly fit inside these vehicles. You see them patrolling the streets on foot; it's like an optical illusion. When they get close, they're only just "tall"—maybe six feet three or four. But at a short distance, they've grown to seven feet at least. At a farther distance, they're giants. They must weigh up to three hundred pounds. Some of the bulk is fat, but most of it is hard muscle, the way a rhinoceros is hard muscle. They tend to look alike, fair- or brown-haired, with buzz cuts. Their ages are anywhere between twenty-nine and forty-nine. Their flushed faces are broad as shovels. They've been trained to smile with their mouths and to use such expressions as "sir," "ma'am," "excuse me, please" deadpan. It's a chilling experience to see a New Jersey cop stretching his mouth in a smile while his eyes are fixed on you like icepicks. Quite a few cops have dimpled cheeks. They give the impression of being husky, overgrown boys who would not utter profanities, let alone obscenities, in the presence of women. Their hands are enormous, the size of a normal man's feet. Their arms are the size of a normal man's thighs. Their necks are the size of a normal man's waist. Their heads are round and heavy as bowling balls and their bodies are built like fire hydrants. Yet they can be startlingly quick on their feet, as killer rhinos and elephants are quick on their feet. They take pride in their blue-gray uniforms, their polished leather boots, visored caps, and chunky belts which contain billy clubs, a holstered revolver, and a small two-way radio. Often they wear dark-tinted mirror-glasses. We citizens have become fearful of our cops, but we admire them, too. Even those of us who are middle-aged—and older—wish to think that cops are Authority, our respected elders. We think that, if we admire them sufficiently, and make public our admiration, they will look kindly upon us. They won't harass us, or injure us. They won't force our cars off the Turnpike during their one-hundred-mile-per-hour pursuits of teenage car thieves from Newark and they won't riddle our bodies with bullets in "cross fire." If we're polite with them, smiling and cowering. If we know the right words. If we're the right people. If we're the right color, neither black nor brown, not "light-skinned" anything.

Of course, the most dangerous cops aren't in uniform. They're "plain-clothes." They look like anyone!—except *larger*.

These cops, uniformed and plainclothes, have many fans among the populace. One of their most vocal fans is the governor of New Jersey, who makes it a point to be seen on TV at least weekly "extolling" cops for their courage and good deeds in fighting crime. Our mayors of cities and suburbs alike "extol" their cops. Caucasian juries routinely acquit cops charged with brutal racist acts, including murder; mostly, Caucasian grand juries refuse to indict them. *Necessary force* is the reason. Politicians are terrified of getting on the wrong side of the cops. All know how devastating a police strike could be, how their administrations would be revealed as powerless, like quadriplegics dumped out of their wheelchairs by high-spirited boys. A police strike would probably be the most disastrous civil upset that could happen to us, more terrifying in its consequences than strikes by firefighters, doctors, hospital workers. It isn't just that an army of cops might go on *strike*, which is a passive act; they might *strike out* at us— they have the weapons, the armored vehicles, and the expertise. They have the zest for hurt, uncultivated in the rest of us.

When a cop is killed, which happens frequently (drug wars? organized crime hits? feuds within the Department?) there are lavish outdoor funerals, a parade of mounted police and stately processions ending with burials presided over by top prelates. The governor, mayors, dignitaries attend. There's an atmosphere of angry sorrow. There's a quickening of the pulse, as the ceremony ends, and an appetite for revenge is aroused. Even on TV news clips, this appetite is powerfully evoked.

So last winter when EXPOSÉ! was preparing its undercover investigation of cops, we knew we were putting ourselves more at risk than usual, and that was fine with S. At least, I said so. I may have thought so. In my three years with the program, I'd been involved with several sensational exposés. Our ratings were consistently high. I had reason to believe I might be invited to *Sixty Minutes,* at triple my salary. EXPOSÉ! had delivered the goods on dishonest charities, insurance and HMO scams, contaminated "organic" foods, corrupt nursing homes, slum landlords who let their welfare-recipient tenants freeze in cold weather or go up in flames when their substandard buildings caught fire. We'd investigated high-class brothels, AIDS-infected cokehead street hookers and their suburban johns, child porn and Internet-sex rings. EXPOSÉ! worked in absolute secrecy and it was said of our team we were beyond reproach— "unswayable, and unbribable."

Even our spouses didn't know what we were investigating. Seeing S.'s chic-sexy new look, M. said, cruelly, "Aren't you getting a little too old for this, darling? Whatever 'this' is."

WE WERE UNDERCOVER, in our disguises, out on the street and on our assignments by March 10. The program would broadcast March 25. Like all media people we worked best under the pressure of a quick deadline. Some of us worked alone, but most of us were in teams of two or three. Always there was an unmarked van close by in which a cameraman was videotaping our every move. Or one of us carried on his person, inside a padded nylon jacket, a video camera. It was a wild season! Every day the media reported murders, rapes, robberies, arson! Dramatic car chases, shoot-outs, and arrests by police. Confessions by criminals. Highly publicized trials. Unreported were rumors of cop-crimes: the "questioning" of black- and brown-skinned young men who were stopped in their vehicles, handcuffed, beaten, in some instances shot, under the pretext of their being "suspects." It was believed that the car-thieving drug-dealing gang kids (blacks, Hispanics) had been nearly eradicated from Newark; there was a rumor we'd been hearing (but wouldn't be able to substantiate, unfortunately) that their bones, tangled with their gang "colors," could be found in lime pits in the Jersey City area. Thousands of homeless people, many of them black, many mentally defective, were said to have been herded into large vans and driven away—where? No one knew. But there were conspicuously fewer in urban areas. Some of us went to shelters in disguise as homeless folks, in soiled, tattered clothing, unshaven, unwashed, staring empty-eyed, and we were sprayed for lice with the others by unsuspecting city workers or volunteers, made to shuffle through long lines for grubby, lukewarm food, and these were depressing experiences as you might imagine, but patrolling cops didn't harass any of us. Maybe we looked too "normal"? Maybe officials recognized us, even in our disguises? With my platinum-blond hair, scruffy beard, glasses with thick lenses, and a cheesy vinyl raincoat like a shower curtain, swaying and staggering on my feet, I must've looked to cop eyes like a loathsome strung-out "fag"—but the only time a cop addressed me, as I sat muttering to myself in a corner, was to say, with deadpan solicitude, "Sir? The last of the coffee is being served." I blinked up at the husky young giant's toothy smile. Were his jaws tightened, his eyes narrowed steely as ice picks? Yet he was smiling. His gloved fingers twitched, but he hadn't laid a finger on *me*.

Another day, in Newark, I was walking with an EXPOSÉ! colleague, a black man named Sherwin, drop-out from Yale Law, and Sherwin's in dark glasses, wild goatee and flashy-pimp outfit, we're jaywalking through traffic, laughing like we're high, what more luscious bait for Newark cops?—and there come up to us two traffic cops, hands on their billy clubs but flashing their trademark smiles, and one of them says politely, "It's recommended that you cross this busy street at the intersection, with the light, for safety's sake." He's grinning so broadly dimples cut into his cheeks like knife wounds. The other, older cop is staring at us with a tight, clamped smile and his eyes filling up with blood. We murmured in fluty voices, "Thank you, officers! We'll *try*." Afterward I said to Sherwin, disappointed, "Y'know, these cops aren't what we've been led to expect. You think they have a bad rep?" Sherwin made a rude sound with his lips. He said contemptuously, "No. We're just having lousy luck. We haven't pushed far enough yet."

But EXPOSÉ!'s reporters, variously disguised, in scattered urban areas of northeast New Jersey, were encountering similar experiences. Jaywalking, simulated public drunkenness, "suspicious behavior"—we citizens were greeted with smiling courtesy. Our women reporters, who'd steeled themselves to be sexually insulted and harassed, were encountering gentlemen cops. After the third or fourth such encounter, the thought passed through my head, *Has someone tipped these guys off? Do they know they're on camera?* But in the next instant, I forgot. I didn't want to think this might be so. That our effort was for nothing; that, from the start, there must have been collusion between WNET top executives and the Jersey police.

A politically motivated collusion, obviously. So EXPOSÉ! was gamely filming material that, when aired, would play like PR for Jersey police.

Yet we kept trying. We knew we were failing, but we kept trying. I'm remembering woozy March nights when S. in his "new look" was cruising certain urban areas alone, hoping for action; or in the company of Sherwin, Randall, Elise. Sometimes a rowdy gang of us cruised together, hoping to draw the attention of brutal but photogenic cops. *We knew they existed! But where were they?* On Saturday night Sherwin and I were making the scene of gay waterfront bars in Hoboken, swaying with our arms around each other's waist along damp cobblestone streets hoping to catch the predatory eyes of cops passing in squad cars, our unmarked van following a half-block behind. One of us, it might've been me, made a playfully lewd signal to a cop-car, and the car braked to an immediate stop, and we steeled ourselves for trouble, but all that happened was a burly cop, must've been seven feet tall, three hundred pounds, stuck his bowling-ball head out of the car window, shook a sausage-forefinger at us and scolded, "Now, boys! Remember 'safe sex.' And don't catch *cold*." The squad car sped around a corner and disappeared and Sherwin called after, trilling, "Yo my mans! C'mon give us boys a *ride!*" But the squad car was gone. (Circling the block? We hoped.) The unmarked van continued to trail behind us, wasting video film. Sherwin said flatly, "The bastards know." I said, "They can't know. EXPOSÉ! has never been found out. And don't we look like the real thing? *We are the real thing.*" Maybe I was a little drunk, and I'd popped a few pills (of the kind once called speed, now "crystal") bought at the bar inside. My eyes glittered like my gold ear studs. I hadn't showered in days—this was part of my disguise—and my body exuded a rich, ripe, musky-sexy fragrance any sharp-nosed homophobic cop could pick up at thirty feet. I wanted something more than this! I wanted a cop-confrontation! I wanted to be broadcast on TV handcuffed, knocked around, on my knees, threatened with having my head beaten in, I wanted my rights as a citizen trampled upon, I wanted to be insulted, debased, I'd be brave and cool with a bloody nose, my family would be amazed at my courage and proud of me, thrilled to know me, wasn't this going to happen? any of it? I was feeling that powerful sexual charge of having aroused someone, even if strangers, except the arousal has come to nothing. Like lightning pumping into only just the earth, meeting no resistance and sparking no fireworks.

But the big cops hunkered in their tank-sized car never reappeared that night.

WHAT WAS BROADCAST on March 25 caused EXPOSÉ! to be laughed at in the media, even on our own turf. An hour of banal footage depicting Jersey cops as model cops: decent, kind, helpful, courteous, and smiling and clearly not racist, not misogynist, and not brutal. In our elaborate disguises we EXPOSÉ! reporters were Hallowe'en trick-or-treaters who'd come away with no treats.

The logic was, EXPOSÉ!'s agenda is to "expose" truth. If our investigation exposed true cop behavior, we had an ethical duty to make it public even if it wasn't anything like what we'd expected.

A few days later some of us were having drinks at The Skids. Some of us were rueful, and some of us were defiant. We guessed maybe we'd been tricked. But we couldn't know. The cop-performances were phony? We'd been fucked over? Some of us tried to see the humor in it. And S. who'd been the most depressed of the crew catches a glimpse of himself in the mirror behind the bar and feels a stab of sexual excitement. That hair, that tan! Those ear studs! But it's a sad, fading excitement. Next morning, he's going to get rid of it all. A return to dull-brown hair, no gold studs. It's over. I had two more drinks, and it was time to leave. I offered to drive one of the girls home but she had her own car. She laughed at me, pressing a forefinger against my lips. You should take a taxi, she said. You're in no condition to drive. Tears leaked from my eyes to everyone's embarrassment. Sherwin said quickly, S. isn't himself; he's taken this hard. *I'll* drive him. But I fled to the men's room and when I returned Sherwin was nowhere in sight. And I thought, Shithead, you've lost Sherwin, too. You let him go. I had a final drink, and set off for home.

Since the EXPOSÉ! broadcast, it seemed to me I was seeing more cops than ever, and they were big husky boys bursting out of their uniforms who could barely fit their bulk into police vehicles. It seemed they were smiling, still. They stood at a distance, hands on their billy clubs. EXPOSÉ! made it clear, *cops are a law-abiding citizen's best friends.* Driving past cop-cars on my way home I flicked my headlights at them and it seemed to me their headlights winked in return.

Then, this happened.

I remember driving up to get in line for a ticket for the Garden State Parkway, maybe the eighth car from the booth, and other lines are equally long, but one or two are moving faster, so as I often do, as everyone does, I switched lanes. And suddenly there's a tall uniformed figure beside my car rapping sharply on the window. A Jersey cop. "All right, mister. Let's see your license and auto registration." He wasn't one of the young husky guys but a little older, a seasoned veteran about my age, coarse-skinned and reddened in the face as if sunburned. I protested, "It isn't illegal to switch lanes, for God's sake. What's the law I broke?" The cop didn't hear. He was getting belligerent. A flame in his close-set ice pick eyes. Drivers of other cars, inching slowly toward the ticket booths, eyed us covertly. I could see these fellow citizens felt no sympathy for me. No pity. I'd violated a law; I was in trouble. I'd be issued a ticket at least, and I deserved a ticket. Nervously, I handed over my driver's license into the cop's gloved hands. He was staring at my photo I.D., and at my chic platinum-blond hair styled short in back, long at the sides. He was staring at my tanned face, my gold ear studs. I searched for the registration in the glove compartment of my car and handed that over, too. I'd begun to tremble. There was no unmarked WNET van behind me, recording this. There was no one watching. The cop was saying with a tight smile I'd better come with him to the station and I asked why, and was told my paperwork wasn't "one-hundred-percent in order." I asked what could be wrong with it? By this time the cop has my car door open and he's hauled me out onto the pavement, fingers like steel gripping my shoulder where the bones feel like plywood in danger of breaking. "Come with me, mister. Now." This big guy, six inches taller than me, sixty pounds heavier, force-walks me to a waiting squad car, cuffs my hands behind my back. I'm whimpering with pain, the metal hurts my tender wrists. I'm stammering, "Look, please. I'm a television reporter. For EXPOSÉ!—we just did an hour's program on police. We're your friends! Didn't you see it?" By now I'm in the rear of the squad car, the cop and his partner are driving back into the city. Siren wailing. We stop at a windowless building the size of a warehouse. Near the docks? The river? Where? I'm dragged out of the car. My left ankle is livid with pain, I can't walk upright, which infuriates the cops. I'm being shaken like a rag doll, against a brick wall. There's a door one of the cops dials us into, punching out a code, and we're inside the building, there's a blast of hard-metal rock music, and a crimson neon sign pulsing

COPLAND   *COPLAND*   *COPLAND*

and it isn't clear to me if this is a cop bar, a hangout for off-duty cops, or if it's an actual precinct in the inner city. Everywhere I look are cops: and they're big, and dramatic. Most are in their shirtsleeves. All of them are wearing badges. They're equipped with billy clubs, holstered revolvers, some are carrying rifles as if they'd only just returned from dangerous missions. Many are wearing mirrored sunglasses. Gloves, boots. Their ham-like thighs strain their regulation trousers. Only their ears appear small, disproportionate to their large heads. The noise in here is deafening, their hearing has atrophied and maybe, with it, their ears? Even in this terrible place S. is trying to reason, to rationalize. But *COPLAND* *COPLAND* *COPLAND* is overwhelming. Video games, vending machines, TV monitors. The rising of terror like backed-up sewage. On every side, cops are laughing. Guffawing. These are hearty hyena laughs, true "belly laughs." These are infectious laughs; you want to join in. Cops are smoking cigarettes and cigars and shouting jokes at one another. There's an enormous curved bar, and cops of all ages and sizes are crowded against the bar. It's like an altar; you want to push in with them; you want to be served. They're drinking draft beer, foaming from the tap. There's a thunderous sound of bowling from close by. Bowling alleys long as city blocks. In the distance, I see giant cops walking awkwardly, with bended knees, to avoid striking their heads against the ceiling. And it's a high ceiling, lost in bluish clouds of smoke. One of the friendly cops featured on EXPOSÉ!—the husky boy who'd been so polite to me in the homeless shelter—is hauling a handcuffed suspect into a back room. The suspect is a skinny, brown-skinned Hispanic teenager, already bleeding from mouth, nose, ears. Some cops are more mature than others, some are lieutenants, sergeants, captains with the insignia of their rank proudly displayed on their shirts. "My" cops are patrolmen, cop-cops with buzz cuts. *Because your case isn't important. Because you are not important. Your suffering, your life.* A booted foot kicks me in the small of the back and I'm on my face, coughing. My platinum-blond hair is being tugged out of my head. My head is being thumped against the floor. My jaws are being prized open, and an enormous cop-cock is being thrust inside, large as as normal man's forearm, and the tip of the cock hard as a man's elbow. *Off-camera, you don't exist. You are not being recorded.* The first cop finishes with me, and another cop straddles me, and another enormous cop-cock is thrust into my mouth. By this time I'm almost unconscious. I'm choking, gagging. My vomit spills onto my cop-assailant, scalding his bloated cock and fouling his blue-gray trousers, and polished leather boots. I'm an object of loathing and disgust. I'm whimpering in pain. I have no name now: not even "S." Cop-fury! I'm being kicked. Loud raucous cop-laughter! Blinding neon ★COPLAND★ ★COPLAND★ Someone, possibly a cop-medic, is thoughtful enough to dump a bucket of water over my head, it's not clean water but I'm grateful, my vision is somewhat cleared and I'm reviving. A drum majorette's baton is being passed from gloved cop-hand to cop-hand. My fawn-colored trousers have been torn from me, my Jockey shorts in shreds, a searing pain erupts between the crack of my ass. They're jamming the baton into me. Or it's a toilet plunger with a wooden handle, they're jamming into me. Laughing and shouting and their heated boys' faces exuding a strange sort of radiance. Their buzz cuts gleaming with sweat and in the smoke-haze of ★COPLAND★ aureoles of radiant light tremble about their heads like halos. It isn't too late, I'm thinking. I can forgive you. Even now, I can forgive you. I'm an American citizen, I'm an optimist, I want to love you. *I love you.* But the cops pay me no heed. It's their game now, it has nothing to do with me. I'm a game-object like a football. I'm sobbing, crawling across the blood-slick floor. The wooden handle dangling from my anus, swaying and lurching. This makes the cops laugh louder. Their superiors, drawn by the hilarity, come to look. Women cops drift about the doorway. They're laughing loudest of all. The women cops are giants, too. Yet their nails are manicured and polished. There's too much blood on the floor, I can't get traction, I can't crawl. There's a sharp stink of piss. Disgusting feces. The cops are angry with me, kicking me seriously now in the back, my spine, in the stomach, my guts. Laughing, leaping out of my way, surprisingly agile for men of their girth, not wanting to soil their handsome polished boots.

Whatever happens next, I've lost the thread.

I know that I was found early in the morning of March 29, in a Dumpster in Hoboken, a forty-minute drive from my home in suburban Lakeview. My naked, beaten body. My abused, broken body. Yet I don't believe the cops meant for me to die, or that I'd be flattened and processed as landfill. I believe they knew I'd be rescued by their fellow city workers, the sanitation men. I was unconscious and in a state of shock, my blood pressure dropping toward zero, but *I didn't die.* That's the crucial fact. If the *COPS* had seriously wanted to kill me they'd have killed me, like their other victims. If they'd wanted to injure my "pretty" face, they'd have injured it. There was a reason, probably a directive from the superintendent of police who's a friend of our billionaire Mister G-d at WNET-TV and for that I'm grateful.

Sure, I complain a lot. But I'm grateful.

So MY TV CAREER ENDED at its zenith, abruptly back in March. It's June now. I'm on a fairly generous disability leave. At the station they've promised I can return when I've "fully recovered" but I know I never will either return, or "fully recover."

My concern right now, this past hour, is that Chop-Chop is missing. Security guards, sharpshooter practicing, might've shot the poor little fellow if he left our property unleashed. And my wife M. and my children K. and C. are often gone, too. I'd been under the impression that they were at work and at school but in fact they're gone on weekends as well as weekdays and often they don't return to 9 Deer Trail Road for days at a time. I've come to the humiliating conclusion that they have another home. Another household. Through the Internet I acquired a "nightscope" telescope and with this device I've seen, or seemed to see, my wife driving her Lexus out of Deer Trail Villas to another private community in Lakeview, turning up the drive at a large English Tudor–style house; there's a car in the driveway I don't recognize. But possibly this isn't M.; my contact lenses don't fit as they once did and my vision is blurred.

Next week, the official start of summer. I'm optimistic. I refuse to despair. Chop-Chop may return. I'm still young, I think.